THE
BRIGHT MESSENGER

BY

ALGERNON BLACKWOOD

AUTHOR OF

" Julius LeVallon," "The Wolves of God," etc.

WILDSIDE PRESS

Printed in the United States of America

To the Unstable

THE BRIGHT MESSENGER

CHAPTER I

EDWARD FILLERY, so far as may be possible to a
man of normal passions and emotions, took a detached
view of life and human nature. At the age of thirty-eight
he still remained a spectator, a searching, critical, analytical,
yet chiefly, perhaps, a sympathetic spectator, before the
great performance whose stage is the planet and whose
performers and auditorium are humanity.

Knowing himself outcast, an unwelcome deadhead at
the play, he had yet felt no bitterness against the parents
whose fierce illicit passion had deprived him of an honour-
able seat. The first shock of resentment over, he had faced
the situation with a tolerance which showed an unusual
charity, an exceptional understanding, in one so young.

He was twenty when he learned the truth about himself. And it was his wondering analysis as to why two
loving humans could be so careless of their offspring's
welfare, when the rest of Nature took such pains in the
matter, that first betrayed, perhaps, his natural aptitude.
He had the innate gift of seeing things as they were,
undisturbed by personal emotion, while yet asking himself
with scientific accuracy why and how they came to be
so. These were invaluable qualities in the line of knowledge
and research he chose for himself as psychologist and
doctor. The terms are somewhat loose. His longing was
to probe the motives of conduct in the first place, and, in
the second, to correct the results of wrong conduct by

removing faulty motives. Psychiatrist and healer, therefore, were his more accurate titles; psychiatrist and healer, in due course, he became.

His father, an engineer of ability and enterprise, prospecting in the remoter parts of the Caucasus for copper, and making a comfortable fortune in so doing, was carried off his feet suddenly by the beauty of a Khaketian peasant girl, daughter of a shepherd in these lonely and majestic mountains, whose intolerable grandeur may well intoxicate a man to madness. A dangerous and disgraceful episode it seems to have been between John Fillery, hitherto of steady moral fibre, and this strange, lovely pagan girl, whose savage father hunted the pair of them high and low for weeks before they finally eluded him in the azalea valleys beyond Artvine.

Great passion, possibly great love, born of this enchanted land whose peaks touch heaven, while their lower turfy slopes are carpeted with lilies, azaleas, rhododendrons, contributed to the birth of Edward, who first saw the light in a secret chamber of a dirty Tiflis house, above the Koura torrent. That same night, when the sun dipped beneath the Black Sea waters two hundred miles to the westward, his mother had looked for the last time upon her northern lover and her wild Caucasian mountains.

Edward, however, persisted, visible emblem of a few weeks' primal passion in a primal land. Intense desire, born in this remote wilderness of amazing loveliness, lent him, perhaps, a strain of illicit, almost unearthly yearning, a secret nostalgia for some lost vale of beauty that held fiercer sunshine, mightier winds and fairer flowers than those he knew in this world.

At the age of four he was brought to England; his Russian memories faded, though not the birthright of his primitive blood. Settling in London, his father increased his fortune as consulting engineer, but did not marry. To the short vehement episode he had given of his very best; he remained true to his gorgeous memory and his sin; the cream of his life, its essence and its perfume, had been spent in those wild wind-swept azalea valleys beyond Artvine. The azalea honey was in his blood, the scent of the lilies in his brain; he still heard the Koura and Rion foaming down towards ancient Colchis. Edward embodied for him the spirit of these sweet, passionate memories. He loved the boy, he cherished and he spoilt him.

But Edward had stuff in him that rendered spoiling harmless. A vigorous, independent youngster, he showed firmness and character as a lad. To the delight of his father he knew his own mind early, reading and studying on his own account, possessed at the same time by a vehement love of nature and outdoor life that was far more than the average English boy's inclination to open air and sport. There lay some primal quality in his blood that was of ancient origin and leaned towards wildness. There seemed almost, at the same time, a faunish strain that turned away from life.

As a tiny little fellow he had that strange touch of creative imagination other children have also known—an invisible playmate. It had no name, as it, apparently, had no sex. The boy's father could trace it directly to no fairy tale read or heard; its origin in the child's mind remained a mystery. But its characteristics were unusual, even for such fanciful imaginings: too full-fledged to have been created gradually by the boy's loneliness, it seemed half goblin and half Nature-spirit; it replaced, at any rate, the little brothers and sisters who were not there, and the father, led by his conscience, possibly, to divine or half divine its origin, met the pretence with sympathetic encouragement.

It came usually with the wind, moreover, and went with the wind, and wind accordingly excited the child. "Listen! Father!" he would exclaim when no air was moving anywhere and the day was still as death. Then: "Plop! So there you are!" as though it had dropped through empty space and landed at his feet. "It came from a tremenjus height," the child explained. "The wind's up *there*, you see, to-day." Which struck the parent's mind as odd, because it proved later true. An upper wind, far in the higher strata of air, came down an hour or so afterwards and blew into a storm.

Fire and flowers, too, were connected with this invisible playmate. "*He'll* make it burn, father," the child said convincingly, when the chimney smoked and the coals refused to catch, and then became very busy with his friend in the grate and about the hearth, just as though he helped and superintended what was being invisibly accomplished. "It's burning better, anyhow," agreed the father, astonished in spite of himself as the coals began to glow and spurt their gassy flames. "Well done; I am very much obliged to you and your little friend."

"But it's the only thing he can do. He likes it. It's his work really, don't you see—keeping up the heat in things."

"Oh, it's his natural job, is it? I see, yes. But my thanks to him, all the same."

"Thank you very much," said grave Edward, aged five, addressing his tiny friend among the fire-irons. "I'm much mobliged to you."

Edward was a bit older when the flower incident took place—with the geranium that no amount of care and coaxing seemed able to keep alive. It had been dying slowly for some days, when Edward announced that he saw its "inside" flitting about the plant, but unable to get back into it. "It's got out, you see, and can't get back into its body again, so it's dying."

"Well, what in the world are we to do about it?" asked his father.

"I'll ask," was the solemn reply. "Now I know!" he cried, delighted, after asking his question of the empty air and listening for the answer. "Of course. Now I see. Look, father, there it is—its spirit!" He stood beside the flower and pointed to the earth in the pot.

"Dear me, yes! Where d'you see it? I—don't see it quite."

"He says I can pick it up and put it back and then the flower will live." The child put out a hand as though picking up something that moved quickly about the stem.

"What's it look like?" asked his father quickly.

"Oh, sort of trinangles and things with lines and corners," was the reply, making a gesture as though he caught it and popped it back into the red drooping blossoms. "There you are! Now you're alive again. Thank you very much, please"—this last remark to the invisible playmate who was superintending.

"A sort of geometrical figure, was it?" inquired the father next day, when, to his surprise, he found the geranium blooming in full health and beauty once again. "That's what you saw, eh?"

"It was its spirit, and it was shiny red, like fire," the child replied. "It's heat. Without these things there'd be no flowers at all."

"Who makes everything grow?" he asked suddenly, a moment later.

"You mean *what* makes them grow."

"Who," he repeated with emphasis. "Who builds the bodies up and looks after them?"

"Ah! the structure, you mean, the form?"

Edward nodded. His father had the feeling he was not being asked for information, but was being cross-examined. A faint pressure, as of uneasiness, touched him.

"They develop automatically—that means naturally, under the laws of nature," he replied.

"And the laws—who keeps them working properly?"

The father, with a mental gulp, replied that God did.

"A beetle's body, for instance, or a daisy's or an elephant's?" persisted the child undeceived by the theological evasion. "Or mine, or a mountain's——?"

John Fillery racked his brain for an answer, while Edward continued his list to include sea-anemones, frost-patterns, fire, wind, moon, sun and stars. All these forms to him were bodies apparently.

"I know!" he exclaimed suddenly with intense conviction, clapping his hands together and standing on his toes.

"Do you, indeed! Then you know more than the rest of us."

"*They do,* of course," came the positive announcement. "The other kind! It's their work. Yours, for instance" —he turned to his playmate, but so naturally and convincingly that a chill ran down his father's spine as he watched —"is fire, isn't it? You showed me once. And water stops you, but wind helps you . . . " and he continued long after his father had left the room.

With advancing years, however, Edward either forgot his playmate or kept its activities to himself. He no longer referred to it, at any rate. His energies demanded a bigger field; he roamed the fields and woods, climbed the hills, stayed out all night to see the sunrise, made fires even when fires were not exactly needed, and hunted with Red Indians and with what he called "Windy-Fire people" everywhere. He was never in the house. He ran wild. Great open spaces, trees and flowers were what he liked. The sea, on the other hand, alarmed him. Only wind and fire comforted him and made him happy and full of life. He was a playmate of wind and fire. Water, in large quantities at any rate, was inimical.

With concealed approval, masking a deep love fulfilled yet incomplete, his father watched the growth of this fiercer strain that mere covert shooting could not satisfy, nor ordinary sporting holidays appease.

"England's too small for you, Edward, isn't it?" he asked once tentatively, when the boy was about fifteen.

"The English people, you mean, father?"

"You find them dull, don't you? And the island a bit cramped—eh?"

Edward waited without replying. He did not quite understand what his indulgent father intended, or was leading up to.

"You'd like to travel and see things and people for yourself, I mean?"

He watched the boy without, as he thought, the latter noticing. The answer pleased but puzzled him.

"We're all much the same, aren't we?" said Edward.

"Well—with differences—yes, we are. But still——"

"It's only the same over and over again, isn't it?" Then, while his father was thinking of this reply, and of what he should say to it, the boy asked suddenly with arresting intensity:

"Are we the only people—the only sort of beings, I mean? Just men and women like us all over the world? No others of any sort—bigger, for instance, or—more wild and wonderful?" Then he added, a thrust of strange yearning in his face and eyes: "More beautiful?" He almost whispered the last words.

His father winced. He divined the origin of that strange inquiry. Upon those immense and lonely mountains, distant in space and time for him, imagination, rich and pagan, ran, he well knew, to vast and mighty beings, superior to human, benignant and maleficent, akin to the stimulating and exhilarating conception of the gods, and certainly non-human.

"Nothing, Edward, that we know of. Why should there be?"

"Oh, I don't know, dad. I just wondered—sometimes. But, as you say, we've not a scrap of evidence, of course."

"Not a scrap," agreed his father. "Poetic legends ain't evidence."

The mind ruled the heart in Edward; he had his father's brains, at any rate; and all his powers and longings focused in a single line that indicated plainly what his career should be. The Public Schools could help him little; he went to Edinburgh to study medicine; he passed eventually with all possible honours; and the day he brought home the news his father, dying, told him the secret of his illegitimate birth.

CHAPTER II

THE subsequent twenty years or so may be summarized.

Alone in the world, of a loving, passionate nature, he deliberately set all thought of marriage on one side as an impossibility, and directed his entire energy into the acquirement of knowledge; reading, studying, experimenting far outside the circle of the ordinary medical man. The attitude of detachment he had adopted became a habit. He believed it was now his nature.

The more he learned of human frailty and human faculties, the greater became the charity he felt towards his fellow-kind. In his own being, it seemed, lay something big, sweet, simple, a generosity that longed to share with others, a tolerance more ready to acquit than to condemn, above all, a great gift of understanding sympathy that, doubtless, was the explanation of his singular insight. Rarely he found it in him to blame; forgiveness, based upon the increasing extent of his experience, seemed his natural view of human mistakes and human infirmities. His one desire, his one hope, was to serve the Race.

Yet he himself remained aloof. He watched the Play but took no part in it. This forgiveness, too, began at home. His grievance had not soured or dejected him, his father's error presenting itself as a problem to be pondered over, rather than a sin to blame. Some day, he promised himself, he would go and see with his own eyes the Khaketian tribe whence his blood was partially derived, whence his un-English yearnings for a wilder scale of personal freedom amid an unstained, majestic Nature were first stolen. The inherited picture of a Caucasian vale of loveliness and liberty lay, indeed, very deep in his nature,

8

emerging always like a symbol when he was profoundly moved. At any crisis in his life it rose beckoning, seductive, haunting beyond words . . . Curious, ill-defined emotions with it, that drove him towards another standard, another state, to something, at any rate, he could neither name nor visualize, yet that seemed to dwarf the only life he knew. About it was a touch of strange unearthly radiance that dimmed existence as he knew it. The shine went out of it. There was involved in this symbolic "Valley" something wholly new both in colour, sound and outline, yet that remained obstinately outside definition.

First, however, he must work, develop himself, and broaden, deepen, extend in every possible way the knowledge of his kind that seemed his only love.

He began in a very practical way, setting up his plate in a mean quarter of the great metropolis, healing, helping, learning with his heart as well as with his brain, observing life at closest quarters from its beginning to its close, his sympathies becoming enriched the more he saw, and his mind groping its way towards clearer insight the more he read, thought, studied. His wealth made him independent; his tastes were simple; his wants few. He observed the great Play from the Pit and Gallery, from the Wings, from Behind the Scenes as well.

Moving then, into the Stalls, into a wealthier neighbourhood, that is, he repeated the experience among another class, finding, however, little difference except in the greater artificiality of his types, the larger proportion of mental and nervous ailments, of hysteria, delusion, imaginary troubles, and the like. The infirmities due to idleness, enflamed vanity and luxury offered a new field, though to him a less attractive one. The farther from simplicity, from the raw facts of living, the more complicated, yet the more trivial, the resulting disabilities. These, however, were quite as real as those, and harder, indeed, to cure. Idle imagination, fostered by opportunity and means, yet forced by conventionality to wear infinite disguises, brought a strange, if far from a noble, crop of disorders into his ken. Yet he accepted them for serious treatment, whatever his private opinion may have been, while his patience, tact and sympathy, backed by his insight and great knowledge, brought him quick success. He was soon in a fair way to become a fashionable doctor.

But the field, he found, was restricted somewhat. His quest was knowledge, not fame or money. He chose his cases where he could, though actually refusing nothing. He specialized more and more with afflictions of a mental kind. He was immensely successful in restoring proportion out of disorder. He revealed people to themselves. He taught them to recover lost hope and confidence. He used little medicine, but stimulated the will towards a revival of fading vitality. Auto-suggestion, rather than suggestion or hypnotism, was his method. He healed. He began to be talked about.

Then, suddenly, his house was sold, his plate was taken down, he vanished.

Human beings object to sudden changes whose secret they have not been told and cannot easily guess; his abrupt disappearance caused talk and rumours, led, of course, by those, chiefly disappointed women, who had most reason to be grateful for past services. But, if the words charlatan and quack were whispered, he did not hear them; he had taken the post of assistant in a lunatic asylum in a northern town, because the work promised him increase of knowledge and experience in his own particular field. The talk he left behind him mattered as little as the small pay attached to the humble duties he had accepted.

London forgot him, but he did not forget what London had taught him.

A new field opened, and in less than two years, opportunity, combined with his undoubted qualifications, saw him Head of an establishment where he could observe at first hand the facts and phenomena that interested him most. Humane treatment, backed by profound insight into the derangements of the poor human creatures under his charge, brought the place into a fame it had never known before. He spent five years there in profound study and experiment; he achieved new results and published them. His *Experimental Psychology* caused a sensation. His name was known. He was an Authority.

At this time he was well past thirty, a tall, dark, distinguished-looking man, of appearance grave and even sombre; imposing, too, with his quiet, piercing eyes, but sombre only until the smile lit up his somewhat rugged face. It was a face that nobody could lie to, but to that smile the suffering heart might tell its inmost secrets with confidence, hope, trust, and without reserve.

There followed several years abroad, in Paris, Rome, St. Petersburg, Moscow; Vienna and Zurich he also visited to test there certain lines of research and to meet personally their originators.

This period was partly a holiday, partly an opportunity to know at first hand the leaders in mental therapeutics, psychology and the rest, and also that he might find time to digest and arrange his own accumulation of knowledge with a view, later, to undertaking the life-work to which his previous experience was but preliminary. Fame had come to him unsought; his published works alone ensured his going down to posterity as a careful but daring and original judge of the human species and its possibilities. It was the supernormal rather than the merely abnormal powers that attracted him. In the subconscious, as, equally, in the superconscious, his deep experience taught him, lay amazing powers of both moral and physical healing, powers as yet but little understood, powers as limitless as they seemed incredible, as mysterious in their operation as they were simple in their accessibility. And auto-suggestion was the means of using them. The great men whom he visited welcomed him with open arms, added to his data, widened yet further his mental outlook. Sought by high and low in many countries and in strangest cases, his experience grew and multiplied, his assortment of unusual knowledge was far-reaching; till he stood finally in wonder and amazement before the human being and its unrealized powers, and his optimism concerning the future progress of the race became more justified with every added fact.

Yet, perhaps, his greatest achievement was the study of himself; it was probably to this deep, intimate and honest research into his own being that his success in helping others was primarily due. For in himself, though mastered and co-ordinated by his steady will, rendered harmless by his saving sense of humour and (as he believed) by the absence of any harboured grievance against others—in his very own being lay all those potential elements of disorder, those loose unravelled threads of alien impulse and suppressed desire, which can make for dangerous disintegration, and thus produce the disturbing results classed generally under alienation and neurosis.

The incongruous elements in him were the gift of nature; γνῶθι σεαυτόν was the saving attitude he brought to that gift, redeeming it. This phrase, borrowed, he remembered with a smile, for the portal of the ancient Mysteries, remained his watchword. He was able to thank the fierce illicit love that furnished his body and his mental make-up for a richer field of first-hand study than years of practice among others could have supplied. He belonged by temperament to the unstable. But—he was aware of it. He realized the two beings in him: the reasoning, scientific man, and the speculative dreamer, visionary, poet. The latter wondered, dreamed among a totally different set of values far below and out of sight. This deeper portion of himself was forever beating up for recognition, clamouring to be used, yet with the strange shyness that reminded him of a loving woman who cannot be certain her passion is returned. It hinted, threatened, wept and even sulked. It rose like a flame, bringing its own light and wind, blessed his whole being with some divine assurance, and then, because not instantly accepted, it retired, leaving him empty, his mind coloured with unearthly yearnings, with poignant regrets, yet perfumed as though the fairness of Spring herself had lit upon his heart and kissed it into blossom on her passage north. It presented its amazing pictures, and withdrew. Elusive, as the half memory of some radiant dream, whose wonder and sweetness have been intense to the point of almost pain, it hovered, floating just out of reach. It lay waiting for that sincere belief which would convince that its passion was returned. And a fleeting picture of a wild Caucasian valley, steeped in sunshine and flowers, was always the first sign of its awakening.

Though not afraid of reason, it seemed somehow independent of the latter's processes. It was his reason, however, he well knew that dimmed the light in its grand, terrible eyes, causing it to withdraw the instant he began to question. Precise, formal thinking shut the engines off and damped the furnaces. His love, his passion, none the less, were there, hiding with belief, until some bright messenger, bringing glad tidings, should reveal the method of harmonious union between reason and vision, between man's trivial normal faculties and his astounding supernormal possibilities.

"This element of feeling in our outlook on Nature is a satisfaction in itself, but our plea for allowing it to operate in our interpretation of Nature is that we get closer to some things through feeling than we do through science. The tendency of feeling is always to see things whole. We cannot, for our life's sake, and for the sake of our philosophical reconstruction, afford to lose in scientific analysis what the poets and artists and the lovers of Nature all see. It is intuitively felt, rather than intellectually perceived, the vision of things as totalities, root and all, all in all; neither fancifully, nor mystically, but sympathetically in their wholeness."

To these words of Professor T. Arthur Thomson's, he heartily subscribed, applying their principle to his own particular field.

CHAPTER III

THE net result of his inquiries and research, when, at the age of nearly forty, he established his own Private Home for unusual, so-called hopeless cases in North-West London—it was free to all, and as Spiritual Clinique he thought of it sometimes with a smile—may be summed up in the single sentence that man is greater than he knows, and that completer realization of his full possibilities lies accessible to his subconscious and superconscious powers. Herein he saw, indeed, the chief hope of progress for humanity.

And it was to the failures, the diseased, the evil and the broken that he owed chiefly his inspiring optimism, since it was largely in collapse that occurred the sporadic upheaval of those super-normal forces which, controlled, co-ordinated, led, must eventually bring about the realization he foresaw.

The purpose, however, of these notes is not to furnish a sensational story of various patients whom he studied, healed, or failed to heal. Its object is to give some details of one case in particular whose outstanding peculiarities affected his theories and convictions, leaving him open-minded still, but with a breath of awe in his heart perhaps, before a possibility his previous knowledge had ruled entirely out of court, even if—which is doubtful—he had ever considered it as a possibility at all.

He had realized early that the individual manifests but an insignificant portion of his being in his ordinary existence, the normal self being the tip of his consciousness only, yet whose fuller expression rises readily to adequate evocation; and it was the study of genius, of prodigies, so-called, and of certain faculties shown sometimes in hysteria, that led him to believe these were small jets from a sea of power that might, indeed ought, to be realizable at will.   The phenomena all pointed, he believed, to powers that seemed as superior to cerebral functions as they were independent of these.

Man's possible field of being, in other words, seemed capable of indefinite extension.   His heart glowed within him as he established, step by step, these greater powers. He dared to foresee a time when the limitations of separate personality would have been destroyed, and the vast brother-hood of the race become literally realized, its practical unity accomplished.

The difficulties were endless and discouraging.   The inventive powers of the bigger self, its astonishing faculty for dramatizing its content in every conceivable form, blocked everywhere the search for truth.

It could, he found, also detach a portion of its content into a series of separate personalities, each with its individual morals, talents, tendencies, each with its distinct and separate memory.   These fragments it could project, so to speak, masquerading convincingly as separate entities, using strange languages, offering detailed knowledge of other conditions, distant in time and space, suggesting, indeed, to the unwary that they were due to obsessing spirits, and leaving the observer in wonder before the potential capacity of the central self disgorging them.

The human depths included, beyond mere telepathy and extended telepathy, an expansion of consciousness so vast as to be, apparently, limitless.   The past, on rare occasions even the future, lay open; the entire planetary memory, stored with rich and pregnant accumulated experience, was accessible and shareable.   New aspects of space and time were equally involved.   A vision of incredible grandeur opened gradually before his eyes.

The surface consciousness of to-day was really rather a trumpery affair; the gross lethargy of the vast majority

vis à vis the greater possibilities afflicted him.   To this
surface consciousness alone was so-called evil possible—
as ignorance.   As "ugly is only half-way to a thing," so
evil is half-way to good.   With the greater powers must
come greater knowledge, shared as by instantaneous wireless over the entire planet, and misunderstanding, chief
obstacle to progress always, would be impossible.   A huge
unity, sense of oneness must follow.   Moral growth would
accompany the increase of faculty.   And here and there,
it seemed to him, the surface ice had thawed already a
little; the pressure of the great deeps below caused cracks
and fissures.   Auto-suggestion, prototype of all suggestion,
offered mysterious hints of the way to reach the stupendous
underworld, as the Christian Scientists, the miraculous
healers, the New Thought movement, saints, prophets, poets,
artists, were finding out.

The subliminal, to state it shortly, might be the divine.
This was the hope, though not yet the actual belief, that
haunted and inspired him.   Behind his personality lurked
this strange gigantic dream, ever beating to get through. . . .

In his Private Home, helping, healing, using his great
gifts of sympathy and insight, he at the same time found
the material for intimate study and legitimate experiment
he sought.   The building had been altered to suit his exact
requirements; there were private suites, each with its door
and staircase to the street; one part of it provided his own
living quarters, shut off entirely from the patients' side;
in another, equally cut off and self-contained, yet within
easy communication of his own rooms, lived Paul Devonham, his valued young assistant.   There was a third private
suite as well.   The entire expenses he defrayed himself.

Here, then, for a year or two he worked indefatigably,
with the measure of success and failure he anticipated;
here he dreamed his great dream of the future of the race,
in whose progress and infinite capacities he hopefully believed.   Work was his love, the advancement of humanity
his god.   The war availed itself of his great powers, as

also of his ready-made establishment, both of which he gave without a thought of self. New material came as well from the battlefields into his ken.

The effect of the terrible five years upon him was in direct proportion to his sincerity. His mind was not the type that shirks conclusions, nor fears to look facts in the face. For really new knowledge he was ever ready to yield all previous theories, to scrap all he had held hitherto for probable. His mind was open, he sought only Truth.

The war, above all the Peace, shook his optimism. If it did not wholly shatter his belief in human progress, it proved such progress to be so slow that his Utopia faded into remotest distance, and his dream of perfectibility became the faintest possible star in his hitherto bright sky of hope.

He felt shocked and stupefied. The reaction was greater than at first he realized. He had often pitied the mind that, aware only of its surface consciousness, uninformed by thrill or shift of the great powers below and above, lived unwarned of its own immenser possibilities. To such, the evidence for extended human faculties must seem explicable by fraud, illusion, derangement, to be classed as abnormal rubbish worthy only of the alienist's attention as diseases. To him such minds, though able, with big intellects among them, had ever seemed a prejudiced, fossilized, prehistoric type. Restricted by their very nature, violently resisting new ideas, they might be intense within their actual scope, but, with vision denied them, they never could be really great.

One effect of the shock he had undergone will be evident by merely stating that he now understood this type of mind a good deal better than before.

CHAPTER IV

THE war was over, though the benefits of the long anticipated peace still kept provocatively, exasperatingly, out of reach, when, about the middle of September, Dr. Fillery received a letter that interested him deeply.

The shattered world was still distraught, uneasy. Nervously eager to resume its former activities, it was yet waiting for the word that should give it the necessary confidence to begin. Doubt, insecurity, uncertainty everywhere dominated human minds. Those who hoped for a renewal of the easy, careless mood of pre-war days were dismayed to find this was impossible; others who had allowed an optimistic idealism to prophesy a New Age, looked about them bewilderingly and in vain for signs of its fair birth. The latter, to whom, perhaps, Dr. Fillery belonged, were more bitterly disappointed, more cruelly shocked, than the former. The race, it seemed to many unshirking eyes, had leaped back centuries at a single spring; the gulf of primal savagery which had gaped wide open for five years, proving the Stone Age close beneath the surface of so-called civilization, had not yet fully closed. Its jaws still dripped blood, hatred, selfishness; the Race was still dislocated by the convincing disproof of progress, horrified at the fierce reality which had displaced the two-pence coloured dream it had been complacently worshipping hitherto. Men in the mass undoubtedly were savages still.

To Dr. Fillery, an honest, though not a necessarily fundamental pessimism, seemed justified. He believed in progress still, but as his habit was, he faced the facts. His attitude lost something of its original enthusiasm. Looking about him, he saw no big constructive movement; the figure who more than any other was altering the face of the world with his ideas as well as his armies, was avowedly destructive only. He found himself a sobered and a saddened man.

His Private Home, having accomplished splendid work, had just discharged its last shell-shocked patient; it was now empty again, the staff, carefully chosen and proved by long service, dismissed on holidays, the building itself renovated and repaired against the arrival later of new patients that were expected.

Devonham, his assistant, away for a period of rest in Switzerland, would be back in a week or two, and Dr. Fillery, before resuming his normal work, found himself with little to do but watch the progress of the cleaners, painters and carpenters at work.

Into this brief time of leisure dropped the strange, perplexing letter with an effect distinctly stimulating. It promised an unusual case, a patient, if patient the case referred to could properly be called, a young man "who if you decide after careful reflection to reject, can be looked after only by the State, which means, of course, an Asylum for the Insane. I know you are no longer head of the Establishment in Liverpool, but that you confine yourself to private work along similar lines, though upon a smaller scale, and that you welcome only cases that have been given up as hopeless. I honour your courage and your sympathy, I know your skill. So far as a cure is conceivable, this one is hopeless certainly, but its unusual, indeed, its unique character, entitles it, I believe, to be placed among your chosen few. Love, sympathy, patience, combined with the closest observation, it urgently demands, and these qualities, associated with unrivalled skill, you must allow me, again, to think you alone possess among healers and helpers of strange minds.

"For over twenty years, in the solitudes of these Jura forests and mountains,' I have cared for him as best I could, and with a devotion a child of my own might have expected. But now, my end not far away, I cannot leave him behind me here uncared for, yet the alternative, the impersonal and formal care of an Institute, must break my heart and his. I turn to you.

"My advanced age and growing infirmities, in these days of unkind travel, prohibit my bringing him over. Can your great heart suggest a means, since I feel sure you will not refuse the care of this strange being whose nature and peculiarities indicate your especial care, and yours alone? Is it too much to wonder if you yourself could come and see him—here in the remote mountain châlet where I have tended and cared for him ever since his mother died in bearing him over twenty years ago?

"I have taught him what seemed wise and best; I have guarded and observed him; he knows little or nothing of an outside world of men and women, and is ignorant of life in the ordinary meaning of the word. What precisely he may be, to what stratum of consciousness he belongs, what kind of being he is, I mean. . . ." The last two lines were then scored through, though left legible. "I feel with Arago, that he is a rash man who pronounces the word 'impossible' anywhere outside the sphere of pure mathematics." More sentences were here scored through.

"Dare I· say—to you, as master, teacher, great open-minded soul—that to *human* life, as we know it, he does not, perhaps, belong?

"In writing—in this letter—I find it impossible to give you full details. I had intended to set them down; my pen refuses; in the plain English at my disposal—well, simply, it is not credible. But I have kept full notes all these years, and the notes belong to you. I enclose an imperfect painting I made of him some four years ago. I am no artist; for background you must imagine what lay beyond my little skill—the blazing glory of the immense wood-fires that he loves to make upon the open mountain side, usually at dawn after a night of prayer and singing, while waiting for the strange power he derives (as we all do, indeed, at second or third hand), from the worship of what is to him his mighty father, the life-giving sun. Wind, as the 'messengers' of the sun, he worships too. . . . Both sun and wind, that is, produce an unusual state approaching ecstasy.

"Counting upon you, I have hypnotized him, suggesting that he forget all the immediate past (in fact to date), and telling him he will like you in place of me—though with him it is an uncertain method.

"I am now old in years. I have lived and loved, suffered and dreamed like most of us; my hands have been warmed at the fires of life, of which, let me add, I am not ignorant. You have known, I believe, my serious, as also my lighter imaginative books; my occasional correspondence with your colleague Paul Devonham has been of help and guidance to me. We are not, therefore, wholly strangers.

"The twenty years spent in these solitudes among simple peasant folk, with a single object of devotion to fill my days, have been, I would tell you, among the best of my long existence. My renouncement of the world was no renouncement. I am enriched with wonder and experience that amaze me, for the world holds possibilities few have ever dreamed of, and that I myself, filled as I am with the memory of their contemplation, can hardly credit even now. Perhaps in an earlier stage of evolution, as Delboeuf believes, man was fully aware of *all* that went on within himself—a region since closed to us, owing to attention being increasingly directed outwards. Into some such region I have had a glimpse, it seems. I feel sometimes there was as much fact as fancy, perhaps, in the wise old Hebrew who stated poetically—recently, too, compared with the stretch of time my science deals with—'The Sons of God took to themselves daughters of the children of men. . . .'"

The letter here broke off, as though interrupted by something unexpected and unusual; it was signed, indeed, "John Mason," but signed in pencil and at the bottom of an unwritten blank sheet. It had not all been written, either, at one time, or on the same day; there were intervals, evidently, perhaps of hours, perhaps of days, between the paragraphs. Dr. Fillery read, re-read, then read again the strange epistle, coming each time to the same conclusion —the writer was dying in the very act of forming the last sentences. Their incoherence, the alteration in the style, were thus explained. He had felt the end of life so close that he had written his signature, probably addressed the envelope as well, knowing the page might never be filled up. It had not been filled up.

Something behind the phrases, behind the intensity of the actual words, beyond the queer touches that revealed a mind betrayed by solitude, the hints possibly of a deluded intelligence—there was something that rang true and stimulated him more than ordinarily. The reference to Devonham, too, was definite enough. Dr. Fillery remembered vaguely a correspondence during recent crowded years with a man named Mason, living away in Switzerland somewhere, and that Devonham had asked him questions from time to time about what he called, with his rough-and-ready and half-humorous classification, "pagan obsession," "worshipper of fire and wind," referring it to the writer of the letters, named John Mason. "Non-human delusion," he had also called it sometimes. They had come to refer to it, he remembered, as "N.H." in fact.

He now looked up those Notes, for the mention of the books caused him an uncomfortable feeling of neglected opportunity, and John Mason was an honoured name.

"You know, I believe . . . my books," the writer said. Could this be, he asked himself anxiously, John Mason, the eminent geologist? Had Devonham not realized who he was? Must he blame his assistant, whose jealous care and judgment saved him so many foolish, futile, un-real cases, reserving what was significant and important only?

The Notes established his mistakes and his assistant's —perhaps intentional?—ignorance. The writer of this

curious letter was unquestionably the author of those fairy
books for children, old and young, whose daring speculations had suggested that other types and races, ages even
before the Neanderthal man, had dwelt side by side with
what is known as modern man upon this time-worn planet.
Behind the literary form of legend and fairy tale, however,
lay a curious conviction. Atlantis was of yesterday compared with earlier civilizations, now extinct by fire and flood
and general upheaval, which once may have inhabited the
globe. The present evolutionary system, buttressed by
Darwin and the rest, was but a little recent insignificant
series, trivial both in time and space, when set beside the
mightier systems that had come and gone. Their evidence
he found, not in clumsy fossils and footprints on cooled
rocks, but in the *minds* of those who had followed and
eventually survived them: memories of Titan Wars and
mighty beings, and gods and goddesses of non-human kind,
to whose different existence the physical conditions of an
over-heated planet presented no impossibility. The human
species, this trumpery, limited, self-satisfied super-animal
man, was not the only type of being.

Yet John Mason, in his day, had held the chair at Edinburgh University, his lectures embodied common-sense and
knowledge, with acutest imaginative insight. His earliest
writings were the text-books of the time. His name, when
Edward Fillery was medical student there, still hovered
like well-loved incense above the old-town towers.

The Notes now intrigued him. No blame attached to
Devonham for having missed the cue, Devonham could not
know everything; geology was not in his line of work and
knowledge; and Mason was a common name. Rather he
blamed himself for not having been struck by the oddness
of the case—the Mason letters, the pagan obsession,
worshipper of wind and fire, the strange "N.H."

"A competent indexer, at any rate," he said to himself
with a smile, as he turned up the details easily.

These were very scanty. Devonham evidently had

deemed the case of questionable value. The letters from Mason, with the answers to them, he could not find.

The slight record was headed *"Mason,* John," followed by an address "Chez Henri Petavel, peasant, Jura Mountains, Vaud, French Switzerland," and details how to reach this apparently remote valley by mule and carriage and foot-path. Name of Mason's protégé not given.

"Sex, male; age—born 1895; parentage, couple of mystical temperament, sincere, but suffering from marked delusions, believers in Magic (various, but chiefly concerned with Nature and natural forces, once known, forgotten to-day, of immense potency, accessible to certain practices of logical but undetailed kind, able apparently to intensify human consciousness).

"Subject, of extremely quick intelligence, yet betrays ignorance of human conditions; intelligence superior to human, though sometimes inferior; long periods of quiescence, followed by immense, almost super-human, activity and energy; worships fire and air, chiefly the former, calling the sun his father and deity.

"Abhors confined space; this shown by intense desire for heat, which, together with free space (air), seem conditions of well-being.

"Fears (as in claustrophobia) both water and solidity (anything massive).

"Has great physical power, yet indifferent to its use; women irresistibly attracted to him, but his attitude towards other sex seems one of gentleness and pity; love means nothing. Has, on the other hand, extraordinarily high ideal of service. Is puzzled by quarrels and differences of personal kind. Half-memories of vast system of myriad workers, ruled by this ideal of harmonious service. Faithful, true, honest; falseness or lies impossible . . . lovable, pathetic, helpless type——"

The Notes broke off abruptly.

Dr. Fillery, wondering a little that his subordinate's brief but suggestive summary had never been brought to his notice before, turned a moment to glance at the rough water-colour drawing he held in his hand. He looked at it for some moments with absorption. The expression of his face was enigmatical. He was more than surprised that Devonham had not drawn his attention to the case in detail. Placing his hand so as to hide the lower portion of the face, he examined the eyes, then turned the portrait upside down, gazing at the eyes afresh. He seemed lost in thought for a considerable time. A faint flush stole into his cheek, and a careful observer might have noticed an increase of light about the skin. He sighed once or twice, and presently, laying the portrait down again, he turned back to the *dossier* upon the table in front of him.

"Very accurate and careful," he said to himself with satisfaction as he noticed the date Devonham had set against the entries—"June 20th, 1914."

The war, therefore, had interrupted the correspondence. Devonham had made further notes of his own in the margin here and there:

"Does this originate primarily from Mason's mind, communicated thence to his protégé?" He agreed with his assistant's query.

"If so, was it transferred to Mason's mind before that? By the father or mother? The mother was, obviously, his—Mason's—great love. Yet the father was his life friend. Mason's great passion was suppressed. He never told it. It found no outlet."

"Admirable," was the comment spoken below his breath.

"Boy born as result of some 'magical' experiment intensely believed (not stated in detail), during course of which father died suddenly.

"Mason tended mother, then lived alone in remote place where all had occurred.

"Did Mason inherit entire content of parents' beliefs, dramatizing this by force of unexpressed but passionate love?

"Did not Mason's mind, thus charged, communicate whole

business to the young mind he has since formed, a plastic mind uninfluenced by normal human surroundings and conditions of ordinary life?

"Transfer of a sex-inspired mania?"

Then followed another note, summarizing evidently Devonham's judgment:

"Not worth F.'s investigation until examined further. N.B.—Look up Mason first opportunity and judge at first hand."

Dr. Fillery, glancing from the papers to the portrait, smiled a little again as he signified approval.

But the last entry interested him still more. It was dated July 13, 1914.

"Mason reports boy's prophecy of great upheaval coming. Entire race slips back into chaos of primitive life again. Entire Western Civilization crumbles. Modern inventions and knowledge vanish. Nature spirits reappear. . . . Desires return of all previous letters. These sent by registered post."

A few scattered notes on separate sheets of paper lay at the end of the carefully typed *dossier*, but these were very incomplete, and Devonham's handwriting, especially when in pencil, was not of the clearest.

"Non-human claim, though absurd, not traceable to any antecedent causes given by letters. What is Mason's past mental and temperamental history? Is he not, through the parents, the cause? Mania seems harmless, both to subject and others. No suffering or unhappiness. Therefore not a case for F., until further examined by self. Better see Mason and his subject first. Wrote July 24th proposing visit."

Dr. Fillery's eyes twinkled. His forehead relaxed. He looked back. He remembered details. Devonham's holiday that year, he recalled, was due on August 1st; he had intended going out mountain climbing in Switzerland.

The final note of all, also in half-legible writing, seemed

to refer to the treatment Mason had asked advice about, and the line Devonham had suggested:

"Natural life close to Nature cannot hurt him. But I advise watch him with fire and with heights—heat, air! That is, he may decide his physical body is irksome and seek to escape it. Teach him natural history—botany, geology, insects, animals, even astronomy, but always giving him reasons and explanations. *Above all*—let him meet girls of his own age and fall in love. Fullest natural expression, but guarded without his knowing it. . . ."

For a long time Dr. Fillery sat with the notes and papers before him, thinking over what he had read. Devonham's advice was clever enough, but without insight, sound and astute, yet lacking divination.

The twinkle in his eyes, caused by the final entry, died away. His face was grave, his manner preoccupied, intense. He gazed long at the portrait in his hand. . . . It was dusk when he finally rose, replaced the *dossier,* locked the cabinet, and went out into another room, and thence into the hall. Taking his hat and stick, he left the house, already composing in his mind the telegram instructing Devonham, while apologizing for the interrupted holiday, to bring the subject of the Notes to England with him. A telegraph girl met him on the very steps of the house. He took the envelope from her, and opened it. He read the message It was dated Bâle, the day before:

"Arriving end week with interesting patient. Details index under Mason. Prepare private suite.

"DEVONHAM."

CHAPTER V

IT was, however, some two weeks later before Dr. Fillery was on his way to the station to meet Devonham and his companion. A slight delay, caused apparently by the necessity of buying an outfit, had intervened and given time for an exchange of letters, but Devonham had contented himself chiefly with telegrams. He did not wish his chief to know too much about the case in advance. "Probably he regrets the Notes already," thought the doctor, as the car made its way slowly across crowded London. "He wants my first unbiased judgment; he's right, of course, but it's too late for that now."

The delay, however, had been of value. The Home was in working order again, the staff returned, the private suite all ready for its interesting occupant, whom in thought he had already named "N.H."; for in the first place he did not know his name as yet, and in the second he felt towards him a certain attitude of tolerant, half-humorous scepticism.

Cut off from his own kind for so many years, educated, perhaps half-educated only, by too speculative and imaginative a mind, equally warped by this long solitude, a mind unduly stretched by the contemplation of immense geological perspectives, filled, too, with heaven knows what strange stories of pantheistic Nature-feeling—"N. H." might be distinctly interesting, but hardly all that Mason had thought him. "Unique" was a word rarely justified; the peculiarities would prove to be mere extravagances that had, of necessity, remained uncorrected by the friction of intercourse with his own kind. The rest was inheritance, equally unpruned; a mind living in a side-eddy, a backwater with Nature. . . .

28

At the same time Dr. Fillery admitted a certain anticipatory excitement he could not wholly account for, an undercurrent of wonder he ascribed to his Khaketian blood.

He had written once only to his assistant, sending briefest instructions to say the rooms would be ready, and that the young man must believe he was an invited guest coming on a visit. "Let him expect complete freedom of movement and occupation without the smallest idea of restraint in any way. He is merely coming to stay for as long as he pleases with a friend of Mason. Impress him with a sense of hearty welcome." And Devonham, replying, had evidently understood the wisdom of this method. "He is also greatly pleased with your name—the sound of it," was stated in the one letter that he wrote, "and as names mean a lot to him, so much the better. The sound of it gives him pleasure; he keeps repeating it over to himself; he already likes you. My name he does not care about, saying it quickly, sharply. But he trusts me. His trust in anyone who shows him kindness is instantaneous and complete. He invariably expects kindness, however, from everyone— gives it himself equally—and is baffled and puzzled by any other treatment."

So Devonham, with "N. H.," who attached importance to names and expected kindness from people as a natural thing, would be in London town within the hour. Straight from his forests and mountains for the first time in his life, he would find himself in the heart of the greatest accumulation of human beings on the planet, the first city of the world, the final expression of civilization as known to the human race.

" 'N. H.' in London town," thought Dr. Fillery, his mouth twitching with the smile that began in his quiet eyes. "Bless the lad! We must make him feel at home and happy. He shall indeed have kindness. He'll need a woman's touch as well." He reflected a moment. "Women are a great help in doubtful cases—the way a man reacts to them," he mused. "Only they must be distinct in type to be of

value." And his mind ran quickly, comprehensively over
the women of his acquaintance, pausing, as it did so, upon
two in particular—a certain Lady Gleeson, and Iraida—
sometimes called Nayan—Khilkoff, the daugher of his
Russian friend, the sculptor.

His mind pondered for some moments the two he had
selected. It was not the first time he had made use of
them. Their effect respectively upon a man was invariably
instinctive and illuminating.

The two were radically different feminine types, as far
removed from one another as pole from pole, yet each
essentially of her sex. Their effect, respectively, upon such
a youth must be of value, and might be even illuminating
to the point of revelation. Both, he felt sure, would not be
indifferent to the new personality.

It was, however, of Nayan Khilkoff that he thought
chiefly. Of that rare, selfless, maternal type which men
in all ages have called saint or angel, she possessed that
power which evoked in them all they could feel of respect,
of purity, of chivalry, that love, in a word, which holds
as a chief ingredient, worship. Her beauty, beyond their
reach, was of the stars; it was the unattainable in her they
loved; her beauty was of the soul. Nayan was spiritual,
not as a result of painful effort and laborious development,
but born so. Her life, moreover, was one of natural service.
Personal love, exclusive devotion to an individual, concentration of her being upon another single being—this seemed
impossible to her. She was at the same time an enigma: there
was an elusive flavour about her that made people a little in
awe of her, a flavour not of this earth, quite. She carried an
impersonal attitude almost to the point of seeming irresponsive to common human things and interests.

The other woman, Lady Gleeson, Angela her Christian
name, was equally a simple type, though her simplicity was
that of the primitive female who is still close to the Stone
Age—a savage. She adorned herself to capture men. She

was the female spider that devours its mates. She wanted slaves. To describe her as selfish were inadequate, for she was unaware that any other ideal existed in life but that of obtaining her own pleasure. There was instinct and emotion, but, of course, no heart. Without morals, conscience or consideration, she was the animal of prey that obeys the call of hunger in the most direct way possible, regardless of consequences to herself or others. Her brain was quick, her personality shallow. When talking she "rattled on." Devonham had well said once: "You can hear her two thoughts clicking, both of them in trousers!" Sir George, recently knighted, successful with large concessions in China, was indulgent. The male splendour of the youth was bound to stimulate her hunger, as his simplicity, his loneliness, and in a sense his pathetic helplessness, would certainly evoke the tenderness in Nayan. "He'll probably like her dear, ridiculous name, too," Dr. Fillery felt, "the nickname they gave her because she's the same to everybody, whichever way you take her—Nayan Khilkoff." Yet her real name was more beautiful—Iraida. And, as he repeated it half aloud, a soft light stole upon his face, shone in the deep clear eyes, and touched even the corners of the rather grim mouth with another, a tenderer expression, before the sternness quickly returned to it.

"N. H." would meet, thus, two main types of female life. He, apparently an exceedingly male being, would face the onslaught of passion and heart, of lust and love, respectively; and it was his reactions to these onslaughts that Fillery wished to observe. They would help his diagnosis, they might guide his treatment.

It was a warm and muggy afternoon, the twilight passing rapidly into darkness now; one of those late autumn days when summer heat flits back, but light is weak. The covered sky increased the clammy warmth, which was damp, unhealthy, devitalizing. No wind stirred. The great city was sticky and depressing. Yet people approved the heat, although it tired them. "It shortens the winter, any-how," was the general verdict, when expressed at all. They referred unconsciously to the general dread of strikes.

London was hurried and confused. An air of feverish overcrowding reigned in the great station, when he left the car and went in on foot. No sign of order, system, direction, was visible. The scene might have been a first rehearsal of some entirely new experiment. Grumbling and complaint rose from all sides in an exasperated chorus. He tried to ascertain how late the train was and on which platform it might be expected, but no one knew for certain, and the grudging replies to questions seemed to say, "You've no right to ask anything, and if you keep on asking there will be a strike. So that's that!"

He listened to the talk and watched the facial expressions and the movements of the half-resigned and half-excited concourse of London citizens. The clock was accurate, and everyone was kind to ladies; stewed tea, stale cake with little stones in it, vile whisky and very weak beer were obtainable at high prices. There were no matches. The machine for supplying platform-tickets was broken. He saw men paying more thought and attention to the comfort of their dogs than to their own. The great, marvellous, stupid, splendid race was puzzled and exasperated. Then, suddenly, the train pulled in, full of returned exiles longing to be back again in "dear old England."

"Thank God, it's come," sighed the crowd. "Good! We're English. Forgive and forget!" and prepared to tip the porters handsomely and carry their own baggage.

The confusion that followed was equally characteristic, and equally remarkable, displaying greatness side by side with its defects. There was no system; all was muddled, yet all was safe. Anyone could claim what luggage they liked, though no one did so, nor dreamed, it seemed, of doing so. There was an air of decent honesty and trust. There were ladies who discovered that all men are savages; there were men—and women—who were savages. People shook hands warmly, smiled with honest affection, said light, careless good-byes that hid genuine emotion; helped one another with parcels, offered one another lifts. There were few taxicabs, one perhaps to every thirty people. And in this general scrimmage, Dr. Fillery, at first, could see no sign of his expected arrivals; he walked from end to end of the platform littered with luggage and thronged with bustling people, but nowhere could he discover the familiar outline of Devonham, nor anyone who answered to the strange picture that already stood forth sharply in his mind.

"There's been a mistake somewhere," he said to himself; "I shall find a telegram when I get back to the house explaining it"—when, suddenly and without apparent cause, there stole upon him a curious lift of freedom—a sharp sense of open spaces he was at a loss to understand. It was accompanied by an increase of light. For a second it occurred to him that the great enclosing roof had rolled back and blown away, letting in air and some lost ray of sunshine. A lovely valley flitted across his thought. Almost he was aware of flowers, of music, of rhythmic movement.

"Edward! there you are. I thought you hadn't come," he heard close behind him, and, turning, saw the figure of Devonham, calm and alert as usual. At his side stood a lean, virile outline of a young man, topping Devonham by several inches, with broad but thin shoulders, figure erect yet flexible, whose shining and inquiring eyes of blue were the most striking feature in a boyish face, where strength, intensity and radiant health combined in an unusual degree.

"Here is our friend, LeVallon," added Devonham, but not before the figure had stepped lightly and quickly forward, already staring at him and shaking his outstretched hand.

So this was "N. H.," and LeVallon was his name. The calm, searching eyes held a touch of bewilderment in them, the eyes of an honest, intelligent animal, thought Fillery quickly, adding in spite of himself and almost simultaneously, "but of a divine animal." It was a look he had never in his life before encountered in any human eyes. Mason's water-colour sketch had caught something, at least, of their innocence and question, of their odd directness and intensity, something, too, of the golden fire in the hair. He wore a broad-brimmed felt hat of Swiss pattern, a Bernese overcoat, a low, soft-collared shirt, with blue tie to match.

Buffeted and pushed by the frenzied travellers, they stood and faced each other, shaking hands, eyes looking into eyes, two strangers, doctor and patient possibly, but friends most certainly, both felt instantly. They liked one another, Once again the scent of flowers danced with light above the piled-up heaps of trunks, rugs, packages. A cool wind from mountains seemed to blow across the dreadful station.

"You've arrived safely," began Dr. Fillery, a little taken aback perhaps. "Welcome! And not too tired, I hope——" when the other interrupted him in a man's deep voice, full of pleasant timbre:

"Fill-er-y," he said, making the "F" sound rather long, "I need you. To see you makes me happy."

"Tired," put in Devonham breathlessly, "good heavens, not he! But I am. Now for a porter and the big luggage. Have you got a taxi?"

"The car is here," said Fillery, letting go with a certain reluctance the hand he held, and paying little attention to anything but the figure before him who used such unexpected language. What was it? What did it mean? Whence came this sudden sense of intensity, light, of order, system, intelligence into the racial scene of muddled turmoil all about him? There seemed an air of speeding up in thought and action near him, compared to which the slow stupidity, unco-ordinated and confused on all sides, became painful, gross, and even ludicrous.

Someone bumped against him with violence, but quite needlessly, since the simplest judgment of weight and distance could have avoided the collision. In such ordinary small details he was aware of another, a higher, standard close. A man on his left, trying to manage several bundles, appeared vividly as of amazing incompetence, with his mis-calculation, his clumsy movement, his hopeless inability to judge cause and effect. Yet he had two arms, ten fingers, two legs, broad shoulders and deep chest. Misdirection of his great strength made it impossible for him to manage the assortment of light parcels. Next to him, however, stood a woman carrying a baby—there was no error there. The panting engine just beyond them, again, set a standard of contemptuous, impersonal intelligence that, obeying Nature's laws, dwarfed the humans generally. But it was another, a quasi-spiritual standard that had flashed to him above all. In some curious way the competent "dead" machinery that obeyed the Law with faultless efficiency, and the woman obeying instinct with equally unconscious skill—these two energies were akin to the new standard he was now startlingly aware of.

He looked up, as though to trace this sudden new con-sciousness of bright, quick, rapid competence—almost as of some immense power building with consistent scheme and system—that had occurred to him; and he met again the direct, yet slightly bewildered eyes that watched him, watched him with confidence, sweetness, and with a ques-tioning intensity he found intriguing, captivating, and oddly stimulating. He felt happiness.

"By yer leave!" roared a porter, as they stepped aside just in time to save being pushed by the laden truck—just in time to save himself, that is, for the other, Fillery noticed, moved like a chamois on its native rocks, so surely, lightly, swiftly was he poised.

"This! Ah, you must excuse it," the doctor exclaimed with a smile of apology almost, "we've not yet had time to settle down after the war, you see." He pointed with a sweep of his hand to the roaring, dim-lit cavern where confusion reigned supreme, the G.H.Q. of travel in the biggest city of the Empire.

"I've got a porter," cried Devonham, beckoning vigorously

a little further down the platform. "You wait there. I'll be along in a minute with the stuff." He was hot, flustered, exhausted.

"You struggle. It was like this all the way. Is there no knowledge?" LeVallon asked in his deep, quiet tones.

"We do," said Fillery. "With us life is always struggle. But there is more system than appears. The confusion is chiefly on the surface."

"It is dark and there is so little air," observed the other. "And they all work against each other."

Fillery laughed into the other's eyes; they laughed together; and it seemed suddenly to the doctor that their beings somehow merged, so that, for a second, he knew the entire content of his companion's mind—as if there was nothing in LeVallon he did not understand.

"You—are a builder," LeVallon said abruptly. But as he said it his companion caught, on the wing as it were, another meaning. He became curiously aware of the smallness, of the remote insignificance of the little planet whereon this dialogue took place, yet at the same time of its superb seductive loveliness. In him rose a feeling, as on wings, that he was not chained in his familiar, daily personality, but that an immense, delicious freedom lay within reach. He could be everywhere at once. He could do everything.

"Wait here while I help Devonham. Then we'll get into the car and be off." He moved away, threading a path with difficulty.

"I wait in peace. I am happy," was the reply.

And with those few phrases, uttered in the quiet, deep voice, sounding in his ears and in his very blood, the older man went towards the spot where Devonham struggled with a porter, a pile of nondescript luggage and a truck: "I wait in peace. . . . You struggle, you work against each other. . . . It is dark, there is little air. . . . You are a builder. . . ."

But not these singular words alone remained alive in his mind; there remained in his heart the sense of that vitality of open spaces, keen air and brighter light he had experienced—and, with it, the security of some higher, faultless standard. His brain, indeed, had recognized a consciousness of swifter reactions, of surer movements, of more intelligent co-ordination, compared to which the people about him behaved like stupid, almost like half-witted beings, the one exception being the instinctive action of the mother in carrying her baby, and the other, the impersonal, accurate, competence of the dead machinery.

But, more than this reasoned change, there burned suddenly in his heart an inexplicable exhilaration and brightness, a wonder that he could attribute only to another mode of life. His Khaketian blood, he knew, might be responsible for part of it, but not for all. The invigorating mountain wind, the sunlight, the rhythmic sound, the scent of wild flowers, these were his own personal interpretations of a quickened sense he could not analyse as yet. As he held the young man's hand, as he gazed into his direct blue eyes, this sense had increased in intensity. LeVallon had some marvellous quality or power that was new to him, while yet not entirely unfamiliar. What was it? And how did the youth perceive this sense in him so surely that he took its presence for granted, accepted, even played upon it? He experienced, as it were, a brilliant intensification of spirit. Some portion of him already knew exactly what LeVallon was.

Across the ugly turmoil and confusion of the huge dingy railway terminus had moved wondrously some simple power that brought in—Beauty. Some very deep and ancient conception had touched him and gone its way again. The stupendous beauty of a simple, common day appeared to him. His subconscious being, of course, was deeply stirred. That was the truth, phrase it as he might. His heart was lifted as by a primal wind at dawn upon some mountain top. The heaviness of the day was gone. Fatigue, too, vanished. The "civilized" folk appeared contemptible and stupid. Something direct from Nature herself poured through him. And it was from the atmosphere of LeVallon this new vitality issued radiating.

He found a moment or two, while alone with Devonham, to exchange a few hurried sentences. As they bent over bags and bundles he asked quick questions. These questions and answers between the two experienced men were brief but significant:

"Yes, quiet as a lamb. Just be kind and sympathetic. You looked up the Notes? Well, that can't be helped now, though I had rather you knew nothing. My mistake, of course."

"The content of his mind is accessible to me—telepathically—in any case."

"But at one remove more distant, because unexpressed."

Fillery laughed. "Quite right. I admit it's a pity. But tell me more about him—anything I ought to know—at once."

"Quiet as a lamb, I told you," repeated the other, "and most of the way over too. Butt puzzled—my God, Edward, his criticisms would make a book."

"Normal? Intelligent criticisms?"

"Intelligent above ordinary. Normal—no."

"Hysteria?"

"Not a sign."

"Health?"

"Perfect, magnificent, as you see. He's less tired now than when we started three days ago, whereas I'm fagged out, though in climbing condition."

"Origin of delusions—any indication?"

Devonham looked up quickly. His eyes flashed a peculiarly searching glance—something watchful in it perhaps. "No delusion at all of any sort. As for origin of his ideas—the parents probably, but stimulated and allowed unchecked growth by Mason. Affected by Nature beyond anything *we* know."

"By Nature. Ah!" He checked himself. "And what peculiarities?" he asked.

"His terror of water, for instance. Crossing the Channel he was like a frightened child. He hid from it, kept his hands over his eyes even, so as not to see it."

"Give any reason?"

"All he said was 'It is unknown, an enemy, and can destroy me. I cannot understand its secret ways. Fire and wind are not in it. I cannot work with it.' No, it was not fear of drowning that he meant. He found comfort, too, in the repetition of your name."

"Appetite, pulse, temperature?" asked Fillery, after a brief pause.

"First two very strong; temperature always slightly above normal."

"Other peculiarities?"

"He became rather excited before a lighted match once —tried to kneel, almost, but I stopped it."

"Fire?"

"That's it. Instinct of worship presumably."

The barrow was laden, the porter was asking where the car was. They prepared to move back to the companion, whom Fillery had never failed to observe carefully over his shoulder during this rapid conversation. "N. H." had not moved the whole time: he stood quietly, looking about him, a curious figure, aloof somehow from his surroundings, so tall and straight and unconcerned he seemed, yet so poised, alert, virile, vigorous. It was not his clothes that made him appear unusual, nor was it his eyes and hair alone, though all three contributed their share. Yet he seemed dressed up, his clothes irksome to him. He was uncommon, an attractive figure, and many a pair of eyes, female eyes especially, Fillery noticed, turned to examine him with undeniable curiosity.

"And women?" the doctor asked quickly in a lowered voice, as they followed the porter's barrow towards Le-Vallon, who already smiled at their approach—the most engaging, trustful, welcoming smile that Fillery had ever seen upon a human countenance.

He lowered his head to catch the reply. But Devonham only laughed and shrugged his shoulders. "All attracted," he mumbled in a half whisper, "and eager to help him."

"And he——?"

"Gentle, astonished, but indifferent, oh, supremely indifferent."

LeVallon came forward to meet them, and Fillery took his hand and led him to the car. The luggage was bundled in, some behind and some on the roof. Fillery and LeVallon sat side by side. The car started.

"We shall get home in half an hour," the doctor mentioned, turning to his companion. "We'll have a good dinner and then get to bed. You are hungry, I know."

"Thank you," was the reply, "thank you, dear Fillery. I want sleep most. Will there be trees and air near me? And stars to see?"

"Your windows open on to a garden with big trees, there will be plenty of fresh air, and you will hear the sparrows chattering at dawn. But London, of course, is not the country. Oh, we'll make you comfortable, never fear."

"Dear Fillery, I thank you," said LeVallon quietly, and without more ado lay back among the soft cushions and closed his eyes. Hardly a word was said the whole way out to the north-west suburb, and when they arrived the "patient" was too overcome with sleep to wish to eat. He went straight to his room, found a hot bath into which he tumbled first, and then leaped into his bed and was sound asleep almost before the door was closed. Upon a table beside the bed Dr. Fillery, with his own hands, arranged bread, butter, eggs and a jug of milk in case of need. Nurse Robbins, an experienced, tactful young woman, he put in special charge. He thought of everything, divining his friend's possible needs instinctively, noticing with his keen practised eye several details for himself at the same time. The splendid physical condition, frame-work, muscular development he noted—no freakish bulky masses produced by gymnastic exercises, but the muscles laid on flowingly, smooth and firm and ample, without a trace of fat, and the whole in the most admirable proportion possible. The leanness was deceptive; the body was of immense power. The quick, certain, unerring movements he noticed too; perfect, swift co-ordination between brain and physical response, no misdirection, no miscalculation, the reactions extremely rapid. He thought with a smile of something between deer and tiger. The poise and balance and accuracy conveyed intense joy of living. Yet above and beyond these was something else he could not name, something that stirred in him wonder, love, a touch of awe, and a haunting suggestion of familiarity.

He saw him into bed, he saw him actually asleep. The strong blue eyes looked up into his own with their intense and innocent gaze for a moment; he held the firm, dry muscular hand; ten seconds later the eyes were closed in sleep, the grip of the powerful but slender fingers relaxed.

"Good night, my friend, and sleep deeply. To-morrow we'll see to everything you need. Be happy here and comfortable with us, for you are welcome and we love you." His voice trembled slightly.

"Good night, dear Fill-er-y," the musical tones replied, and he was off.

The windows were wide open. "N. H." had thrown aside the pyjamas and blankets. On this cool, damp night of late autumn he covered his big, warm, lithe body with a single sheet only.

Fillery went out quietly, an expression of keen approval and enjoyment on his face—not a smile exactly, but that look of deep content, betraying a fine inner excitement of happiness, which is the mother of all smiles. As he softly opened the door the draught blew through from the open windows, stirring the white curtains by the bed. It came from the big damp garden where the trees stood, already nearly leafless, and where no flowers were. And yet a scent of flowers came faintly with it. He caught an echo of faint sound like music. There was the invigorating hint of forests too. It seemed a living wind that blew into the house.

Dr. Fillery paused a moment, sniffed with surprise and sharp enjoyment, listened intently, then switched the light off and went out, closing the door behind him. There was a flash of wonder in his eyes, and a thrill of some remote inexplicable happiness ran through his nerves. An instant of complete comprehension had been his, as if another consciousness had, for that swift instant, identified itself with his own.

CHAPTER VI

EDWARD FILLERY was glad that Paul Devonham, good friend and skillful colleague, was his assistant; for Devonham, competent as himself in knowledge and experience, found explanations for all things, and had in his natural temperament a quality of sane judgment which corrected extravagances.

Devonham was agnostic, because reason ruled his life. Devoid of imagination, he had no temptations. Speculative, within limits, he might be, but he belonged not to the unstable. Not that he thought he knew everything, but that he refused to base action on what he regarded as unknown. A clue into the unknown he would follow up as keenly, carefully, as Fillery himself, but he went step by step, with caution, declining to move further until the last step was of hardened concrete. To the powers of the subconscious self he set drastic limits, admitting their existence of course, but attaching small value to their use or development. His own deeper being had never stirred or wakened. Of this under-sea, this vast background in himself, he remained placidly uninformed. A comprehensive view of a problem—the flash of vision he never knew— thus was perhaps denied him, but so far as he went he was very safe and sure. And his chief was the first to appreciate his value. He appreciated it particularly now, as the two men sat smoking after their late dinner, discussing details of the new inmate of the Home.

Fillery, aware of the strong pull upon his own mixed blood, aware of a half-wild instinctive sympathy towards "N. H.," almost of a natural desire now, having seen him, to believe him "unique" in several ways, and, therefore, conscious of a readiness to accept more than any evidence yet justified—feeling these symptoms clearly, and remembering vividly his experiences in the railway station, he was glad, for truth's sake, that Devonham was there to clip extravagance before it injured judgment. A weak man, aware of his own frailties, excels a stronger one who thinks he has none at all. The two colleagues were a powerful combination.

"In your view, it's merely a case of a secondary—anyhow of a divided—personality?" he asked, as soon as the other had recovered a little from his journey, and was digesting his meal comfortably over a pipe. "You have seen more of him than I have. Of insanity, at any rate, there is no sign at all, I take it? His relations with his environment are sound?"

"None whatever." Devonham answered both questions at once. "Exactly."

He took off his pince-nez, cleaned them with his handkerchief, and then replaced them carefully. This gave him time to reflect, as though he was not quite sure where to begin his story.

"There are certainly indications," he went on slowly, "of a divided personality, though of an unusual kind. The margin between the two—between the normal and the secondary self—is so very slight. It is not clearly defined, I mean. They sometimes merge and interpenetrate. The frontier is almost indistinguishable."

Fillery raised his eyebrows.

"You feel uncertain which is the main self, and which the split-off secondary personality?" he inquired, with surprise.

Devonham nodded. "I'm extremely puzzled," he admitted. "LeVallon's most marked self, the best defined, the richest, the most fully developed, seems to me what *we* should call his Secondary Self—this 'Nature-being' that worships wind and fire, is terrified by a large body of water, is ignorant of human ways, probably also quite *un*-moral, yet alive with a kind of instinctive wisdom we credit usually to the animal kingdom—though far beyond anything animals can claim——"

"Briefly, what we mean by the term 'N. H.,'" suggested Fillery, not anxious for too many details at the moment.

"Exactly. And I propose we always refer to that aspect of him as 'N. H.,' the other, the normal ordinary man, being LeVallon, his right name." He smiled faintly.

"Agreed," replied his chief. "We shall always know then exactly which one we're talking of at a given moment. Now," he went on, "to come to the chief point, and before you give me details of what happened abroad, let me hear your own main conclusion. What is LeVallon? What is 'N. H.'?"

Devonham hesitated for some time. It was evident his respect for his chief made him cautious. There was an eternal battle between these two, keen though always good-natured, even humorous, the victory not invariably perhaps with the assistant. Later evidence had often proved Fillery's swifter imagination correct after all, or, alternately, shown him to be wrong. They kept an accurate score of the points won and lost by either.

"You can always revise your conclusions later," Fillery reminded him slyly. "Call it a preliminary conclusion for the moment. You've not had time yet for a careful study, I know."

But Devonham this time did not smile at the rally, and his chief noticed it with secret approval. Here was something new, big, serious, it seemed. Devonham, apparently, was already too interested to care who scored or did not score. His Notes of 1914 indeed betrayed his genuine zeal sufficiently.

"LeVallon," he said at length—"to begin with him! I think LeVallon—without any flavour of 'N. H.'—is a fine specimen of a normal human being. His physique is magnificent, as you have seen, his health and strength exceptional. The brain, so far as I have been able to judge,

functions quite normally. The intelligence, also normal, is
much above the average in quickness, receptivity of ideas,
and judgment based on these. The emotional development,
however, puzzles me; the emotions are not entirely normal.
But"—he paused again, a grave expression on his face—
"to answer your question as well as my limited observation
of him, of LeVallon, allows—I repeat that I consider him
a normal young man, though with peculiarities and idiosyncrasies of his own, as with most other normal young fellows
who are individuals, that is," he added quickly, "and not
turned out in bundles cut to measure."

"So much for LeVallon. Now what about 'N. H.' ?"

He repeated the question, fixing the assistant with his
steady gaze. He had noticed the confusion in the reply.

"My dear Edward——" began Devonham, after a considerable pause. Then he stuck fast, sighed, settled his
glasses carefully upon his aquiline, sharp nose, and relapsed
into silence. His forehead became wrinkled, his mouth
much pursed.

"Out with it, Paul! This isn't a Court of Law. I shan't
behead you if you're wrong." Yet Fillery, too, spoke
gravely.

The other kept his eyes down; his face still wore a
puzzled look. Fillery detected a new expression on the
keen, thoughtful features, and he was pleased to see it.

"To give you the truth," resumed his assistant, "and all
question of who is right or who is wrong aside, I tell you
frankly—I am not sure. I confess myself up against it.
It—er—gives me the creeps a little——" He laughed
awkwardly. That swift watchful look, as of a man who
plays a part, flashed and vanished.

"Your feeling, anyhow?" insisted his friend. "Your
general feeling?"

"A general judgment based on general feeling," said the
other in a quiet tone, "has little value. It is based, necessarily, as you know, upon intuition, which I temperamentally
dislike. It has no facts to go upon. I distrust generaliza-

tions." He took a deep breath, inhaled a lot of smoke, exhaled it with relief, and made an effort. It went against the grain in him to be caught without an explanation.

" 'N. H.' in my opinion, and so far as my limited observation of him——"

Fillery allowed himself a laugh of amused impatience. "Leave out the personal extras for once, and burn your bridges. Tell me finally what you think about 'N. H.' We're not scoring points now."

Thus faced with an alternative, Devonham found his sense of humour again and forgot himself. It cost him an effort, but he obeyed the bigger and less personal mind.

"I really don't know exactly *what* he is," he confessed again. "He puzzles me completely. It *may* be"—he shrugged his shoulders, compelled by his temperament to hedge—"that he represents, as I first thought, the content of his parents' minds, the subsequent addition of Mason's mind included."

"That's possible, usual and comprehensible enough," put in the doctor, watching him with amused concentration, but with an inner excitement scarcely concealed.

"Or" resumed Devonham, "it *may* be that through these——"

"Through his mental inheritance from his parents and from Mason, yes——"

"——he taps the most primitive stores and layers of racial memory we know. The world-memory, if I dare put it so, full proof being lacking, is open to him——"

"Through his subconscious powers, of course?"

"That is your usual theory, isn't it? We have there, at any rate, a working hypothesis, with a great mass of evidence—generally speaking—behind it."

"Don't be cynical, Paul. Is this 'N. H.' merely a Secondary Personality, or is it the real central self? That's the whole point."

"You jump ahead, as usual," replied Devonham, really smiling for the first time, though his face instantly grew serious again. "Edward," he went on, "I do not know, I cannot say, I dare not—dare not guess. 'N. H.' is something entirely new to me, and I admit it." He seemed to find his stride, to forget himself. "I feel far from cynical. 'N. H.,' in my opinion, is exceptional. My notes suggested it long ago. He has, for instance—at least, so it seems to me—peculiar powers."

"Ah!"

"Of suggestion, let us put it."

"Of suggestion, yes. Get on with it, there's a good fellow. I felt myself an extraordinary vitality about him. I noticed it at once at Charing Cross."

"I saw you did." Devonham looked hard at him. "You were humming to yourself, you know."

"I didn't know," was the surprised reply, "but I can well believe it. I felt a curious pleasure and exhilaration."

Devonham, shrugging his shoulders slightly, resumed: "During the 'LeVallon' periods he is ordinary, though unusually observant, critical and intelligent; during the 'N. H.' periods he becomes—er—super-normal. If you felt this—felt anything in the station, it was because something in you—called up the 'N. H.' aspect."

"It's quick of you to guess that," said Fillery, with quick appreciation. "You noticed a change in me, well—but the other——? He divined my 'foreign' blood, you think?"

"It is enough that you responded and felt kinship. Put it that way. 'N. H.' seems to me"—he took a deeper breath and gave a sort of gasp—"in some ways—a unique—being —as I said before."

"Tell me, if you can," said Fillery, lighting his own pipe and settling back into his chair, "tell me a little about your first meeting with him in the Jura Mountains, what happened and so forth. I remember, of course, your Notes. After your telegram, I read 'em carefully." He glanced round at his companion. "They were very honest, Paul, I thought. Eh?" He was unable to refuse himself the pleasure of the little dig. "Honest you always are," he added. "We couldn't work together otherwise, could we?"

Devonham, deep in his own thoughts, did not accept the challenge. He turned in his chair, puffing at his pipe.

"I can give you briefly what happened and how things went," he said. "The place, then, first: an ordinary peasant châlet in a remote Jura valley, difficult of access, situated among what they call the upper pastures. I reached it by *diligence* and mule late in the afternoon. A peasant in a lower valley directed me, adding that 'le monsieur anglais' was dead and buried two days before——"

"Mason, that is?"

The other nodded. "And adding that 'le fou'——"

"LeVallon, of course?"

"——would eat me alive at sight. He spoke with respect, however, even awe. He hoped I had come to take him away. The countryside was afraid of him.

"The valley struck me as intolerably lonely, but of unusual beauty. Big forests, great rocks, and tumbling streams among cliffs and pastures made it exceptional. The châlet was simple, clean and comfortable. It was really an ideal spot for a thinker or a student. The first thing I noticed was a fire burning on a pile of rock in front of the building. The sun was setting, and its last rays lit the entire little glen—a mere gully between precipices and forest slopes—but especially lit up the pile of rocks where the fire burned, so that I saw the smoke, blue, red and yellow, and the figure kneeling before it. This figure was a man, half naked, and of magnificent proportions. When I shouted——"

"You *would* shout, of course." Yet he did not say it critically.

"——the figure rose and turned and came to meet me. It was LeVallon."

Devonham paused a moment. Fillery's eyes were fixed upon him.

"I admit," Devonham went on, conscious of the other's inquiring and intent expression, "I was surprised a bit." He smiled his faint, unwilling smile. "The figure made me start. I was aware of an emotion I am not subject to —what I called just now the creeps. I thought, at last, I had really seen a—a vision. He looked so huge, so wonderful, so radiant. It was, of course, the effect of coloured smoke and magnifying sunset, added to his semi-nakedness. To the waist he was stripped. But, at first, his size, his splendour, a kind of radiance borrowed from the sunlight and the fire, seemed to enlarge him beyond human. He seemed to dominate, even to fill the little valley.

"I stood still, uncertain of my feelings. There was, I think, a trace of fear in me. I waited for him to come up to me. He did so. He stretched out a hand. I took it. And what do you think he said?"

Fillery, the inner excitement and delight increasing in him as he listened, stared in silence. There was no lightness in him now.

"'Are you Fillery?' That's what he said, and the first words he uttered. 'Are you Fillery?' But spoken in a way I find difficult to reproduce. He made the name sound like a rush of wind. 'F,' of course, involves a draught of breath between the teeth, I know. But *he* made the name sound exactly like a gush of wind through branches—that's the nearest I can get to it."

"Well—and then?"

"Don't be impatient, Edward. I try to be accurate. But really—what happened next is a bit beyond any experience that we—I—have yet come across. And, as to what I felt —well, I was tired, hungry, thirsty. I wanted, normally, rest and food and drink. Yet all these were utterly forgotten. For a moment or two—I admit it—I felt as if I had come face to face with something not of this earth quite." He grinned. "A touch of gooseflesh came to me for the first time in my life. The fellow's size and radiance in the sunlight, the fact that he stood there worshipping

fire—always, to me, the most wonderful of natural phenomena—his grandeur and nakedness—the way he pro-
nounced your name even—all this—er—upset my judgment
for the moment." He paused again. He hesitated. "A
visual hallucination, due to fatigue, can be, of course, very
detailed sometimes," he added, a note of challenge in his
tone.

Fillery watched his friend narrowly, as he stumbled
among the details of what he evidently found a difficult,
almost an impossible description.

"Natural enough," he put in. "You'd hardly be human
yourself if you felt nothing at such a sight."

"The loneliness, too, increased the effect," went on the
other, "for there was no one nearer than the peasants who
had directed me a thousand feet below, nor was there
another building of any sort in sight. Anyhow, it seemed,
I managed my strange emotions all right, for the young
man took to me at once. He left the fire, if reluctantly,
singing to himself a sort of low chanting melody, with
perhaps five or six notes at most in it, and far from
unmusical——"

"He explained the fire? Was he actually worshipping,
I mean?"

"It was certainly worship, judging by the expression of
his face and his gestures of reverence and happiness. But
I asked no questions. I thought it best just to accept, or
appear to accept, the whole thing as natural. He said something about the Equinox, but I did not catch it properly
and did not ask. This had evidently been taught him. It
was, however, the 22nd of September, oddly enough, though
the gales had not yet come."

"So you got into the châlet next?" asked the other,
noticing the gaps, the incoherence.

"He put his coat on, sat down with me to a meal of
bread and milk and cheese—meat there seemed none in
the building anywhere. This meal was, if you understand
me, obeying a mere habit automatically. He did just what

it had been his habit to do with Mason all these years. He got the stuff himself—quickly, effectively, no fumbling anywhere—and, from that moment, hardly spoke again until we left two days later. I mean that literally. All he said, when I tried to make him talk, was, 'You are not Fillery,' or 'Take me to Fillery. I need him.'

"I almost felt that I was living with some marvellously trained animal, of extraordinary intelligence, gentle, docile, friendly, but unhappy because it had lost its accustomed master. But on the other hand—I admit it—I was conscious of a certain power in his personality beyond me to explain. That, really, is the best description I can give you."

"You mentioned the name of Mason?" asked Fillery, avoiding a dozen more obvious and natural questions.

"Several times. But his only reply was a smile, while he repeated the name himself, adding your own after it: 'Mason Fillery, Mason Fillery,' he would say, smiling with quiet happiness. 'I like Fillery!' "

"The nights?"

"Briefly—I was glad to see the dawn. We had separate rooms, my own being the one probably where Mason had died a few days before. But it was not that I minded in the least. It was the feeling—the knowledge in fact—that my companion was up and about all night in the building or out of doors. I heard him moving, singing quietly to himself, the wooden veranda creaked beneath his tread. He was active all through the darkness and cannot have slept at all. When I came down soon after dawn he was running over the slopes a mile away, running towards the châlet, too, with the speed and lightness of a deer. He had been to some height, I think, to see the sun rise and probably to worship it——"

"And your journey? You got him away easily?"

"He was only too ready to leave, for it meant coming to *you*. I arranged with the peasants below to have the châlet closed up, took my charge to Neuchâtel, and thence to Berne, where I bought him an outfit, and arrived in due course, as you know, at Charing Cross."

"His first sight of cities, people, trains, steamers and the rest, I take it. Any reactions?"

"The troubles I anticipated did not materialize. He came like a lamb, the most helpless and pathetic lamb I ever saw. He stared but asked no questions. I think he was half dazed, even stupefied with it all."

"Stupefied?"

"An odd word to use, I know. I should have said perhaps 'automatic' rather. He was so open to my suggestions, doing what my mind expected him to do, but nothing more —ah! with one exception."

Fillery meant to hear an account of that exception, though the other would willingly have foregone its telling evidently. It was related, Fillery felt sure, to the unusual powers Devonham had mentioned.

"Oh, you shall hear it," said the latter quickly, "for what it's worth. There's no need to exaggerate, of course." He told it rapidly, accurately, no doubt, because his mind was honest, yet without comment or expression in his voice and face. He supplied no atmosphere.

"I had got him like a lamb, as I told you, to Paris, and it was during the Customs examination the—er—little thing occurred. The man, searching through his trunk, pulled out a packet of flat papers and opened it. He looked them over with puzzled interest, turning them upside down to examine them from every possible angle. Then he asked a trifle unpleasantly what they were. I hadn't the smallest idea myself, I had never seen them before; they were very carefully wrapped up. LeVallon, whose sudden excitement increased the official's interest, told him that they were star-and-weather maps. It doubtless was the truth; he had made them with Mason; but they were queer-looking papers to have at such a time, hidden away, too, at the bottom of the trunk; and LeVallon's manner and expression did not help to disarm the man's evident suspicion. He asked a

number of pointed questions in a very disagreeable way—
who made them, for what purpose, how they were used,
and whether they were connected with aviation. I trans-
lated, of course. I explained their innocence——"

"LeVallon's excitement?" asked Fillery. "What form
did it take? Rudeness, anger, violence of any sort?" He
was aware his friend would have liked to shirk these
details.

"Nothing of the kind." He hesitated briefly, then went
on. "He behaved, rather, as though—well, as a devout
Catholic might have behaved if his crucifix or some holy
relic were being mauled. The maps were sacred. Symbols
possibly. Heaven knows what! He tried to take them
back. The official, as a natural result, became still more
suspicious and, of course, offensive too. My explanations
and expostulations were quite useless, for he didn't even
listen to them."

Devonham was now approaching the part of the story
he least wished to describe. He played for time. He gave
details of the ensuing altercation.

"What happened in the end?" Fillery at length interrupted. "What did LeVallon do? There were no arrests,
I take it?" he added with a smile.

Paul coughed and fidgeted. He told the literal truth,
however.

"LeVallon, after listening for a long time to the conversation he could not understand, suddenly took his fingers
off the papers. The man's dirty hand still held them tightly
on the grimy counter. LeVallon began—or—he suddenly
began to breathe—well—heavily rather."

"Rhythmically?"

"Heavily," insisted the other. "In a curious way, anyhow," he added, determined to keep strictly to the truth,
"not unlike Heathcote when he put himself automatically
into trance and then told us what was going on at the
other end of England. You remember the case." He
paused a moment again, as if to recall exactly what had

occurred. "It's not easy to describe, Edward," he continued, looking up. "You remember that huge draughty hall where they examine luggage at the Lyons Station. I can't explain it. But that breathing somehow caught the draughts, used them possibly, in any case increased them. A wind came through the great hall. I can't explain it," he repeated, "I can only tell you what happened. That wind most certainly came pouring steadily through, for I felt it myself, and saw it blow upon the fluttering papers. The heat in the *salle* at the same moment seemed to grow intense. Not an oppressive heat, though. Radiant heat, rather. It felt, I mean, like a fierce sunlight. I looked up, almost expecting to see a great light from which it came. It was then—at this very moment—the Frenchman turned as if someone touched him."

"*You* felt anything, Paul?"

"Yes," admitted the other slowly.

Fillery waited.

"A—what I must call—a thrill." His voice was lower now.

"Of——?" his Chief persisted.

Devonham waited a full ten seconds before reply. He again shrugged his shoulders a little. Apparently he sought his words with honest care that included also intense reluctance and disapproval:

"Loveliness, romance, enchantment; but, above all, I think—power." He ground out the confession slowly. "By power I mean a sort of confidence and happiness."

"Increase of vitality, call it. Intensification of your consciousness."

"Possibly. A bigger perspective suddenly, a bigger scale of life; something—er—a bit wild, but certainly—er— uncommonly stimulating. The best word, I think, is liberty, perhaps. An immense and careless sense of liberty." And Fillery, knowing the value of superlatives in Devonham's cautious mind, felt satisfied. He asked quietly what the official did next.

"Stood stock still at first. Then his face changed; he smiled; he looked up understandingly, sympathetically, at LeVallon. He spoke: 'My father, too,' he said with admiration, 'had a big telescope. Monsieur is an astronomer.'

"'One of the greatest,' I added quickly; 'these charts are of infinite value to France.' No sense of comedy touched me anywhere, the ludicrous was absent. The man bowed, as carefully, respect in every gesture, he replaced the maps, marked the trunk with his piece of chalk, and let us go, helping in every way he could."

Devonham drew a long breath, glad that he had relieved himself of his unwelcome duty. He had told the literal truth.

"Of course, of course," Fillery said, half to himself perhaps. "A breath of bigger consciousness, his imagination touched, the subconscious wakened, and intelligence the natural result." He turned to his colleague. "Interesting, Paul, very," he added in a louder tone, "and not easy to explain, I grant. The official we do not know, but you, at any rate, are not a good subject for hypnotic suggestion!"

For some time Devonham said nothing. Presently he spoke:

"Fillery, I tell you—really I love the fellow. He's the most lovable thing in human shape I ever saw. He gets into your heart so strangely. We must heal him."

The other sighed, quickly smothering it, yet not before Devonham had noticed it. They did not look at one another for some seconds, and there was a certain tenseness, a sense of deep emotion in the air that each, possibly, sought to hide from the other.

Devonham was the first to break the silence that had fallen between them.

"To be quite frank—it's LeVallon that appeals most to me," he said, as if to himself, "whereas you, Edward, I believe, are more—more interested in the other aspect of him. It's 'N. H.' that interests you."

No challenge was intended, yet the glove was flung.

Fillery said nothing for a minute or two. Then he looked up, and their eyes met across the smoke-laden atmosphere. It was close on midnight. The world lay very still and hushed about the house.

"It is," he said quietly, "a pathetic and inspiring case. He is deserving of"—he chose his words slowly and with care—"our very best," he concluded shortly.

"And now," he added quickly, "you're tired out, and I ought to have let you have a night's sleep before taxing you like this." He poured out two glasses of whisky. "Let us drink anyhow to success and healing of body, mind—and soul."

"Body, mind and—nerves," said Devonham slowly, as he drank the toast.

"The reason I had none of the trouble I anticipated," remarked Devonham, as he sipped the reviving liquor, "is simple enough."

"There are two periods, of course. I guessed that."

"Exactly. There is the LeVallon period, when he is quiescent, normal, very charming into the bargain, more like a good child or trained animal or happy peasant, if you like it better, than a grown man. And there is the 'N. H.' period, when he is—otherwise."

"Ah!"

"I arrived just at the transition moment, so to speak. It was during the change I reached the châlet."

"Precisely." Fillery looked up, smiled and nodded.

"That's about the truth," repeated Devonham, putting his glass down. He thought for a moment, then added slowly, "I think that fire of his, the worship, singing—at the autumnal equinox—marked the change. 'N. H,' at once after that, slipped back into the unconscious state. Le-Vallon emerged. It was with LeVallon only or chiefly, *I* had to deal. He became so very quiet, dazed a little, half there, as we call it, and almost entirely silent. He retained little, if any, memory of the 'N. H.' period, although it lies, I think, just beneath the surface only. The LeVallon personality, you see, is not very positive, is it? It seems a quiet, negative state, a condition almost of rest, in fact."

Fillery listening attentively, made no rejoinder.

"We may expect," continued Devonham, "these alternating states, I think. The frontier between them is, as I said, a narrow one. Indeed, often they merge or interpenetrate In my judgment, the main, important part of his consciousness, that parent Self, is LeVallon—*not* 'N. H.'" The voice was slightly strident.

"Ah!"

It so happened that, in the act of exchanging these last words, they both looked up toward the ceiling, where a moth buzzed round and round, banging itself occasionally against the electric light. Whether it was this that drew their sight upwards simultaneously, or whether it was that some other sound in the stillness of the night had caught their strained attention, is uncertain. The same thought, at any rate, was in both minds at that instant, the same freight of meaning trailing behind it invisibly across the air. Their hearts burned within them; the two faces upward turned, the lips a little parted as when listening is intense, the heads thrown back. For in the room above that ceiling, asleep at this moment, lay the subject of their long discussion; only a few inches of lath and plaster separated them from the strange being who, dropping out of space, as it were, had come to make his home with them. A being, lonely utterly in the world, unique in kind perhaps, his nature as yet undecipherable, lay trustingly unconscious in that upper chamber. The two men felt the gravity, the responsibility of their charge. The same thought had vividly touched them both at the same instant.

A few minutes later they were still standing, facing one another. They were of a height, but compared to Fillery's big frame and rugged head, his friend's appearance was almost slight. Devonham, for all his qualifications, looked painfully like a shopwalker. They exchanged this steady

gaze for a few seconds without speaking. Then the older
man said quietly:

"Paul, I understand, and I respect your reticence. I think
I can agree with it."

He placed a hand upon the other's shoulder, smiling
gently, even tenderly.

"You have told me much, but you have not told me *all!*
The chief part—you have intentionally omitted."

"For the present, at any rate," was the reply, given without flinching.

"Your reasons are sound, your judgment perhaps right.
I ask no questions. What happened, what you saw, at the
châlet; the 'peculiar powers' you mentioned; all, in fact,
that you think it wise to keep to yourself for the moment,
I leave there willingly."

He spoke gravely, sincere emotion in the eyes and tone.
It was in a lower voice he added:

"The responsibility, of course, is yours."

Devonham returned the steady gaze, pondering his reply
a moment.

"I can—and do accept it," he answered. "You have read
my thoughts correctly as usual, Edward. I think you know
quite enough already—what with my Notes and Mason's
letter—even too much. Besides, why complicate it with an
account of what were doubtless mere mental pictures—
hallucinations—on my part? This is a matter," he went
on slowly, "a case, we dare not trifle with; there may be
strange and terrible afflictions in it later; we must remain
unbiased." The anxiety deepened on his face.

"True, true," murmured the other. "God bless the boy!
May his own gods bless him!"

"In other words, it will need your clearest, soundest
judgment, your finest skill, your very best, as you said
yourself just now." He used a firmer, yet also a softer
tone suddenly: "Edward, you know your own mind, its
contents, its suppressions, its origin; your refusal of the

love of women, your deep powerful dreams that you have suppressed and put away. Promise me"—the voice and manner were very earnest—"that you will not communicate these to him in any way, and that you will keep your judgment absolutely unbiased and untainted." He looked at his old friend and paused. "Only your purest judgment of what is to come can help. You promise."

Fillery sighed a scarcely noticeable sigh. "I promise you, Paul. You are wise—and you are right," he said. "On the other hand, let me say one thing to you in my turn. This theory of heredity and of mental telepathic transference—the idea that all his mind's content is derived from his parents and from Mason—we cannot, remember, force this transference and interchange *too* far. I ask only this: be fair and open yourself with all that follows."

Devonham raised his voice: "Nor can we, apparently, sets limits to it, Edward. But—to be fair and open-minded —I give my promise too."

Thus, in the little downstairs room of a Private Home for Incurable Mental Cases, *not* a Lunatic Asylum, though sometimes perhaps next door to it, these two men, deeply intrigued by a new "Case" that passed their understanding, as it exceeded their knowledge, practice and experience, swore to each other to observe carefully, to report faithfully, and to experiment, if experiment proved necessary, with honest and affectionate uprightness.

Their views were, obviously, not the same. Devonham, temperamentally opposed to radical innovations, believed it was a case of divided personality—hundreds of such cases had passed through their hands. Forced to accept extended telepathy—that all minds can on occasion share one another's content, and that even a racial and a world-memory can be tapped—he feared that his Chief might influence LeVallon, and twist, thus, the phenomena to a special end. He knew Edward Fillery's story. He feared, for the sake of truth, the mental transference. He had, perhaps, other fears as well.

Fillery, on the other hand, believing as much, and know-ing more than his colleague, saw in "N. H." a unique pos-sibility. He was thrilled and startled with a half-impossible hope. He felt as if someone ran beside his life, bearing impossible glad tidings, an unexpected, half-incredible figure, the tidings marvellously bright. He hoped, he already wished to think, that "N. H." might shadow forth a promise of some magical advance for the ultimate benefit of the Race. . . .

The thinkers were crying on the housetops that progress was a myth, that each wave of civilization at its height reached the same average level without ever passing further. The menace to the present civilization, already crumbling, was in full swing everywhere; knowledge, culture, learning threatened in due course with the chaos of destruction that has so far been the invariable rule. The one hope of saving the world, cried religion, lay in substituting spiritual for material values—a Utopian dream at best. The one chance, said science, on the other hand, was that civilization to-day is continuous and not isolated.

The best hope, believed Fillery, the only hope, lay in raising the individual by the drawing up into full conscious-ness of the limitless powers now hidden and inactive in his deeper self—the so-called subliminal faculties. With these greater powers must come also greater moral development.

Already, with his uncanny insight, derived from knowl-edge of himself, he had piercingly divined in "N. H." a being, whatever he might be, whose nature acted auto-matically and directly upon the subconscious self in every-body.

That bright messenger, running past his life, had looked, as with fire and tempest, straight into his eyes.

It was long after one o'clock when the two men said good-night, and went to their rooms. Devonham was soon in bed, though not soon asleep. Exhausted physically though he was, his mind burned actively. His recent memories were vivid. All he had purposely held back from Fillery returned with power. . . .

The uncertainty whether he had experienced hallucination, or had actually, as by telepathic transfer from LeVallon, touched another state of consciousness, kept sleep far away. . . .

His brain was far too charged for easy slumber. He feared for his dear, faithful friend, his colleague, the skilful, experienced, yet sorely tempted mind—tempted by Nature and by natural weaknesses of birth and origin— who now shared with him the care and healing of a Case that troubled his being too deeply for slumber to come quickly.

Yet he had done well to keep these memories from Edward Fillery. If Fillery once knew what *he* knew, his judgment and his scientific diagnosis must be drawn hopelessly away from what he considered the best treatment: the suppression of "N. H." and the making permanent of "LeVallon." . . .

He fell asleep eventually, towards dawn, dreaming impossible, radiant dreams of a world he might have hoped for, yet could not, within the limits of his little cautious, accurate mind, believe in. Dreams that inspire, yet sadden, haunted his release from normal consciousness. Someone had walked upon his life, leaving a growth of everlasting flowers in their magical tread, though his mind—his stolid, cautious mind—had no courage for the plucking. . . .

And while he slept, as the hours slipped from west to east, his chief and colleague, lying also sleepless, rose suddenly before the late autumn dawn, and walked quietly along the corridor towards the Private Suite where the new patient rested. His mind was quiet, yet his inner mind alert. His thoughts, his hopes, his dreams, these lay, perhaps, beyond human computation. He was calmer far than his assistant, though more strangely tempted.

It was just growing light, the corridor was cold. A cool, damp air came through the open windows and the linoleum felt like ice against the feet. The house lay dead and silent. Pausing a moment by a window, he listened to the chattering of early sparrows. He felt chill and hungry, unrested too, though far from sleepy. He was aware of London—bleak, heavy, stolid London town. The troubles of modern life, of Labour, Politics, Taxes, cost of living, all the common, daily things came in with the cheerless morning air.

He reached the door he sought, and very softly opened it.

The radiance met him in the face, so that he almost gasped. The scent of flowers, the sting of sharp, keen forest winds, the exhilaration of some distant mountain-top. There was, actually, a tang of dawn, known only to those who have tasted the heights at sunrise with the heart. And into his heart, singing with happy confidence, rose a sense of supreme joy and confidence that mastered all little earthly woes and pains, and walked among the stars.

The occupant of the bed lay very still. His shining hair was spread upon the pillow. The splendid limbs were motionless. The chest and arms were bare, the single covering sheet tossed off. The strange, wild face wore happiness and peace upon its skin, the features very calm, the mouth relaxed. It almost seemed a god lay sleeping there upon a little human bed.

How long he stood and stared he did not know, but suddenly, the light increased. The curtains stirred about the bed.

With a marvellous touch the separate details merged and quickened into life. The room was changed. The occupant of the bed moved very swiftly, as through the open window came the first touch of exhilarating light. Gold stole across the lintel, breaking over the roofs of slates beyond. The leafless elm trees shimmered faintly. The telegraph wires shone. There was a running sparkle. It was dawn.

The figure leaped, danced—no other word describes it

—to the open window where the light and air gushed in, spread wide its arms, lowered its radiant head, began to sing in low, melodious rhythmic chant—and Fillery, as silently as he had come, withdrew and closed the door unseen. His heart moved strangely, but—his promise held him. . . .

CHAPTER VII

THE following days it seemed to both Fillery and Devonham that their discussion of the first night had been pitched in too intense, too serious a key. Their patient was so commonplace again, so ordinary. He made himself quite at home, seemed contented and uncurious, taking it for granted he had come to stay for ever, apparently.

Apart from his strange beauty, his size, virility and a general impression he conveyed of immense energies he was too easy-going to make use of, he might have passed for a peasant, a countryman to whom city life was new; but an educated, or at least half-educated, countryman. He was so big, yet never gauche. He was neither stupid nor ill-informed; the garden interested him, he knew much about the trees and flowers, birds and insects too. He discussed the weather, prevailing wind, moisture, prospects of change and so forth with a judgment based on what seemed a natural, instinctive knowledge. The gardener looked on him with obvious respect.

"Such nice manners and such a steady eye," Mrs. Soames, the matron, mentioned, too, approvingly to Devonham. "But a lot in him he doesn't understand himself, unless I'm wrong. Not much the matter with his nerves, anyhow. Once he's married—unless I'm much mistaken—eh, sir?"

He was quiet, talking little, and spent the morning over the books Fillery had placed purposely in his sitting-room, books on simple physics, natural history and astronomy. It was the latter that absorbed him most; he pored over them by the hour.

Fillery explained the situation so far as he thought wise. The young man was honesty and simple innocence, but only vaguely interested in the life of the great city he now experienced for the first time. He had in his luggage a copy of the Will by which Mason had left him everything, and he was pleased to know himself well provided for. Of Mason, however, he had only a dim, uncertain, almost an impersonal memory, as of someone encountered in a dream.

"I suppose something's happened to me," he said to Fillery, his language normal and quite ordinary again. He spoke with a slight foreign accent. "There was somebody, of course, who looked after me and lived with me, but I can't remember who or where it was. I was very happy," he added, "and yet . . . I miss something."

Dr. Fillery, remembering his promise, did not press him.

"It will all come back by degrees," he remarked in a sympathetic tone. "In the meantime, you must make yourself at home here with us, for as long as you like. You are quite free in every way. I want you to be happy here."

"I live with you always," was the reply. "There are things I want to tell you, ask you too." He paused, looking thoughtful. "There was someone I told all to once."

"Come to me with everything. I'll help you always, so far as I can." He placed a hand upon his knee.

"There are feelings, big feelings I cannot reach quite, but that make me feel different"—he smiled beautifully—"from—others." Quick as lightning he had changed the sentence at the last word, substituting "others" for "you." Had he been aware of a slight uneasy emotion in his listener's heart? It had hardly betrayed itself by any visible sign, yet he had instantly divined its presence. Such evidences of a subtle, intimate, understanding were not lacking. Yet Fillery admirably restrained himself.

"There are bright places I have lost," he went on frankly, no sign of shy reserve in him. "I feel confused, lost somewhere, as if I didn't belong here. I feel"—he used an odd word—"doubled." His face shaded a little.

"Big overpowering London is bound to affect you," put in Fillery, who had noticed the rapid discernment, "after living among woods and mountains, as you have lived, for years. All will come right in a little time; we must settle down a bit first——"

"Woods and mountains," repeated the other, in a half-dreamy voice, his eyes betraying an effort to follow thought elsewhere. "Of course, yes—woods and mountains and hot living sunlight—and the winds——"

His companion shifted the conversation a little. He suggested a line of reading and study. . . . They talked also of such ordinary but necessary things as providing a wardrobe, of food, exercise, companionship of his own age, and so forth—all the commonplace details of ordinary daily life, in fact. The exchange betrayed nothing of interest, nothing unusual. They mentioned theatres, music, painting, and, beyond the natural curiosity of youth that was ignorant of these, no detail was revealed that need have attracted the attention of anybody, neither of doctor, psychologist, nor student of human nature. With the single exception that the past years had been obliterated from memory, though much that had been acquired in them remained, there was not noticeable peculiarity of any sort. Both language and point of view were normal.

This was obviously LeVallon. The "N. H." personality scarcely cast a shadow even. Yet "N. H.," the doctor was quick to see, lay ready and waiting just below the surface. There was no doubt in *his* mind which was the central self and which its transient projection, the secondary personality. Again, as he sat and talked, he had the odd impression that someone with bright tidings ran swiftly past his life, perhaps towards it.

The swift messenger was certainly not LeVallon. LeVallon, indeed, was but a shadow cast before this glad, bright visitant. Thus he felt, at any rate. LeVallon was an empty simulacrum left behind while "N. H." rested, or was active upon other things, things natural to him, elsewhere. LeVallon was an arm, a limb, a feeler that "N. H." thrust out. At Charing Cross, for instance, for a brief moment only, "N. H." had peered across his shoulder, then withdrawn again. In the car had sat by his side LeVallon. The being he now chatted with was also LeVallon only.

But in his own heart, deep down, hidden yet eager to break loose, lay his own deeper self that burned within him. This, the important part of him, yearned towards "N. H." And up rose the strange symbol that always appeared when his deepest, perhaps his subliminal self was stirred. That lost radiant valley in the haunted Caucasus shone close and brimming over , . . with light, with flowers, with splendid winds and fire, symbols of a vaster, grander, happier life, though perhaps a life not yet within the range of normal human consciousness. . . . The fiery symbol flashed and passed.

Curious thoughts and pictures rose flaming in his mind, persistent ideas that bore no possible relation to his intellectual, reasoning life. Passing across the background of his brain, as with waves of heat and colour, they were correlated somewhere with harmonious sound. Music, that is, came with them, as though inspiration brought its own sound with it that made singing natural. They haunted him, these vague, pleasurable phantasmagoria that were connected, he felt sure, with music, as with childhood's lost imaginings. For a long time he searched in vain for their source and origin. Then, suddenly, he remembered. He heard his father's gruff, humorous voice: "There's not a scrap of evidence, of course. . . ." And, sharply, vividly, the buried memory gave up its dead. His childish question went crashing through the air: "Are we the only beings in the world?"

"Nothing is ever lost," he reminded himself with a smile that Devonham assuredly never saw. "Every seed must bear its fruit in time."

And emotion surged through him from the remorseless records of his underself. The childhood's love, with its correlative of deep, absolute belief, returned upon him, linked on somehow to that old familiar symbol he knew to mean his awakening subconscious being—a flowering Caucasian vale of sun and wind. A belief, he realized, especially a belief of childhood, remains for ever inexpugnable, eternal, prolific seed of future harvests.

The unstable in him betrayed its ineradicable, dangerous streak. There rose upon him in a cloud strange notions that inflamed imagination sweetly. Later reading, indeed, had laid flesh upon the skeleton of the boyish notion, though derived in the first instance he certainly knew not whence. The literature and tradition of the East, he recalled, peopled the elements with conscious life, to which the world's fairy-tales—remnant of lost knowledge possibly—added nerves and heart and blood. In all human bodies, at any rate, dwelt not necessarily always human spirits, human souls. . . .

He checked himself with a smile he would have liked to call a chuckle, but that yet held some inexplicable happiness at its heart. His rugged, eager face, its expression bitten deeply by experience, turned curiously young. There rushed through him the Eastern conception of another system of life, another evolution, deathless, divine, important, the Order of the *Devas,* a series of Nature Beings entirely apart from human categories. They included many degrees, from fairies to planetary spirits, the gods, so called; and their duties, work and purposes were concerned, he remembered, with carrying out the Laws of Nature, the busy tending of all forms and structures, from the elaborately marvellous infusoria in a drop of stagnant water, the growth of crystals, the upbuilding of flowers and trees, of insects, animals, humans, to the guidance and guardianship of those vaster forms of heavenly bodies, the stars, the planets and the mighty suns, whose gigantic "bodies," inhabited by immenser consciousness, people empty space. . . . A noble, useful, selfless work, God's messengers. . . .

He checked himself again, as the rich, ancient notion flitted across his stirring memory.

"Delightful, picturesque conceptions of the planet's young, fair ignorance!" he reminded himself, smiling as before.

Whereupon rose, bursting through his momentary dream, with full-fledged power, the great hope of his own reasoned, scientific Dream—that man is greater than he knows, and that the progress of the Race was demonstrable.

For, to the subliminal powers of an awakened Race these Nature Beings with their special faculties, must lie open and accessible. The human and the non-human could unite! Nature must come back into the hearts of men and win them again to simple, natural life with love, with joy, with naked beauty. Death and disease must vanish, hope and purity return. The Race must develop, grow, become in the true sense *universal.* It could know God!

The vision flashed upon him with extraordinary conviction, so that he forgot for the moment how securely he belonged to the unstable. The smile of happiness spread, as it were, over his entire being. He glowed and pulsed with its delicious inward fire. Light filled his being for an instant—an instant of intoxicating belief and certainty and vision. The instant inspiration of a dream went lost and vanished. He had drawn upon childhood and legendary reading for the substance of a moment's happiness. He shook himself, so to speak. He remembered his patients and his duties, his colleague too. . . .

Nothing, meanwhile, occurred to arouse interest or attention. Le Vallon was quite docile, ordinary; he needed no watching; he slept well, ate well, spent his leisure with his books and in the garden. He complained often of the lack of sunlight, and sometimes he might be seen taking some deep breaths of air into his lungs by the open window or on the balcony. The phases of the moon, too, interested him, and he asked once when the full moon would come and then, when Devonham told him, he corrected the date the latter gave, proving him two hours wrong. But, on the whole, there seemed little to differentiate him from the usual young man whose physique had developed in advance of his mental faculties; his knowledge in some respects certainly was backward, as in the case of arrested development. He seemed an intelligent countryman, but an unusually intelligent countryman, though all the time another under-intelligence shone brightly, betraying itself in remarks and judgments oddly phrased.

Dr. Fillery took him, during the following day or two, to concerts, theatres, cinemas. He enjoyed them all. Yet in the theatres he was inclined to let his attention wander. The degree of alertness varied oddly. His critical standard, moreover, was curiously exacting; he demanded the real creative interpretation of a part, and was quick to detect a lack of inspiration, of fine technique, of true conception in a player. Reasons he failed to give, and argument seemed impossible to him, but if voice or gesture or imaginative touch failed anywhere, he lost interest in the performer from that moment.

"He has poor breath," he remarked. "He only imitates. He is outside." Or, "She pretends. She does not feel and know. Feeling—the feeling that comes of fire—she has not felt."

"She does not understand her part, you mean?" suggested Fillery.

"She does not burn with it," was the reply.

At concerts he behaved individually too. They bored as well as puzzled him; the music hardly stirred him. He showed signs of distress at anything classical, though Wagner, Debussy, the Russians, moved him and produced excitement.

"He," was his remark, with emphasis, "has *heard*. He gives me freedom. I could fly and go away. He sets me free . . ." and then he would say no more, not even in reply to questions. He could not define the freedom he referred to, nor could he say where he could go away *to*.

But his face lit up, he smiled his delightful smile, he looked happy. "Stars," he added once in a tone of interest, in reply to repeated questions, "stars, wind, fire, away from *this!*"—he tapped his head and breast—"I feel more alive and real."

"It's real and true, that music? That's what you feel?"

"It's beyond this," he replied, again tapping his body. *"They have heard."*

The cinema interested him more. Yets its limits seemed to perplex him more than its wonder thrilled him. He accepted it as a simple, natural, universal thing.

"They stay always on the sheet," he observed with evident surprise. "And I hear nothing. They do not even sing. Sound and movement go together!"

"The speaking will come," explained Fillery. "Those are pictures merely."

"I understand. Yet sound is natural, isn't it? They ought to be heard."

"Speech," agreed his companion, "is natural, but singing isn't."

"Are they not alive enough to sing?" was the reply, spoken to himself rather than to his neighbour, who was so attentive to his least response. "Do they only sing when"—Fillery heard it and felt something leap within him—"when they are paid or have an audience?" he finished the sentence quickly.

"No one sings naturally of their own accord—not in cities, at any rate," was the reply.

LeVallon laughed, as though he understood at once.

"There is no sun and wind," he murmured. "Of course. They cannot."

It was the cinemas that provided most material for observation, Fillery found. There was in a cinema performance something that excited his companion, but excited him more than the doctor felt he was justified in encouraging. Obviously the other side of him, the "N. H." aspect, came up to breathe under the stimulus of the rapid, world-embracing, space-and-time destroying pictures on the screen. Concerts did not stimulate him, it seemed, but rather puzzled him. He remained wholly the commonplace LeVallon— with one exception: he drew involved patterns on the edge of his programmes, patterns of a very complicated yet accurate kind, as though he almost saw the sounds that poured into his ears. And these ornamented programmes Dr. Fillery preserved. Sound—music—seemed to belong to his interpretation of movement. About the cinema, however, there seemed something almost familiar, something he already knew and understood, the sound belonging to movement only lacking.

Apart from these small incidents, LeVallon showed nothing unusual, nothing that a yokel untaught yet of natural intelligence might not have shown. His language, perhaps, was singular, but, having been educated by one mind only, and in a region of lonely forests and mountains, remote from civilized life, there was nothing inexplicable in the odd words he chose, nor in the peculiar—if subtle and penetrating—phrases that he used. Invariably he recognized the spontaneous, creative power as distinguished from the derivative that merely imitated.

He found ways of expressing himself almost immediately, both in speech and writing, however, and with a perfection far beyond the reach of a half-educated country lad; and this swift aptitude was puzzling until its explanation suddenly was laid bare. He absorbed, his companion realized at last, as by telepathy, the content of his own, of Fillery's mind, acquiring the latter's mood, language, ideas, as though the two formed one being.

The discovery startled the doctor. Yet what startled him still more was the further discovery, made a little later, that he himself could, on occasions, become so identified with his patient that the slightest shade of thought or feeling rose spontaneously in his own mind too.

He remained, otherwise, almost entirely "LeVallon"; and, after a full report made to Devonham, and the detailed discussion thereon that followed, Dr. Fillery had no evidence to contradict the latter's opinion: "LeVallon is the real true self. The other personality—'N. H.' as we call it —is a mere digest and accumulation of material supplied by his parents and by Mason."

"Let us wait and see what happens when 'N. H.' appears and *does* something," Fillery was content to reply.

"If," answered Devonham, with sceptical emphasis, "it ever does appear."

"You think it won't?" asked Fillery.

"With proper treatment," said Devonham decisively, "I see no reason why 'N. H.' should not become happily merged in the parent self—in LeVallon, and a permanent cure result."

He put his glasses straight and stared at his chief, as much as to say "You promised."

"Perhaps," said Fillery. "But, in my judgment, 'LeVallon' is too slight to count at all. I believe the whole, real, parent Self is 'N. H.,' and the only life LeVallon has at all is that which peeps up through him—from 'N. H.'"

Fillery returned his serious look.

"If 'N. H.' is the real self, and I am right," he added slowly, "you, Paul, will have to revise your whole position."

"I shall," returned Devonham. "But—you will allow this—it is a lot to expect. I see no reason to believe in anything more than a subconscious mind of unusual content, and possibly of unusual powers and extent," he added with reluctance.

"It is," said Fillery significantly, "a lot to expect—as you said just now. I grant you that. Yet I feel it possible that——" he hesitated.

Devonham looked uncomfortable. He fidgeted. He did not like the pause. A sense of exasperation rose in him, as though he knew something of what was coming.

"Paul," went on his chief abruptly in a tone that dropped instinctively to a lower key—almost a touch of awe lay behind it—"you admit no deity, I know, but you admit purpose, design, intelligence."

"Well," replied the other patiently, long experience having taught him iron restraint, "it's a blundering, imperfect system, inadequately organized—if you care to call that intelligence. It's of an extremely intricate complexity. I admit that. Deity I consider an unnecessary assumption."

"The love and hate of atoms alone bowls you over," was the unexpected comment. "The word 'Laws' explains nothing. A machine obeys the laws, but intelligence conceived that machine—and a man repairs and keeps it going. Who—what—keeps the daisy going, the crystal, the creative thought in the imagination? An egg becomes a leaf-eating caterpillar, which in turn becomes a honey-eating butterfly with wings. A yolk turns into feathers. Is that accomplished without intelligence?"

"Ask our new patient," interrupted Devonham, wiping his glasses with unnecessary thoroughness.

"Which?"

Devonham startled, looked up without his glasses. It seemed the question made him uneasy. Putting the glasses on suddenly, he stared at his chief.

"I see what you mean, Edward," he said earnestly, his interest deeply captured. "Be careful. We know nothing, remember, nothing of life. Don't jump ahead like this or take your dreams for reality. We have our duty—in a case like this."

Fillery smiled, as though to convey that he remembered his promise.

"Humanity," he replied, "is a very small section of the universe. Compared to the minuter forms of life, which *may* be quite as important, if not more so, the human section is even negligible; while, compared to the possibility of greater forms——" He broke off abruptly. "As you say, Paul, we know nothing of life after all, do we? Nothing, less than nothing! We observe and classify a few results, that's all. We must beware of narrow prejudice, at any rate—you and I."

His eyes lost their light, his speech dried up, his ideas, dreams, speculations returned to him unrewarded, unexpressed. With natures in whom the subconscious never stirred, natures through whom its magical fires cast no faintest upward gleam, intercourse was ever sterile, unproductive. Such natures had no background. Even a fact, with them, was detached from its true big life, its full significance, its divine potentialities! . . .

"We must beware of prejudice," he repeated quietly. "We seek truth only."

"We must beware," replied Devonham, as he shrugged his shoulders, "of suggestion—of auto-suggestion above all. We must remember how repressed desires dramatize themselves—especially," he added significantly, "when aided by imagination. We seek only facts." On his face appeared swiftly, before it vanished again, an expression of keen anxiety, almost of affliction, yet tempered, as it were, by surprise and wonder, by pity possibly, and certainly by affection.

CHAPTER VIII

TO Devonham, meanwhile, LeVallon's behaviour was polite and kind and distant; he did not show distrust of any sort, but he betrayed a certain diffidence, reserve and caution. Trust he felt; sympathy he did not feel. To the amusement of Fillery, he suggested almost a kind of mild contempt when dealing with him, and this amusement was increased by the fact that it obviously annoyed Devonham, while it gratified his chief. For towards Fillery, LeVallon behaved with an intimate and understanding sympathy that proved his instantaneous affection based upon mutual comprehension. It seemed that LeVallon and Fillery had known one another always.

It was doubtless, due to this innate sympathy between them that Edward Fillery's rare gift of absorbing the content of another's mind, even to the point of taking on that other's conditions, physical and emotional at the same time, was so successful. By means of a highly developed power of auto-suggestion, he had learned so to identify his own mind, thought, feeling with those of a patient, that there resulted a kind of merging by which he literally became that patient. He felt with him. As a subject sees the pictures in the hypnotiser's mind, perceives his thoughts, divines his slightest will, so Fillery, reversing the process, could realize for the moment exactly what his patient was thinking, feeling, desiring. It was of great use to him in his strange practice.

This gift, naturally, varied in degree, and was not invariably successful. In some cases he only felt, the emotion alone being thus transferred; in others he only saw what the patient saw, or thought he saw, the accompanying

77

emotion being omitted; in others again, as in cases of vision at a distance, either of time or space, he had been able to follow the "travelling sight" of his patient, whose consciousness in trance was operating far away, and thus to check for subsequent verification exactly what that patient saw. He had shared strange experiences with others—with a man, for instance, in whom sight was transferred to the tip of his index finger, so that he could read a book by passing that finger along the printed line; with a woman, again, in whom "exteriorized consciousness" manifested itself, so that, if the air several inches from her face was pinched or struck, the impact was received and an actual bruise produced upon her skin.

This extension of consciousness, its seeds already in his nature, he had trained and developed to a point where he could almost rely upon auto-suggestion bringing about quickly the desired conditions. Its success, however, as mentioned, was variable. With "N. H.," especially now, this variableness was marked; sometimes it was so easily accomplished as to seem natural and without a conscious effort, while at other times it failed completely. Since it was in no sense an attempt to transfer anything from his own mind to that of the patient, Fillery felt that his promise to his colleague was not involved.

The following scene describes the first time in which the process took place with his new patient. Fillery himself wrote down the words, supplied the detailed description, filled in the emotion and psychology, but exactly as these occurred and as he felt them, both when these took place, respectively, in his own consciousness and in that of his patient. Part of the time he was present, part of it he was not visibly so, being screened from observation, yet so placed that he could note everything that happened. It is clear, however, that his mind was so intimately *en rapport* with the thoughts and feelings of "N. H.," that he experienced in his own being all that "N. H." experienced. The description was written immediately after the occurrence, though some of it, the spoken language in particular, was jotted down in his hiding place at the actual moment.

The interlacing of the two minds, their interpenetration, as it were, one occasionally dominating the other, is curious to trace and far from difficult to disentangle. Similarly the interweaving of LeVallon and "N. H." is noticeable. The description given by Devonham of the portion of the occurrence he witnessed personally, or heard about from Nurse Robbins and the attendants—this description reduces the whole thing to the commonplace level of "a slight seizure accompanied by signs of violence and moments of delirium due to excitement and fatigue, and soon cured by sleep."

The occurrence took place precisely at the period when the moon was at the full.

CHAPTER IX

THE body I'm in and using is 22, as they call it, and from a man named Mason, a geologist, I receive sums of money, regularly paid, with which I live. They call it "live." A roof and walls protect me, who do not need protection; my body, which it irks, is covered with wool and cloth and stuff, fitting me as bark fits a tree and yet not part of me; my feet, which love the touch of earth and yearn for it, are cased in dead dried skin called leather; even my head and hair, which crave the sun and wind, are covered with another piece of dead dried skin, shaped like a shell, but an ugly shell, in which, were it shaped otherwise, the wind and rustling leaves might sing with flowers.

Before 22 I remember nothing—nothing definite, that is. I opened my eyes in a soft, but not refreshing case standing on four iron legs, and well off the ground, and covered with coarse white coverings piled thickly on my body. It was a bed. Slabs of transparent stuff kept out the living sunshine for which I hungered; thick solid walls shut off the wind; no stars or moon showed overhead, because an enormous lid hid every bit of sky. No dew, therefore, lay upon the sheets. I smelt no earth, no leaves, no flowers. No single natural sound entered except the chattering of dirty sparrows which had lost its freshness. I was in a hospital.

One comely figure alone gave me a little joy. It was soft and slim and graceful, with a smell of fern and morning in its hair, though that hair was lustreless and balled up in ugly lumps, with strips of thin metal in it. They called it nurse and sister. It was the first moving thing I saw when my eyes opened on my limited and enclosed surroundings. My heart beat quicker, a flash of thin joy

came up in me. I had seen something similar before somewhere; it reminded me, I mean, of something I had known
elsewhere; though but a shabby, lifeless, clumsy copy of
this other glorious thing. Though not real, it stirred this
faint memory of reality, so that I caught at the skirts of
moonlight, stars and flowers reflected in a forest pool where
my companion played for long periods of happiness between our work. The perfume and the eyes did that. I
watched it for a bit, as it moved away, came close and
looked at me. When the eyes met mine, a wave of life,
but of little life, surged faintly through me.

They were dim and pitiful, these eyes; mournful, unlit,
unseeing. The stars had set in them; dull shadows crowded.
They were so small. They were hungry too. They were
unsatisfied. For some minutes it puzzled me, then I understood. That was the word—unsatisfied. Ah, but I could
alter that! I could comfort, help, at any rate. My strength,
though horribly clipped and blocked, could manage a little
thing like that! My smaller rhythms I could put into it.

The eyes, the smile, the whole soft comely bundle, so
pitifully hungry and unsatisfied, I rose and seized, pressing
it close inside my own great arms, and burying it all against
my breast. I crushed it, but very gently, as I might crush
a sapling. My lips were amid the ferny hair. I breathed
upon it willingly, glad to help.

It was a poor unfinished thing, I felt at once, soft and
yielding where it should have been resilient and elastic as
fresh turf; the perfume had no body, it faded instantly;
there was so little life in it.

But, as I held it in my big embrace, smothering its
hunger as best I could within my wave of being, this bundle,
this poor pitiful bundle, screamed and struggled to get free.
It bit and scratched and uttered sounds like those squeaks
the less swift creatures make when the swifter overtake
them.

I was too surprised to keep it to me; I relaxed my hold.
The instant I did so the figure, thus released, stood upright

like a young birch the wind sets free. The figure looked
alive. The hair fell loose, untidily, the puny face wore
colour, the eyes had fire in them. I saw that fire. It was
a message. Memory stirred faintly in me.

"Ah!" I cried.. "I've helped you anyhow a little!"

The scene that followed filled me with such trouble and
bewilderment that I cannot recall exactly what occurred.
The figure seemed to spit at me, yet not with grace and
invitation. There was no sign of gratitude. I was entirely
misunderstood, it seemed. Bells rang, as the figure rushed
to the door and flung it open. It called aloud; similar,
though quite lifeless figures came in answer and filled the
room. A doctor—Devonham, they called him—followed
them. I was most carefully examined in a dozen curious
ways that tickled my skin a little so that I smiled. But I
lay quite still and silent, watching the whole performance
with a confusion in my being that baffled my comprehend-
ing what was going on. Most of the figures were frightened.

Then the doctor gave place to Fillery, whose name has
rhythm.

To him I spoke at once:

"I wished to comfort and revive her," I told him. "She
is so starved. I was most gentle. She brings a message
only."

He made no reply, but gazed at me with the corners of
his mouth both twitching, and in his eyes—ah, his eyes had
more of the sun in them—a flash of something that had
known fire, at least, if it had not kept it.

"My God! I worship thee," I murmured at the glimpse
of the Power I must own as Master and creator of my
being. "Even when thou art playful, I adore thee and
obey."

Then four other figures, shaped like the doctor but wholly
mechanical, a mere blind weight operating through them,
held my arms and legs. Not the least desire to move was
in me luckily. I say "luckily," because, had I wished it,
I could have flung them through the roof, blown down the

little walls, caught up a dozen figures in my arms, and rushed forth with them towards the Powers of Fire and Wind to which I belonged.

Could I? I felt that I could. The sight of the true fire, small though it was, in the comely figure's and the doctor's eyes, had set me in touch again with my home and origin. This touch I had somehow lost; I had been "ill," with what they called nervous disorder and injured reason. The lost touch was now restored. But, luckily, as I said, there was no desire in me to set free these other figures, to help them in any way, after the reception my first kindly effort had experienced. I lay quite still, held by these four grotesque and puny mechanisms. The comely one, with the others similar to her, had withdrawn. I felt very kindly towards them all, but especially towards the doctor, Fillery, who had shown that he knew my deity and origin. None of them were worth much trouble, anyhow. I felt that too. A mild, sweet-toned contempt was in me.

"Dangerous," was a word I caught them whispering as they went. I laughed a little. The four faces over me made odd grimaces, tightening their lips, and gripping my legs and arms with greater effort. The doctor—Fillery— noticed it.

"Easy, remember," he addressed the four. "There's really no need to hold. It won't recur." I nodded. We understood one another. And, with a smile at me, he left the room, saying he would come back after a short interval. A link with my source, a brother as it were, went with him. I was lonely. . . .

I began to hum songs to myself, little fragments of a great natural music I had once known but lost, and I noticed that the four figures, as I sang, relaxed their grip of my limbs considerably. To tell the truth, I forgot that they were holding me; their grip, anyhow, was but a thread I could snap without the smallest effort. The songs were happiness in me. Upon free leaping rhythms I careered with an exhilarating rush of liberty; all about space I soared and sank; I was picked up, flung far, riding the crest of immense waves of orderly vibration` that delighted me. I let myself go a bit, let my voice out, I mean. No effort accompanied my singing. It was automatic, like breathing almost. It was natural to me. These rhythmical sounds and the patterns that they wove in space were the outlines of forms it was my work to build. This expressed my nature. Only my power was blocked and stifled in this confining body. The fire and air which were my tools I could not control. I have forgotten—forgotten——!

"Got a voice, ain't he?" observed one of the figures admiringly.

"Lunies can do 'most anything they have a mind to."

"Grand Opera isn't it."

"Yes," mentioned the fourth, "but he'll lift the roof off presently. We'd better stop him before there's any trouble."

I stopped of myself, however: their remarks interested me. Also while I had been singing, although I called it humming only, they had gradually let go of me, and were now sitting down on my bed and staring with quite pleasant faces. All their dim eight eyes were fixed on me. Their forms were not built well.

"Where did you get that from, Guv'nor?" asked the one who had spoken first. "Can you give me the name of it?"

The sound of his own voice was like the scratching of a pin after the enormous rhythm that now ceased.

"Ain't printed, is it?" he went on, as I stared, not understanding what he meant. "I've got a sister at the Halls," he explained. "She'd make a hit with that kind of thing. Gave me quite a twist inside to hear it," he added, turning to the others.

The others agreed solemnly with dull stupid faces. I lay and listened to their talk. I longed to help them. I had forgotten how.

"A bit churchy, I thought it," said one. "But, I confess, it stirred me up."

"Churchy or not, it's the stuff," insisted the first.

"Oh, it's the stuff to give 'em, right enough." And they looked at me admiringly again. "Where did you get it, if I may ask?" replied Number One in a more respectful tone. His face looked quite polite. The lips stretched, showing yellow teeth. It was his smile. But his eyes were a little more real. Oh, where was my fire? I could have built the outline better so that he was real and might express far more. I have forgotten——!

"I hear it," I told him, "because I'm in it. It's all about me. It never stops. It's what we build with——"

Number One seemed greatly interested.

"Hear it, do you? Why, that's odd now. You see"— he looked at his companions apologetically, as though he knew they would not believe him—"my father was like that. He heard his music, he always used to say, but we laughed at him. He was a composer by trade. Oh, his stuff was printed too. Of course," he added, "there's musical talent in the family," as though that explained everything. He turned to me again. "Give us a little more, Mister—if you don't object, that is," he added. And his face was soft as he said it. "Only gentle like—if you don't mind."

"Yes, keep it down a bit," another put in, looking anxiously in the direction of the closed door. He patted the air with his open palm, slowly, carefully, as though he patted an animal that might rise and fly at him.

I hummed again for them, but this time with my lips closed. The waves of rhythm caught me up and away. I soared and flew and dropped and rose again upon their huge coloured crests. Curtains and sheets of quiet flame in palest gold flared shimmering through the sound, while winds that were full of hurricanes and cyclones swept down to lift the fire and dance with it in spirals. The perfume of great flowers rose. There were flowers everywhere, and stars shone through it all like showers of gold. Ah! I began to remember something. It was flowers and stars as well as human forms we worked to build. . . .

But I kept the fire from leaping into actual flame; the mighty winds I held back. Even thus pent and checked, their powerful volume made the atmosphere shake and pulse about us. Only I could not control them now. . . . With an effort I came back, came down, as it were, and saw the funny little faces staring at me with opened eyes and mouths, and yellow teeth, pale gums, their skins gone whitish, their figures rigid with their tense emotion. They were so poorly made, the patterns so imperfect. The new respect in their manner was marked plainly. Suddenly all four turned together towards the door. I stopped. The doctor had returned. But it was Fillery again. I liked the feel of him.

"He wanted to sing, sir, so we let him. It seemed to relieve him a bit," they explained quickly and with an air of helpless apology.

"Good, good," said the doctor. "Quite good. Any normal expression that brings relief is good." He dismissed them. They went out, casting back at me expressions of puzzled thanks and interest. The door closed behind them. The doctor seated himself beside me and took my hand. I liked his touch. His hand was alive, at any rate, although within my own it felt rather like a dying branch or bunch of leaves I grasped. The life, if thin, was real.

"Where's the rest of it?" I asked him, meaning the music. "I used to have it all. It's left me, gone away. What's cut it off?"

"You're not cut off really," he said gently. "You can always get into it again when you really need it." He gazed at me steadily for a minute, then said in his quiet voice— a full, nice tone with wind through a forest running in it: "Mason. . . . Dr. Mason. . . ."

He said no more, but watched me. The name stirred something in me I could not get at quite. I could not reach down to it. I was troubled by a memory I could not seize.

"Mason," I repeated, returning his strong gaze. "What
—who—was Mason? And where?" I connected the name
with a sense of liberty, also with great winds and pools of
fire, with great figures of golden skin and radiant faces, with
music, too, the music that had left me.

"You've forgotten for the moment," came the deep running voice I liked. "He looked after you for twenty years.
He gave his life for you. He loved you. He loved your
mother. Your father was his friend."

"Has he gone—gone back?"

"He's dead."

"I can get after him though," I said, for the name touched
me with a sense of lost companionship I wanted, though
the reference to my father and mother left me cold. "I
can easily catch him up. When I move with my wind and
fire, the fastest things stand still." My own speed, once
I was free again, I knew outpaced easily the swiftest bird,
outpaced light itself."

"Yes," agreed the doctor; "only he doesn't want that
now. You can always catch him up when the time comes.
Besides, he's waiting for you anyhow."

I knew that was true. I sank back comforted upon the
stuffy pillows and lay silent. This tinkling chatter wearied
me. It was like trickling wind. I wanted the flood of
hurricanes, the pulse of storms. My building, shaping
powers, my great companions—oh! where were they?

"He taught you himself, taught you all you know," I
heard the tinkling go on again, "but he kept you away
from life, thinking it was best. He was afraid for you,
afraid for others too. He kept you in the woods and mountains where, as he believed, you could alone express yourself
and so be happy. A hundred times, in babyhood and early
childhood, you nearly died. He nursed you back to life.
His own life he renounced. Now he is dead. He has left
you all his money."

He paused. I said no word. Faint memories passed
through my mind, but nothing I could hold and seize. The

money I did not understand at all, except that it was necessary.

"He thought at first that you could not possibly live to
manhood. To his surprise you survived everything—ill-
ness, accident, disaster of every sort and kind. Then, as
you grew up, he realized his mistake. Instead of keeping
you away from life, he ought to have introduced you to it
and explained it—as I and Devonham are now trying to
do. You could not live for ever alone in woods and
mountains; when he was gone there would be no one to
look after you and guide you."

The trickling of wind went on and on. I hardly listened
to it. He did it for his own pleasure, I suppose. It pleased
and soothed him possibly. Yet I remembered every syllable.
It was a small detail to keep fresh when my real memory
covered the whole planet.

"Before he died, he recognized his mistake and faced the
position boldly. It was some years before the end; he was
hale and hearty still, yet the end, he knew, was in sight.
While the power was still strong in him, therefore, he did
the only thing left to him to do. He used his great powers.
He used suggestion. He hypnotized you, telling you to forget—from the moment of his death, but not before—forget
everything—— It was only partially successful."

The door opened, the comely figure glanced in, then
vanished.

"She wants more help from me," I interrupted the
monotonous tinkling instantly, for pity stirred in me again
as I saw her eager, hungry and unsatisfied little eyes. "Call
her back. I feel quite willing. It is one of the lower
forms we made. I can improve it."

Dr. Fillery, as he was called, looked at me steadily, his
mouth twitching at the corners as before, a flash of fire
flitting through his eyes. The fire made me like and trust
him; the twitching, too, I liked, for it meant he knew how
absurd he was. Yet he was bigger than the other figures.

"You can't do that," he said, "you mustn't," and then laughed outright. "It isn't done, you know—here."

"Why not, sir?" I asked, using the terms the figures used. "I feel like that."

"Of course, you do. But all you feel can't be expressed except at the proper times and places. The consent of the other party always is involved," he went on slowly, "when it's a question of expressing—anything you feel."

This puzzled me, because in this particular instance the other party had asked me with her eyes to comfort her. I told him this. He laughed still more. Caught by the sound —it was just like wind passing among tall grasses on a mountain ridge—I forgot what he was talking about for the moment. The sound carried me away towards my own rhythms.

"You've got such amazing insight," he went on tinkling to himself, for I heard, although I did not listen. "You read the heart too easily, too quickly. You must learn to hide your knowledge." The laughter which ran with the words then ended, and I came back to the last thing I had definitely listened to—"express, expressing," was the phrase he used.

"You told me that self-expression is the purpose for which I'm here——?"

"I believe it is," he agreed, more solemnly.

"Only sometimes, then?"

"Exactly. If that expression involves another in pain or trouble or discomfort——"

"Ah! I have to choose, you mean. I have to know first what the other feels about it."

I began to understand better. It was a game. And all games delighted me.

"You may put it roughly so, yes," he explained, "you're very quick. I'll give you a rule to guide you," he went on. I listened with an effort; this tinkling soon wearied me; I could not think long or much; my way, it seemed,

was feeling. "Ask yourself always how what you do will
affect another," Dr. Fillery concluded. "That's a safe rule
for you."

"That is of children," I observed. We stared at each
other a moment. "Both sides keep it?" I asked.

"Childish," he agreed, "it certainly is. Both sides, yes,
keep it."

I sighed, and the sigh seemed to rise from my very feet,
passing through my whole being. He looked at me most
kindly then, asking why I sighed.

"I used to be free," I told him. "This is not liberty.
And why are we not all free together?"

"It is liberty for two instead of only for one," he said,
"and so, in the long run, liberty for all."

"So that's where they are," I remarked, but to myself and
not to him. "Not further than that." For what I had once
known, but now, it seemed, forgotten, was far beyond such
a foolish little game. We had lived without such tiny
tricks. We lived openly and unafraid. We worked in
harmony. We lived. Yes—but who was "we"? That was
the part I had forgotten.

"It's the growth and development of civilization," I heard
the little drift of wind go whistling thinly, "and it won't
take you long to become quite civilized at this rate, more
civilized, indeed, than most—with your swift intelligence
and lightning insight."

"Civilization," I repeated to myself. Then I looked at
his eyes which hid carefully in their depths somewhere that
tiny cherished flame I loved. "Your ways are really very
simple," I said. "It's all easy enough to learn. It is so
small."

"A man studying ants," he tinkled, "finds them small,
but far from simple. You may find complications later. If
so, come to me."

I promised him, and the fire gleamed faintly in his eyes
a moment. "He entrusted you to me. Your mother," he
added softly, "was the woman he loved."

"Civilization," I repeated, for the word set going an odd new rhythm in me that I rather liked, and that tired me less than the other things he said. "What is it then? You are a Race, you told me."

"A Race of human beings, of men and women developing——"

"The comely ones?"

"Are the women. Together we make up the Race."

"And civilization?"

"Is realizing that we are a community, learning, growing, all its members living for the others as well as for themselves."

Dr. Fillery told me then about men and women and sex, how children are made, and what enormous and endless work was necessary merely to keep them all alive and clothed and sheltered before they could accomplish anything else of any sort at all. Half the labour of the majority was simply to keep alive at all. It was an ugly little system he described. Much I did not hear, because my thinking powers gave out. Some of it gave me an awful feeling he called pain. The confusion and imperfection seemed beyond repair, even beyond the worth of being part of it, of belonging to it at all. Moreover, the making of children, without which the whole thing must end, gave me spasms of irritation he called laughter. Only the Comely Ones, and what he told me of them, made me want to sing.

"The men," I said, "but do they see that it is ugly and ludicrous and——"

"Comic," he helped me.

"Do they know," I asked, taking his unknown words, "that it's comic?"

"The glamour," he said, "conceals it from them. To the best among them it is sacred even."

"And the Comely Ones?"

"It is their chief mission," he replied. "Always remember that. It's sacred." He fixed his kind eyes gravely on my face.

"Ah, worship, you mean," I said. "I understand." Again we stared for some minutes. "Yet all are not comely, are they?'" I asked presently.

The fire again shone faintly in his eyes as he watched me a moment without answering. It caught me away. I am not sure I heard his words, but I think they ran like this:

"That's just the point where civilization—so far—has always stopped."

I remember he ceased tinkling then; our talk ceased too. I was exhausted. He told me to remember what he had said, and to lie down and rest. He rang the bell, and a man, one of the four who had held me, came in.

"Ask Nurse Robbins to come here a moment, please," he said. And a moment later the Comely One entered softly and stood beside my bed. She did not look at me. Dr. Fillery began again his little tinkling. ". . . wishes to apologize to you most sincerely, nurse, for his mistake. He meant no harm, believe me. There is no danger in him, nor will he ever repeat it. His ignorance of our ways, I must ask you to believe——"

"Oh, it's nothing, sir," she interrupted. "I've quite forgotten it already. And usually he's as good as gold and perfectly quiet." She blushed, glancing shyly at me with clear invitation.

"It will not recur," repeated the Doctor positively. "He has promised me. He is very, very sorry and ashamed."

The nurse looked more boldly a moment. I saw her silver teeth. I saw the hint of soft fire in her poor pitiful eyes, but far, far away and, as she thought, safely hidden.

"Pitiful one, I will not touch you," I said instantly. "I know that you are sacred."

I noticed at once that her sweet natural perfume increased about her as I said the words, but her eyes were lowered, though she smiled a little, and her little cheeks grew coloured. I saw her small teeth of silvery marble again. Our work was visible. I liked it.

"You have promised me," said Dr. Fillery, rising to go out.

"I promise," I said, while the Comely One was arranging my pillows and sheets with quick, clever hands, sometimes touching my cheek on purpose as she did so. "I will not worship, unless it is commanded of me first. The increased sweetness of her smell will tell me."

But indeed already I had forgotten her, and I no longer realized who it was that tripped about my bed, doing numerous little things to make me comfortable. My friend, the understanding one, companion of my big friend, Mason, who was dead, also had left the room. His twitching mouth, his laughter, and his shining eyes were gone. I was aware that the Comely One remained, doing all manner of little things about me and my bed, unnecessary things, but my pity and my worship were not asked, so I forgot her. My thinking had wearied me, and my feeling was not touched. I began to hum softly to myself; my giant rhythms rose; I went forth towards my Powers of Wind and Fire, full of my own natural joy. I forgot the Race with its men, its women, its rules and games, its tiny tricks, its civilization. I was free for a little with my own.

One detail interfered a little with the rhythms, but only for a second and very faintly even then. The Comely One's face grew dark.

"He's gone off asleep—actually," I heard her mutter, as she left the room with a fling of her little skirts, shutting the door behind her with a bang.

That bang was far away. I was already rising and falling in that natural happy state which to me meant freedom. It is hard to tell about, but that dear Fillery knows, I am sure, exactly what I know, though he has forgotten it. He has known us somewhere, I feel. He understands our service. But, like me, he has forgotten too.

What really happened to me? Where did I go, what did I see and feel when my rhythms took me off?

Thinking is nowhere in it—I can tell him that. I am conscious of the Sun.

One difficulty is that my being here confuses me. Here I am already caught, confined and straitened. I am within certain limits. I can only move in three ways, three measurements, three dimensions. The space I am in here allows only little rhythms; they are coarse and slow and heavy, and beat against confining walls as it were, are thrown back, cross and recross each other, so that while they themselves grow less, their confusion grows greater. The forms and outlines I can build with them are poor and clumsy and insignificant. Spirals I cannot make. Then I forget.

Into these small rhythms I cannot compress myself; the squeezing hurts. Yet neither can I make them bigger to suit myself. I would break forth towards the Sun.

Thus I feel cramped, confused and crippled. It is almost impossible to tell of my big rhythms, for it is an attempt to tell of one thing in terms of another. How can I fix fire and wind upon the point of a pin, for instance, and examine them through a magnifying-glass? The Sun remains. What I experience, really, when I go off into my own freedom is release. My rhythms are of the Sun. They are his messengers, they are my law, they are my life and happiness. By means of them I fulfill the purpose of my being. I work, so Fillery calls it. I build.

That, at any rate, is literally true. My thinking stops at that point, perhaps; but "I think" I mean by "release" —that I escape back from being trapped by all these separate little individualities, human beings each working on his own, for his own, and against all the others—escape from this stifling tangle into the sweep of my big rhythms which work together and in unison. I search for lost companions, but do not find them—the golden skins and ıadiant faces, the mighty figures and the splendid shapes.

They work without effort, however. That is another difference.

I, too, work, only I work with them, and never against

them. I can draw upon them as they can draw upon me.
We do draw on one another. We know harmony. Service
is our method and system.

My dear Fillery also wants to know who "we" are. How
can I tell him? The moment I try to "think," I seem to
forget. This forgetting, indeed, is one of the limits against
which I bang myself, so that I am flung back upon the
tangle of criss-cross, tiny rhythms which confuse and
obliterate the very thing he wants to know. Yet the Sun I
never forget—father of fire and wind.. My companions are
lost temporarily. I am shut off from them. It seems I
cannot have them and the Race at the same time. I yearn
and suffer to rejoin them. The service we all know together
is great joy. Of love, this love between two isolated individuals the Race counts the best thing they have—we know
nothing.

Now, here is one thing I can understand quite clearly:

I have watched and helped the Race, as he calls it, for
countless ages. Yet from outside it. Never till now have
I been inside its limits with it. And a dim sense of having
watched it through a veil or curtain comes to me. I can
faintly recall that I tried to urge my big rhythms in among
its members, as great waves of heat or sound might be
launched upon an ant-heap. I used to try to force and project my vast rhythms into their tiny ones, hoping to make
these latter swell and rise and grow—but never with success.
Though a few members, here and there, felt them and
struggled to obey and use their splendid swing, the rest did
not seem to notice them at all. . . . Indeed, they objected
to the struggling efforts of the few who did feel them, for
their own small accustomed rhythms were interfered with.
The few were generally broken into little pieces and pushed
violently out of the way.

And this made me feel pitiful, I remember dimly; because
these smaller rhythms, though insignificant, were exquisite.
They were of extraordinary beauty. Could they only have
been increased, the Race that knew and used them must

have changed my own which, though huge and splendid of their kind, lacked the intense, perfect loveliness of the smaller kind.

The Race, had it accepted mine and mastered them, must have carried themselves and me towards still mightier rhythms which I alone could never reach.

This, then, is clear to me, though very faint now. Fillery, who can think for a long time, instead of like me for seconds only, will understand what I mean. For if I tell him what "we" did, he may be able to think out what "we" were.

"Your work?" he asked me too.

I'm not sure I know what he means by "work." We were incessantly active, but not for ourselves. There was no effort. There was easy and sure accomplishment—in the sense that nothing could stop or hinder our fulfilling our own natures. Obstacles, indeed, helped our power and made it greater, for everything feeds fire and opposition adds to the pressure of wind. Our main activity was to make perfect forms. We were form-builders. Apart from this, our "work" was to maintain and keep active all rhythms less than our own, yet of our kind. I speak of my own kind alone. We had no desire to be known outside our kind. We worked and moved and built up swiftly, but out of sight—an endless service.

"You are the Powers behind what we call Nature, then?" the dear Fillery asked me. "You operate behind growing things, even behind inanimate things like trees and stones and flowers. Your big rhythms, as you call them, are our Laws of Nature. Your own particular department, your own elements evidently, were heat and air."

I could not answer that. But, as he said it, I saw in his grey eyes the flash of fire which so few of his Race possessed; and I felt vaguely that he was one of the struggling members who was aware of the big rhythms and who would be put away in little pieces later by the rest. It made me pitiful. "Forget your own tiny rhythms," I said, "and come over to us. But bring your tiny rhythms with you because they are so exquisitely lovely. We shall increase them."

He did not answer me. His mouth twitched at the corners, and he had an attack of that irritation which, he says, is relieved and expressed by laughter. Yet the face shone.

The laughter, however, was a very quick, full, natural answer, all the same. It was happy and enthusiastic. I saw that laughter made his rhythms bigger at once. Then laughter was probably the means to use. It was a sort of bridge.

"Your instantaneous comprehension of our things puzzles me," he said. "You grasp our affairs in all their relations so swiftly. Yet it is all new to you." His voice and face made me wish to stroke and help him, he was so dear and eager. "How do you manage it?" he asked point blank. "Our things are surely foreign to your nature."

"But they are of children," I told him. "They are small and so very simple. There are no difficulties. Your language is block letters because your self-expression, as you call it, is so limited. It all comes to me at a glance. I and my kind can remember a million tiniest details without effort."

He did not laugh, but his face looked full of questions. I could not help him further. "A scrap, probably, of what you've taught us," I heard him mumble, though no further questions came. "Well," he went on presently, while I lay and watched the pale fire slip in tiny waves about his eyes, "remember this: since our alphabet is so easy to you, follow it, stick to it, do not go outside it. There's a good rule that will save trouble for others as well as for yourself."

"I remember and I try. But it is not always easy. I get so cramped and stiff and lifeless with it."

"This sunless, chilly England, of course, cannot feed you," he said. "The sense of beauty in our Race, too, is very poor."

Once he suddenly looked up and fixed his eyes on my face. His manner became very earnest.

"Now, listen to me," he said. "I'm going to read you something; I want you to tell me what you make of it. It's private; that is, I have no right to show it to others, but as no one would understand it—with the exception possibly of yourself—secrecy is not of importance." And his mouth twitched a little.

He drew a sheaf of papers from an inner pocket, and I saw they were covered with fine writing. I laughed; this writing always made me laugh—it was so laborious and slow. The writing I knew best, of course, lay all over and inside the earth and skies. The privacy also made me laugh, so strange seemed the idea to me, and so impossible—this idea of secrecy. It was such an admission of ignorance.

"I will understand it quickest by reading it," I said. "I take in a page at once—in your block letters."

But he preferred to read it out himself, so that he could note the effect upon me, he explained, of definite passages. He saw that I guessed his purpose, and we laughed together a moment. "When you tire of listening," he said, "just tell me and I'll pause." I gave him my hand to hold. "It helps me to stay here," I explained, and he nodded as he grasped me in his warm firm clasp.

"It's written by one who *may* have known you and your big rhythms, though I can't be sure," he added. "One of —er—my patients wrote it, someone who believed she was in communication with a kind of immense Nature-spirit."

Then he began to read in his clear, windy voice:

"'I sit and weave. I feel strange; as if I had so much consciousness that words cannot explain it. The failure of others makes my work more hard, but my own purposes never fail. I am associated with those who need me. The universal doors are open to me. I compass Creation.'"

But already I began to hum my songs, though to please him I kept the music low, and he, dear Fillery, did not bid me stop, but only tightened his grasp upon my hand. I listened with pleasure and satisfaction. Therefore I hummed.

" 'I am silent, seeking no expression, needing no communication, satisfied with the life that is in me. I do not even wish to be known about——' "

"That's where your Race," I put in, "is to me as children. All they do must be shouted about so loud or they think it has not happened."

" 'I do not wish to be forced to obtrude myself,' " he went on. " 'There are hosts like me. We do not want that which does not belong to us. We do not want that hindrance, that opposition which rouses an undesirable consciousness; for without that opposition we could never have known of disobedience. We are formless. The formless is the real. That cannot die. It is eternal.' "

Again he tightened his grasp, and this time also laid his eyes a moment on my own, over the top of his paper, so that I kept my music back with a great effort. For it was hard not to express myself when my own came calling in this fashion.

He continued reading aloud. He selected passages now, instead of going straight through the pages. The words helped memory in me; flashes of what I had forgotten came back in sheets of colour and waves of music; the phrases built little spirals, as it were, between two states. Of these two states, I now divined, he understood one perfectly—his own, and the other—mine—partially. Yet he had a little of both, I knew, in himself. With me it was similar, only the understood state was not the same with us. To the Race, of course, what he read would have no meaning.

"The Comely One and the four figures," I said, "how they would turn white and run if they could hear you, showing their yellow teeth and dim eyes!"

His face remained grave and eager, though I could see the laughter running about beneath the tight brown skin as he went on reading his little bits.

" 'We heard nothing of man, and were rarely even con-

scious of him, although he benefited by our work in all that
sustained and conditioned him. The wise are silent, the
foolish speak, and the children are thus led astray, for
wisdom is not knowledge, it is a realization of the scheme
and of one's own part in it.' "

He took a firmer, broader grip of my hand as he read the
next bit. I felt the tremble of his excitement run into my
wrist and arm. His voice deepened and shook. It was like
a little storm:

" 'Then, suddenly, we heard man's triumphant voice. We
became conscious of him as an evolving entity. Our Work
had told. We had built his form and processes so faithfully. We knew that when he reached his height we must
be submissive to his will.' "

A gust of memory flashed by me as I heard. Those small
but perfect, exquisite, lovely rhythms!

"Who called me here? Whose voice reached after me,
bringing me into this undesirable consciousness?" I cried
aloud, as the memory went tearing by, then vanished before
I could recover it. At the same time Fillery let go my hand,
and the little bridge was snapped. I felt what he called
pain. It passed at once. I found his hand again, but the
bridge was not rebuilt. How white his skin had grown, I
noticed, as I looked up at his face. But the eyes shone
grandly. "I shall find the way," I said. "We shall go back
together to our eternal home."

He went on reading as though I had not interrupted, but
I found it less easy to listen now.

I realized then that he was gone. He had left the room,
though I had not seen him go. I had been away.

It was some days ago that this occurred. It was to-day,
a few hours ago, that I seized the Comely One and tried to
comfort her, poor hungry member of this little Race.

But both occurrences help us—help dear Fillery and myself—to understand how difficult it is to answer his questions
and tell him exactly what he wants to know.

"How long, O Lord, how long!" I hear his yearning

cry. "Yet other beings cannot help us; they can only tell us what their own part is."

After the door had clicked I knew release for a bit—release from a state I partially understood and so found irksome, into another where I felt at home and so found pleasurable. In the big rhythms my nature expressed itself apparently. I rose, seeking my lost companions. They—the Devonham and his busy little figures—called it sleep. It may be "sleep." But I find there what I seek yet have forgotten, and that with me were dear Fillery and another —a Comely One whom *he* brings—as though we belong together and have a common origin. But this other Comely One—who is it?

CHAPTER X

ABOUT a week after the arrival of LeVallon in London,
Dr. Fillery came out of the Home one morning early,
upon some uninteresting private business. He had left
"LeVallon" happy with his books and garden, Devonham
was with him to answer questions or direct his energies;
the other "cases" in the establishment were moving nicely
towards a cure.

The November air was clear and almost bright; no
personal worries troubled him. His mind felt free and
light.

It was one of those mornings when Nature slips, very
close and sweet, into the heart, so close and sweet that the
mind wonders why people quarrel and disagree, when it
is so easy to forgive, and the planet seems but a big, lovely,
happy garden, evil an impossible nightmare, and personal
needs few and simple.

He walked by cross roads towards Primrose Hill, entering Regent's Park near the Zoo. An early white frost was
rapidly melting in the sun. The sky showed a faint tinge
of blue. He saw floating sea-gulls. These, and a faint
breeze that stirred the yellowing last leaves of autumn, gave
his heart a sudden lift.

And this lift was in the direction of a forbidden corner.
He was aware of some exquisite dawn-wind far away
stirring a million flowers, dew sparkled, streams splashed
and murmured. A valley gleamed and vanished, yet left
across his mind its shining trail. . . . For this lift of his
heart made him soar into a region where it was only too
easy to override temptation. Fillery, however, though his
invisible being soared, kept both visible feet firmly on

the ground. The surface was slippery, being melted by
the sun, but frost kept the earth hard and frozen underneath. His balance never was in danger. He remained
detached and a spectator.

She walked beside him nevertheless, a figure of purity
and radiance, perfumed, soft, delicious. She was so
ignorant of life. That was her wonder partly; for beauty
was her accident and, while admirable, was not a determining factor. Life, in its cruder sense, she did not know,
though moving through the thick of it. It neither touched
nor soiled her; she brushed its dirt and dust aside as though
a non-conducting atmosphere surrounded her. Her emotions, deep and searching, had remained untorn. A quality
of pristine innocence belonged to her, as though, in the
noisy clamour of ambitious civilized life, she remained still
aware of Eden. Her grace, her loveliness, her simplicity
moved by his side as naturally, it seemed to him, as air
or perfume.

"Iraida," he murmured to himself, with a smile of joy.
"Nayan Khilkoff. All the men worship and adore you,
yet respect you too. They cannot touch you. You remain
aloof, unstained." And, remembering LeVallon's remarks
in cinema and theatre, he could have sung at this mere
thought of her.

"Untouched by coarseness, something unearthly about
your loveliness of soul, a baby, a saint, and to all the men
in Khilkoff's Studio, a mother. Where do you really come
· from? Whence do you derive? Your lovely soul can have
no dealings with our common flesh. How many young
fellows have you saved already, how many floundering
characters redeemed! They crave your earthly, physical
love. Instead you surprise and disappoint and shock them
into safety again—by giving to them Love. . . . !"

And, as he half repeated his vivid thoughts aloud, he
suddenly saw her coming towards him from the ornamental
water, and instantly, wondering what he should say to her,
his mind contracted. The thing in him that sang went

backward into silence. He put a brake upon himself. But he watched her coming nearer, wondering what brought her so luckily into Regent's Park, and all the way from Chelsea, at such an hour. She moved so lightly, sweetly; she was so intangible and lovely. He feared her eyes, her voice.

They drew nearer. From looking to right and left, he raised his head. She was close, quite close, a hundred yards away. That walk, that swing, that poise of head and neck he could not mistake anywhere. His whole being glowed, thrilled, and yet contracted as in pain.

A sentence about the weather, about her own, her father's, health, about his calling to see them shortly, rose to his lips. He turned his eyes away, then again looked up. They were now not twenty yards apart; in another moment he would have raised his hat, when, with a sensation of cold disappointment in him, she went past in totally irresponsive silence. It was a stranger—a shop girl, a charwoman, a bus-conductor's wife—anybody but she whom he had thought.

How could he have been so utterly mistaken? It amazed him. It was, indeed, months since they had met, yet his knowledge of her appearance was so accurate and detailed that such an error seemed incredible. He had experienced, besides, the actual thrill.

The phenomenon, however, was not new to him. Often had he experienced it, much as others have. He knew, from this, that she was somewhere near, coming deliciously, deliberately towards him, moving every minute firmly nearer, from a point in great London town which she had left just at the precise moment which would time her crossing his own path later. They would meet presently, if not now. Fate had arranged all details, and something in him was aware of it before it happened.

The phenomenon, as a matter of fact, was repeated twice again in the next half-hour: he saw her—on both occasions beyond the possibility of question—coming towards him, yet each time it was a complete stranger masquerading in her guise.

It meant, he knew, that their two minds—hearts, too, he wondered, with a sense of secret happiness, enjoyed intensely then instantly suppressed—were wirelessing to one another across the vast city, and that both transmitter and receiver, their physical bodies, would meet shortly round the corner, or along the crowded street. Strong currents of desiring thought, he knew, he hoped, he wondered, were trying to shape the crude world nearer to the heart's desire, causing the various intervening passers-by to assume the desirable form and outline in advance.

He reflected, following the habit of his eager mind; this wireless discovery, after all, was the discovery of a universal principle in Nature. It was common to all forms of life, a faint beginning of that advance towards marvellous inter-communicating, semi-telepathic brotherhood he had always hoped for, believed in. . . . Even plants, he remembered, according to Bosé. . . .

Then, suddenly, half-way down Baker Street he found her close beside him.

She was dressed so becomingly, so naturally, that no particular detail caught his eye, although she wore more colour than was usual in the dull climate known to English people. There was a touch of fur and there were flowers, but these were part of her appearance as a whole, and the hat was so exactly right, though it was here that English-women generally went wrong, that he could not remember afterwards what it was like. It was as suitable as natural hair. It looked as if she had grown it. The shining eyes were what he chiefly noticed. They seemed to increase the pale sunlight in the dingy street.

She was so close that he caught her perfume almost before he recognized her, and a sense of happiness invaded his whole being instantly, as he took the slender hand emerging from a muff and held it for a moment. The casual sentences he had half prepared fled like a flock of birds surprised.   Their eyes met. . . . And instantly the sun rose over a far Khaketian valley; he was aware of joy, of peace, of deep contentment, London obliterated, the entire world elsewhere.   He knew the thrill, the ecstasy of some long-forgotten dawn. . . .

But in that brief second while he held her hand and gazed into her eyes, there flashed before him a sudden apparition. With lightning rapidity this picture darted past between them, paused for the tiniest fraction of a second, and was gone again. So swiftly the figure shot across that the very glance he gave her was intercepted, its angle changed, its meaning altered. He started involuntarily, for he knew that vision, the bright rushing messenger, someone who brought glad tidings. And this time he recognized it —it was the figure of "N. H."

The outward start, the slight wavering of the eyelids, both were noticed, though not understood, much less interpreted by the young woman facing him.

"You are as much surprised as I am," he heard the pleasant, low-pitched voice before his face. "I thought you were abroad. Father and I came back from Sark only yesterday."

"I haven't left town," he replied. "It was Devonham went to Switzerland."

He was thinking of her pleasant voice, and wondering how a mere voice could soothe and bless and comfort in this way. The picture of the flashing figure, too, preoccupied him. His various mind was ever busy with several trains of thought at once, though all correlated. Why, he was wondering, should that picture of "N. H." leave a sense of chill upon his heart? Why had the first radiance of this meeting thus already dimmed a little? Her nearness, too, confused him as of old, making his manner a trifle brusque and not quite natural, until he found his centre of control again. He looked quickly up and down the street, moved aside to let some people pass, then turned to the girl again. "Your holiday has done you good, Iraida," he said quietly; "I hope your father enjoyed it too."

"We both enjoyed ourselves," she answered, watching him, something of a protective air about her. "I wish you had been with us, for that would have made it perfect. I was thinking that only this morning—as I walked across Hyde Park."

"How nice of you! I believe I, too, was thinking of you both, as I walked through Regent's Park." He smiled for the first time.

"It's very odd," she went on, "though *you* can explain it probably," she added, with a smile that met his own, increasing it, "or, at any rate, Dr. Devonham could—but I've seen you several times this morning already—in the last half-hour. I've seen you in other people in the street, I mean. Yet I wasn't thinking of you at the actual moment, it's two months since we've met, and I imagined you were abroad."

"Odd, yes," he said, half shyly, half curtly. "It's an experience many have, I believe."

She gazed up at him. "It's very natural, I think, when people like each other, Edward, and are in sympathy."

"Yet it happens with people who don't like each other too," he objected, and at the same moment was vexed that he had used the words.

Iraida Khilkoff laughed. He had the feeling that she read his thoughts as easily as if they were printed in red letters on his grey felt hat.

"There must be *some* bond between them, though," she remarked, "an emotion, I mean, whatever it may be—even hatred."

"Probably, Nayan," he agreed. "It's you now, not Devonham, that wants to explain things. I think I must take you into the Firm, you could take charge of the female patients with great success."

Whereupon she looked up at him with such a grave

mothering expression that he was aware of her secret power, her central source of strength in dealing with men. Her innocence and truth were an atmosphere about her, protecting her as naturally and neatly as the clothes upon her body. She believed in men. He felt like a child beside her.

"I'm in the Firm already," she said, "for you made me a partner years ago when I was so high," and her small gloved hand indicated the stature of a little girl. "You taught me first."

He remembered the bleak northern town where fifteen years ago he had known her father as a patient for some minor ailment, and the friendship that grew out of the relationship. He remembered the child of nine or ten who sat on his knee and repeated to him the Russian fairy tales her mother told her; he recalled the charm, the wonder, the extraordinary power of belief. Her words brought back again that flowered Caucasian valley in the sunlight and this, again, flashed upon the screen the strange bright figure that had already once intercepted their glance, as though it somehow came between them. . . .

"You have one advantage over me," he rejoined presently, "for in my Clinique the people know that they need treatment, whereas in the Studio you catch your patients unawares. They do not know they're ill. You heal them without their being aware that they need healing."

"Yet some of our *habitués* have found their way later to your consulting-room," she reminded him.

"Merely to finish what you had first begun—a sort of convalescence. You work in the big, raw world, I in a mere specialized corner of it."

He turned away, lest the power in her eyes overcome him. The traffic thundered past, the people crowded, jostling them. He could have stood there talking to her all day long, the London street forgotten or full of flowers and Eden's trees and rippling summer streams. The pale sunlight caught her face beside him and made it shine. . . .

He longed to take her in his arms and fly through the dawn for ever, for his clean mind saw her without clothing, her hair loose in the wind, her white shape fleeing from him, yet beckoning across a gleaming shoulder that he must overtake and capture her. . . .

"I'm on my way to St. Dunstan's," he heard the musical voice. "A friend of father's. . . . Come with me, will you?" And with her muff she touched his arm, trying to make him turn her way. But just as he felt the touch he saw the bright figure again. Swifter than himself and far more powerful, it leaped dancing past and carried her away before his very eyes. She waved her hand, her eyes faded like stars into the distance of some unearthly spring —and she was gone. A pang of peculiar anguish seized him, as the mental picture flashed with the speed of light and vanished. For the figure seemed of elemental power, taking its own with perfect ease. . . .

He shook his head. "I'll come to see you to-morrow instead," he told her. "I'll come to the Studio in the afternoon, if you'll both be in. I'd like to bring a friend with me, if I may."

"Good-bye then." She took his hand and kept it. "I shall expect you to tell me all about this—friend. I knew you had something on your mind, for your thoughts have been elsewhere all the time."

"Julian LeVallon," he replied quickly. "He's staying with me indefinitely." His face grew stern a moment about the mouth. "I think he may need you," he added with abrupt significance.

"Julian LeVallon," she repeated, the name sounding very musical the way her slightly foreign accent touched it. "And what nationality may that be?"

Dr. Fillery hesitated. "His parents, Nayan, I believe, were English," he said. "He has lived all his life in the Jura Mountains, alone with an old scholar, poet and geologist, who brought him up. Of our modern life he knows little. I think you may——" He broke off. "His mother died when he was born," he concluded.

"And of women he knows nothing," she replied, understandingly, "so that he will probably fall in love with the first he sees—with Nayan."

"I hope so, Nayan, and he will be safe with you."

She watched her companion's face for a minute or two with her clear searching eyes. She smiled. But his own face wore a mask now; no figure this time flashed between their deep understanding gaze.

"A woman, you think, can teach and help him more than a man," she said, without lowering her eyes.

"Probably—perhaps, at any rate. The material, I must warn you at once, is new and strange, I want him to meet you."

"Then I *am* in the Firm," was all she answered, "and you can't do without me." She let go the hand she had held all this time, and turned from him, looking once across her shoulder as he, too, went upon his way.

"About three o'clock we shall expect you—and Mr. Julian LeVallon," she added. "The Prometheans are coming too, as of course you know, but that won't matter. Father has let the Studio to them."

"The more the merrier," he answered, raised his hat, and went on at a rapid pace up Baker Street.

But with him up the London street went a flock of thoughts, hopes, fears and memories that were hard to disentangle. Lost, forgotten dreams went with him too. He had known that one day he must be "executed," yet with his own hands he had just slipped the noose about his neck. Detachment from life, he realized, keeping aloof from the emotions that touch one's fellow beings, can only be, after all, a pose. In his case it was evidently a pose assumed for safety and self-protection, an artificial attitude he wore to keep his heart from error. His love, born of some far unearthly valley, undoubtedly consumed him, while yet he said it nay. . . .

He had himself suggested bringing together the girl and "N. H." There had been no need to do this. Yet he had deliberately offered it, and she had instantly accepted. Even while he said the words there was a volcano of emotion in him, several motives fighting to combine. The fear for himself, being selfish, he had set aside at once; there was also the fear for her—the odd certainty in him that at last her woman's nature would be waked; lastly, the fear for "N. H." himself. And here he clashed with his promise to Devonham. Behind the simple proposal lay these various threads of motive, emotion and qualification.

Now, as he hurried along the street, they rushed to and fro about his mind, each at its own speed and with its own impetuous strength. It was the last one, however, the certainty that her mere presence must evoke the "N. H." personality, banishing the commonplace LeVallon; it was this that, in the end, perhaps troubled him most. An intuitive conviction assured him that this was bound to be the result of their meeting. LeVallon would sink down out of sight; "N. H." would emerge triumphant and vital, bringing his elemental power with him. The girl would summon him. . . .

"I must tell Paul first," he decided. "I must consult his judgment. Otherwise I'm breaking my promise. If Paul is against it, I will send an excuse. . . ."

With this proviso, he dismissed the matter from his mind, noting only how clearly it revealed his own keen desire to let LeVallon disappear and "N. H." become active. He himself yearned for the interest, stimulus and companionship of the strange new being that was "N. H."

The other aspect of the problem he dismissed quickly too: he would lose Nayan. Yes, but he had never possessed the right to hold her. He was strong, indifferent, detached. . . . His life in any case was a sacrifice upon the altar of a mistake with regard to which he had not been consulted. His whole existence must be passed in worship before this altar, unless he was to admit himself a failure. His ideal possession of the girl, he consoled himself, need know no change. To watch her womanhood, hitherto untouched by any man, to watch this bloom and ripen at the bidding of another must mean pain. But he faced the loss. And a curious sense of compensation lay in it somewhere—the strange notion that she and he would share "N. H." in a sense between them. He was already aware of a deep subtle kinship between the three of them, a kinship hardly of this physical world. And, after all, the interests of "N. H." must come first. He had chosen his life, accepted it, at any rate; he must remain true to his high ideal. This strange being, blown by the winds of chance into his keeping, must be his first consideration.

"LeVallon" needed no special help, neither from himself, nor from her, nor from others. "LeVallon" was ordinary enough, if not commonplace, his only interest being at those thin places in his being where the submerged personality of "N. H." peeped through. Paul Devonham, he felt convinced, was wrong in thinking "N. H." to be the transient manifestation.

It was the reverse that Dr. Fillery believed to be the truth. He saw in "N. H." almost a new type of being altogether. In that physical body warred two personalities certainly, but "N. H." was the important one, and LeVallon merely the transient outer one, masquerading on the surface merely, a kind of automatic and mechanical personality, gleaned, picked up, trained and educated, as it were, by the few years spent among the human herd.

And this "N. H." needed help, the best, the wisest possible. Both male and female help "N. H." demanded. He, Edward Fillery, could supply the former, but the latter could be furnished only by some woman in whom innocence, truth and a natural mother-love—the three deepest feminine qualities—were happily combined. Nayan possessed them all. "N. H.," the strange bright messenger, bringing perhaps glad tidings into life, had need of her.

And Fillery, as his thoughts ran down these sad and happy paths of that lost valley in his blood, realized the meaning of the flashing intuition that had pained yet gladdened him half an hour before with its convincing symbolic picture.

This private Eden secreted in his depths he revealed to no one, though Paul, his intimate friend and keen assistant, divined its general neighbourhood and geography to some extent. It was the girl who invariably opened its ivory gates for him. They had but to meet and talk a moment, when, with a sudden drift of wonder, beauty, wildness, this Khaketian inheritance rose before him. Its sunny brilliance, its flowers, its perfumes seduced and caught him away. The unearthly mood stole over him. Thought took wings of imagination and soared beyond the planet. He foresaw, easily, the effect she would produce upon "LeVallon." . . .

He came back to earth again at the door of the Home, smiling, as so often before, at these brief wanderings in his secret Eden, yet perfectly able to pigeon-hole the experience, each detail explained, labelled, docketed, and therefore harmless. . . .

He found Devonham in the study and at once told him of his suggestion and its possible results, and his assistant, resting before lunch after a long morning's work, looked up at him with his quick, observant air. Noticing the light in the eyes, the softer expression about the mouth, the general appearance of a strong and recent stimulus, he easily divined their origin, and showed his pleasure in his face. He longed for his old friend to be humanized and steadied by some deep romance. There was a curious new watchful attitude also about him, though cleverly concealed.

"I'm glad the Khilkoffs are back in town," he said easily. "As for LeVallon—he's been quiet and uninteresting all the morning. He needs the human touch, as I already said, and the Studio atmosphere, especially if the Prometheans are to be there, seems the very thing."

"And Nayan——?"

"Her influence is good for any man, young or old, and

if LeVallon worships at her shrine like the rest of 'em,
so much the better. You remember my Notes. Nothing
will help towards his finding his real self quicker than
an abandoned passion—unreturned."

"Unreturned?"

"You can't think she will give to LeVallon what so
many——?"

"But may she not," the other interrupted, "stimulate
'N. H.' rather than LeVallon?"

Devonham was surprised—he had quickly divined the
subconscious fear and jealousy. For this detached, impersonal attitude he was not prepared. Only the keenest
observer could have noticed the sharp, anxious watchful-
ness he hid so well.

"Edward, there's only one thing I feel we—you rather
—have to be careful about. And the girl has nothing
to do with *that*. In your blood, remember, lies an unearthly spiritual vagrancy which you must not, dare not,
communicate to him, if you ever hope to see him cured."

Devonham regarded him keenly as he said it. He
was as earnest as his chief, but the difference between
the two men was fundamental, probably unbridgeable as
well. The affection, trust, respect each felt for the other
was sincere. Devonham, however, having never known
a thought, a feeling, much less an actual experience, outside the normal gamut of humanity, regarded all such as
pathogenic. Fillery, who had tasted the amazing, dangerous sweetness of such experiences, in his own being,
had another standard.

"You must not exaggerate," observed Fillery, slowly.
"Your phrase, though, is good. 'Spiritual vagrancy' is
an apt description, I admit. Yet to the 'spiritual,' if it
exists, the whole universe lies open, remember, too."

They laughed together. Then, suddenly, Devonham
rose, and a new inexpressible uneasiness was in his face.
He thrust his hands deep into his trouser pockets, turned
his eyes hard upon the floor, stood with his legs apart.

Abruptly turning, he came a full step closer. "Edward," he said, furious with himself, and yet fiercely determined to be honest, "I may as well tell you frankly—though explanation lies beyond me—there's something in this—this case I don't quite like." Behind his lowered eyelids his observation never failed.

Quick as a flash, his companion took him up. "For yourself, for others, or for himself?" he asked, while a secret touch of joy ran through him.

"For myself perhaps," was the immediate rejoinder. "It's intolerable. It's the panic sense he touches in me. I admit it frankly. I've had—once or twice—the desire to turn and run. But what I mean is—we've got to be uncommonly careful with him," he ended lamely.

"LeVallon you refer to? Or 'N. H.'?"

" 'N. H.' "

"The panic sense," repeated Fillery to himself more than to his friend. "The old, old thing. I understand."

"Also," Devonham went on presently, "I must tell you that since he came here there's been a change in every patient in the building—without exception." He looked over his shoulder as though he heard a sound. He listened certainly, but his mind was sharply centred on his friend.

"For the better, yes," said Fillery at once. "Increased vitality, I've noticed too."

"Precisely," whispered the other, still listening.

There came a pause between them.

"And when we have found the real, the central self," pursued Fillery presently. "When we have found the essential being—what is it?"

"Exactly," replied Devonham with extraordinary emphasis. *"What is it?"* But even then he did not look up to meet the other's glance.

CHAPTER XI

THE meeting with Dr. Fillery and his friends, the Khilkoffs, father and daughter, had, for one reason or another, to be postponed for a week, during which brief time even, no single day wasted, LeVallon's education proceeded rapidly. He was exceedingly quick to learn the usages of civilized society in a big city, adapting himself with an ease born surely of quick intelligence to the requirements and conventions of ordinary life.

In his perception of the rights of others, particularly, he showed a natural aptitude; he had good manners, that is, instinctively; in certain houses where Fillery took him purposely, he behaved with a courtesy and tact that belong usually to what England calls a gentleman. Except to Fillery and Devonham, he talked little, but was an excellent and sympathetic listener, a quality that helped him to make his way. With Mrs. Soames, the stern and even forbidding matron, he made such headway, that it was noticed with a surprise, including laughter. He might have been her adopted son.

"She's got a new pet," said Devonham, with a laugh. "Mason taught him well. His aptitude for natural history is obvious; after a few years' study he'll make a name for himself. The 'N. H.' side will disappear now more and more, unless *you* stimulate it for your own ends——" He broke off, speaking lightly still, but with a carelessness some might have guessed assumed.

"You forget," put in his Chief, "I promised."

Devonham looked at him shrewdly. "I doubt," he said, "whether you can help yourself, Edward," the expression in his eyes for a moment almost severe.

116

Fillery remained thoughtful, making no immediate reply.

"We must remember," he said presently, "that he's now in the quiescent state. Nothing has again occurred to bring 'N. H.' uppermost again."

Devonham turned upon his friend. "I see no reason why 'N. H.' "—he spoke with emphasis—"should ever get uppermost again. In my opinion we can make this quiescent state—LeVallon—the permanent one."

"We can't keep him in a cage like Mrs. Soames's mice and parrot. Are you, for instance, against my taking him to the Studio? Do you think it's a mistake to let him meet the Prometheans?"

"That's just where Mason went wrong," returned Devonham. "He kept him in a cage. The boy met only a few peasants, trees, plants, animals and birds. The sun, making him feel happy, became his deity. The rain he hated. The wind inspired and invigorated him. If we now introduce the human element wisely, I see no danger. If he can stand the Khi—the Studio and the Prometheans, he can stand anything. He may be considered cured."

The door opened and a tall, radiant figure with bright eyes and untidy shining hair came into the room, carrying an open book.

"Mrs. Soames says I've nothing to do with stars," said a deep musical voice, "and that I had better stick to animals and plants. She says that star-gazing never was good for anyone except astronomers who warn us about tides, eclipses and dangerous comets."

He held out the big book, open at an enlarged stellar photograph. "What, please, is a galaxy, a star that is suddenly brilliant, then disappears in a few weeks, and a nebula?"

Before either of the astonished men could answer, LeVallon turned to Devonham, his face wearing the gravity and intense curiosity of a child. "And, please, are *you* the only sort of being in the universe? Mrs. Soames says that the earth is the only inhabited place. Aren't there other beings besides you anywhere? The Earth is such a little planet, and the solar system, according to this book, is one of the smallest too."

"My dear fellow," Devonham said gently, "do not bother your head with useless speculations. Our only valuable field of study is this planet, for it is all we know or ever can know. Whether the universe holds other beings or not, can be of no importance to us at present."

LeVallon stared fixedly at him, saying nothing. Something of his natural radiance dimmed a little. "Then what are all these things that I remember I've forgotten?" he asked, his blue eyes troubled.

"It will take you all your lifetime to understand beings like me, and like yourself and like Dr. Fillery. Don't waste time speculating about possible inhabitants in other stars."

He spoke good-humouredly, but firmly, as one who laid down certain definite lines to be followed, while Dr. Fillery, watching, made no audible comment. Once long ago he had asked his own father a somewhat similar question.

"But I shall so soon get to the end of you," replied LeVallon, a disappointed expression on his face. "I may speculate *then?*" he asked.

"When you get to the end of me and of yourself and of Dr. Fillery—yes, then you may speculate to your heart's content," said Devonham in a kindly tone. "But it will take you longer than you think perhaps. Besides, there are women, too, remember. You will find them more complicated still."

A curious look stole into the other's eager eyes. He turned suddenly towards the older man who had his confidence so completely. There was in the movement, in the incipient gesture that he made with his arms, his hands, almost with his head and face as well, something of appeal that set the doctor's nerves alert. And the change of voice—it was lower now and more musical than before—increased the nameless message that flashed to his brain and heart. There was a hint of song, of chanting almost, in the tone. There was music in him. For the voice, Fillery realized suddenly, brought in the over-tones, somewhat in the way good teachers of singing and voice production know. There was the depth, sonority, singing quality which means that the "harmonics" are made audible, as with a violin played in perfect tune. The sound seemed produced not by the vocal cords alone, but by the entire being, so to speak. Yet, "LeVallon's" voice had not this rich power, he noticed. Its appearance was a sign that "N. H." was stirring into activity and utterance.

"Women, yes," the young man repeated to himself. "Women—bring back something. Their eyes make me remember——" he turned abruptly to the open book upon the doctor's knee. "It's something to do with stars, these memories," he went on eagerly, the voice resonant. "Stars, women, memories . . . where are they all gone to . . . ? Why have I lost . . . ? What is it that . . . ?"

It seemed as if a veil passed from his face, a thin transparency that dimmed the shining effect his hair and eyes and radiant health produced. A far-away expression followed it.

"'N. H.'!" Devonham quickly flashed the whispered warning. And in the same instant, Fillery rose, holding out the open book.

"Come, LeVallon," he said, putting a hand upon his shoulder, "we'll go into my room for an hour, and I'll tell you all about the galaxies and nebulæ. You shall as' as many questions as you like. Devonham is a very busy man and has duties to attend to just now."

He moved across to open the door, and LeVallon, his face changing more and more, went with him; the light in his eyes increased; he smiled, the far-away expression passed a little.

"Dr. Devonham is quite right in what he says about

useless speculations," continued Fillery, as they went out
arm in arm together, "but we çan play a bit with thought
and imagination, for all that—you and I. 'Let your
thought wander like an insect which is allowed to fly in
the air, but is at the same time confined by a thread.'
Come along, we'll have an hour's play. We'll travel
together among the golden stars, eh?"

"Play!" exclaimed the youth, looking up with flashing eyes. "Ah! in the Spring we play! Our work with
sap, roots, crystals, fire, all finished out of sight, so that
their results followed of their own accord." He was
talking at great speed in a low voice, a deep, rolling
voice, and half to himself. "Spring is our holiday, the
forms made perfect and ready for the power to rush
through, and we rush with it, playing everywhere——"

"Spring is the wine of life, yes," put in Fillery, caught
away momentarily by something behind the words he
listened to, as though a rhythm swept him. "Creative
life racing up and flooding into every form and body
everywhere. It brings wonder, joy—play, as you call it."

"We—we build the way——" The youth broke off
abruptly as they reached the study door. Something
flowed down and back in him, emptying face and manner
of a mood which had striven for utterance, then passed.
He returned to the previous talk about the stars again:

"Who attends to them? Who looks after them?" he
inquired, a deep, peculiar interest in his manner, his eyes
turning a little darker.

"What we call the laws of Nature," was the reply,
"which are, after all, merely our 'descriptive formulæ
summing up certain regularities of recurrence,' the laws
under which they were first set alight and then sent
whirling into space. Under these same laws they will
all eventually burn out and come to rest. They will be
dead."

"Dead," repeated the other, as though he did not
understand. "They are the children of the laws," he

stated, rather than asked. "Are the laws kind and faithful? They never tire?"

Fillery explained with one-half of his nature, and still as to a child. The other half of him lay under firm restraint according to his promise. He outlined in general terms man's knowledge of the stars. "The laws never tire," he said.

"But the stars end! They burn out, stop, and die! You said so."

The other replied with something judicious and cautious about time and its immense duration. But he was startled.

"And those who attend to the laws," came then the words that startled him, "who keeps them working so that they do not tire?"

It was something in the tone of voice perhaps that, once again, produced in his listener the extraordinary sudden feeling that Humanity was, after all, but an insignificant, a microscopic detail in the Universe; that it was, say, a mere ant-heap in the colossal jungle crowded with other minuter as well as immenser life of every sort and kind, and, moreover, that "N. H." was aware of this "other life," or at least of some vast section of it, and had been, if he were not still, associated with it. The two letters by which he was designated acquired a deeper meaning than before.

A rich glow came into the young face, and into the eyes, growing ever darker, a look of burning; the skin had the effect of radiating; the breathing became of a sudden deep and rhythmical. The whole figure seemed to grow larger, expanding as though it extended already and half filled the room. Into the atmosphere about it poured, as though heat and light rushed through it, a strange effect of power.

"You'd like to visit them, perhaps—wouldn't you?" asked Fillery gently.

"I feel——" began the other, then stopped short.

"You feel it would interest you," the doctor helped—
then saw his mistake.

"I feel," repeated the youth. The sentence was complete. "I am there."

"Ah! when you feel you're there, you *are* there?"

The other nodded.

He leaned forward. "*I* know," he whispered as with
sudden joy. "*You* help me to remember, Fillery." The
voice, though whispering, was strong; it vibrated full of
over-tones and under-tones. The sound of the "F" was
like a wind in branches. "You wonderful, *you* know too!
It is the same with flowers, with everything. We build
with wind and fire." He stopped, rubbing a hand across
his forehead a moment. "Wind and fire," he went on,
but this time to himself, "my splendid mighty ones. . . ."
Dropping his hand, he flashed an amazing look of enthusiasm and power into his companion's face. The
look held in concentrated form something of the power
that seemed pulsing and throbbing in his atmosphere.
"Help me to remember, dear Fillery," his voice rang out
aloud like singing. "Remember with me why we both
are here. When we remember we can go back where
we belong."

The glow went from his face and eyes as though an
inner lamp had been suddenly extinguished. The power
left both voice and atmosphere. He sank back in his
chair, his great sensitive hands spread over the table
where the star charts lay, as through the open window
came the crash and clatter of an aeroplane tearing, like
some violent, monstrous insect, through the sunlight.

A look of pain came into his eyes. "It goes again.
I've lost it."

"We were talking about the stars and the laws of
Nature," said Fillery quickly, though his voice was shaking, "when that noisy flying-machine disturbed us." He
leaned over, taking his companion's hand. His heart was
beating. He smelt the open spaces. The blood ran wildly

in his veins. It was with the utmost difficulty he found simple, common words to use. "You must not ask too much at once. We will learn slowly—there is so much we have to learn together."

LeVallon's smile was beautiful, but it was the smile of "LeVallon" again only.

"Thank you, dear Fillery," he replied, and the talk continued as between a tutor and his backward pupil. . . . But for some time afterwards the "tutor's" mind and heart, while attending to LeVallon now, went travelling, it seemed, with "N. H." There was this strange division in his being . . . for "N. H." appealed with power to a part of him, perhaps the greatest, that had never yet found expression, much less satisfaction.

Many a talk together of this kind, with occasional semi-irruptions of "N. H.," he had already enjoyed with his new patient, and LeVallon was by now fairly well instructed in the general history of our little world, briefly but picturesquely given. Evolution had been outlined and explained, the rise of man sketched vividly, the great war, and the planet's present state of chaos described in a way that furnished a clear enough synopsis of where humanity now stood. LeVallon was able to hold his own in conversation with others; he might pass for a simple-minded but not ill-informed young man, and both Paul Devonham and Edward Fillery, though each for different reasons, were, therefore, well satisfied with the young human being entrusted to their care, a human being to be eventually discharged from the Home, healed and cured of extravagances, made harmonious with himself, able to make his own way in the world alone. To Devonham it appeared already certain that, within a reasonable time, LeVallon would find himself happily at home among his fellow kind, a normal, even a gifted young man with a future before him. "N. H." would disappear and be forgotten, absorbed back into the parent Self. To his colleague, on the other hand, another vision of his future opened. Sooner or later it was LeVallon that would disappear and "N. H." remain in full control, a strange, possibly a new type of being, not alone marvellously gifted, but who might even throw light upon a vista of research and knowledge hitherto unknown to humanity, and with benefits for the Race as yet beyond the reach of any wildest prophecy.

Both men, therefore, went gladly with him to the Khilkoff Studio that early November afternoon, anxious to observe him, his conduct, attitude, among the curious set of people to be found there on the Prometheans' Society day, and to note any reactions he might show in such a milieu. Each felt fully justified in doing so, though they would have kept an ordinary "hysterical" patient safely from the place. LeVallon, however, betrayed no trace of hysteria in any meaning of the word, big or little; he was stable as a navvy, betraying no undesirable reaction to the various well-known danger points. The visit might be something of an experiment perhaps, but an experiment, a test, they were justified in taking. Yet Devonham on no account would have allowed his chief to go alone. He had insisted on accompanying them.

And to both men, as they went towards Chelsea, their quiet companion with them, came the feeling that the visit might possibly prove one of them right, the other wrong. Fillery expected that Nayan Khilkoff alone, to say nothing of the effect of the other queer folk who might be present, must surely evoke the "N. H." personality now lying quiescent and inactive below the threshold of LeVallon. The charm and beauty of the girl he had never known to fail with any male, for she had that in her which was bound to stimulate the highest in the opposite sex. The excitement of the wild, questing, picturesque, if unbalanced, minds who would fill the place, must also, though in quite another way, affect the *real* self of anyone who came in contact with their fantastic and imaginative atmosphere.   Attraction or repulsion must certainly be felt.   He expected at any rate a vital clue.

"Ivan Khilkoff," he told LeVallon, as they went along in the car, "is a Russian, a painter and sculptor of talent, a good-hearted and silent sort of old fellow, who has remained very poor because he refuses to advertise himself or commercialize his art, and because his work is not the kind of thing the English buy.   His daughter, Nayan, teaches the piano and Russian.   She is beautiful and sweet and pure, but of an independent and rather impersonal character.   She has never fallen in love, for instance, though most men fall in love with her.   I hope you may like and understand each other."

"Thank you," said LeVallon, listening attentively, but with no great interest apparently.   "I will try very much to like her and her father too."

"The Studio is a very big one, it is really two studios knocked into one, their living rooms opening out of it. One half of the place, being so large, they sometimes let out for meetings, dances and that sort of thing, earning a little money in that way.   It is rented this evening by a Society called the Prometheans—a group of people whose inquisitive temperaments lead them to believe, or half believe——"

"To imagine, if not deliberately to manufacture," put in Devonham.

"——to imagine, let us call it," continued the other with a twinkle, "that there are other worlds, other powers, other states of consciousness and knowledge open to them outside and beyond the present ones we are familiar with."

"They *know* these?" asked LeVallon, looking up with signs of interest.   "They have experienced them?"

"They know and experience," replied Fillery, "according to their imaginations and desires, those with a touch of creative imagination claiming the most definite results, those without it being merely imitative.   They report their experiences, that is, but cannot—or rarely show the results to others. You will hear their talk and judge accordingly. They are interesting enough in their way. They have, at any rate, one thing of value—that they are open to new ideas. Such people have existed in every age of the world's history, but after an upheaval, such as the great war has been, they become more active and more numerous, because the nervous system, reacting from a tremendous strain, produces exaggeration. Any world is better than an uncomfortable one in revolution, they think. They are, as a rule, sincere and honest folk. They add a touch of colour to the commonplace——"

"Tuppence coloured," murmured Devonham below his breath.

"And they believe so much in other worlds to conquer, other regions, bigger states of consciousness, other powers," concluded Fillery, ignoring the interruption, "that they are half in this world, half in the next. Hence Dr. Devonham's name, the name by which he sometimes laughs at them—of Half Breeds."

LeVallon's eyes, he saw, were very big; his interest and attention were excited.

"They will probably welcome you with open arms," he added, "if you care to join them. They consider themselves pioneers of a larger life. They are not mere spiritualists—oh no! They are familiar with all the newest theories, and realize that an alternative hypothesis can explain all so-called psychic phenomena without dragging spirits in. It is in exaggerating results they go mostly wrong."

"Eccentrics," Devonham remarked, "out of the circle, and hysterical to a man. They accomplish nothing. They are invariably dreamers, usually of doubtful morals and honesty, and always unworthy of serious attention. But they may amuse you for an hour."

"We all find it difficult to believe what we have never experienced," mentioned Fillery, turning to his colleague with a hearty laugh, in which the latter readily joined, for their skirmishes usually brought in laughter at the end. Just now, moreover, they were talking with a purpose, and it was wise and good that LeVallon should listen and take in what he could—hearing both sides. He watched and listened certainly with open eyes and ears, as he sat between them on the wide front seat, but saying, as usual, very little.

The car turned down a narrow lane with slackening speed and slowed up before a dingy building with faded Virginia creepers sprawling about stained dirty walls. The neighbourhood was depressing, patched and dishevelled, and almost bordering on a slum. The November light was passing into early twilight.

"You," said LeVallon abruptly, turning round and staring at Devonham, "make everything seem unreal to me. I do not understand you. You know so much. Why is so little real to you?"

But Devonham, in the act of getting out of the car, made no reply, and probably had not heard the words, or, if he had heard, thought them more suitable for Fillery.

CHAPTER XII

THE Prometheans were evidently in full attendance; possibly the rumour had reached them that Dr. Fillery was coming. No one announced the latter's arrival, there was no servant visible; the party hung up their hats and coats in a passage, then walked into the lofty, dim-lit studio which was already filled with people and the hum of many voices.

At once, standing in a hesitating group beside the door, they were observed by everyone in the room. All asked, it seemed, "Who is this stranger they have brought?" Fillery caught the curious atmosphere in that first moment, an instant whiff, as it were, of excitement, interest, something picturesque, if possibly foolish, fantastic, too, yet faintly stimulating, breathing along his extremely sensitive nerves.

He glanced at his companions. Devonham, it struck him, looked more than ever like a floor-walker come to supervise, say, a Department where the sales and assistants were not satisfactory or—he laughed inwardly as the simile occurred to him—a free-thinker entering a church whose teaching he disapproved, even despised, and whose congregation touched his contemptuous pity. "Who would ever guess," thought his friend and colleague, "the sincerity and depth of knowledge in that insignificant appearance? Paul hides his value well!" He noticed, in his quick fashion, touched by humour, the hard challenging eyes, the aquiline nose on which a pair of pince-nez balanced uneasily, the narrow shoulders, the poorly fitting clothes. The heart, of course, remained invisible. Yet suddenly he felt glad that Devonham was with him. "Nothing unstable there," he reflected,

128

"and stability combined with competence is rare." This rapid judgment, it occurred to him, was possibly a warning from his own subconscious being. . . . A red flag signalled, flickered, vanished.

He glanced next at LeVallon, towering above the other. LeVallon was now well dressed in London clothes that suited him, though, for that matter, any clothes must have looked well upon a male figure so virile and upstanding. His great shoulders, his leanness, covered so beautifully with muscle, his height, his colouring, his radiant air; above all, his strange, big penetrating eyes, marked him as a figure one would notice anywhere. He stood, somehow, alone, apart, though the ingredients that contributed to this strange air of aloofness would be hard to define.

It was chiefly, perhaps, the poise of the great powerful frame that helped towards this odd setting in isolation and independence. Motionless, he gazed about him quietly, but it was the way he stood that singled him out from other men. Even in his stillness there was grace; neither hands nor feet, though it was difficult to describe exactly how he placed them or used them, were separate from this poise of perfect balance. To put it colloquially, he knew what to do with his extremities. Self-consciousness, in sight of this ardent throng, the first he had encountered at close, intimate quarters, was entirely absent.

This Fillery noticed instantly, but other impressions followed during the few brief seconds while they waited by the door; and first, the odd effect of tremendous power he managed to convey. Nothing could have been less aggressive than the tentative, questioning, half inquiring, half wondering attitude in which he stood, waiting to be introduced to the buzzing throng of humans; yet there hung about him like an atmosphere this potential strength, of confidence, of superiority, even of beauty too, that not only contributed much to the aloofness already mentioned, but also contrived to make the others, men and women, in the crowded room—insignificant. Somehow they seemed pale and ineffective against a larger grandeur, a scale entirely beyond their reach.

"Gigantic" was the word that leaped into the mind, but another perhaps leaped with it—"elemental."

Fillery was aware of envy, oddly enough, of pride as well. His heart warmed more than ever to him. Almost, he could have then and there recalled his promise given to Devonham, cancelling it contemptuously with a word of self-apology for his smallness and his lack of faith. . . .

LeVallon, aware of a sympathetic mind occupied closely with himself, turned in that moment, and their eyes met squarely; a smile of deep, inner understanding passed swiftly between them over Devonham's head and shoulders. In which moment, exactly, a short, bearded man, detaching himself from the crowd, came forward and greeted them with sincere pleasure in his voice and manner. He was broad-shouldered, lean, his clothes hung loosely; his glance was keen but kindly. Introductions followed, and Khilkoff's sharp eye rested for some seconds with unconcealed admiration upon LeVallon, as he held his hand. His discerning sculptor's glance seemed to appraise his stature and proportions, while he bade him welcome to the Studio. His big head and short neck, his mane of hair, the width of his face, with its squat nose and high cheek-bones, the half ferocious eyes, the heavy jaw and something sprawling about the mouth, gave him a leonine expression. And his voice was not unlike a deep-toned growl, for all its cordiality.

A stir, meanwhile, ran through the room, more heads turned in their direction; they had long ago been observed; they were being now examined.

"Nayan," Khilkoff was saying, while he still held Le-Vallon's hand as though its size and grip contented him, "had a late Russian lesson. She will be here shortly, and very glad to make your acquaintance," looking up at Le-Vallon, as the new-comer. His gruffness and brevity had something pleasing in them. "To-day the Studio is not

entirely mine," he explained. "I want you to come when
I'm alone. Some studies I made in Sark this summer may
interest you." He turned to Fillery. "That lonely place
was good for both of us," he said; "it gave me new life
and inspiration, and Nayan benefited immensely too. She
looks more like a nymph than ever."

He shook hands with Devonham, smiling more grimly.
"I'm surprised you, too, have honoured us," he exclaimed
with genuine surprise. "Come to damn them all as usual,
probably! Good! Your common-sense and healthy criticism are needed in these days—cool, cleaning winds in an
over-heated conservatory." He broke off abruptly and
looked down at LeVallon's hand he was still holding. He
examined it for a second with care and admiration, then
turned his eye upon the young man's figure. He grunted.

"When I know you better," he said, with a growl of
earnest meaning, "I shall ask a favour, a great favour, of
you. So, beware!"

"Thank you," replied LeVallon, and at the sound of his
voice the sculptor's interest deepened. A gleam shone in
his eye.

"You've begun some work," said Fillery, "and models
are hard to come by, I imagine." His eye never left Le-
Vallon.

Khilkoff chuckled. "Thought-reader!" he exclaimed.
"If Povey heard that, he'd make you join the Society at
once—as honorary member or vice-president. Anything to
get you in. Dr. Fillery understands us all too well," he
went on to LeVallon. "In Sark, that lonely island in the
sea, I began four figures—four elemental figures—of earth,
air, fire and water—a group, of course. The air figure,
I've done——"

"With Nayan as model," suggested Fillery, smiling.

"One morning, yes, I caught her bathing from a rock,
hair streaming in the wind, no clothes on, white foam from
the big breakers fluttering about her, slim, shining, unconscious and half dancing, fierce sunlight all over her. Ah"

—he broke off—"here's Povey coming. I mustn't monopolize you all. Devonham, you know most of 'em. Make yourselves at home." He turned to LeVallon again, with a touch of something gentler, almost of respect, thought Fillery, as he noticed the delicate change of voice and manner quickly. "Come, Mr. LeVallon," he said courteously, "I should like to show you the figure as I've done it. We'll go for a moment into my own private rooms. But it's a model for fire I'm looking for, as Fillery guessed. You may be interested." He led him off. LeVallon went with evident content, and the advance of skirmishes that were already approaching for introductions was temporarily defeated.

For the three men standing by the door had formed a noticeable group, and Khilkoff's presence added to their value. Dr. Fillery, known and much respected, regarded with a touch of awe by many, had not come for nothing, it was doubtless argued; his colleague, moreover, accompanied him, and he, too, was known to the Society, though not much cultivated by its members owing to his downright, critical way of talking. They deemed him prejudiced, unsympathetic. It was the third member of the group, LeVallon, who had quickly caught all eyes, and the attention immediately paid to him by their host set the value of a special and important guest upon him instantly. All watched him led away by Khilkoff to the private quarters of the Studio, where none at first presumed to follow them; but it was the eyes of the women that remained glued to the open door where they had disappeared, waiting with careful interest for their reappearance. In particular Lady Gleeson, the "pretty Lady Gleeson," watched from the corner where she sat alone, sipping some refreshment.

Fillery and Devonham, having observed the signs about them, exchanged a glance; their charge was safe for the moment, at any rate; they felt relieved; yet it was for the entry of Nayan, the daughter, that both waited with interest and impatience, as, meanwhile, the bolder ones among the crowd came up one by one and captured them.

"Oh, Dr. Fillery, I *am* glad to see you here. I thought you were always too busy for unscientific people like us. Yet, in a way, we're all seekers, are we not? I've been reading your Physiology book, and I *did* so want to ask you about something in it. I wonder if you'd mind."

He shook hands with a young-old woman, wearing bobbed hair and glasses, and speaking with an intense, respectful, yet self-apologetic manner.

"You've forgotten me, but I *quite* understand. You see *so* many people. I'm Miss Lance. I sent you my little magazine, 'Simplicity,' once, and you acknowledged it *so* sweetly, though, of course, I understood you had not the time to write for it." She continued for several minutes, smiling up at him, her hands clasping and unclasping themselves behind a back clothed with some glittering coloured material that rather fascinated him by its sheen. She kept raising herself on her toes and sinking back again in a series of jerky rhythms.

He gave her his delightful smile.

"Oh, Dr. Fillery!" she exclaimed, with pleasure, leading him to a divan, upon which he let himself down in such a position that he could observe the door from the street as well as the door where LeVallon had disappeared. "This is really too good-natured of you. Your book set me on fire simply"—her eyes wandering to the other door—"and what a wonderful looking person you've brought with you——"

"I fear it's not very easy reading," he interposed patiently.

"To me it was too delightful for words," she rattled on, pleased by the compliment implied. "I devour *all* your books and always review them myself in the magazine. I wouldn't trust them to anyone else. I simply can't tell you how physiology stimulates me. Humanity needs imaginative books, especially just now." She broke off with a deprecatory smile. "I do what I can," she added, as he made no remark, "to make them known, though in such a very small way, I fear." Her interest, however, was divided, the two powerful attractions making her quite incoherent. "Your friend," she ventured again, "he must be Eastern perhaps? Or is that merely sunburn? He looks *most* unusual."

"Sunburn merely, Miss Lance. You must have a chat with him later."

"Oh, thank you, *thank* you, Dr. Fillery. I do so love unusual people. . . ."

He listened gravely. He was gentle, while she confided to him her little inner hopes and dreams about the "simple life." She introduced adjectives she believed would sound correct, if spoken very quickly, until, between the torrent of "psychical," "physiological" and once or twice, "psychological," she became positively incoherent in a final entanglement from which there was no issue but a convulsive gesture. None the less, she was bathed in bliss. She monopolized the great man for a whole ten minutes on a divan where everybody could see that they talked earnestly, intimately, perhaps even intellectually, together side by side.

He observed the room, meanwhile, without her noticing it, scanning the buzzing throng with interest. There was confusion somewhere, something was lacking, no system prevailed; he was aware of a general sense of waiting for a leader. All looked, he knew, for Nayan to appear. Without her presence, there was no centre, for, though not a member of the Society herself, she was the heart always of their gatherings, without which they straggled somewhat aimlessly. And "heart," he remembered, with a smile that Miss Lance took proudly for herself, was the appropriate word. Nayan mothered them. They were but children, after all. . . .

"When you talk of a 'New Age,' what *exactly* do you mean? I wish you'd define the term for me," Devonham meanwhile was saying to an interlocutor, not far away, while with a corner of his eye he watched both Fillery and the private door. He still stood near the entrance, looking more than ever like a disapproving floor-walker in a big department store, and it was with H. Millington Povey that he talked, the Honorary Secretary of the Society. The

Secretary had aimed at Fillery, but Miss Lance had been too quick for him. He was obliged to put up with Devonham as second best, and his temper suffered accordingly. He was in aggressive mood.

Povey, facing him, was talking with almost violent zeal. A small, thin, nervous man, on the verge of middle age, his head prematurely bald, with wildish tufts of patchy hair, a thin, scraggy neck that he lengthened and shortened between high hunched shoulders, Povey resembled an eager vulture. His keen bright eyes, hooked nose, and a habit of twisting head and neck apart from his body, which held motionless, increased this likeness to a bird of prey. Possessed of considerable powers of organization, he kept the Society together. It was he who insisted upon some special "psychic gift" as a qualification of membership; an applicant must prove this gift to a committee of Povey's choosing, though these proofs were never circulated for general reading in the Society's Reports. Talkers, dreamers, faddists were not desired; a member must possess some definite abnormal power before he could be elected. He must be clairvoyant or clairaudient, an automatic writer, trance-painter, medium, ghost-seer, prophet, priest or king.

Members, therefore, stated their special qualification to each other without false modesty: "I'm a trance medium," for instance; "Oh, really! *I* see auras, of course"; while others had written automatic poetry, spoken in trance— "inspirational speakers," that is—photographed a spirit, appeared to someone at a distance, or dreamed a prophetic dream that later had come true. Mediums, spirit-photographers, and prophetic dreamers were, perhaps, the most popular qualifications to offer, but there were many who remembered past lives and not a few could leave their bodies consciously at will.

Memberships cost two guineas, the hat was occasionally passed round for special purposes, there was a monthly dinner in Soho, when members stood up, like saved sinners at a revivalist meeting, and gave personal testimony of conversion or related some new strange incident. The Prometheans were full of stolen fire and life.

Among them were ambitious souls who desired to start a new religion, deeming the Church past hope. Others, like the water-dowsers and telepathists, were humbler. There was an Inner Circle which sought to revive the Mysteries, and gave very private performances of dramatic and symbolic kind, based upon recovered secret knowledge, at the solstices and equinoxes. New Thought members despised these, believing nothing connected with the past had value; they looked ahead; "live in the present," "do it now" was their watchword. Astrologers were numerous too. These cast horoscopes, or, for a small fee, revealed one's secret name, true colour, lucky number, day of the week and month, and so forth. One lady had a tame "Elemental." Students of Magic and Casters of Spells, wearers of talismans and intricate designs in precious or inferior metal, according to taste and means, were well represented, and one and all believed, of course, in spirits.

None, however, belonged to any Sect of the day, whatever it might be; they wore no labels; they were seekers, questers, inquirers whom no set of rules or dogmas dared confine within fixed limits. An entirely open mind and no prejudices, they prided themselves, distinguished them.

"Define it in scientific terms, this New Age—I cannot," replied Povey in his shrill voice, "for science deals only with the examination of the known. Yet you only have to look round you at the world to-day to see its obvious signs. Humanity is changing, new powers everywhere——"

Devonham interrupted unkindly, before the other could assume he had proved something by merely stating it:

"What *are* these signs, if I may ask?" he questioned sharply. "For if you can name them, we can examine them —er—scientifically." He used the word with malice, knowing it was ever on the Promethean lips.

"There you are, at cross-purposes at once," declared Povey. "I refer to hints, half-lights, intuitions, signs that only the most sensitive among us, those with psychic divination, with spiritual discernment—that only the privileged and those developed in advance of the Race—can know. And, instantly you produce your microscope, as though I offered you the muscles of a tadpole to dissect."

They glared at one another. "We shall never get progress your way," Povey fumed, withdrawing his head and neck between his shoulders.

"Returning to the Middle Ages, on the other hand," mentioned Devonham, "seems like advancing in a circle, doesn't it?"

"Dr. Devonham," interrupted a pretty, fair-haired girl with an intense manner, "forgive me for breaking up your interesting talk, but you come so seldom, you know, and there's a lady here who is dying to be introduced. She has just seen crimson flashing in your aura, and she wants to ask—do you mind *very* much?" She smiled so sweetly at him, and at Mr. Povey, too, who was said to be engaged to her, though none believed it, that annoyance was not possible. "She says she simply *must* ask you if you were feeling anger. Anger, you know, produces red or crimson in one's visible atmosphere," she explained charmingly. She led him off, forgetting, however, her purpose *en route*, since they presently sat down side by side in a quiet corner and began to enjoy what seemed an interesting tête-à-tête, while the aura-seeing lady waited impatiently and observed them, without the aid of clairvoyance, from a distance.

"And *your* qualifications for membership?" asked Devonham. "I wonder if I may ask——?"

"But you'd laugh at me, if I told you," she answered simply, fingering a silver talisman that hung from her neck, a six-pointed star with zodiacal signs traced round a rose, *rosa mystica*, evidently. "I'm so afraid of doctors."

Devonham shook his head decidedly, asserting vehemently his interest, whereupon she told him her little private dream delightfully, without pose or affectation, yet shyly and so sincerely that he proved his assertion by a genuine interest.

"And does that protect you among your daily troubles?"
he asked, pointing to her little silver talisman. He had
already commented sympathetically upon her account of
saving her new puppies from drowning, having dreamed
the night before that she saw them gasping in a pail of
water, the cruel under-gardener looking on. "Do you wear
it always, or only on special occasions like this?"

"Oh, Miss Milligan made that," she told him, blushing
a little. "She's rather poor. She earns her living by de-
signing——"

"Oh!"

"But I don't mean *that*. She tells you your Sign and
works it in metal for you. I bought one. Mine is Pisces."
She became earnest. "I was born in Pisces, you see."

"And what does Pisces do for you?" he inquired, remembering the heightened colour. The sincerity of this Rose
Mystica delighted him, and he already anticipated her reply
with interest. Here, he felt, was the credulous, religious
type in its naked purity, forced to believe in something
marvellous.

"Well, if you wear your Sign next your skin it brings
good luck—it makes the things you want happen." The
blush reappeared becomingly. She did not lower her eyes.

"Have your things happened then?"

She hesitated. "Well, I've had an awfully good time
ever since I wore it——"

"Proposals?" he asked gently.

"Dr. Devonham!" she exclaimed. "How ever did you
guess?" She looked very charming in her innocent confusion.

He laughed. "If you don't take it off at once," he told
her solemnly, "you may get another."

"It was two in a single week," she confided a little
tremulously. "Fancy!"

"The important thing, then," he suggested, "is to wear
your talisman at the right moment, and with the right
person."

But she corrected him promptly.

"Oh, no. It brings the right moment and the right person together, don't you see, and if the other person is a Pisces person, you understand each other, of course, at once."

"Would that I too were Pisces!" he exclaimed, seeing that she was flattered by his interest. "I'm probably"— taking a sign at random—"Scorpio."

"No," she said with grave disappointment, "I'm afraid you're Capricornus, you know. I can tell by your nose and eyes—and cleverness. But—I wanted really to ask you," she went on half shyly, "if I might——" She stuck fast.

"You want to know," he said, glancing at her with quick understanding, "who *he* is." He pointed to the door. "Isn't that it?"

She nodded her head, while a divine little blush spread over her face. Devonham became more interested. "Why?" he asked. "Did he impress you so?"

"*Rather,*" she replied with emphasis, and there was something in her earnestness curiously convincing. A sincere impression had been registered.

"His appearance, you mean?"

She nodded again; the blush deepened; but it was not, he saw, an ordinary blush. The sensitive young girl had awe in her. "He's a friend of Dr. Fillery's," he told her; "a young man who's lived in the wilds all his life. But, tell me—why are you so interested? Did he make any particular impression on you?"

He watched her. His own thoughts dropped back suddenly to a strange memory of woods and mountains . . . a sunset, a blazing fire . . . a hint of panic.

"Yes," she said, her tone lower, "he did."

"Something *very* definite?"

She made no answer.

"What did you see?" he persisted gently. From woods and mountains, memory stepped back to a railway station and a customs official. . . .

Her manner, obviously truthful, had deep wonder, mystery, even worship in it. He was aware of a nervous reaction he disliked, almost a chill. He listened for her next words with an interest he could hardly account for.

"Wings," she replied, an odd hush in her voice. "I thought of wings. He seemed to carry me off the earth with great rushing wings, as the wind blows a leaf. It was too lovely: I felt like a dancing flame. I thought he was——"

"What?" Something in his mind held its breath a moment.

"You *won't* laugh, Dr. Devonham, will you? I thought —for a second—of—an angel." Her voice died away.

For a second the part of his mood that held its breath struggled between anger and laughter. A moment's confusion in him there certainly was.

"That makes two in the room," he said gently, recovering himself. He smiled. But she did not hear the playful compliment; she did not see the smile. "You've a delightful, poetic little soul," he added under his breath, watching the big earnest eyes whose rapt expression met his own so honestly. Having made her confession she was still engrossed, absorbed, he saw, in her own emotion. . . . So this was the picture that LeVallon, by his mere appearance alone, left upon an impressionable young girl, an impression, he realized, that was profound and true and absolute, whatever value her own individual interpretation of it might have. Her mention of space, wind, fire, speed, he noticed in particular—"off the earth . . . rushing wind . . . dancing flame . . . an angel!"

It was easy, of course, to jeer. Yet, somehow, he did not jeer at all.

She relapsed into silence, which proved how great had been the emotional discharge accompanying the confession, temporarily exhausting her. Dr. Devonham keenly registered the small, important details.

"Entertaining an angel unawares in a Chelsea Studio,"

he said, laughingly; then reminding her presently that there was a lady who was "dying to be introduced" to him, made his escape, and for the next ten minutes found himself listening to a disquisition on auras which described "visible atmospheres whose colour changes with emotion . . . radio-activity . . . the halo worn by saints" . . . the effect of light noticed about very good people and of blackness that the wicked emanated, and ending up with the "radiant atmosphere that shone round the figure of Christ and was believed to show the most lovely and complicated geometrical designs."

"God geometrizes—you, doubtless, know the ancient saying?" Mrs. Towzer said it like a challenge.

"I have heard it," admitted her listener shortly, his first opportunity of making himself audible. "Plato said some other fine things too——"

"I felt sure you were feeling cross just now," the lady went on, "because I saw lines and arrows of crimson darting and flashing through your aura while you were talking to Mr. Povey. He *is* very annoying sometimes, isn't he? I often wonder where all our subscriptions go to. I never could understand a balance-sheet. Can you?"

But Devonham, having noticed Dr. Fillery moving across the room, did not answer, even if he heard the question. Fillery, he saw, was now standing near the door where Khilkoff and LeVallon had disappeared to see the sculpture, an oddly rapt expression on his face. He was talking with a member called Father Collins. The buzz of voices, the incessant kaleidoscope of colour and moving figures, made the atmosphere a little electric. Extricating himself with a neat excuse, he crossed towards his colleague, but the latter was already surrounded before he reached him. A forest of coloured scarves, odd coiffures, gleaming talismans, intervened; he saw men's faces of intense, eager, preoccupied expression, old and young, long hair and bald; there was a new perfume in the air, incense evidently; tea, coffee, lemonade were being served, with stronger drink for the few who liked it, and cigarettes were everywhere. The note everywhere was *exalté* rather.

Out of the excited throng his eyes then by chance, apparently, picked up the figure of Lady Gleeson, smoking her cigarette alone in a big armchair, a half-empty glass of wine-cup beside her. She caught his attention instantly, this "pretty Lady Gleeson," although personally he found neither title nor adjective justified. The dark hair framed a very white skin. The face was shallow, trivial, yet with a direct intensity in the shining eyes that won for her the reputation of being attractive to certain men. Her smile added to the notoriety she loved, a curious smile that lifted the lip oddly, showing the little pointed teeth. To him, it seemed somehow a face that had been over-kissed; everything had been kissed out of it; the mouth, the lips, were worn and barren in an appearance otherwise still young. She was very expensively dressed, and deemed her legs of such symmetry that it were a shame to hide them; clad in tight silk stockings, and looking like strips of polished steel, they were now visible almost to the knee, where the edge of the skirt, neatly trimmed in fur, cut them off sharply. Some wag in the Society, paraphrasing the syllables of her name, wittily if unkindly, had christened her *fille de joie*. When she heard it she was rather pleased than otherwise.

Lady Gleeson, too, he saw now, was watching the private door. The same moment, as so often occurred between himself and his colleague at some significant point in time and space, he was aware of Fillery's eye upon his own across the intervening heads and shoulders. Fillery, also, had noticed that Lady Gleeson watched that door. His changed position in the room was partly explained.

A slightly cynical smile touched Dr. Devonham's lips, but vanished again quickly, as he approached the lady, bowed politely, and asked if he might bring her some refreshment. He was too discerning to say "more" refreshment. But she dotted every i, she had no half tones.

"Thanks, kind Dr. Devonham," she said in a decided tone, her voice thin, a trifle husky, yet not entirely unmusical. It held a strange throaty quality. "It's so absurdly light," she added, holding out the glass she first emptied. "The mystics don't hold with anything strong apparently. But I'm tired, and you discovered it. That's clever of you. It'll do me good."

He, malevolently, assured her that it would.

"Who's your friend?" she asked point blank, with an air that meant to have a proper answer, as he brought the glass and took a chair near her. "He looks unusual. More like a hurdle-race champion than a visionary." A sneer lurked in the voice. She fixed her determined clear grey eyes upon his, eyes sparkling with interest, curiosity in life, desire, the last-named quality of unmistakable kind. "I think I should like to know him perhaps." It was mentioned as a favour to the other.

Devonham, who disliked and disapproved of all these people collectively, felt angry suddenly with Fillery for having brought LeVallon among them. It was after all a foolish experiment; the atmosphere was dangerous for anyone of unstable, possibly of hysterical temperament. He had vengeance to discharge. He answered with deliberate malice, leading her on that he might watch her reactions. She was so transparently sincere.

"I hardly think Mr. LeVallon would interest you," he said lightly. "He is neither modern nor educated. He has spent his life in the backwoods, and knows nothing but plants and stars and weather and—animals. You would find him dull."

"No man with a face and figure like that can be dull," she said quickly, her eyes alight.

He glanced at her rings, the jewelry round her neck, her expensive gown that would keep a patient for a year or two. He remembered her millionaire South African husband who was her foolish slave. She lived, he knew,

entirely for her own small, selfish pleasure. Although he
meant to use her, his gorge rose. He produced his happiest
smile.

"You are a keen observer, Lady Gleeson," he remarked.
"He doesn't look quite ordinary, I admit." After a pause
he added, "It's a curious thing, but Mr. LeVallon doesn't
care for the charms that we other men succumb to so easily.
He seems indifferent. What he wants is knowledge only.
. . . Apparently he's more interested in stars than in girls."

"Rubbish," she rejoined. "He hasn't met any in his
woods, that's all."

Her directness rather disconcerted him. At the same
time, it charmed him a little, though he did not know it.
His dislike of the woman, however, remained. The idle,
self-centred rich annoyed him. They were so useless. The
fabulous jewelry hanging upon such trash now stirred his
bile. He was conscious of the lust for pleasure in her.

"Yet, after all, he's rather an interesting fellow perhaps,"
he told her, as with an air of sudden enthusiasm. "Do you
know he talks of rather wonderful things, too. Mere
dreams, of course, yet, for all that, out of the ordinary. He
has vague memories, it seems, of another state of existence
altogether. He speaks sometimes of—of marvellous women,
compared to whom our women here, our little dressed-up
dolls, seem commonplace and insignificant." And, to his
keen enjoyment, Lady Gleeson took the bait with open
mouth. She recrossed her shapely legs. She wriggled a
little in her chair. Her be-ringed fingers began fidgeting
along the priceless necklace.

"Just what I should expect," she replied in her throaty
voice, "from a young man who looks as he does."

She began to play her own cards then, mentioning that
her husband was interested in Dr. Fillery's Clinique. Devonham, however, at once headed her off. He described the
work of the Home with enthusiasm. "It's fortunate that
Dr. Fillery is rich," he observed carelessly, "and can follow
out his own ideas exactly as he likes. I, personally, should

never have joined him had he been dependent upon the
mere philanthropist."

"How wise of you," she returned. "And I should never
have joined this mad Society but for the chance of coming
across unusual people. Now, your Mr. LeVallon is one.
You may introduce him to me," she repeated as an
ultimatum.

Her directness was the one thing he admired in her.
At her own level, she was real. He was aware of the
semi-erotic atmosphere about these Meetings and realized
that Lady Gleeson came in search of excitement, also that
she was too sincere to hide it. She wore her insignia
unconcealed. Her talisman was of base metal, the one cheap
thing she wore, yet real. This foolish woman, after all,
might be of use unwittingly. She might capture LeVallon,
if only for a moment, before Nayan Khilkoff enchanted
him with that wondrous sweetness to which no man could
remain indifferent. For he had long ago divined the natural,
unspoken passion between his Chief and the daughter of
his host, and with his whole heart he desired to advance it.

"My husband, too, would like to meet him, I'm sure,"
he heard her saying, while he smiled at the reappearance
of the gilded bait. "My husband, you know, is interested
in spirit photography and Dr. Frood's unconscious theories."

He rose, without even a smile. "I'll try and find him
at once," he said, "and bring him to you. I only hope,"
he added as an afterthought, "that Miss Khilkoff hasn't
monopolized him already——"

"She hasn't come," Lady Gleeson betrayed herself.
Instinctively she knew her rival, he saw, with an inward
chuckle, as he rose to fetch the desired male.

He found him the centre of a little group just inside
the door leading into the sculptor's private studio, where
Khilkoff had evidently been showing his new group of
elemental figures. Fillery, a few feet away, observing
everything at close range, was still talking eagerly with
Father Collins. LeVallon and Kempster, the pacifist, were

in the middle of an earnest talk, of which Devonham caught an interesting fragment. Kempster's qualification for membership was an occasional display of telepathy. He was a neat little man exceedingly well dressed, over-dressed in fact, for his tailor's dummy appearance betrayed that he thought too much about his personal appearance. LeVallon, towering over him like some flaming giant, spoke quietly, but with rare good sense, it seemed. Fillery's condensed education had worked wonders on his mind. Devonham was astonished. About the pair others had collected, listening, sometimes interjecting opinions of their own, many women among them leaning against the furniture or sitting on cushions and movable, dump-like divans on the floor. It was a picturesque little scene. But LeVallon somehow dwarfed the others.

"I really think," Kempster was saying, "we might now become a comfortable little third-rate Power—like Spain, for instance—enjoy ourselves a bit, live on our splendid past, and take the sun in ease." He looked about him with a self-satisfied smirk, as though he had himself played a fine rôle in the splendid past.

LeVallon's reply surprised him perhaps, but it surprised Devonham still more. The real, the central self, LeVallon, he thought with satisfaction, was waking and developing. His choice of words was odd too.

"No, no! *You*—the English are the leaders of the world; the best quality is in you. If *you* give up, the world goes down and backwards." The deep, musical tones vibrated through the little room. The speaker, though so quiet, had the air of a powerful athlete, ready to strike. His pose was admirable. Faces turned up and stared. There was a murmur of approval.

"We're so tired of that talk," replied Kempster, no whit disconcerted by the evident signs of his unpopularity. "Each race should take its turn. We've borne the white man's burden long enough. Why not drop it, and let another nation do its bit? We've earned a rest, I think."

His precise, high voice was persuasive. He was a good public speaker, wholly impervious to another point of view. But the resonant tones of LeVallon's rejoinder seemed to bury him, voice, exquisite clothes and all.

"There *is* no other—unless you hand it back to weaker shoulders. No other race has the qualities of generosity, of big careless courage of the unselfish kind required. Above all, you alone have the chivalry."

Two things Devonham noted as he heard: behind the natural resonance in the big voice lay a curious deepness that made him think of thunder, a volume of sound suppressed, potential, roaring, which, if let loose, might overwhelm, submerge. It belonged to an earnestness as yet unsuspected in him, a strength of conviction based on a great purpose that was evidently subconscious in him, as though he served it, belonged to it, without realizing that he did so. He stood there like some new young prophet, proclaiming a message not entirely his own. Also he said "you" in place of the natural "we."

Devonham listened attentively. Here, too, at any rate, was an exchange of ideas above the "psychic" level he so disliked.

LeVallon, he noticed at once, showed no evidence of emotion, though his eyes shone brightly and his voice was earnest.

"America——" began Kempster, but was knocked down by a fact before he could continue.

"Has deliberately made itself a Province again. America saw the ideal, then drew back, afraid. It is once more provincial, cut off from the planet, a big island again, concerned with local affairs of its own. Your Democracy has failed."

"As it always must," put in Kempster, glad perhaps to shift the point, when he found no ready answer. "The wider the circle from which statesmen are drawn, the lower the level of ability. We should be patriotic for ideas, not for places. The success of one country means the downfall

of another. That's not spiritual. . . ." He continued at
high speed, but Devonham missed the words. He was too
preoccupied with the other's language, penetration, point
of view. LeVallon had, indeed, progressed. There was
nothing of the alternative personality in this, nothing of
the wild, strange, nature-being whom he called "N. H."

"Patriotism, of course, is vulgar rubbish," he heard
Kempster finishing his tirade. "It is local, provincial. The
world is a whole."

But LeVallon did not let him escape so easily. It was
admirable really. This half-educated countryman from the
woods and mountains had a clear, concentrated mind. He
had risen too. Whence came his comprehensive outlook?

"Chivalry—you call it sporting instinct—is the first essential of a race that is to lead the world. It is a topmost
quality. Your race has it. It has come down even into
your play. It is instinctive in you more than any other.
And chivalry is unselfish. It is divine. You have conquered the sun. The hot races all obey you."

The thunder broke through the strange but simple words
which, in that voice, and with that quiet earnestness, carried
some weight of meaning in them that print cannot convey.
The women gazed at him with unconcealed, if not with
understanding admiration. "Lead us, inspire us, at any
rate!" their eyes said plainly; "but love us, O love us,
passionately, above all!"

Devonham, hardly able to believe his ears and eyes,
turned to see if Fillery had heard the scrap of talk. Judging by the expression on his face, he had not heard it.
Father Collins seemed saying things that held his attention
too closely. Yet Fillery, for all his apparent absorption,
had heard it, though he read it otherwise than his somewhat literal colleague. It was, nevertheless, an interesting
revelation to him, since it proved to him again how unreal
"LeVallon" was; how easily, quickly this educated simulacrum caught up, assimilated and reproduced as his own,

yet honestly, whatever was in the air at the moment. For
the words he had spoken were not his own, but Fillery's.
They lay, or something like them lay, unuttered in Fillery's
mind just at that very moment. Yet, even while listening
attentively to Father Collins, his close interest in LeVallon
was so keen, so watchful, that another portion of his mind
was listening to this second conversation, even taking part
in it inaudibly. LeVallon caught his language from the
air. . . .

Devonham made his opportunity, leading LeVallon off
to be introduced to Lady Gleeson, who still sat waiting for
them on the divan in the outer studio.

As they made their way through the buzzing throng into
the larger room, Devonham guessed suddenly that Lady
Gleeson must somehow have heard in advance that Le-
Vallon would be present; her flair for new men was
singular; the sexual instinct, unduly developed, seemed
aware of its prey anywhere within a big radius. He owed
his friend a hint of guidance possibly. "A little woman,"
he explained as they crossed over, "who has a weakness
for big men and will probably pay you compliments. She
comes here to amuse herself with what she calls 'the
freaks.' Sometimes she lends her great house for the meetings. Her husband's a millionaire." To which the other,
in his deep, quiet voice, replied: "Thank you, Dr. Devonham."

"She's known as 'the pretty Lady Gleeson.' "

"That?" exclaimed the other, looking towards her.

"Hush!" his companion warned him.

As they approached, Lady Gleeson, waiting with keen
impatience, saw them coming and made her preparations.
The frown of annoyance at the long delay was replaced by
a smile of welcome that lifted the upper lip on one side
only, showing the white even teeth with odd effect. She
stared at LeVallon, thought Devonham, as a wolf eyes its
prey. Deftly lowering her dress—betraying thereby that

she knew it was too high, and a detail now best omitted from the picture—she half rose from her seat as they came up. The instinctive art of deference, though instantly corrected, did not escape Paul Devonham's too observant eye.

"You were kind enough to say I might introduce my friend," murmured he. "Mr. LeVallon is new to our big London, and a stranger among all these people."

LeVallon bowed in his calm, dignified fashion, saying no word, but Lady Gleeson put her hand out, and, finding his own, shook it with her air of brilliant welcome. Determination lay in her smile and in her gesture, in her voice as well, as she said familiarly at once: "But, Mr. LeVallon, how tall *are* you, really? You seem to me a perfect giant." She made room for him beside her on the divan. "Everybody here looks undersized beside you!" She became intense.

"I am six feet and three inches," he replied literally, but without expression in his face. There was no smile. He was examining her as frankly as she examined him. Devonham was examining the pair of them. The lack of interest, the cold indifference in LeVallon, he reflected, must put the young woman on her mettle, accustomed as she was to quick submission in her victims.

LeVallon, however, did not accept the offered seat; perhaps he had not noticed the invitation. He showed no interest, though polite and gentle.

"He towers over all of us," Devonham put in, to help an awkward pause. Yet he meant it more than literally; the empty prettiness of the shallow little face before him, the triviality of Miss Rosa Mystica, the cheapness of Povey, Kempster, Mrs. Towzer, the foolish air of otherworldly expectancy in the whole room, of deliberate exaggeration, of eyes big with wonder for sensation as story followed story—all this came upon him with its note of poverty and tawdriness as he used the words.

Something in the atmosphere of LeVallon had this effect

—whence did it come? he questioned, puzzled—of dwarfing all about him.

"All London, remember, isn't like this," he heard Lady Gleeson saying, a dangerous purr audible in the throaty voice. "Do sit down here and tell me what you think about it. I feel you don't belong here quite, do you know? London cramps you, doesn't it? And you find the women dull and insipid?" She deliberately made more room, patting the cushions invitingly with a flashing hand, that alone, thought Devonham contemptuously, could have endowed at least two big Cliniques. "Tell me about yourself, Mr. LeVallon. I'm dying to hear about your life in the woods and mountains. Do talk to me. I *am* so bored!"

What followed surprised Devonham more than any of the three perhaps. He ascribed it to what Fillery had called the "natural gentleman," while Lady Gleeson, doubtless, ascribed it to her own personal witchery.

With that easy grace of his he sat down instantly beside her on the low divan, his height and big frame contriving the awkward movement without a sign of clumsiness. His indifference was obvious—to Devonham, but the vain eyes of the woman did not notice it.

"That's better," she again welcomed him with a happy laugh. She edged closer a little. "Now, do make yourself comfortable"—she arranged the cushions again—"and please tell me about your wild life in the forests, or wherever it was. You know a lot about the stars, I hear." She devoured his face and figure with her shining eyes.

The upper lip was lifted for a second above a gleaming tooth. Devonham had the feeling she was about to eat him, licking her lips already in anticipation. He himself would be dismissed, he well knew, in another moment, for Lady Gleeson would not tolerate a third person at the meal. Before he was sent about his business, however, he had the good fortune to hear LeVallon's opening answer to the foolish invitation. Amazement filled him. He wished

Fillery could have heard it with him, seen the play of expression on the faces too—the bewilderment of sensational hunger for something new in Lady Gleeson's staring eyes, arrested instantaneously; the calm, cold look of power, yet power tempered by a touch of pity, in LeVallon's glance, a glance that was only barely aware of her proximity. He smiled as he spoke, and the smile increased his natural radiance. He looked extraordinarily handsome, yet with a new touch of strangeness that held even the cautious doctor momentarily almost spellbound.

"Stars—yes, but I rarely see them here in London, and they seem so far away. They comfort me. They bring me—they and women bring me—nearest to a condition that is gone from me. I have lost it." He looked straight into her face, so that she blinked and screwed up her eyes, while her breathing came more rapidly. "But stars and women," he went on, his voice vibrating with music in spite of its quietness, "remind me that it is recoverable. Both give me this sweet message. I read it in stars and in the eyes of women. And it is true because no words convey it. For women cannot express themselves, I see; and stars, too, are silent—here."

The same soft thunder as before sounded below the gently spoken words; Lady Gleeson was trembling a little; she made a movement by means of which she shifted herself yet nearer to her companion in what seemed a natural and unconscious way. It was doubtless his proximity rather than his words that stirred her. Her face was set, though the lips quivered a trifle and the voice was less shrill than usual as she spoke, holding out her empty glass.

"Thank you, Dr. Devonham," she said icily.

The determined gesture, a toss of the head, with the glare of sharp impatience in the eyes, he could not ignore; yet he accepted his curt dismissal slowly enough to catch her murmured words to LeVallon:

"How wonderful! How wonderful you are! And what sort of women . . . ?" followed him as he moved away.

In his heart rose again an uncomfortable memory of a
Jura valley blazing in the sunset, and of a half-naked figure
worshipping before a great wood fire on the rocks. . . .
He fancied he caught, too, in the voice, a suggestion of a
lilt, a chanting resonance, that increased his uneasiness
further. One thing was certain: it was not quite the ordinary "LeVallon" that answered the silly woman. The
reaction was of a different kind. Was, then, the other self
awake and stirring? Was it "N. H." after all, as his
colleague claimed?

Allowing a considerable interval to pass, he returned with
a glass—of lemonade—reaching the divan in its dimlit
corner just in time to see a flashing hand withdrawn quickly
from LeVallon's arm, and to intercept a glance that told
him the intrigue evidently had not developed altogether
according to Lady Gleeson's plan, although her air was one
of confidence and keenest self-satisfaction. LeVallon sat
like a marble figure, cold, indifferent, looking straight before him, listening, if only with half an ear, to a stream
of words whose import it was not difficult to guess.

This Devonham's practised eye read in the flashing look
she shot at him, and in the quick way she thanked him.

"Coffee, dear Dr. Devonham, I asked for."

Her move was so quick, his desire to watch them a
moment longer together so keen, that for an instant he
appeared to hesitate. It was more than appearance; he did
hesitate—an instant merely, yet long enough for Lady
Gleeson to shoot at him a second swift glance of concentrated virulence, and also long enough for LeVallon to
spring lightly to his feet, take the glass from his hand and
vanish in the direction of the refreshment table before anything could prevent. "I will get your coffee for you," still
sounded in the air, so quickly was the adroit manœuvre
executed. LeVallon had cleverly escaped.

"How stupid of me," said Devonham quickly, referring
to the pretended mistake. Lady Gleeson made no reply.
Her inward fury betrayed itself, however, in the tight-set

lips and the hard glitter of her brilliant little eyes. "He won't be a moment," the other added. "Do you find him interesting? He's not very talkative as a rule, but perhaps with you——" He hardly knew what words he used.

The look she gave him stopped him, so intense was the bitterness in the eyes. His interruption, then, must indeed have been worse—or better?—timed than he had imagined. She made no pretence of speaking. Turning her glance in the direction whence the coffee must presently appear, she waited, and Devonham might have been a dummy for all the sign she gave of his being there. He had made an enemy for life, he felt, a feeling confirmed by what almost immediately then followed. Neither the coffee nor its bearer came that evening to pretty Lady Gleeson in the way she had desired. She laid the blame at Devonham's door.

For at that moment, as he stood before her, secretly enjoying her anger a little, yet feeling foolish, perhaps, as well, a chord sounded on the piano, and a hush passed instantly over the entire room. Someone was about to sing. Nayan Khilkoff had come in, unnoticed, by the door of the private room. Her singing invariably formed a part of these entertainments. The song, too, was the one invariably asked for, its music written by herself.

All talk and movement stopped at the sound of the little prelude, as though a tap had been turned off. Even Devonham, most unmusical of men, prepared to listen with enjoyment. He tried to see Nayan at the piano, but too many people came between. He saw, instead, LeVallon standing close at his side, the cup of coffee in his hand. He had that instant returned.

"For Lady Gleeson. Will you pass it to her? Who's going to sing?" he whispered all in the same breath. And Devonham told him, as he bent down to give the cup. "Nayan Khilkoff. Hush! It's a lovely song. I know it —'The Vagrant's Epitaph.' "

They stood motionless to listen, as the pure voice of the

girl, singing very simply but with the sweetness and truth of sincere feeling, filled the room. Every word, too, was clearly audible:

"Change was his mistress; Chance his counsellor.
   Love could not hold him; Duty forged no chain.
The wide seas and the mountains called him,
   And grey dawns saw his camp-fires in the rain.

"Sweet hands might tremble!—aye, but he must go.
   Revel might hold him for a little space;
But, turning past the laughter and the lamps,
   His eyes must ever catch the luring Face.

"Dear eyes might question! Yea, and melt again;
   Rare lips a-quiver, silently implore;
But he must ever turn his furtive head,
   And hear that other summons at the door.

"Change was his mistress; Chance his counsellor.
   The dark firs knew his whistle up the trail.
Why tarries he to-day? . . . And yesternight
   Adventure lit her stars without avail."

CHAPTER XIII

LADY GLEESON, owing to an outraged vanity and jealousy she was unable to control, missed the final scene, for before the song was actually finished she was gone. Being near a passage that was draped only by a curtain, she slipped out easily, flung herself into a luxurious motor, and vanished into the bleak autumn night.

She had seen enough. Her little heart raged with selfish fury. What followed was told her later by word of mouth.

Never could she forgive herself that she had left the studio before the thing had happened. She blamed Devonham for that too.

For LeVallon, it appears, having passed the cup of coffee to her through a third person—in itself an insult of indifference and neglect—stood absorbed in the words and music of the song. Being head and shoulders above the throng, he easily saw the girl at the piano. No one, unless it was Fillery, a few yards away, watched him as closely as did Devonham and Lady Gleeson, though all three for different reasons. It was Devonham, however, who made the most accurate note of what he saw, though Fillery's memory was possibly the truer, since his own inner being supplied the fuller and more sympathetic interpretation.

LeVallon, tall and poised, stood there like a great figure shaped in bronze. He was very calm. His bright hair seemed to rise a little; his eyes, steady and wondering, gazed fixedly; his features, though set, were mobile in the sense that any instant they might leap into the alive and fluid expression of some strong emotion. His whole being, in a word, stood at attention, alert for instant action of some uncontrollable, perhaps terrific kind. "He seemed like a

156

glowing pillar of metal that must burst into flame the very next instant," as a Member told Lady Gleeson later.

Devonham watched him.   LeVallon seemed transfixed. He stared above the intervening tousled heads.   He drew a series of deep breaths that squared his shoulders and made his chest expand.   His very muscles ached apparently for instant action.   An intensity of wondering joy and admiration that lit his face made the eyes shine like stars. He watched the singing girl as a tiger watches the keeper who brings its long-expected food.   The instant the bar is up, it springs, it leaps, it carries off, devours.   Only, in this case, there were no bars.   Nor was the wild desire for nourishment of a carnal kind.   It was companionship, it was intercourse with his own that he desired so intensely.

"He divines the motherhood in her," thought Fillery, watching closely, pain and happiness mingled in his heart. "The protective, selfless, upbuilding power lies close to Nature."   And as this flashed across him he caught a glimpse by chance of its exact opposite—in Lady Gleeson's peering, glittering eyes—the destructive lust, the selfish passion, the bird of prey.

"The dark firs knew his whistle up the trail," the song in that soft true voice drew to its close.   LeVallon was trembling.

"Good Heavens!" thought Devonham.   "Is it 'N. H.' ? Is it 'N. H.,' after all, waking—rising to take possession?" He, too, trembled.

It was here that Lady Gleeson, close, intuitive observer of her escaping prey, rose up and slipped away, her going hardly noticed by the half-entranced, half-dreaming hearts about her, each intent upon its own small heaven of neat desire.   She went as unobtrusively as an animal that is aware of untoward conditions and surroundings, showing her teeth, feeling her claws, yet knowing herself helpless. Not even Devonham, his mind ever keenly alert, observed her going.   Fillery, alone, conscious of LeVallon's eyes across the room, took note of it.   She left, her violent little will intent upon vengeance of a later victory that she still promised herself with concentrated passion.

Yet Devonham, though he failed to notice the slim animal of prey in exit, noticed this—that the face he watched so closely changed quickly even as he watched, and that the new expression, growing upon it as heat grows upon metal set in a flame, was an expression he had seen before. He had seen it in that lonely mountain valley where a setting sun poured gold upon a burning pyre, upon a dancing, chanting figure, upon a human face he now watched in this ridiculous little Chelsea studio. The sharpness of the air, the very perfume, stole over him as he stared, perplexed, excited and uneasy. That strange, wild, innocent and tender face, that power, that infinite yearning! LeVallon had disappeared. It was "N. H." that stood and watched the singer at the little modern piano.

Then with the end of the song came the rush, the bustle of applause, the confusion of many people rising, trotting forward, all talking at once, all moving towards the singer —when LeVallon, hitherto motionless as a statue, suddenly leaped past and through them like a vehement wind through a whirl of crackling dead leaves. Only his deft, skilful movement, of poise and perfect balance combined with accurate swiftness, could have managed it without bruised bodies and angry cries. There was no clumsiness, no visible effort, no appearance of undue speed. He seemed to move quietly, though he moved like fire. In a moment he was by the piano, and Nayan, in the act of rising from her stool, gazed straight up into his great lighted eyes.

It was singular how all made way for him, drew back, looked on. Confusion threatened. Emotion surged like a rising sea. Without a leader there might easily have been tumult; even a scene. But Fillery was there. His figure intervened at once.

"Nayan," he said in a steady voice, "this is my friend, Mr. LeVallon. He wants to thank you."

But, before she could answer, LeVallon, his hand upon her arm, said quickly, yet so quietly that few heard the actual words, perhaps—his voice resonant, his eyes alight with joy: "You are here too—with me, with Fillery. We are all exiles together. But you know the way out—the way back! You remember! . . ."

She stared with delicious wonder into his eyes as he went on:

"O star and woman! Your voice is wind and fire. Come!" And he tried to seize her. "We will go back together. We work here in vain! . . ." His arms were round her; almost their faces touched.

The girl rose instantly, took a step towards him, then hung back; the stool fell over with a crash; a hubbub of voices rose in the room behind; Povey, Kempster, a dozen Members with them, pressed up; the women, with half-shocked, half-frightened eyes, gaped and gasped over the forest of intervening male shoulders. A universal shuffle followed. The confusion was absurd and futile. Both male and female stood aghast and stupid before what they saw, for behind the mere words and gestures there was something that filled the little scene with a strange shaking power, touching the panic sense.

LeVallon lifted her across his shoulders.

The beautiful girl was radiant, the man wore the sudden semblance of a god. Their very stature increased. They stood alone. Yet Fillery, close by, stood with them. There seemed a magic circle none dared cross about the three. Something immense, unearthly, had come into the room, bursting its little space. Even Devonham, breaking with vehemence through the human ring, came to a sudden halt.

In a voice of thunder—though it was not actually loud —LeVallon cried:

"Their little personal loves! They cannot understand!" He bore Nayan in his arms as wind might lift a loose flower and whirl it aloft. "Come back with me, come home! The

Sun forgets us here, the Wind is silent. There is no Fire. Our work, our service calls us." He turned to Fillery. "You too. Come!"

His voice boomed like a thundering wind against the astonished frightened faces staring at him. It rose to a cry of intense emotion: "We are in little exile here! In our wrong place, cut off from the service of our gods! We will go back!" He started, with the girl flung across his frame. He took one stride. The others shuffled back with one accord.

"The other summons at the door. But, Edward!—you —you too!"

It was Nayan's voice, as the girl clung willingly to the great neck and arms, the voice of the girl all loved and worshipped and thought wonderful beyond temptation; it was this familiar sound that ran through the bewildered, startled throng like an electric shock. They could not believe their eyes, their ears. They stood transfixed.

Within their circle stood LeVallon, holding the girl, almost embracing her, while she lay helpless with happiness upon his huge enfolding arms. He paused, looked round at Fillery a moment. None dared approach. The men gazed, wondering, and with faculties arrested; the women stared, stock still, with beating hearts. All felt a lifting, splendid wonder they could not understand. Devonham, mute and motionless before an inexplicable thing, found himself bereft of judgment. Analysis and precedent, for once, both failed. He looked round in vain for Khilkoff.

Fillery alone seemed master of himself, a look of suffering and joy shone in his face; one hand lay steady upon LeVallon's arm.

Within the little circle these three figures formed a definite group, filling the beholders, for the first time in their so-called "psychic" experience, with the thrill of something utterly beyond their ken—something genuine at last. For there seemed about the group, though emanating, as with shining power, from the figure of LeVallon chiefly, some radiating force, some elemental vigour they could not comprehend. Its presence made the scene possible, even right.

"Edward—you too! What is it, O, what is it? There are flowers—great winds! I see the fire——!"

A searching tenderness in her tone broke almost beyond the limits of the known human voice.

There swept over the onlookers a wave of incredible emotion then, as they saw LeVallon move towards them, as though he would pass through them and escape. He seemed in that moment stupendous, irresistible. He looked divine. The girl lay in his arms like some young radiant child. He did not kiss her, no sign of a caress was seen; he did no ordinary, human thing. His towering figure, carrying his burden almost negligently, came out of the circle "like a tide" towards them, as one described it later —or as a poem that appeared later in "Simplicity" began:

> "With his hair of wind
> And his eyes of fire
> And his face of infinite desire . . ."

He swept nearer. They stirred again in a confused and troubled shuffle, opening a way. They shrank back farther. They shivered, like crying shingle a vast wave draws back. Only Fillery stood still, making no sign or movement; upon his face that look of joy and pain—wild joy and searching pain—no one, perhaps, but Devonham understood.

"Wind and fire!" boomed LeVallon's tremendous voice. "We return to our divine, eternal service. O Wind and Fire! We come back at last!" An immense rhythm swept across the room.

Then it was, without announcement of word or action, that Nayan, suddenly leaping from the great enfolding arms, stood upright between the two figures, one hand outstretched towards—Fillery.

At which moment, emerging apparently from nowhere, Khilkoff appeared upon the scene. During the music he had left the studio to find certain sketches he wished to show to LeVallon; he had witnessed nothing, therefore, of what had just occurred. He now stood still, staring in sheer surprise. The people in a ring, gazing with excited, rapt expression into the circle they thus formed, looked like an audience watching some performance that dazed and stupefied them, in which Fillery, LeVallon and Nayan— his own daughter—were the players. He took it for an impromptu charade, perhaps, something spontaneously arranged during his absence. Yet he was obviously staggered.

As he entered, the girl had just leaped from the arms that held her, and run towards Fillery, who stood erect and motionless in the centre of the circle; and LeVallon's wild splendid cry in that instant shook its grand music across the vaulted room. So well acted, so dramatic, so real was the scene thus interrupted that Khilkoff stood staring in silence, thinking chiefly, as he said afterwards, that the young man's pose and attitude were exactly—magnificently—what he wanted for the figure of Fire and Wind in his elemental group.

This enthusiastic thought, with the attempt to engrave it permanently in his memory, filled his mind completely for an instant, when there broke in upon it again that resonant voice, half cry, half chant, vibrating with depth and music, yet quiet too:

"Wind and Fire! My Wind and Fire! O Sun—your messengers are come for us! . . . Oh, come with power and take us with you! . . ." Its rhythm was gigantic.

So extraordinary was the volume, yet the sweetness, too, in the voice, though its actual loudness was not great— so arresting was its quality, that Khilkoff, as he put it afterwards, thought he heard an entirely new sound, a sound his ears had never known before. He, like the rest of the astonished audience, was caught spell-bound. But for an instant only. For at once there followed another voice, releasing the momentary spell, and, with the accompanying action, warned him that what he saw was no mere game of acting. This was real.

"I hear that other summons at the door! . . ."

Her hands were outstretched, her eyes alight with yearning, she was oblivious of everyone but Fillery, LeVallon and herself.

And her father, then, breaking through the crowding figures, packed shoulder to shoulder nearest to him, entered the circle. His mind was confused, perhaps, for vague ideas of some undesirable hypnotic influence, of some foolish experiment that had become too real, passed through it. He knew one thing only—this scene, whether real or acted, pretence or sincere, must be stopped. The look on his daughter's face—entirely new and strange to him—was all the evidence he needed. He shouldered his way through like an angry bear, making inarticulate noises, growling.

But, before he reached the actors, before Nayan reached Fillery's side, and while the voice of the girl and of Le-Vallon still seemed to echo simultaneously in the air, a new thing happened that changed the scene completely. In these few brief seconds, indeed, so much was concentrated, and with such rapidity, that it was small wonder the reports of individual witnesses differed afterwards, almost as if each one had seen a separate detail of the crowded picture. Its incredibility, too, bewildered minds accustomed to imagined dreams rather than to real action.

LeVallon, at any rate, all agreed, turned with that ease and swiftness peculiarly his own, caught Nayan again into the air, and with one arm swung her back across his shoulder. He moved, then, so irresistibly, with a great striding rush in the direction of the door into the street, and so rapidly, that the onlookers once more drew back instinctively pell mell, tumbling over each other in their frightened haste.

This, all agreed, had happened. One second they saw

LeVallon carrying the girl off, the next—a flash of intense and vivid brilliance entered the big studio, flooding all detail with a blaze of violent light. There was a loud report, there was a violent shock.

"The Messengers! Our Messengers! . . ." The thunder of LeVallon's cry was audible.

The same instant this dazzling splendour, so sparkling it was almost painful, became eclipsed again. There was complete obliteration. Darkness descended like a blow. An inky blackness reigned. No single thing was visible. There came a terrific splitting sound.

The effect of overwhelming sudden blackness was natural enough. In every mind danced still the vivid memory of that last amazing picture they had seen: Khilkoff, with alarmed face, breaking violently into the circle where his daughter, Nayan, swinging from those giant shoulders, looked back imploringly at Dr. Fillery, who stood motionless as though carved in stone, a smile of curious happiness yet pain upon his features. Yet the figure of LeVallon dominated. His radiant beauty, his air of superb strength, his ease, his power, his wild swiftness. Something unearthly glowed about him. He looked a god. The extraordinary idea flashed into Fillery's mind that some big energy as of inter-stellar spaces lay about him, as though great Sirius called down along his light-years of distance into the little tumbled Chelsea room.

This was the picture, set one instant in dazzling violet brilliance, then drowned in blackness, that still hung shining with intense reality before every mind.

The following confusion had a moment of real and troubling panic; women screamed, some fell upon their knees; men called for light; various cries were heard; there was a general roar:

"To the door, all men to the door! He's controlled! There's an Elemental in him!" It was Povey's shrill tones that pierced.

"Strike a match!" shouted Kempster. "The electric light
has fused. Stay where you are. Don't move—everybody.
"Lightning," the clear voice of Devonham was heard.
"Keep your heads. It's only a thunderstorm!"

Matches were struck, extinguished, lit again; a patch
of dim light shone here and there upon a throng of huddled
people; someone found a candle that shed a flickering glare
upon the walls and ceiling, but only made the shadows
chiefly visible. It was an unreal, fantastic scene.

A moment later there descended a hurricane gust of
wind against the building, with splintering glass as though
from a hail of bullets, that extinguished candle and matches,
and plunged the scene again into total darkness. A terrific
clap of thunder, followed immediately by a rushing sound
of rain that poured in a flood upon the floor, completed
the scene of terror and confusion. The huge north window
had blown in.

The consternation was, for some moments, dangerous,
for true panic may become an unmanageable thing, and
this panic was unquestionably real. The superstitious
thread that lies in every human being, stretched and
shivered, beginning to weave its swift, ominous pattern.
The elements dominated the human too completely just
then even for the sense of wonder that was usually so
active in the Society's mental make-up to assert itself in-
telligently. Most of them lost their heads. All associated
that picture of LeVallon and the girl with this terrific
demonstration of overpowering elemental violence. Povey's
startled cry had given them the lead. The human touch
thus added the flavour of something both personal and
supernatural.

Some stood screaming, whimpering, unable to move;
some were numb; others cried for help; not a few remained
on their knees; the name of God was audible here and
there; many collapsed and several women fainted. To one
and all came the realization of that panic fear which dis-

locates and paralyses. This was a manifestation of elemental power that had intelligence somewhere driving too suggestively behind it. . . .

It was Devonham and Khilkoff who kept their heads and saved the situation. The sudden storm was, indeed, of extreme violence and ferocity; the force of the wind, with the nearness of the terrible lightning and the consequent volume of the overwhelming thunder, werē certainly bewildering. But a thunderstorm, they began to realize, was a thunderstorm.

"Everyone stay exactly where he is," suddenly shouted Khilkoff through the darkness. His voice brought comfort. "I'll light candles in the inner studio." He did so a moment later; the faint light was reassuring; a pause in the storm came to his assistance, the wind had passed, the rain had ceased, there was no more lightning. With a whispered word to Devonham, he disappeared through the door into the passage: "You look after 'em; I must find my girl."

"One by one, now," called Devonham. "Take careful steps! Avoid the broken glass!"

Voices answered from dark corners, as the inner room began to fill; all saw the candle light and came to it by degrees. "Povey, Kempster, Imson, Father Collins! Each man bring a lady with him. It's only a thunderstorm. Keep your heads!"

The smaller room filled gradually, people with white faces and staring eyes coming, singly or in couples, within the pale radiance of the flickering candle light. Feet splashed through pools of water; the furniture, the clothing, were soaked; the heat in the air, despite the great broken window, was stifling. One or two women were helped, some were carried; there were cries and exclamations, a noise of splintered glass being trodden on or kicked aside; drinks were brought for those who had fainted; order was restored bit by bit. The collective consciousness resumed gradually its comforting sway. The herd found strength in contact. A single cry—in a woman's voice—"Pan was among

us! . . ." was instantly smothered, drowned in a chorus
of "Hush! Hush!" as though a mere name might bring a
repetition of a terror none could bear again.

The entire scene had lasted perhaps five minutes, possibly
less. The violent storm that had hung low over London,
accumulating probably for hours, had dissipated itself in
a single prodigious explosion, and was gone. Through the
gaping north window, torn and shattered, shone the stars.
More candles were brought and lighted, food and drink
followed, a few cuts from broken glass were attended to,
and calm in a measure came back to the battered and shaken
yet thrilled and delighted Prometheans.

But all eyes looked for a couple who were not there; a
hundred heads turned searching, for in every heart lay one
chief question. Yet, oddly enough, none asked aloud; the
names of Nayan and LeVallon were not spoken audibly;
some touch of awe, it seemed, clung to a memory still burning in each individual mind; it was an awe that none would
willingly revive just then. The whole occurrence had been
too devastating, too sudden; it all had been too real.

There was little talk, nor was there the whispered discussion even that might have been expected; individual
recovery was slow and hesitating. What had happened
lay still too close for the comfort of detailed comparison
or analysis by word of mouth. With common accord the
matter was avoided. Discussions must wait. It would fill
many days with wonder afterwards. . . .

It was with a sense of general relief, therefore, that the
throng of guests, bedraggled somewhat in appearance, eyes
still bright with traces of uncommon excitement, their
breath uneven and their attitude still nervous, saw the door
into the passage open and frame the figure of their returning host. He held a lighted candle. His bearded face
looked grim, but his slow deep voice was quiet and reassuring—he smiled, his words were commonplace.

"You must excuse my daughter," he said firmly, "but
she sends her excuses, and begs to be forgiven for not

coming to bid you all good-night. The lightning—the electricity—has upset her. I have advised her to go to bed."

A sigh of relief from everybody came in answer. They were only too glad to take the hint and go.

"The little impromptu act we had prepared for you we cannot give now," he added, anticipating questions. "The storm prevented the second part. We must give it another time instead."

CHAPTER XIV

K HILKOFF, Edward Fillery and Paul Devonham, between them, it seems, were wise in their generation. The story spread that the scene in the Studio had been nothing but a bit of inspired impromptu acting, to which the coincidence of the storm had lent a touch of unexpected conviction where, otherwise, all would have ended in a laugh and a round or two of amused applause.

The spreading of an undesirable story, thus, was to a great extent prevented, its discussion remaining confined, chiefly, among the few startled witnesses. Yet the Prometheans, of course, knew a supernatural occurrence when they saw one. They were not to be so easily deprived of their treasured privilege. Thrilled to their marrows, individually and collectively, they committed their versions to writing, drew up reports, compared notes and, generally, made the feast last as long as possible. It was, moreover, a semi-sacred feast for them. Its value increased portentously. It bound the Society together with fresh life. It attracted many new members. Povey and his committee increased the subscription and announced an entrance fee in addition.

The various accounts offered by the Members, curious as these were, may be left aside for the moment, since the version of the occurrence as given by Edward Fillery comes first in interest. His report, however, was made only to himself; he mentioned it in full to no one, not even to Paul Devonham. He felt unable to share it with any living being. Only one result of his conclusions he shared openly enough with his assistant: he withdrew his promise.

Upon certain details, the two men agreed with interest

—that everybody in the room, men and women, were on the *qui vive* the moment LeVallon made his entrance. His appearance struck a note. All were aware of an unusual presence. Interest and curiosity rose like a vapour, heads all turned one way as though the same wind blew them, there was a buzz and murmur of whispered voices, as though the figure of LeVallon woke into response the same taut wire in every heart. "Who on earth is that? What is he?" was legible in a hundred questioning eyes. All, in a word, were aware of something unaccustomed.

Upon this detail—and in support of the Society's claim to special "psychic" perception, it must be mentioned— Fillery and Devonham were at one. But another detail, too, found them in agreement. It was not the tempest that caused the panic; it was LeVallon himself. Something about LeVallon had produced the abrupt and singular sense of panic terror.

Fillery was glad; he was satisfied, at any rate. The transient, unreal personality called "LeVallon" had disappeared and, as he believed, for ever; a surface apparition after all, it had been educated, superimposed, the result of imitation and quick learning, a phantom masquerading as an intelligent human being. It was merely an acquired surface-self, a physical, almost an automatic intelligence. The deep nature underneath had now broken out. It was the sudden irruption of "N. H." that touched the subconscious self of everyone in the room with its strange authentic shock. "N. H." was in full possession.

Towards this real Self he felt attraction, yearning, even love. He had felt this from the very beginning. Why, or what it was, he did not pretend to know as yet. Towards "N. H." he reacted as towards his own son, as to a comrade, ancient friend, proved intimate and natural playmate even. The strange tie was difficult to describe. In himself, though faint by comparison, lay something akin in sympathy and understanding. . . . They belonged together in the same unknown region. The girl, of course, belonged there too, but more completely, more absolutely, even than himself. He foresaw the risks, the dangers. His heart, with a leap of joy, accepted the responsibilities.

Unlike Devonham, he had not come that afternoon to scoff; his smile at the vagaries of what his assistant called "hysterical psychics" had no bitterness, no contempt. If their excesses were pathogenic often, he believed with Lombroso that genius and hysteria draw upon a common origin sometimes, also that, from among this unstable material, there emerged on occasions hints of undeniable value. To the want of balance was chiefly due the ineffectiveness of these hints. This class, dissatisfied with present things, kicking over the traces which herd together the dull normal crowd into the safe but uninteresting commonplace, but kicking, of course, too wildly, alone offered hints of powers that might one day, obedient to laws at present unknown, become of value to the race. They were temperamentally open to occasional, if misguided, inspiration, and all inspiration, the evidence overwhelmingly showed, is due to an intense, but hidden mental activity. The hidden nine-tenths of the self peeped out here and there periodically. These people were, at heart, alert to new ideas. The herd instinct was weak in them. They were individuals.

Fillery had not come to scoff. His chief purpose on this particular occasion had been to observe any reactions produced in LeVallon by the atmosphere of these unbalanced yet questing minds, and by the introduction to a girl, whose beauty, physical and moral, he considered far far above the standard of other women. Iraida Khilkoff, as he saw her, rose head and shoulders, like some magical flower in a fairy-tale, beyond her feminine kind.

His hopes had in both respects proved justified. LeVallon was gone. "N. H." had swept up commandingly into full possession.

If it is the attitude of mind that interprets details in a given scene, it is the heart that determines their selection. Devonham saw collective hallucination, delusion, humbug —useless and undesirable weeds, where his chief saw strange imperfect growths that might one day become flowers in a marvellous garden. That this garden blossomed upon the sunny slopes of a lost Caucasian valley had a significance he did not shirk. Always he was honest with himself. It was this symbolic valley he longed to people. Its radiant loveliness stirred a forgotten music in his heart, he watched golden bees sipping that wild azalea honey, of which even the natives may not rob them without the dangerous delight of exaltation; his nostrils caught the delicious perfumes, his cheek felt the touch of happy winds . . . as he stood by the door with Devonham and LeVallon, looking round the crowded Chelsea studio.

Aware of this association stirring in his blood, he believed he had himself well in hand; he knew already in advance that a spirit moved upon the face of those waters that were his inmost self; he had that intuitive divination which anticipates a change of spiritual weather. The wind was rising, the atmosphere lay prepared, already the flowers bent their heads one way. All his powers of self-control might well be called upon before the entertainment ended. Glancing a moment at LeVallon, tall, erect and poised beside him, he was conscious—it was an instant of vivid self-revelation—that he steadied himself in doing so. He borrowed, as it were, something of that poise, that calm simplicity, that potential energy, that modest confidence. Some latent power breathed through the great stalwart figure by his side; the strength was not his own; LeVallon emanated this power unconsciously.

Khilkoff, as described, had then led the youth away to see the sculpture, Devonham was captured by a Member, and Fillery found himself alone. He looked about him, noticing here and there individuals whom he knew. Lady Gleeson he saw at once on her divan in the corner, with her cigarette, her jewels, her glass, her background of millions through which an indulgent husband floated like a shadow. His eye rested on her a second only, then passed in search of something less insignificant. Miss Lance, who had heard of his books and dared to pretend knowledge of them, monopolised him for ten minutes. A little tactful kindness managed her easily, while he watched the door where LeVallon had disappeared with Khilkoff, and through which Nayan might any moment now enter. Already his thoughts framed these two together in a picture; his heart saw them playing hand in hand among the flowers of the Hidden Valley, one flying, the other following, a radiance of sunny fire and a speed of lifting winds about them both, yet he himself, oddly enough, not far away. He, too, was somehow with them. While listening with his mind to what Miss Lance was saying, his heart went out playing with this splendid pair. . . . He would not lose her finally, it seemed; some subtle kinship held them together in this trinity. The heart in him played wild against the mind.

He caught Devonham's eye upon him, and a sudden smile that Miss Lance fortunately appropriated to herself, ran over his too thoughtful face. For Devonham's attitude towards the case, his original Notes, his obvious conceal-ment of experiences in the Jura Mountains, flashed across him with a flavour of something half comic, half pathetic. "With all that knowledge, with all the accumulation of data, Paul stops short of Wonder!" he thought to himself, his eyes fixed solemnly upon Miss Lance's face. He remem-bered Coleridge: "All knowledge begins and ends with wonder, but the first wonder is the child of ignorance, while the second wonder is the parent of adoration." A thousand years, and the dear fellow will still regard adoration as hysteria! He chuckled audibly, to his companion's surprise, since the moment was not appropriate for chuckling.

Making his peace with his neighbour, he presently left her for a position nearer to the door, Father Collins pro-viding the opportunity.

Father Collins, as he was called, half affectionately, half in awe, as of a parent with a cane, was an individual. He had been evangelical, high church, Anglican, Roman Catholic, in turn, and finally Buddhist. Believing in reincarnation, he did not look for progress in humanity; the planet resembled a form at school—individuals passed into it and out of it, but the average of the form remained the same The fifth form was always the fifth form. Earth's history showed no advance as a whole, though individuals did. He looked forward, therefore, to no Utopia, nor shared the pessimism of the thinkers who despaired of progress.

A man of intense convictions, yet open mind, he was not ashamed to move. Before the Buddhist phase, he had been icily agnostic. He thought, but also he felt. He had vision and intuition; he had investigated for himself. His mind was of the imaginative-scientific order. Buddhism, his latest phase, attracted him because it was "a scientific, logical system rather than a religion based on revelation." He belonged eminently to the unstable. He found no resting place. He came to the meetings of the Society to listen rather than to talk. His net was far flung, catching anything and everything in the way of new ideas, experiments, theories, beliefs, especially powers. He tested for himself, then accepted or discarded. The more extravagant the theory, the greater its appeal to him. Behind a grim, even a repulsive ugliness, he hid a heart of milk and honey. In his face was nobility, yet something slovenly ran through it like a streak.

He loved his kind and longed to help them to the light. Although a rolling stone, spiritually, his naked sincerity won respect. He was composed, however, of several personalities, and hence, since these often clashed, he was accused of insincerity too. The essay that lost him his pulpit and parish, "The Ever-moving Truth, or Proof Impossible," was the poignant confession of an honest intellect where faith and unbelief came face to face with facts. The Bishop, naturally, preferred the room of "Father" Collins to his company.

"I should like you to meet my friend," Fillery mentioned, after some preliminary talk. "He would interest you. You might help him possibly." He mentioned a few essential details. "Perhaps you will call one day—you know my address—and make his acquaintance. His mind, owing to his lonely and isolated youth, is *tabula rasa*. For the same reason, a primitive Nature is his Deity."

Father Collins raised his bushy dark eyebrows.

"I took note of him the moment he came in," he replied. "I was wondering who he was—and what! I'll come one day with pleasure. The innocence on his face surprised me. Is he—may I ask it—friend or patient?"

"Both."

"I see," said the other, without hesitation. He added: "You are experimenting?"

"Studying. I should value the help—the view of a religious temperament."

Father Collins looked grim to ugliness. The touch of nobility appeared.

"I know your ideals, Dr. Fillery; I know your work," he said gruffly. "In you lies more true religion than in a thousand bishops. I should trust your treatment of an unusual case. If," he added slowly, "I can help him, so much the better." He then looked up suddenly, his manner as if galvanized: "Unless *he* can perhaps help us."

The words struck Fillery on the raw, as it were. They startled him. He stared into the other's eyes. "What makes you think that? What do you mean exactly?"

Father Collins returned his gaze unflinchingly. He made an odd reply. "Your friend," he said, "looks to me—like a man who—might start a new religion—Nature for instance —back to Nature being, in my opinion, always a possible solution of over-civilization and its degeneracy." The streak of something slovenly crept into the nobility, smudging it, so to speak, with a blur.

Dr. Fillery, for a moment, waited, listening with his heart.

"And find a million followers at once," continued the other, as though he had not noticed. "His voice, his manner, his stature, his face, but above all—something he brings with him. Whatever his nature, he's a natural leader. And a sincere, unselfish leader is what people are asking for nowadays."

His black bushy eyebrows dropped, darkening the grim, clean-shaven face. "You noticed, of course—*you*—the women's eyes?" he mentioned. "It isn't, you know, so much what a man says, nor entirely his looks, that excite favour or disfavour with women. It's something he emanates— unconsciously. They can't analyze it, but they never fail to recognize it."

Fillery moved sideways a little, so that he could watch the inner studio better. The discernment of his companion was somewhat unexpected. It disconcerted him. All his knowledge, all his experience clustered about his mind as thick as bees, yet he felt unable to select the item he needed. The sunshine upon his Inner Valley burned a brighter fire. He saw the flowers glow. The wind ran sweet and magical. He began to watch himself more closely.

"LeVallon is an interesting being," he admitted finally, "but you make big deductions surely. A mind like yours," he added, "must have its reasons?"

"Power," replied the other promptly; "power. 'The earlier generations,' said Emerson, 'saw God face to face; *we* through their eyes. Why should not we also enjoy an original relation to Nature?' Your friend has this original relation, I feel; he stands close—terribly close—to Nature. He brings open spaces even into this bargain sale——" He drew a deep breath. "There is a power about him——"

"Perhaps," interrupted the other.

"Not of this earth."

"You mean that literally?"

"Not of this earth quite—not of humanity, so to speak," repeated Father Collins half irritably, as though his intel-

ligence had been insulted. "That's the best way I can
describe how it strikes me. Ask one of the women. Ask
Nayan, for instance. Whatever he is, your friend is
elemental."

Like a shock of fire the unusual words ran deep into
Fillery's heart, but, at that same instant a stirring of the
figures beyond the door caught his attention. His main
interest revived. The inner door of the private studio, he
thought, had opened.

"Elemental!" he repeated, his interest torn in two directions simultaneously. He looked at his companion keenly,
searchingly. "You—a man like you—does not use such
words——" He kept an eye upon the inner studio.

"Without meaning," the other caught him up at once.
"No. I mean it. Nor do I use such words idly to a man
—Fillery—like you." He stopped. "He has what you
have," came the quick blunt statement; "only in your case
it's indirect, while in his it's direct—essential."

They looked at each other. Two minds, packed with
knowledge and softened with experience of their kind,
though from different points of view, met each other fairly.
A bridge existed. It was crossed. Few words were necessary, it seemed. Each understood the other.

"Elemental," repeated Fillery, his pulse quickening half
painfully.

At which instant he knew the inner door *had* opened.
Nayan had come in. The same instant almost she had
gone out again. So quick, indeed, was the interval between her appearance and disappearance, that Fillery's
version of what he then witnessed in those few seconds
might have been ascribed by a third person who saw it
with him to his imagination largely. Imaginative, at any
rate, the version was; whether it was on that account unreal
is another matter. The swift, tiny scene, however, no one
witnessed but himself. Even Devonham, unusually alert
with professional anxiety, missed it; as did also the watch-

ful Lady Gleeson, whom jealousy made clairvoyante almost. Khilkoff and LeVallon, standing sideways to the door, were equally unaware that it had opened, then quickly closed again. None saw, apparently, the radiant, lovely outline.

It was a curtained door leading out of the far end of the inner studio into a passage which had an exit to the street; Fillery was so placed that he could see it over his companion's shoulder; Khilkoff, LeVallon and the little group about them stood in his direct line of sight against the dark background of the curtain. The light in this far corner was so dim that Fillery was not aware the curtained door had swung open until he actually saw the figure of Nayan Khilkoff framed suddenly in the clear space, the white passage wall behind her. She wore gloves, hat and furs, having come, evidently, straight from the street. Ten seconds, perhaps twenty, she stood there, gazing with a sudden fixed intensity at LeVallon, whose figure, almost close enough for touch, was sideways to her, the face in profile.

She stopped abruptly as though a shock ran through her. She remained motionless. She stared, an expression in her eyes as of life momentarily arrested by wild, glorious, intense surprise. The lips were parted; one gloved hand still held the swinging curtained door. To Fillery it seemed as if a flame leaped into her eyes. The entire face lit up. She seemed spellbound with delight.

This leap of light was the first sign he witnessed. The same second her eyes lifted a fraction of an inch, changed their focus, and, gazing past LeVallon, looked straight across the room into his own.

In his mind at that instant still rang the singular words of Father Collins; in his heart still hung the picture of the flowered valley: it was across this atmosphere the eyes of the girl flashed their message like a stroke of lightning. It came as a cry, almost a call for help, an audible message whose syllables fled down the valley, yearning sweet, yet a tone of poignant farewell within the following wind. It

was a moment of delicious joy, of exquisite pain, of a
blissful, searching dream beyond this world. . . .

He stood spellbound himself a moment. The look in
the girl's big eloquent eyes threatened a cherished dream
that lay too close to his own life. He was aware of collapse,
of ruin; that old peculiar anguish seized him. He remembered her words in Baker Street a few days before: "Please
bring your friend"—the accompanying pain they caused.
And now he caught the echo on that following wind along
the distant valley. The cry in her eyes came to him:

"Why—O why—do you bring this to me? It must take
your place. It must put out—You!"

The reasoning and the inspirational self in him knew
this momentary confusion, as the cry fled down the wind.

> "O follow, follow
> Through the caverns hollow
> As the song floats, thou pursue
> Where the wild bee never flew . . ."

The curtained door swung to again; the face and figure
were no longer there; Nayan had withdrawn quickly,
noticed by none but himself. She had gone up to make
herself ready for her father's guests; in a few minutes she
would come down again to play hostess as her custom
was. . . . It was so ordinary. It was so dislocating. . . .
For at that moment it seemed as if all the feminine forces
of the universe, whatever these may be, focused in her,
and poured against him their concentrated stream to allure,
enchant, subdue. He trembled. He remembered Devonham's admission of the panic sense.

"It's the air," said a voice beside him, "all this tobacco
smoke and scent, and no ventilation."

Father Collins was speaking, only he had completely forgotten that Father Collins was in the world. The steadying
hand upon his arm made him realize that he had swayed a
moment.

"The perfume chiefly," the voice continued. "All this cheap nasty stuff these women use. It's enough to sicken any healthy man. Nobody knows his own smell, they say." He laughed a little.

Collins was tactful. He talked on easily of nothing in particular, so that his companion might let the occasion slip, or comment on it, as he wished.

"Worse than incense." Fillery gave him the clue perhaps intentionally, certainly with gratitude. He made an effort. He found control. "It intoxicates the imagination, doesn't it?" That note of sweet farewell still hung with enchanting sadness in his brain. He still saw those yearning eyes. He heard that cry. And yet the conflict in his nature bewildered him—as though he found two persons in him, one weeping while the other sang.

Father Collins smiled, and Fillery then knew that he, too, had seen the girl framed in the doorway, intercepted the glance as well. No shadow of resentment crossed his heart as he heard him add: "She, too, perhaps belongs elsewhere." The phrase, however, brought to his own personal dream the conviction of another understanding mind. "As you yourself do, too," was added in a thrilling whisper suddenly.

Fillery turned with a start to meet his eye. "But *where?*"

"That is *your* problem," said Father Collins promptly. "You are the expert—even though you think—mistakenly —that your heart is robbed." His voice held the sympathy and tenderness of a woman taught by suffering. The nobility was in his face again, untarnished now. His words, his tone, his manner caught Fillery in amazement. It did not surprise him that Father Collins had been quick enough to understand, but it did surprise him that a man so entangled in one formal creed after another, so netted by the conventional thought of various religious Systems, and therefore stuffed with old, rigid, commonplace ideas—it did, indeed surprise him to feel this sudden atmosphere of vision and prophecy that abruptly shone about him. The extravagant, fantastic side of the man he had forgotten.

"Where?" he repeated, gazing at him. "Where, indeed?"

"Where the wild bee never flew . . . perhaps!"

Father Collins's eyebrows shot up as though worked by artificial springs. His eyes, changing extraordinarily, turned very keen. He seemed several persons at once. He looked like—contradictory description—a spiritual Jesuit. The ugly mouth—thank Heaven, thought Fillery—showed lines of hidden humour. His sanity, at any rate, was unquestioned. Father Collins watched the planet with his soul, not with his brain alone. But which of his many personalities was now in the ascendancy, no man, least of all himself, could tell. His companion, the expert in him automatically aware of the simultaneous irruption and disruption, waited almost professionally for any outburst that might follow. "Arcades ambo," he reflected, making a stern attempt to keep his balance.

"The subconscious, remember, doesn't explain everything," came the words. "Not everything," he added with emphasis. "As with heredity"—he looked keenly half humorously, half sympathetically at the doctor—"there are gaps and lapses. The recent upheaval has been more than an inter-tribal war. It was a planetary event. It has shaken our nature fundamentally, radically. The human mind has been shocked, broken, dislocated. The prevalent hysteria is not an ordinary hysteria, nor are the new powers—perhaps—quite ordinary either."

"Mental history repeats itself," Fillery put in, now more master of himself again. "Unbalance has always followed upheaval. The removal of known, familiar foundations always lets in extravagance of wildest dissatisfaction, search and question."

"Upheaval of this kind," rejoined the other gravely, "there has never been since human beings walked the earth.

Our fabulous old world trembles in the balance." And, as he said it, the dreamer shone in the light below the big, black eyebrows, noticed quickly by his companion. "Old ideals have been smashed beyond recovery. The gods men knew have been killed, like Tommy, in the trenches. The past is likewise dead, its dreams of progress buried with it by a Black Maria. The human mind and heart stand everywhere empty and bereft, while their hungry and unanswered questions search the stars for something new."

"Well, well," said Fillery gently, half stirred, half amused by the odd language. "You may be right. But mental history has always shown a desire for something new after each separate collapse. Signs and wonders are a recurrent hunger, remember. In the days of Abraham, of Paul, of Moses it was the same."

"Questions to-day," replied the other, "are based on an immense accumulated knowledge unknown to Moses or to Abraham's time. The phenomenon, I grant you, is the same, but—the shock, the dislocation, the shattering upheaval comes in the twentieth century upon minds grounded in deep scientific wisdom. It was formerly a shock to the superstitious ignorance of intuitive feeling merely. To-day it is organized scientific knowledge that meets the earthquake."

"You mentioned gaps and lapses," said Fillery, deeply interested, but still half professionally, perhaps, in spite of his preoccupations. "You think, perhaps, those gaps——?" One eye watched the inner studio. The unstable in him gained more and more the upper hand.

"I mean," replied Father Collins, now fairly launched upon his secret hobby, evidently his qualification for membership in the Society, "I mean, Edward Fillery, that the time is ripe, if ever, for a new revelation. If Man is the only type of being in the universe, well and good. We see his finish plainly, for the war has shown that progress is a myth. Man remains, in spite of all conceivable scientific knowledge, a savage, of low degree, irredeemable, and intellect, as a reconstructive force, but of small account."

"It seems so, I admit."

"But if"—Father Collins said it as calmly as though he spoke of some new food or hygienic treatment merely —"if mankind is not the only life in the universe, if, for instance, there exist—and why not?—other evolutionary systems besides our own somewhat trumpery type—other schemes and other beings—perhaps parallel, perhaps quite different—perhaps in more direct contact with the sources of life—a purer emanation, so to say——"

He hesitated, realizing perhaps that in speaking to a man of Edward Fillery's standing he must choose his words, or at least present his case convincingly, while aware that his inability to do so made him only more extravagant and incoherent.

"Yes, quite so," Fillery helped him, noting all the time the suppressed intensity, the half-concealed conviction of an *idée fixe* behind the calmness, while the balance of his own attention remained concentrated on the group about LeVallon. "If, as you suggest, there *are* other types of life——" He spoke encouragingly. He had noticed the slovenly streak spread and widen, breaking down, as it were, the structure of the face. He was aware also of the increasing insecurity in himself.

"Now is the moment," cried the other; "now is the time for their appearance."

He turned as though he had hit a target unexpectedly.

"Now," he repeated, "is the opportunity for their manifestation. The human mind lies open everywhere. It is blank, receptive, ready. On all sides it waits ready and inviting. The gaps are provided. If there is any other life, it should break through and come among us—*now!*"

Fillery, startled, withdrew for the first time his attention from that inner room. With keen eyes he gazed at his companion. With an abrupt, unpleasant shock it occurred to him that all he heard was borrowed, filched, stolen out of his own mind. Before words came to him, the other spoke:

"Your friend," he mentioned quietly, but with intentional significance, "and patient."

"LeVallon!"

But it was at this moment that Nayan Khilkoff, entering again without her hat and furs, had moved straight to the piano, seated herself, and began to sing.

CHAPTER XV

TO retail the following scene as Dr. Fillery saw it in detail is not necessary, the sequence of acts, of physical events being already known. The reactions of his heart and mind, however, have importance. What he felt, thought, hoped and feared, what he believed as well, his point of view in a word, remain essential.

Edward Fillery, being what he was, witnessed it from his own individual angle; his mind, with his heredity, his soul, with its mysterious background, these held the glasses to his eyes, adjusting, as with a Zeiss instrument, each eye separately. In his case the analyst and thinker checked the unstable dreamer with acute exactitude. This was his special gift. He studied himself best while studying others. His sight, moreover, was exceptionally keen, his glasses of consummate workmanship. He saw, it seems, considerably beyond the normal range. He believed, at least, that he did so.

He saw, for instance, that the girl, while her fingers ran over the keys before she sang, searched the room and found LeVallon in a second. Following her rapid glance, he took in the picture that she also saw—LeVallon, coffee cup in hand, before Lady Gleeson languishing on the divan, and Devonham just beside them. LeVallon was obviously unaware of Lady Gleeson's presence; he had forgotten her existence. Devonham, a floor-walker with nothing particular to do at the moment, looked uncomfortable and ill at ease, scared a little, fearing a scene, a possible outbreak even. The meaning of the group was easily read. The girl herself, undoubtedly, read it clearly too.

This flashed upon the cinema screen, and Fillery divined it without the help of tedious letterpress.

The same instant he was aware that the girl and LeVallon looked for the first time straight into each other's faces, and that both seemed simultaneously caught into the air as though a star had lifted them. Not even a question lay in their clear eyes. It was an instantaneous understanding, so complete and perfect that the expression of happy surprise was too convicing to be missed even by the slow-witted Lady Gleeson. Vanity usually delays intelligence, and her vanity was abnormal. But she saw the expression on the two faces, and interpreted it aright. Fillery noticed that she squirmed; she would presently, he felt positive, disappear. Before the singing ended he had seen her slink away.

The song began. He had heard it before, "The Vagrant's Epitaph," sung by the same clear, sweet voice, had felt his heart stirred by the true simple feeling she put into it. He knew every word and every bar; the music was her own. He loved it. Both words and music awoke in him invariably a picture of his own lost valley, a physical desire to be over the hills and far away with the homeless liberty of winds and stars and waters, and at the same time, its spiritual equivalent—a yearning that the Race should discover the immense fair region of its greater hidden self and enjoy its new powers without restraint. All this was familiar to him. But now, as she sang, there came another, deeper meaning that sublimated the essential spirit of it, lifting it out of the known ditch of space and time. Never yet had he heard such yearning passion, such untold desire in her voice. The physical vagrancy changed subtly, exquisitely, to a symbol of a vaster meaning—a spiritual vagrancy that suddenly captured him in bitter pain. "Love could not hold him, Duty forged no chain"—as he listened to the sweetness, struck him between the joints of armour he had not realized before was so insecurely bound about him. The anguish of lonely souls, alien among their kind, hungry for companionship they might not find, unclothed, uncared for, desired of none and understanding none— this rose tumultuously in his blood. "The wide seas and the mountains called him . . ." the words and music pierced him like a flame. "Revel might hold him for a little space . . ."—her voice made it sound like a description of man's brief moment on the whirling planet, tasting adventure with men and women, playing a moment with love and hope and fear, till, "turning past the laughter and the lamps," he heard that "other summons at the door."

' This bigger version, this deeper meaning, caught at him with power as he heard the song in the sweet, familiar voice, and realized in a flash that what he felt faintly LeVallon felt terrifically. His own detachment was a pose, a shadow, at best a bodiless yearning; in LeVallon it was a reality of consuming fire. Also it was an explanation of the girl's own singular aloofness from the world of admiring men. Both belonged, as Father Collins put it, "elsewhere."

He watched them. LeVallon's eyes, he saw, remained fixed and motionless on the singer; her own did not leave the notes for a single moment; the words and music poured into the room like a shower of dancing silver. The personality of the girl flowed out with them to meet the newly-found companion they addressed. An extraordinary thing then happened: to Fillery it almost seemed that there formed then and there between them a new vehicle—as it were, a body—that gave expression to their own great secret. Something in each of them, unable to manifest through their minds, their brains, their earthly bodies, formed for itself an elastic subtle vehicle, using the sound, the words, the feeling for this purpose—and as literally as a human spirit uses the familiar physical body for its manifestation.

The experience was amazing, but it was real. He watched it carefully. In the room about him, formed on the waves of this sweet singing, shaped by feeling that found normally no other expression, inspired by emotions, yearnings, desires alien to their normal kind, these two created between them a new vehicle or body that could and did express all this.

They heard that "other summons at the door. . . ." And they were off.

Yet he, too, heard the summons, and in the depths of his being he answered to it. His essential weakness, wearing the guise of strength, rose naked. . . .

These thoughts and feelings lay unexpressed, perhaps —too deep actually, too remote from any experience he had yet known, to find actual words, even in his mind. What did find expression, in thought at any rate, was that, before his very eyes, he witnessed the transfiguring change come over Nayan. Like some flower that has been growing in the shade, then meets the flood of sunshine for the first time, she knew a fresh tide of life sweep over her entire being. She seemed to blossom, breaking almost into flower and fruit before his very eyes, as though sun and wind brought her into a sudden bloom of exquisite maturity. He was aware of rich, deep purple, the faint gold of fruits and flowers, the creamy softness of a rose, the amber of wild grapes bathed in sparkling dew. The luscious promise of the Spring matured about her whole presentment into full summer glory. And it was the sun and wind of LeVallon's enigmatic, stimulating presence close to her that caused the miracle. The essential flower of her life poured forth to meet his own, as he had always felt it must. LeVallon's was the mighty wind that lifted her, was the sun in whose heat she basked, expanded, soared. She experienced a strange increase of her natural vitality and being. Her consciousness knew an abrupt intensification.

The signs, in that brief moment, were as clear to Fillery's divining heart as though he read them in black printed letters on a page of whitest paper. He knew the cipher and the code. He watched the signals flash. They had not even spoken, yet the relationship was established beyond doubt.

He witnessed the first exchange; the wireless message of joy and sympathy that flashed he intercepted.

Through his extremely rapid mind, as he watched, poured memories, reflections, judgments in concentrated form, yet calmly, steadily, though against a background of deep and troubled emotion. There seemed actually a disruption of his personality. Father Collins, standing beside him, divined nothing, he believed, of his agitation, standing, mere figure of a man, listening to the music with attentive pleasure; at least, he gave no outward sign. . . .

The song drew to its close. Once Nayan raised her eyes, instantly finding those of LeVallon across the room, then shifting again for a fleeting second with a rapidly changing focus to his own. He met them without a quiver; he caught again her tender, searching question; he sent no answer back.

In his own heart burned, however, a score of questions that beat against his soul for answers. What was it that each had found thus intuitively within the other? Was it her maternal instinct only that was reached as with all other men hitherto, was it at last the woman in her that leaped towards its own divine, creative sun, or was it that hidden, nameless aspect of her which had never yet found a vehicle for manifestation among her own kind and had therefore remained hitherto unexpressed—bodiless?

The answer to this he found easily enough. No jealousy stirred; pain for himself had been long ago uprooted. Yet pain of a kind he felt. Would LeVallon injure, drag her down, bring suffering, perhaps of an atrocious sort, into her hitherto so innocent life? Was she yet qualified to withstand the fierce fire, the rushing wind, that the full force of his strange nature must bring to bear upon her?

His questions went prophesying, flying like swift birds to such great distances that no audible answers could return. His pain, at any rate, chiefly was for her. He divined that she was frightened, yet exhilarated, before the unexpected apparition of an unusual presence, Accustomed to smaller jets of admiration from smaller men, this deep flood overwhelmed her. This motionless figure watching her among the shadows, listening to her singing, devouring her beauty with an innocence, power, worship she had never yet encountered—could she, Fillery asked himself, withstand its elemental flood and not be broken by its waves?

For at the back of all his questions, haunting his prophecies, filling his hopes and fears with substance, stood one outstanding certainty:

The motionless figure in the shadows was not LeVallon. It was "N. H."

The thing he had expected had now happened. Instinctively he turned to find his colleague.

For what followed, Fillery, of course, was as unprepared as anyone. In some way, difficult to describe, the whole thing had a strangely natural, almost an inevitable touch. The exaggeration that others felt he was not conscious of. He never, for a single moment, lost his head. The wonder of the elemental violence appealed and stimulated without once touching the sense of fear, much less of panic, in him.

Searching for Devonham's familiar figure, he found it in the seat that Lady Gleeson had vacated shortly before, but the face turned away towards the inner room, so that it was not possible to catch his eye. It was an attentive, critical, almost anxious expression his chief surprised, and while a faint smile perhaps flitted across his own mouth, he became aware that Father Collins—he had again completely forgotten his proximity—was staring with a curious intentness at him. The same instant the song came to an end. Into the brief pause of a second before the applause burst forth, Father Collins's voice was suddenly audible in his ear:

"LeVallon's gone," Fillery was saying to himself, " 'N. H.' is in control," when his neighbour's words broke in. The two sentences were simultaneously in his mind:

"A man in *his own place* is the Ruler of his Fate!"

And Fillery's astonishment was only equalled by the fact that the grim face was soft with sympathy, and that in the eyes shone moisture that was close to tears. Before he could reply, however, the applause burst forth, making an uproar against which no voice could possibly contend. The subsequent events, following so swiftly, made rejoinder equally out of the question, nor did he see Father Collins again that evening.

These Fillery witnessed much as already described through Devonham's eyes. The storm, the panic took place as told. Yet a detail here and there belong to Fillery's version, for they were a part of his own being. He had, for instance, a warning that something was about to happen, although warning seems not quite the faithful word. He saw the Valley for one fleeting second, the three familiar figures, Nayan, "N. H.," himself, flying through the bright sunshine before a wind that stirred a million flowers. In the farthest possible background of his mind it shone an instant. The shutter dropped again, it vanished.

Yet enough to set him on the alert. Into the air about him, into his heart as well, fell an exhilarating and immense refreshment. It rose, as it were, from the most deeply submerged portion of his own hidden being, now stirred, even actually summoned, into activity.

The shutter meanwhile rose and fell and rose again; the Valley reappeared and vanished, then reappeared again.

For the truth came smashing against him—smashing his being open, and bursting the doors of his carefully instructed, carefully guarded nature. The doors flung from their hinges and a blinding light poured in and flooded the strangest possible hidden corners.

He saw what followed with an accuracy of observation impossible to anyone else, with an intimate sympathy the others could not feel—because he himself took part in the entire scene. But the scene, for him, was not the Chelsea studio with its tobacco smoke and perfume, it was the Caucasian valley whence his own blood derived. Clean, fragrant winds swept past him across mighty space. The walls melted into distances of forest and mountain peaks, the ceiling was a dome of stainless blue, the floor ran deep in flowers. A drenching sunshine of crystal purity bathed the world. It was across bright emerald turf that he saw "N. H." dance forward like a wind of power, cry with a joyful resonant voice to the radiant girl who stood laughing, half hiding, yet at the same time beckoning, that she should fly with him. He caught and lifted her, her hair, the whiteness of her skin flashing in the sun like some marvellous bird in the act of taking wing, for before he had touched her she leapt through the air to meet his outstretched arms. Yet one hand, one silvery arm, waved towards himself, towards Fillery; their fingers met and clasped; the three of them, three dancing, free and joyful figures, fled like the wind across the enormous mountains, but fled, he knew beyond all question—*home*.

He saw this in the space of those few seconds in which Nayan was swung over the youth's shoulders beside the piano. The two scenes ran parallel, as it were, before his eyes, outer and inner sight keeping equal pace together. His balance and judgment here were never once disturbed. In the studio: he had just introduced LeVallon to the girl and the latter had caught her up. In the valley: she had leapt into his arms and the three of them were off.

It was this inner interpretation, keeping always level pace with what was happening outwardly, that furnished Fillery with the hint of an astounding explanation. The figure in the valley, it flashed to him, was, of course, "N. H." in all his natural splendour, but a figure unknown surely to all records of humanity as such. Here danced and sang a happy radiant being, by whom the limitations of the human species were not experienced, even if the species were familiar to him at all. A being from another system, another evolution, an elemental being, whose ideal, development, mode of existence, were not those of men and women. "N. H." was not a human being, a human soul, a human spirit. He belonged elsewhere and otherwise. Under the guise of LeVallon he had drifted in. He inhabited LeVallon's frame.

In the Studio, at this instant, Fillery heard him using the singular words already noted, and in the Studio they sounded, indeed, senseless, foolish, even mad. It was, he realized, an attempt to stammer in human language some meaning that lay beyond, outside it. In the Valley, however, and at the same moment, they sounded natural and true. The evolutionary system to which "N. H." belonged, from which he had in some as yet unknown manner passed into humanity, but to which, though almost entirely forgotten, he yearned with his whole being to return—this other system had, it seemed, its own conditions, its own methods of advance, its ideals and its duties. Were, then, its inhabitants —this flashed upon him in the delicious wind and sunshine —the workers in what men call the natural kingdoms, the builders of form and structure, the directing powers that expressed themselves through the elemental energies everywhere behind the laws of Nature? Was this their tireless and wondrous service in the planet, in the universe itself?

"N. H." called the girl to service, not to personal love. Alone, cut off from his own kind, alien and derelict amid the conditions of a humanity strange, perhaps unknown to him, he sought companionship where he could. Drawn instinctively to the more impersonal types, such as Fillery and the girl, he felt there the nearest approach to what he recognized as his own kind; their ideal of selfless service was a beacon that he understood; he would return to his own kingdom, carrying them both with him. From somewhere, at any rate, this all flashed into his too willing mind. . . .

At which second precisely in Fillery's valley-vision, Khilkoff entered, and—yet before he could take action—the lightning struck and the sudden explosion of the ferocious storm blackened out both the outer and the inner scene.

The shock of elemental violence, the astounding revelation

as well that an entirely new type had possibly come within his ken, this, combined with the emotional disturbance caused by the change produced in Nayan, seemed enough to upset the equilibrium of even the most balanced mind. The darkness added its touch of helplessness besides. Yet Fillery never for a moment lost his head. Two natures in him, cause of his radical instability, merged for a moment in amazing harmony. The panic now dominating all about him seemed so small a thing compared to the shattering discovery life had just offered to him. Across it, finding his way past kneeling women and shrieking girls, drenched to the skin by the flood of entering rain, moving over splintered glass, he found the figure he sought, as though by some instinctive sympathy. They came together in the darkness. Their hands met easily. A moment later they were in the street, and "N. H.'s" instinctive terror amid the sheets of falling water, an element hostile to his own natural fire, made it a simple matter to get him home—in Lady Gleeson's motor car.

CHAPTER XVI

WHEN relative order had been restored, Devonham realized, of course, that his colleague had cleverly spirited away their "patient"; also that the sculptor had carried off his daughter. Relieved to escape from the atmosphere of what he considered collective hysteria, he had borrowed mackintosh and umbrella, and declining several offers of a lift, had walked the four miles to his house in the rain and wind. The exercise helped to work off the emotion in him; his mind cleared healthily; personal bias gave way to honest and unprejudiced reflection; there was much that interested him deeply, at the same time puzzled and bewildered him beyond anything he had yet experienced. He reached the house with a mind steady if unsatisfied; but the emotions caused by prejudice had gone. His main anxiety centred about his chief.

He was glad to notice a light in an upper window, for it meant, he hoped, that LeVallon was now safely home. While his latchkey sought its hole, however, this light was extinguished, and when the door opened, it was Fillery himself who greeted him, a finger on his lips.

"Quietly!" he whispered. "I've just got him to bed and put his light out. He's asleep already." Paul noticed his manner instantly—its happiness. There was a glow of mysterious joy and wonder in his atmosphere that made the other hostile at once.

They went together towards that inner room where so often together they had already talked both moon and sun to bed. Cold food lay on the table, and while they satisfied their hunger, the rain outside poured down with a steady drenching sound. The wind had dropped. The suburb lay silent and deserted. It was long past midnight. The

195

house was very still, only the occasional step of a night-
nurse audible in the passages and rooms upstairs. They
would not be disturbed.

"You got him home all right, then?" Paul asked presently,
keeping his voice low.

He had been observing his friend closely; the evident
pleasure and satisfaction in the face annoyed him; the light
in the eyes at the same time profoundly troubled him. Not
only did he love his chief for himself, he set high value
on his work as well. It would be deplorable, a tragedy,
if judgment were destroyed by personal bias and desire.
He felt uneasy and distressed.

Fillery nodded, then gave an account of what had happened, but obviously an account of outward events merely;
he did not wish, evidently, to argue or explain. The strong,
rugged face was lit up, the eyes were shining; some inner
enthusiasm pervaded his whole being. Evidently he felt
very sure of something—something that both pleased and
stimulated him.

His account of what had happened was brief enough,
little more than a statement of the facts.

Finding himself close to LeVallon when the darkness
came, he had kept hold of him and hurried him out of the
house at once. The sudden blackness, it seemed, had made
LeVallon quiet again, though he kept asking excitedly for
the girl. When assured that he would soon see her, he
became obedient as a lamb. The absence of light apparently
had a calming influence. They found, of course, no taxis,
but commandeered the first available private car, Fillery
using the authoritative influence of his name. And it was
Lady Gleeson's car, Lady Gleeson herself inside it. She
had thought things over, put two and two together, and
had come back. Her car might be of use. It was. For
the rain was falling in sheets and bucketfuls, the road had
become a river of water, and Fillery's automobile, ordered
for an hour later, had not put in an appearance. It was
the rain that saved the situation. . . .

An exasperated expression crossed Devonham's face as he heard this detail emphasized. He had meant to listen without interruption. The enigmatical reference to the rain proved too much for him.

"Why 'the rain'? What d'you mean exactly, Edward?"

"Water," was the reply, made in a significant tone that further annoyed his listener's sense of judgment. "You remember the Channel, surely! Water and fire mutually destroy each other. They are hostile elements."

There was a look almost of amusement on his face as he said it. Devonham kept a tight hold upon his tongue. It was not impatience or surprise he felt, though both were strong; it was perhaps sorrow.

"And so Lady Gleeson drove you home?"

He waited with devouring interest for further details. The throng of questions, criticisms and emotions surging in him he repressed with admirable restraint.

Lady Gleeson, yes, had driven the party home. Fillery made her sit on the back seat alone, while he occupied the front one, LeVallon beside him, but as far back among the deep cushions as possible. The doctor held his hand. At any other time, Devonham could have laughed; but he saw no comedy now. Lady Gleeson, it seemed, was awed by the seriousness of the "Chief," whom, even at the best of times, she feared a little. Her vanity, however, persuaded her evidently that she was somehow the centre of interest.

Yet Devonham, as he listened, had difficulty in persuading himself that he was in the twentieth century, and that the man who spoke was his colleague and a man of the day as well.

"LeVallon talked little, and that little to himself or to me. He seemed unaware that a third person was present at all. Though quiet enough, there was suppressed vehemence still about him. He said various things: that *'she* belonged to us,' for instance; that he 'knew his own'; that *she* was 'filled with fire in exile'; and that he would 'take her back.' Also that I, too, must go with them both. He often mentioned the sun, saying more than once that the sun had 'sent its messengers.' Obviously, it was not the ordinary sun he referred to, but some source of central heat and fire he seems aware of——"

"You, I suppose, Edward," put in his listener quickly, "said nothing to encourage all this? Nothing that could suggest or stimulate?"

Fillery ignored, even if he noticed, the tone of the question. "I kept silence rather. I said very little. I let him talk. I had to keep an eye on the woman, too."

"You certainly had your hands full—a dual personality and a nymphomaniac."

"She helped me, without knowing it. All he said about the girl, she evidently took to herself. When he begged me to keep the water out, she drew the window up the last half-inch. . . . The water frightened him; she was sympathetic, and her sympathy seemed to reach him, though I doubt if he was aware of her presence at all until the last minute almost——"

"And 'at the last minute'?"

"She leaned forward suddenly and took both his hands. I had let go of the one I held and was just about to open the door, when I heard her say excitedly that I must let her come and see him, or that he must call on her; she was sure she could help him; he must tell her everything. . . . I turned to look. . . . LeVallon, startled into what I believe was his first consciousness of her presence, stared into her eyes, and leaned forward among his cushions a little, so that their faces were close together. Before I could interfere, she had flung her bare arms about his neck and kissed him. She then sat back again, turning to me, and repeating again and again that he needed a woman's care and that she must help and mother him. She was excited, but she knew what she was saying. She showed neither shame nor the least confusion. She tasted—of course with her it cannot last—a bigger world. She was most determined."

"*His* reaction?" inquired Devonham, amused in spite of his graver emotions of uneasiness and exasperation.

"None whatever. I scarcely think he realized he had been kissed. His interest was so entirely elsewhere. I saw his face a moment among the white ermine, the bare arms and jewels that enveloped him." Fillery frowned faintly. "The car had almost stopped. Lady Gleeson was leaning back again. He looked at me, and his voice was intense and eager: 'Dear Fillery,' he said, 'we have found each other, I have found her. She knows, she remembers the way back. Here we can do so little.'

"Lady Gleeson, however, had interpreted the words in another way.

" 'I'll come to-morrow to see you,' she said at once intensely. 'You *must* let me come,'—the last words addressed to me, of course."

The two men looked at one another a moment in silence, and for the first time during the conversation they exchanged a smile. . . .

"I got him to bed," Fillery concluded. "In ten minutes he was sound asleep." And his eyes indicated the room overhead.

He leaned back, and quietly began to fill his pipe. The account was over.

As though a great spring suddenly released him, Paul Devonham stood up. His untidy hair hung wild, his glasses were crooked on his big nose, his tie askew. His whole manner bristled with accumulated challenge and disagreement.

"*Who?*" he cried. "*Who?* Edward, I ask you?"

His colleague, yet knowing exactly what he meant, looked up questioningly. He looked him full in the face.

"Hush!" he said quietly. "You'll wake him."

He gazed with happy penetrating eyes at his companion. "Paul," he added gently, "do you really mean it? Have you still the faintest doubt?"

The moment had drama in it of unusual kind. The conflict between these two honest and unselfish minds was vital. The moment, too, was chosen, the place as well—this small, quiet room in a commonplace suburb of the greatest city on the planet, drenched by earthly rain and battered by earthly wind from the heart of an equinoctial storm; the mighty universe outside, breaking with wondrous, incredible impossibilities upon a mind that listened and a mind that could not hear; and upstairs, separated from them by a few carpenter's boards, an assortment of "souls," either derelict and ruined, or gifted supernormally, masters of space and time perhaps, yet all waiting to be healed by the best knowledge known to the race—and one among them, about whom the conflict raged . . . sound asleep . . . while wind and water stormed, while lightning fires lit the distant horizons, while the great sun lay hidden, and darkness crept soundlessly to and fro. . . .

"Have you still the slightest doubt, Paul?" repeated Fillery. "You know the evidence. You have an open mind."

Then Devonham, still standing over his Chief, let out the storm that had accumulated in him over-long. He talked like a book. He talked like several books. It seemed almost that he distrusted his own personal judgment.

"Edward," he began solemnly—not knowing that he quoted—"you, above all men, understand the lower recesses of the human heart, that gloomy, gigantic oubliette in which our million ancestors writhe together inextricably, and each man's planetary past is buried alive——"

Fillery nodded quietly his acquiescence.

"You, of all men, know our packed, limitless subterranean life," Devonham went on, "and its impenetrable depths. You understand telepathy, 'extended telepathy' as well, and how a given mind may tap not only forgotten individual memories, but memories of his family, his race, even planetary memories into the bargain, the memory, in fact, of every being that ever lived, right down to Adam, if you will——"

"Agreed," murmured the other, listening patiently, while he puffed his pipe and heard the rain and wind. "I know all that. I know it, at any rate, as a possible theory."

"You also know," continued Devonham in a slightly less strident tone, "your own—forgive me, Edward—your own idiosyncrasies, your weaknesses, your dynamic accumulated repressions, your strange physical heritage and spiritual —I repeat the phrase—your spiritual vagrancies towards— towards——" He broke off suddenly, unable to find the words he wanted.

"I'm illegitimate, born of a pagan passion," mentioned the other calmly. "In that sense, if you like, I have in me a 'complex' against the race, against humanity—as such."

He smiled patiently, and it was the patience, the evident conviction of superiority that exasperated his cautious, accurate colleague.

"If I love humanity, I also tolerate it perhaps, for I try to heal it," added Fillery. "But, believe me, Paul, I do not lose my scientific judgment."

"Edward," burst out the other, "how can you think it possible, then—that *he* is other than the result of tendencies transmitted by his mad parents, or acquired from Mason, who taught him all he knows, or—if you will—that he has these hysterical faculties—supernormal as we may call them —which tap some racial, even, if you will, some planetary past——"

He again broke off, unable to express his whole thought, his entire emotion, in a few words.

"I accept all that," said Fillery, still calmly, quietly, "but perhaps now—in the interest of truth"—his tone was grave, his words obviously chosen carefully—"if now I feel it necessary to go beyond it! My strange heritage," he added, "is even possibly a help and guide. How," he asked, a trace of passion for the first time visible in his manner, "shall we venture—how decide—for we are not wholly ignorant, you and I—between what is possible and impossible? Is this trivial planet, then," he asked, his voice rising suddenly, ominously perhaps, "our sole criterion? Dare we not venture—beyond—a little? The scientific mind should be the last to dogmatize as to the possibilities of this life of ours. . . ."

The authority of chief, the old tie of respectful and affectionate friendship, the admiring wonder that pertained to a daring speculator who had often proved himself right in face of violent opposition—all these affected Devonham. He did not weaken, but for an instant he knew, perhaps, the existence of a vast, incredible horizon in his friend's mind, though one he dared not contemplate. Possibly, he understood in this passing moment a huger world, a new outlook that scorned limit, though yet an outlook that his accurate, smaller spirit shrank from.

He found, at any rate, his own words futile. "You remember," he offered—"'We need only suppose the continuity of our own consciousness with a mother sea, to allow for exceptional waves occasionally pouring over the dam.'"

"Good, yes," said Fillery. "But that 'mother sea,' what may it not include? Dare we set limits to it?"

And, as he said it, Fillery, emotion visible in him, rose suddenly from his chair. He stood up and faced his colleague.

"Let us come to the point," he said in a clear, steady voice. "It all lies—doesn't it?—in that question you asked——"

"*Who?*" came at once from Devonham's lips, as he stood, looking oddly stiff and rigid opposite his Chief. There was a touch of defiance in his tone. "*Who?*" He repeated his original question.

No pause intervened. Fillery's reply came sharp and firm:

"'N. H.,'" he said.

An interval of silence followed, then, between the two men, as they looked into each other's eyes. Fillery waited for his assistant to speak, but no word came.

"LeVallon,' the older man continued, "is the transient, acquired personality. It does not interest us. There is no real LeVallon. The sole reality is—'N. H.'"

He spoke with the earnestness of deep conviction. There was still no reply or comment from the other.

"Paul," he continued, steadying his voice and placing a hand upon his colleague's shoulder, "I am going to ask you to—consider our arrangement—cancelled. I must——"

Then, before he could finish what he had to say, the other had said it for him:

"Edward, I give you back your promise."

He shrugged his shoulders ever so slightly, but there was no unpleasant, no antagonistic touch now either in voice or manner. There was, rather, a graver earnestness than there had been hitherto, a hint of reluctant acquiescence, but also there was an emotion that included certainly affection. No such fundamental disagreement had ever come between them during all their years of work together. "You understand," he added slowly, "what you are doing —what is involved." His tone almost suggested that he spoke to a patient, a loved patient, but one over whom he had no control. He sighed.

"I belong, Paul, myself to the unstable—if that is what you mean," said his old friend gently, "and with all of danger, or of wonder, it involves."

The faint movement of the shoulders again was noticeable. "We need not put it that way, Edward," was the quiet rejoinder; "for that, if true, can only help your insight, your understanding, and your judgment." He hesitated a moment or two, searching his mind carefully for words. Fillery waited. "But it involves—I think"— he went on presently in a firmer voice—"*his* fate as well. He must become permanently—one or other."

No pause followed. There was a smile of curious happiness on Fillery's face as he instantly answered in a tone of absolute conviction:

"There lies the root of our disagreement, Paul. There is no 'other.' I am positive for once. There is only one, and that one is—'N. H.'"

"Umph!" his friend grunted. Behind the exclamation hid an attitude confirmed, as though he had come suddenly to a big decision.

"You see, Paul—I *know*."

CHAPTER XVII

I T was not long after the scene in the Studio that the
Prometheans foregathered at dinner in the back room
of the small French restaurant in Soho and discussed the
event. The prices were moderate, conditions free and easy.
It was a favourite haunt of Members.

To-night, moreover, there was likely to be a good
attendance. The word had gone out.

The Studio scene had, of course, been the subject of
much discussion already. The night of its occurrence it
had been talked over till dawn in more than one flat, and
during the following days the Society, as a whole, thought
of little else. Those who had not been present had to be
informed, and those who had witnessed it found it an
absorbing topic of speculation. The first words that passed
when one member met another in the street was: "What
did you make of that storm? Wasn't it amazing? Did
your solar plexus vibrate? Mine did! And the light, the
colour, the vibrations—weren't they terrific? What do you
think *he* is?" It was rumoured that the Secretary was
asking for individual reports. Excitement and interest were
general, though the accounts of individual witnesses differed
extraordinarily. It seemed impossible that all had seen and
heard the same thing.

The back room was pleasantly filled to-night, for it was
somehow known that Millington Povey, and possibly Father
Collins, too, were coming. Miss Milligan, the astrologist,
was there early, arriving with Mrs. Towzer, who saw auras
and had already, it was rumoured, painted automatically
a strange rendering of "forces" that were visible to her
clairvoyantly during the occurrence. Miss Lance, in shin-

ing beads and a glittering scarf, arrived on their heels, an account of the scene in her pocket—to be published in her magazine "Simplicity" after she had modified it according to what she picked up from hearing other, and better, descriptions.

, Kempster, immaculate as ever, ordering his food as he ordered his clothes, like a connoisseur, was one of the first to establish himself in a comfortable seat. He knew how to look after himself, and was already eating in his neat dainty way while the others still stood about studying the big white *menu* with its illegible hieroglyphics in smudged violet ink. He supplemented his meals with special patent foods of vegetarian kind he brought with him. He had dried bananas in one pocket and spirit photographs in another, and he was invariably pulling out the wrong thing. Meat he avoided. "A man is what he eats," he held, and animal blood was fatal to psychic development. To eat pig or cow was to absorb undesirable characteristics.

Next to him sat Lattimer, a lanky man of thirty, with loose clothes, long hair, and eyes of strange intensity. Known as "occultist and alchemist," he was also a chemist of some repute. His life was ruled by a master-desire and a master-fear: the former, that he might one day project his double consciously; the latter, that in his next earthly incarnation he might be—the prospect made him shudder —a woman. He sought to keep his thought as concrete as possible, the male quality.

He believed that the nervous centre of the physical body which controlled all such unearthly, if not definitely "spiritual," impulses, was the solar plexus. For him it was *the* important portion of his anatomy, the seat of intuition. Brain came second.

. "The fellow," he declared emphatically, "stirred my solar plexus, my *kundalini*—that's all I know." He referred, as all understood, to the latent power the *yogis* claim lies coiled, but only rarely manifested, in that great nervous centre.

His statement, he knew, would meet with general approval and understanding. It was the literal Kempster who spoiled his opening:

"Paul Devonham," said the latter, "thinks it's merely a secondary personality that emerged. I had a long argument with him about it——"

"Never argue with the once-born," declared Povey flatly, producing his pet sentence. "It's waste of time. Only older souls, with the experience of many earthly lives stored in their beings, are knowledgeable." He filled his glass and poured out for others, Lattimer and Mrs. Towzer alone declining, though for different reasons.

"It destroys the 'sight,'" explained the former. "Alcohol sets up coarse vibrations that ruin clairvoyance."

"I decided to deny myself till the war is over," was Mrs. Towzer's reason, and when Povey reminded her of the armistice, she mentioned that Turkey hadn't "signed yet."

"I think his soul——" began Miss Lance.

"If he *has* a soul," put in Povey, electrically.

"—is hardly in his body at all," concluded Miss Lance, less convincingly than originally intended.

"It was love at first sight. His sign is Fire and hers is Air," Miss Milligan said. "That's certain. *Of course* they came together."

"A clear case of memory, at any rate," insisted Kempster. "Two old souls meeting again for the first time for thousands of years, probably. Love at first sight, or hate, for that matter, is always memory, isn't it?" He disliked the astrology explanation; it was not mysterious enough, too mathematical and exact to please him.

"Secondary personalities *are* invariably memories of former selves, of course," agreed young Dickson, the theosophist, who was on the verge now of becoming a psycho-analyst and had already discarded Freud for Jung. "If not memories of past lives, then they're desires suppressed in this one."

"The less you think, the more you know," suggested

Miss Lance. She distrusted intellect and believed that another faculty, called instinct or intuition, according to which word first occurred to her, was the way to knowledge. She was about to quote Bergson upside down, when Povey, foreseeing an interval of boredom, took command:

"One thing we know, at any rate," he began judiciously; "we aren't the only beings in the universe. There are non-human intelligences, both vast and small. The old world-wide legends can't be built on nothing. In every age of history—the reports are universal—we have pretty good evidence for other forms of life than humans——"

"Though never yet in human *form*," put in Lattimer, yet sympathetically. "Their bodies, I mean, aren't human," he added.

"Exactly. That's true. But the gods, the fauns, the satyrs, the elemental beings, as we call 'em—sylphs, undines, gnomes and salamanders—to say nothing of fairies et hoc genus omne—there must be *some* reasonable foundation for their persistence through all the ages."

"They all belong to the *Deva* Evolution," Dickson mentioned with conviction. "In the East it's been known and recognized for centuries, hasn't it? Another evolutionary system that runs parallel to ours. From planetary spirits down to elementals, they're concerned with the building up of form in the various kingdoms——"

"Yes, yes," Povey interrupted impatiently. Dickson was stealing what he had meant to say himself and to say, he flattered himself, far better. "We know all *that*, of course. They stand behind what we call the laws of nature, non-human activities and intelligences of every grade and kind. They work for humanity in a way, are in other space and time, deathless, of course, yet—in some strange way, always eager to cross the gulf fixed between the two and so find a soul. They are impersonal in a sense, as impersonal as, say, wind and fire through which some of them operate as bodies."

He paused and looked about him, noting the interested attention he awaked.

"There *may* be times," he went on, "there probably *are* certain occasions, when the gulf is more crossable than others." He laid down his knife and fork as a sympathetic murmur proved that the point he was leading up to was favourably understood already. "We have had this war, for instance," he stated, his voice taking on a more significant and mysterious tone. "Dislodged by the huge upheaval, man's soul is on the march again." He paused once more. "*They,*" he concluded, lowering his voice still more, and emphasizing the pronoun, "are possibly already among us! Who knows?"

He glanced round. "We do; we know," was the expression on most faces. All knew precisely what he meant and to whom he referred, at any rate.

"You might get him to come and lecture to us," said Dickson, the first to break the pause. "You might ask Dr. Fillery. *You* know him."

"That's an idea——" began the Secretary, when there was a commotion near the door. His face showed annoyance.

It was the arrival of Toogood that at this moment disturbed the atmosphere and robbed Povey of the effect he aimed at. It provided Kempster, however, with an idea at the same time. "Here's a psychometrist!" he exclaimed, making room for him. "He might get a bit of his hair or clothing and psychometrize it. He might tell us about his past, if not exactly *what* he is."

The suggestion, however, found no seconder, for it seemed that the new arrival was not particularly welcomed. Judging by the glances, the varying shades of greeting, too, he was not fully trusted, perhaps, this broad, fleshy man of thirty-five, with complexion blotchy, an over-sensual mouth and eyes a trifle shifty. His claim to membership was two-fold: he remembered past lives, and had the strange power of psychometry. An archæologist by trade, his gift of psychometry—by which he claimed to hold an object and tell its past, its pedigree, its history—was of great use to him in his calling. Without further trouble he could tell whether such an object was genuine or sham. Dealers in antiquities offered him big fees—but "No, no; I cannot prostitute my powers, you see"—and he remained poor accordingly.

In his past lives he had been either a famous Pharaoh, or Cleopatra—according to his audience of the moment and its male or female character—but usually Cleopatra, because, on the whole, there was more money and less risk in her. He lectured—for a fee. Lately, however, he had been Pharaoh, having got into grave trouble over the Cleopatra claim, even to the point of being threatened with expulsion from the Society. His attitude during the war, besides, had been unsatisfactory—it was felt he had selfishly protected himself on the grounds of being physically unfit. Apart from archæology, too, his chief preoccupation, derived from past lives of course, was sex, in the form of other men's wives, his own wife and children being, naturally, very recent and somewhat negligible ties.

His gift of psychometry, none the less, was considered proved—in spite of the backward and indifferent dealers. His mind was quick and not unsubtle. He became now au fait with the trend of the conversation in a very few seconds, but he had not been present at the Studio when the occurrence all discussed had taken place.

"Hair would be best," he advised tentatively, sipping his whisky-and-soda. He had already dined. "It's a part of himself, you see. Better than mere clothing, I mean. It's extremely vital, hair. It grows after death."

"If I can get it for you, I will," said Povey. "He may be lecturing for us before long. I'll try."

"With psychometry and a good photograph," Kempster suggested, "a time exposure, if possible, we ought to get *some* evidence, at any rate. It's first-hand evidence we want, of course, isn't it? What do you think of this, for instance, I wonder?" He turned to Lattimer, drawing something from his pocket and showing it. "It's a time exposure at night of a haunted tree. You'll notice a queer sort of elemental form *inside* the trunk and branches. Oh!" He replaced the shrivelled banana in his pocket, and drew out the photograph without a smile. "This," he explained, waving it, "is what I meant." They fell to discussing it.

Meanwhile, Povey, anxious to resume his lecture, made an effort to recover his command of the group-atmosphere which Toogood had disturbed. The latter had a "personal magnetism" which made the women like him in spite of their distrust.

"I was just saying," he resumed, patting the elbow of the psychometrist, "that this strange event we've been discussing—you weren't present, I believe, at the time, but, of course, you've heard about it—has features which seem to point to something radically new, or at least of very rare occurrence. As Lattimer mentioned, a human body has never yet, so far as we know, been occupied, obsessed, by a non-human entity, but that, after all, is no reason why it should not ever happen. What is a body, anyhow? What is an entity, too?" Povey's thought was wandering, evidently; the thread of his first discourse was broken; he floundered. "Man, anyway, is more than a mere chemical machine," he went on, "a crystallization of the primitive nebulæ, though the instrument he uses, the body he works through, is undoubtedly thus describable. Now, we know there are all kinds of non-human intelligences busy on our planet, in the Universe itself as well. Why, then, I ask, should not one of these——?"

He paused, unable to find himself, his confusion obvious. He was as glad of the interruption that was then provided by the arrival of Imson as his audience was. Toogood certainly was not sorry; he need find no immediate answer. He sipped his drink and made mental notes.

Imson arrived in a rough brown ulster with the collar

turned up about his ears, a low flannel shirt, not strictly clean, lying loosely round his neck. His colourless face was of somewhat flabby texture, due probably to his diet, but its simple, honest expression was attractive, the smile engaging. The touch of foolishness might have been child-like innocence, even saintliness some thought, and though he was well over forty, the unlined skin made him look more like thirty. He enjoyed a physiognomy not unlike that of a horse or sheep. His big, brown eyes stared wide open at the world, expecting wonder and finding it. His hobby was inspirational poems. One lay in his breast pocket now. He burned to read it aloud.

Pat Imson's ideal was an odd one—detachment; the desire to avoid all ties that must bring him back to future incarnations on the earth, to eschew making fresh Karma, in a word. He considered himself an "old soul," and was rather weary of it all—of existence and development, that is. To take no part in life meant to escape from those tangles for whose unravelling the law of rebirth dragged the soul back again and again. To sow no Causes was to have no harvest of Effects to reap with toil and perspiration. Action, of course, there must be, but "indifference to results of action" was the secret. Imson, none the less, was always entangled with wives and children. Having divorced one wife, and been divorced by another, he had recently married a third; a flock of children streamed behind him; he was a good father, if a strange husband.

"It's old Karma I have to work off," he would explain, referring to the wives. "If I avoid the experience I shall only have to come back again. There's no good shirking old Karma." He gave this explanation to the wives themselves, not only to his friends. "Face it and it's done with, worked off, you see." That is, it had to be done nicely, kindly, generously.

An entire absence of the sense of humour was, of course, his natural gift, yet a certain quaint wisdom helped to fill the dangerous vacuum. He was known usually as "Pat."

"Come on, Pat," said Povey, making room for him at his side. "How's Karma? We're just talking about Le-Vallon and the Studio business. What do you make of it? You were there, weren't you?" The others listened, attentively, for Imson had a reputation for "seeing true."

"I saw it, yes," replied Imson, ordering his dinner with indifference—soup, fried potatoes, salad, cheese and coffee —but declining the offered wine. The group waited for his next remark, but none was forthcoming. He sat crumbling his bread into the soup and stirring the mixture with his spoon.

"Did you see the light about him, Mr. Imson?" asked Miss Lance. "The brilliant aura of golden yellow that he wore? *I* thought—it sounds exaggerated, I know—but to me it seemed even brighter than the lightning. Did you notice it?"

"Well," said Imson slowly, putting his spoon down. "I'm not often clairvoyant, you know. I did notice, however, a sort of radiance about him. But with hair like that, it's difficult to be certain——"

"Full of lovely patterns," said Mrs. Towzer. "Geometrical patterns."

"Like astrological designs," mentioned Miss Milligan. "He's Leo, of course—fire."

"Almost as though he brought or caused the lightning— as if it actually emanated out of his atmosphere somehow," claimed Miss Lance, for it was *her* conversation after all.

"I saw nothing of that," replied Imson quietly. "No, I can't say I saw anything *exactly* like that." He added honestly, with his engaging smile that had earned for him in some quarters the nickname of "The Sheep": "I was looking at Nayan, you see, most of the time."

A smile flickered round the table, for rumour had it that the girl had once seemed to him as possible "Karma."

"So was I," put in Kempster with kindly intention, though his sympathy was evidently not needed. Imson was too simple even to feel embarrassment. "She came to life suddenly for the first time since I've known her. It was amazing." To which Imson, busy over his salad-dressing, made no reply.

Povey, lighting his pipe and puffing out thick clouds of smoke, was cleverer. "LeVallon's effect upon her, whatever it was, seemed instantaneous," he informed the table. "I never saw a clearer case of two souls coming together in a flash."

"As I said just now," Kempster quickly mentioned.

"They are similar," said Imson, looking up, while the group waited expectantly.

"Similar," repeated Kempster. "Ah!"

"It was the surprise in her face that struck me most," observed Povey quickly, making an internal note of Imson's adjective, but knowing that indirect methods would draw him out better than point-blank questions. "LeVallon showed it too. It was an unexpected recognition on both sides. They are 'similar,' as you say; both at the same stage of development, whatever that stage may be. The expression on both faces——"

"Escape," exclaimed Imson, giving at last the kernel of what he had to say. And the effect upon the group was electrical. A visible thrill ran round the Soho table.

"The very word," exclaimed Povey and Miss Lance together. "Escape!" But neither of them knew exactly what they meant, nor what Imson himself meant.

"LeVallon has, of course, already escaped," the latter went on quietly. "He is no longer caught by causes and effects as we are here. He's got out of it all long ago—if he was ever in it at all."

"If he ever was in it at all," said Povey quickly. "You noticed that too. You're very discerning, Pat."

"Clairvoyant," mentioned Miss Lance.

"I've seen them in dreams like that," returned Imson calmly. "I often see them, of course." He referred to his qualification for membership. "The great figures I see in dream have just that unearthly expression."

"Unearthly," said Mrs. Towzer with excitement.

"Non-human," mentioned Kempster suggestively.

"Not of this world, anyhow," suggested Miss Lance mysteriously.

"Divine?" inquired Miss Milligan below her breath.

"Really," murmured Toogood, "I must get a bit of his hair and psychometrize it at once." He was sipping a second glass of whisky.

Imson looked round at each face in turn, apparently seeing nothing that need increase his attachment to the planet by way of fresh Karma.

"The *Deva* world," he said briefly, .after a pause. "Probably he's come to take Nayan off with him. She— I always said so—has a strong strain of the elemental kingdom in her. She may be his *Devi*. LeVallon, I'm sure, is here for the first time. He's one of the non-human evolution. He's slipped in. A *Deva* himself probably." It was as though he said that the waiter was Swiss or French, or that the proprietor's daughter had Italian blood in her.

Povey looked round him with an air of triumph.

"Ah!" he announced, as who should say, "You all thought my version a bit wild, but here's confirmation from an unbiased witness."

"Oh, well, I can't be certain," Imson reminded the group. If he deceived them enough to change their lives in any respect, it involved fresh Karma for himself. Care was indicated. "I can't be positive, can I?" he hedged. "Only —I must say—the great deva-figures I've seen in dream have exactly that look and expression."

"That's interesting, Pat," Povey put in, "because, before you came, I was suggesting a similar explanation for his air of immense potential power. The elemental atmosphere he brought—we all noticed it, of course."

"Elemental *is* the only word," Miss Lance inserted. "A great Nature Being." She was thinking of her magazine.

"He struck me as being so close to Nature that he seemed literally part of it."

"That would explain the lightning and the strange cry he gave about 'messengers,' " replied Imson, wiping the oil from his chin and sprinkling his *petit suisse* with powdered sugar. "It's quite likely enough."

"I wish you'd jot down what you think—a little report of what you saw and felt," the Secretary mentioned. "It would be of great value. I thought of making a collection of the different versions and accounts."

"They might be published some day," thought Miss Lance. "Let's all," she added aloud with emphasis.

Imson nodded agreement, making no audible reply, while the conversation ran on, gathering impetus as it went, growing wilder possibly, but also more picturesque. A man in the street, listening behind a curtain, must have deemed the talkers suffering from delusion, mad; a good psychologist, on the other hand, similarly screened, and knowing the antecedent facts, the Studio scene, at any rate, must have been struck by one outstanding detail—the effect, namely, upon one and all of the person they discussed. They had seen him for an hour or so among a crowd, a young man whose name they hardly knew; only a few had spoken to him; there had been, it seemed, neither time nor opportunity for him to produce upon one and all the impression he undoubtedly had produced. For in every mind, upon every heart, LeVallon's mere presence had evidently graven an unforgettable image, scored an undecipherable hieroglyph. Each felt, it seemed, the hint of a personality their knowledge could not explain, nor any earthly explanation satisfy. The consciousness in each one, perhaps, had been quickened. Hence, possibly, the extravagance of their conversation. Yet, since all reported differently, collective hysteria seemed discounted.

Meanwhile, as the talk continued, and the wings of

imaginative speculation fanned the thick tobacco smoke, others had dropped in, both male and female members, and the group now filled the little room to the walls. The same magnet drew them all, in each heart burned the same huge question mark: Who—what—is this LeVallon? What was the meaning of the scene in Khilkoff's Studio?

Here, too, was a curious and significant fact about the gathering—the amount of knowledge, true or otherwise, they had managed to collect about LeVallon. One way or another, no one could say exactly how, the Society had picked up an astonishing array of detail they now shared together. It was known where he had spent his youth, also how, and with whom, as well as something of the different views about him held by Dr. Devonham and Edward Fillery. To such temperaments as theirs the strange, the unusual, came automatically perhaps, percolating into their minds as though a collective power of thought-reading operated. Garbled, fanciful, askew, their information may have been, but a great deal of it was not far wrong.

Imson, for instance, provided an account of LeVallon's birth, to which all listened spellbound. He evaded all questions as to how he knew of it. "His parents," he assured the room, "practised the old forgotten magic; his father, at any rate, was an expert, if not an initiate, with all the rites and formulæ of ancient times in his memory. LeVallon was born as the result of an experiment, its origins dating back so far that they concerned life upon another planet, I believe, a planet nearer to the sun. The tremendous winds and heat were vehicles of deity, you see—*there.*"

"The parents, you mean, had former lives upon another planet?" asked someone in a hushed tone. "Or he himself?"

"The parents—and Mason. Mason was involved in the experiment that resulted in the birth of LeVallon here to-day."

"The experiment—what was it exactly?" inquired Lattimer, while Toogood surreptitiously made notes on his rather dirty cuff.

Imson shrugged his shoulders very slightly.

"Some of it came to me in sleep," he mentioned, producing a paper from his pocket and beginning to read it aloud before anyone could stop him.

"When the sun was younger, and moon and stars
    Were thrilled with my human birth,
And the winds fled shouting the wondrous news
    As they circled the sea and the earth,

"From the fight for money and worldly fame
    I drew one magical soul
Who came to me over the star-lit sea
    As the needle turns to the Pole.

"Conceived in the hour the stars foretold,
    This son of the winds I bore,
And I taught him the secrets of——"

"Yes," interrupted Povey audaciously, "but the experiment you were telling us about——?"

A murmur of approving voices helped him.

"Oh, the experiment, yes, well—all I know is," he went on with conviction, calmly replacing the poem in his pocket, "that it concerned an old rite, involving the evocation of some elemental being or nature-spirit the three of them had already evoked millions of years before, but had not banished again. The experiment they made to-day was to restore it to its proper sphere. In order to do so, they had to evoke it again, and, of course"—he glanced round, as though all present were familiar with the formula of magical practices—"it could come only through the channel of a human system."

"Of course, yes," murmured a dozen voices, while eyes grew bigger and a pin dropping must have been audible.

"Well"—Imson spoke very slowly now, each word clear

as a bell—"the father, who was officiating, failed. He could not stand the strain. His heart stopped beating. He died —just when *it* was there, he dropped dead."

"What happened to *it?*" asked Povey, too interested to care that he no longer led the room. "You said it could only use a human system as channel——"

"It did so," explained Imson.

The information produced a pause of several seconds. Some of the members, like Toogood, though openly, were making pencil notes upon cuffs or backs of envelopes.

"But the channel was neither Mason nor the woman." The effect of this negative information was as nothing compared to the startling interest produced by the speaker's next words: "It took the easiest channel, the line of least resistance—the unborn body of the child."

Povey, seizing his opportunity, leaped into the silence:

"Whose body, now full grown, and named LeVallon, came to the Studio!" he exclaimed, looking round at the group, as though he had himself given the explanation all had just listened to. "A human body tenanted by a nature-spirit, one of the form-builders—a *Deva*. . . ."

CHAPTER XVIII

FOR all the wildness of the talk, this group of the Unstable was a coherent and consistent entity, using a language each item in it understood. They knew what they were after. Alcohol, coffee, tobacco, underfeeding, these helped or hindered, respectively, the expression of an ideal that, nevertheless, was common to them all; and if the minds represented were unbalanced, or merely speculative, poetic, one genuine quest and sympathy bound all together into a coherent, and who shall say unintelligent or valueless, unit. The unstable enjoyed an extreme sensitiveness to varied experience, with flexible adaptability to all possible new conditions, whereas the stable, with their rigid mental organizations, remained uninformed, stagnant, even fossilized.

In other rooms about the great lamp-lit city sat, doubtless, other similar groups at the very same moment, discussing the shibboleths of other faiths, of other dreams, of other ideas, systems, notions, philosophies, all interpretative of the earth in which little humanity dwells, cut off and isolated, apparently, from the rest of the stupendous universe. A listener, screened from view, a listener not in sympathy with the particular group he observed, and puzzled, therefore, by the language used, must have deemed he listened to harmless, if boring, madness. For each group uses its own language, and the lowest common denominator, though plainly printed in the world's old scriptures, has not yet become adopted by the world at large.

Into this particular group, a little later in the evening, and when the wings of imagination had increased their sweep a trifle dangerously perhaps—into the room, like the arrival of a policeman rather, dropped Father Collins. He came rarely to the Prometheans' restaurant. There was a general sense of drawing breath as he appeared. A pause followed. Something of the cold street air came with him. He wore his big black felt hat, his shabby opera cloak, and clutched firmly—he had no gloves on—the heavy gnarled stick he had cut for his collection in a Cingalese forest years ago, when he was studying with a Buddhist priest. The folds of his voluminous cloak, as he took it off, sent the hanging smoke-clouds in a whirl. His personality stirred the mental atmosphere as well. The women looked up and stared, respectful welcome in their eyes; several of the men rose to shake hands; there was a general shuffling of chairs.

"Bring another *moulin à vent* and a clean glass," Povey said at once to the hovering waiter.

"It's raw and bitter in the street and a fog coming down thickly," mentioned Father Collins. He exhaled noisily and with comfortable relief, as he squeezed himself towards the chair Povey placed for him and looked round genially, nodding and shaking hands with those he knew. "But you're warm and cosy enough in here"—he sat down with unexpected heaviness, and smiled at everybody—"and well fed, too, I'll be bound."

"'The body must be comfortable before the mind can enjoy itself,'" said Phillipps, an untidy member who disliked asceticism. "Starvation produces hallucination, not vision." His glance took in the unused glasses. His qualification was a vision of an uncle at the moment of death, and the uncle had left him money. He had written a wordy pamphlet describing it.

"I'll have an omelette, then, I think," Father Collins told the waiter, as the red wine arrived. "And some fried potatoes. A bit of cheese to follow, and coffee, yes." He filled his glass. He had not come to argue or to preach, and Phillipps's challenge passed unnoticed. Phillipps, who had been leading the talk of late, resented the new arrival, but felt his annoyance modify as he saw his own glass generously filled. Povey, too, accepted a glass, while saying with a false vehemence, "No, no," his finger against the rim.

A change stole over the room, for the new personality was not negligible; he brought his atmosphere with him. The wild talk, it was felt now, would not be quite suitable. Father Collins had the reputation of being something of a scholar; they were not quite sure of him; none knew him very intimately; he had a rumoured past as well that lent a flavour of respect. One story had it that "dabbling in magic" had lost him his position in the Church. Yet he was deemed an asset to the Society.

Whatever it was, the key changed sharply. Imson's eyes and ears grew wider, the hand of Miss Lance went instinctively to her hair and combs, Miss Milligan sought through her mind for a remark at once instructive and uncommon, Mrs. Towzer looked past him searchingly lest his aura escape her before she caught its colour, and Kempster, smoothing his immaculate coat, had an air of being in his present surroundings merely by chance. Toogood, quickly scanning his notes, wondered whether, if called upon, he was to be Pharaoh or Cleopatra. One and all, that is, took on a soberer gait. This semi-clerical visit complicated. The presence of Father Collins was a compliment. What he had to say—about LeVallon and the Studio scene—was, anyhow, assured of breathless interest.

Povey led off. "We were just talking over the other night," he observed, "the night at the Studio, you remember. The storm and so on. It was a singular occurrence, though, of course, we needn't, we *mustn't* exaggerate it." And while he thus, as Secretary, set the note, Father Collins sipped his wine and beamed upon the group. He made no comment. "You were there, weren't you?" continued Povey, sipping his own comforting glass. "I think I saw you. Fillery, you may have noticed," he added, "brought—a friend."

"LeVallon, yes," said the other in a tone that startled them. "A most unusual fellow, wasn't he?" He was attacking the omelette now. "A Greek God, if ever I saw one," he added. And the silence in the crowded room became abruptly noticeable. Miss Milligan, feeling her zodiacal garter slipping, waited to pull it up. Imson's brown eyes grew wider. Kempster held his breath. Toogood borrowed a cigar and waited for someone to offer him a match before he lit it.

"Delicious," added Father Collins. "Cooked to a turn." the omelette slid about his plate.

But the silence continued, and he realized the position suddenly. Emptying his glass and casually refilling it, he turned and faced the eager group about him.

"You want to know what *I* thought about it all," he said. "You've been discussing LeVallon, Nayan and the rest, I see." He looked round as though he were in the lost pulpit that was his right. After a pause he asked point blank: "And what do *you* all think of it? How did it strike you all? For myself, I confess"—he took another sip and paused—"I am full of wonder and question," he finished abruptly.

It was Imson, the fearless, wondering Pat Imson, who first found his tongue.

"We think," he ventured, "LeVallon is probably of *Deva* origin."

The others, while admiring his courage, seemed unsympathetic suddenly. Such phraseology, probably meaningless to the respected guest, was out of place. Eyes were cast down, or looked generally elsewhere. Povey, remembering that the Society was not solely Eastern, glared at the speaker. Father Collins, however, was not perturbed.

"Possibly," he remarked with a courteous smile. "The origin of us all is doubtful and confused. We know not whence we come, of course, and all that. Nor can we ever tell exactly who our neighbour is, or what. LeVallon," he went on, "since you all ask me"—he looked round again

—"is—for me—an undecipherable being. I am," he added, his words falling into open mouths and extended eyes and ears, "somewhat puzzled. But more—I am enormously stimulated and intrigued."

All gazed at him. Father Collins was in his element. The rapt silence that met him was precisely what he had a right to expect from his lost pulpit. He had come, probably, merely to listen and to watch. The opportunity provided by a respectful audience was too much for him. An inspiration tempted him.

"I am inclined to believe," he resumed suddenly in a simple tone, "that he is—a Messenger."

The sentence might have dropped from Sirius upon a listening planet. The babble that followed must, to an ordinary man, have seemed confusion. Everyone spoke with a rush into his neighbour's ear. All bubbled. "I always thought so, I told you so, that was exactly what I meant just now"—and so on. All found their tongues, at any rate, if Povey, as Secretary, led the turmoil:

"Something outside our normal evolution, you mean?" he asked judiciously. "Such a conception is possible, of course."

"A Messenger!" ran on the babel of male and female voices.

It was here that Father Collins failed. The "unstable" in him came suddenly uppermost. The "ecstatic" in his being took the reins. The wondering and expectant audience suited him. The red wine helped as well. When he said "Messenger" he had meant merely someone who brought a message. The expression of nobility merged more and more in the slovenly aspect. Like a priest in the pulpit, whom none can answer and to whom all must listen, he had his text, though that text had been suggested actually by the conversation he had just heard. He had not brought it with him. It occurred to him merely then and there. His mind reflected, in a word, the collective idea that was in the air about him, and he proceeded to

sum it up and give expression to it. This was his gift,
his fatal gift—a ready sensitiveness, a plausible exposition.
He caught the prevailing mood, the collective notion, then
dramatized it. Before he left the pulpit he invariably,
however, convinced himself that what he had said in it
was true, inspired, a revelation—for that moment.

"A Messenger," he announced, thrusting his glass aside
with an impatient gesture as though noticing for the first
time that it was there. "A Messenger," he repeated, the
automatic emphasis in his voice already persuading him that
he believed what he was about to say, "sent among us from
who knows what distant sphere"—he drew himself up and
looked about him—"and for who can guess on what
mysterious and splendid mission."

His eye swept his audience, his hand removed the glass
yet farther lest, it impede free gesture. It was, however,
as Povey noticed, empty now. "We, of course," he went on
impressively, lowering his voice, *"we,* a mere handful in
the world, but alert and watchful, all of us—we know that
some great new teaching is expected"—he threw out another
challenging glance—"but none of us can know whence it
may come nor in what way it shall manifest." His voice
dropped dramatically. "Whether as a thief in the night,
or with a blare of trumpets, none of us can tell. But—we
expect it and are ready. . To *us,* therefore, perhaps, as to
the twelve fishermen of old, may be entrusted the privilege
of accepting it, the work of spreading it among a hostile
and unbelieving world, even perhaps the final sacrifice of
—of suffering for it."

He paused, quickly took in the general effect of his words,
picked up here and there a hint of question, and realized
that he had begun on too exalted a note. Detecting this
breath of caution in the collective mind that was his inspiration, he instantly shifted his key.

"LeVallon," he resumed, instinctively emphasizing the
conviction in his voice so that the change of key might be
less noticeable, "undoubtedly—believes himself to be—some

such divine Messenger. . . ." It was consummate hedging.

The sermon needs no full report. The audience, without realizing it, witnessed what is known as an "inspirational address," where a speaker, naturally gifted with a certain facile eloquence, gathers his inspiration, takes his changing cues as well, from the collective mind that listens to him. Father Collins, quite honestly doubtless, altered his key automatically. He no longer said that LeVallon *was* a Messenger, but that he "believed himself" to be one. Like Balaam, he said things he had not at first thought of saying. He talked for some ten minutes without stopping. He said "all sorts of things," according to the expression of critical doubt, of wonder, of question, of rejection or acceptance, on the particular face he gazed at. At regular intervals he inserted, with considerable effect, his favourite sentence: "A man in his *own* place is the Ruler of his Fate."

He developed his idea that LeVallon "believed himself to be such and such . . ." but declared that the conception had been put into the youth during his life of exile in the mountains—the Society had already acquired this information and extended it—and had *"felt himself into"* the rôle until he had become its actual embodiment.

"He does not think, he does not reason," he explained. "He feels—he *feels with*. Now, to 'feel with' anything is to become it in the end. It is the only way of true knowledge, of course, of true understanding. If I want to understand, say, an Arab, I must *feel with* that Arab to the point—for the moment—of actually becoming him. And this strange youth has spent his time, his best years, mark you—his creative years, *feeling with* the elemental forces of Nature until he has actually becomes—at moments—one with them."

He paused again and stared about him. He saw faces shocked, astonished, startled, but not hostile. He continued rapidly: "There lies the danger. One may get caught, get stuck. Lose the desire to return to one's normal self.

Which means, of course, remaining out of relation with one's environment—mad. Only a man in his *own* place is the ruler of his luck. . . ."

He noticed suddenly the look of disappointment on several faces. He swiftly hedged.

"On the other hand," he went on, making his voice and manner more impressive than before, "it may be—who can say indeed?—it may be that he is in relation with another environment altogether, a much vaster environment, an extended environment of which the rest of humanity is unaware. The privilege of tasting something of an extended environment some of us here already enjoy. What we all know as *human* activities are doubtless but a fragment of life—the conscious phenomena merely of some larger whole of which we are aware in fleeting seconds only—by mood, by hint, by suggestive hauntings, so to speak —by faint shadows of unfamiliar, nameless shape cast across our daily life from some intenser sun we normally cannot see! LeVallon may be, as some of us think and hope, a Messenger to show us the way into a yet farther field of consciousness. . . .

"It is a fine, a noble, an inspiring hope, at any rate," he assured the room. "Unless some such Messenger comes into the world, showing us how to extend our knowledge, we can get no farther; we shall never know more than we know now; we shall only go on multiplying our channels for observing the same old things. . . ."

He closed his little address finally on a word as to what attitude should be adopted to any new experience of amazing and incredible kind. To a Society such as the one he had the honour of belonging to was left the guidance of the perverse and ignorant generations outside of it, "the lethargic and unresponsive majority," as he styled them.

"We must not resist," he declared bravely. "We must accept with confidence, above all without fear." He leaned back in his chair, somewhat exhausted, for the source of his inspiration was evidently weakening. His words came less spontaneously, less easily; he hesitated, sighed, looked from face to face for help he did not find. His glass was empty. "We're here," he concluded lamely, "without being consulted, and we may safely leave to the Powers that brought us here the results of such acceptance."

"Quite so," agreed Povey, sighing audibly. "Denial will get us nowhere." He filled up Father Collins's glass and his own. "I think most of us are ready enough to accept any new experience that comes, and to accept it without fear." He drained his own glass and looked about him. "But the point is—how did LeVallon produce the effect upon us all—the effect he did produce? He may be non-human, or he may be merely mad. He may, as Imson says, come to us by some godless chance from another evolutionary system—of which, mind you, we have as yet no positive knowledge—or he may be a Messenger, as Father Collins suggests, from some divine source, bringing new teaching. But, in the name of Magic, how did he manage it? In other words—what is he?"

For Povey could be very ruthless when he chose. It was this ruthlessness, perhaps, that made him such an efficient secretary. The note of extravagance in his language had possibly another inspiration.

An awkward pause, at any rate, followed his remarks. Father Collins had comforted and blessed the group. Povey introduced cold water rather.

"There's this—and there's that," remarked Miss Milligan, tactfully.

"Those among us," added Miss Lance with sympathy, "who have The Sight, know at least what they have seen. Still, I think we are indebted to Father Collins for—his guidance."

"If we knew exactly what he is," mentioned Mrs. Towzer, referring to LeVallon, "we should know exactly where we are."

They got up to go. There was a fumbling among crowded hat-pegs.

"What is he?" offered Kempster. "He certainly made us all sit up and take notice."

"No mere earthly figure," suggested Imson, "could have produced the effect *he* did. In my poem—it came to me in sleep——"

Father Collins held his glass unsteadily to the light. "A Messenger," he interrupted with authority, "would affect us all differently, remember."

The talk continued in this fashion for a considerable time, while all searched for wraps and coats. The waiter brought the bill amid general confusion, but no one noticed him. All were otherwise engaged. Povey paid it finally, putting it down to the Entertainment Account.

"Remember," he said, as they stood in a group on the restaurant steps, each wondering who would provide a lift home, "remember, we have all got to write out an account of what we saw and heard at the Studio. These reports will be valuable. They will appear in our 'Psychic Bulletin' first. Then I'll have them bound into a volume. And I shall try and get LeVallon to give us a lecture too. Tickets will be extra, of course, but each member can bring a friend. I'll let you all know the date in due course."

CHAPTER XIX

WHILE the Prometheans thus, individually and collectively fermenting, floundered between old and new interpretations of a strange occurrence, in another part of London something was happening, of its kind so real, so interesting, that one and all would eagerly have renounced a favourite shibboleth or pet desire to witness it. Kempster would have eaten a raw beefsteak, Lattimer have agreed to rebirth as a woman, Mrs. Towzer have swallowed whisky neat, and even Toogood have written a signed confession that his "psychometry," was intelligent guesswork.

It is the destiny, however, of such students of the wonderful to receive their data invariably at second or third hand; the data may deal with genuine occurrences, but the student seems never himself present at the time. From books, from reports, from accounts of someone who knew an actual witness, the student generally receives the version he then proceeds to study and elaborate.

In this particular instance, moreover, no version ever reached their ears at all, either at second or third hand, because the only witness of what happened was Edward Fillery, and he mentioned it to no one. Its reality, its interpretation likewise, remained authoritative only for that expert, if unstable, mind that experienced the one and divined the other.

His conversation with Devonham over, and the latter having retired to his room, Fillery paid a last visit to the patient who was now his private care, instead of merely an inmate of the institution that was half a Home and half a Spiritual Clinique. The figure lay sleeping quietly, the lean, muscular body bare to the wind that blew upon it from the open window. Graceful, motionless, both pillow

230

and coverings rejected, "N. H." breathed the calm, regular breath of deepest slumber. The light from the door just touched the face and folded hands, the features wore no expression of any kind, the hair, drawn back from the forehead and temples, almost seemed to shine.

Through the window came the rustle of the tossing branches, but the night air, though damp, was neither raw nor biting, and Fillery did not replace the sheets upon the great sleeping body. He withdrew as softly as he entered. Knowing he would not close an eye that night, he left the house silently and walked out into the deserted streets. . . .

The rain had ceased, but the wet wind rushed in gusts against him, the soft blows and heavy moisture acting as balm to his somewhat tired nerves. As with great elemental hands, the windy darkness stroked him, soothing away the intense excitement he had felt, muting a thousand eager questions. They stroked his brain into a gentler silence gradually. "Don't think, don't think," night whispered all about him, "but feel, feel, feel. What you want to know will come to you by feeling now." He obeyed instinctively. Down the long, empty streets he passed, swinging his stick, tapping the lampposts, noting how steady their light held in the wind, noting the tossing trees in little gardens, noting occasionally rifts of moonlight between the racing clouds, but relinquishing all attempt to think.

He counted the steps between the lamp-posts as he swung along, leaving the kerb at each crossing with his left foot, taking the new one with his right, planting each boot safely in the centre of each paving stone, establishing, in a word, a sort of rhythm as he moved. He did so, however, without being consciously aware of it. He was not aware, indeed, of anything but that he swung along with this pleasant rhythmical stride that rested his body, though the exercise was vigorous.

And the night laid her deep peace upon him as he went. . . .

The streets grew narrower, twisted, turned and ran uphill; the houses became larger, spaced farther apart, less numerous, their gardens bigger, with groups of trees instead of isolated specimens. He emerged suddenly upon the open heath, tasting a newer, sweeter air. The huge city lay below him now, but the rough, shouting wind drowned its distant roar completely. For a time he stood and watched its twinkling lights across the vapours that hung between, then turned towards the little pond. He knew it well. Its waves flew dancing happily. The familiar outline of Jack Straw's Castle loomed beyond. The square enclosure of the anti-aircraft gun rattled with a metallic sound in the wind. . . .

He had been walking for the best part of two hours now, thinking nothing but feeling only, and his surface-consciousness, perhaps, lay still, inactive. The mind was quiescent certainly, his being subdued and lulled by the rhythmic movement which had gained upon his entire system. The sails of his ship hung idly, becalmed above the profound deeps below. It was these deeps, the mysterious and inexhaustible region below the surface, that now began to stir. There stole upon him a dim prophetic sense as of horizons lifting and letting in new light. He glanced about him. The moon was brighter certainly, the flying scud was thinning, though the dawn was still some hours away. But it was not the light of moon or sun or stars he looked for; it was no outer light.

The little waves fell splashing at his feet. He watched them for a long time, keeping very still; his heart, his mind, his nerves, his muscles, all were very still. . . . He became aware that new big powers were alert and close, hovering above the world, feathering the Race like wings of mighty birds. The waters were being troubled. . . .

He turned and walked slowly, but ever with the same pleasant rhythm that was in him, to the pine trees, where he paused a minute, listening to the branches shaking and singing, then retraced his steps along the ridge, every yard of which, though blurred in darkness, he knew and recog-

nized. Below, on his left lay London, on his right stretched
the familiar country, though now invisible, past Hendon
with its Welsh Harp, Wembley, and on towards Harrow,
whose church steeple would catch the sunrise before very
long. He reached the little pond again and heard its small
waves rushing and tumbling in the south-west wind. He
stood and watched them, listening to their musical wash and
gurgle.

The waters, yes, were being troubled. . . . Despite the
buffeting wind, the world lay even stiller now about him;
no single human being had he seen; even stiller than before,
too, lay heart and mind within him; the latter held no single
picture. He was aware, yes, of horizons lifting, of great
powers alert and close; the interior light increased. He
felt, but he did not think. Into the empty chamber of his
being, swept and garnished, flashed suddenly, then, as in
picture form, the memory of "N. H." All that he knew
about him came at once: Paul's notes and journey, the London scenes and talks, his own observations, deductions,
questionings, his dreams, and fears and yearnings, his hope
and wonder—all came in a clapping instant, complete and
simultaneous. Into his opened subconscious being floated
the power and the presence of that bright messenger who
brought glad tidings to his life.

"N. H." stood beside him, whispering with lips that were
the darkness, and with words that were the wind. It was
the power and presence of "N. H." that lifted the horizon
and let in light. His body lay sleeping miles away in that
bed against an open window. This was his real presence.
Without words, as without thought, understanding came.
The appeal of "N. H." was direct to the subliminal mind;
it was the hidden nine-tenths he stimulated; hence came the
intensification of consciousness in all who had to do with
him. And it operated now. Fillery was aware of defying
time and space, as though there were no limits to his being.
Faith lights fires. . . . Perception wandered down those
dusky by-ways *behind* the mind that lead through trackless

depths where the massed heritage of the world-soul, lit sometimes by a flashing light, reveal incredible, incalculable things. One of those flashes came now. Through the fissures, as it were, of his unstable being rose the marvellous, uncanny gleam. His eyes were opened and he saw.

The label, he realized, was incorrect, inadequate—"N. H." was a misnomer; more than human, both different to and greater than, came nearer to the truth. A being from other conditions certainly, belonging to another order; an order whose work was unremitting service rendered with joy and faithfulness; a hierarchy whose service included the entire universe, the stars and suns and nebulæ, earth with her frail humanity but an insignificant fraction of it all. . . .

He came, of course, from that central sea of energy whence all life, pushing irresistibly outwards into form, first arises. Like human beings, he came thence undoubtedly, but more directly than they, in more intimate relations, therefore, with the elemental powers that build up form and shape the destinies of matter. One only of a mighty host of varying degrees and powers, his services lay interwoven with the very heart and processes of Nature herself. The energies of heat and air, essentials of all life everywhere, were his handmaidens; he worked with fire and wind; in the forms he helped to build he set enthusiasm and energy aglow. . . .

From stars and fire-mist he came now into humanity, using the limited instrument of a human mechanism, a mechanism he must learn to master without breaking it. A human brain and nerves confined him. He could deal with essences only, those essential, buried, semi-elemental powers that lie ever waiting below the threshold of all human consciousness, linking men, did they but know it, direct with the sea of universal life which is inexhaustible, independent of space and time. The fraction of his nature which had manifested as a transient surface-personality—LeVallon— was gone for ever, merged in the real self below.

His origin was already forgotten; no memory of it lay in his present brain; he must suffer training, education, and he turned instinctively to those whose ideal, like his own, was one of impersonal service. To a woman he turned, and to a man. His recognition, guided by Nature, was sure and accurate. It must take time and patience, sympathy and love, faith, belief and trust, and the labour must be borne by one man chiefly—by Fillery, into whose life had come this strange bright messenger carrying glad tidings . . . to prove at last that man was greater than he knew, that the hope for Humanity, for the deteriorating Race, for crumbling Civilization, lay in drawing out into full practical consciousness the divine powers concealed below the threshold of every single man and woman. . . .

But how, in what practical manner, what instrument could they use? The human mechanism, the brain, the mind, afforded inadequate means of manifestation; new wines into old skins meant disaster; knowledge, power beyond the experience of the Race needed a better instrument than the one the Race had painfully evolved for present uses. New powers of unknown kinds, as already in those rare cases when the supernormal forces emerged, could only strain the machinery and cause disorder. A new order of consciousness required another, a different equipment. And the idea flashed into him, as in the Studio when he watched "N. H." and the girl—Father Collins had divined its possibility as well—the idea of a group consciousness, a collective group-soul. What a single individual might not be able to resist at first without disaster, many—a group in harmony—two or three gathered together in unison—these might provide the way, the means, the instrument—the body.

"The personal merged in the impersonal," he exclaimed to the night about him, already aware that words, expression, failed even at this early stage of understanding. "Beauty, Art! Where words, form, colour end, we shall construct, while yet using these as far as they go, a new vehicle, a new——"

"Good evenin'," said a gruff voice. "Good evenin', sir," it added more respectfully, after a second's inspection. "Turned out quite fine after the storm."

Aware of the policeman suddenly, Fillery started and turned round abruptly. Evidently he had uttered his thoughts aloud, probably had cried and shouted them. He could think of nothing in the world to say.

"It was a terrible storm. I hardly ever see the likes of it." The man was looking at him still with doubtful curiosity.

"Extraordinary, yes." Dr. Fillery managed to find a few natural words. It was an early hour in the morning to be out, and his position by the pond, he now realized, might have suggested an undesirable intention. "It made sleep impossible, and I came out to—to take a walk. I'm a doctor, Dr. Fillery—the Fillery Home."

"Yes, sir," said the man, apparently satisfied. He looked at the sky. "All blown away again," he remarked, "and the moon that nice and bright——"

Fillery offered something in reply, then moved away. The moon, he noticed, was indeed nice and bright now; the heavy lower vapours all had vanished, and thin cirrus clouds at a great height moved slowly before an upper wind; the stars shone clearly, and a faint line of colour gave a hint of dawn not far away.

He glanced at his watch. It was nearly half-past four.

"It's impossible, impossible," he thought to himself, the pictures he had been seeing still hanging before his eyes. "It was all feeling—merely feeling. My blood, my heritage asserting themselves upon an over-tired system! Too much repression evidently. I must find an outlet. My Caucasian Valley again!"

He walked rapidly. His mind began to work, and thinking made an effort to replace feeling. He watched himself. His everyday surface-consciousness partially resumed its sway. The policeman, of course, had interrupted the flow and inrush of another state just at the moment when a flash of direct knowledge was about to blaze. It concerned "N. H.," his new patient. In another moment he would have known exactly what and who he was, whence he came, the purpose and the powers that attended him. The policeman—and inner laughter ran through him at this juxtaposition of the practical and the transcendental—had interfered with an interesting expansion of his being. An extension of consciousness, perhaps a touch of cosmic consciousness, was on the way. The first faint quiver of its coming, magical with wondrous joy, had touched him. Its cause, its origin, he knew not, yet he could trace both to the effect produced upon him by "N. H." Of that he was sure. This effect his reasoning mind, with busy analysis and criticism, had hitherto partially suppressed, even at its first manifestation in Charing Cross Station. To-night, criticism silent and analysis inactive, it had found an outlet. his own deep inner stillness had been its opportunity. Then came the practical, honest, simple policeman, the censor, who received so much a week to keep people in the way they ought to follow, the safe, broad way. . . .

He smiled, as he walked rapidly along the deserted streets. He knew so well the method and process of these abnormal states in others. As he swung along, not tired now, but rested, rather, and invigorated, the rhythm of motion established itself again. "N. H." a Nature Spirit! A Nature Being! Another order of life entering humanity for the first time, that humanity for whose welfare it—or was it he?—had worked, with hosts of similar beings, during incalculable ages. . . .

He smiled, remembering the policeman again. There was always a policeman, or a censor. Oh, the exits beyond safe normal states of being, the exits into extended fields of consciousness, into an outer life which the majority, led by the best minds of the day, deny with an oath—these were well guarded! His smile, as he thought of it, ran from his lips and settled in the eyes, lingering a moment there before it died away. . . .

How quiet, yet unfamiliar, the suburb of the huge city lay about him in pale half-light. The Studio scene, how distant it seemed now in space and time; it had happened weeks ago in another city somewhere. Devonham, his cautious, experienced assistant, how far away! He belonged to another age. The Prometheans were part of a dream in childhood, a dream of pantomime or harlequinade whose extravagance yet conveyed symbolic meaning. Two figures alone retained a reality that refused to be dismissed—a mysterious, enigmatic youth, a radiant girl—with perhaps a third—a broken priest. . . .

The rhythm, meanwhile, gained upon him, and, as it did so, thinking once more withdrew and feeling stole back softly. His being became more harmonized, more one with itself, more open to inspiration. . . . "N. H.," whose work was service, service everywhere, not merely in that tiny corner of the universe called Humanity. . . . "N. H.," who could neither age nor die. . . . What was the hidden link that bound them? Had they not served and played together in some lost Caucasian valley, leaped with the sun's hot fire, flown in the winds of dawn . . . sung, laughed and danced at their service, with a radiant sylph-like girl who had at last enticed them into the confinement of a limited human form? . . . Did not that valley symbolize, indeed, another state of existence, another order of consciousness altogether that lay beyond any known present experience or description . . .?

The dawn, meanwhile, grew nearer and a pallid light ran down the dreadful streets. . . . He reached at length the foot of the hill upon whose shoulder his own house stood. The familiar sights stirred more familiar currents of feeling, and these in turn sought words. . . .

The crowding houses, with their tight-shut windows, followed and pressed after as he climbed. They swarmed behind him. How choked and airless it all was. He thought of the heavy-footed routine of the thousands who occupied these pretentious buildings. Here lived a section of the greatest city on the planet, almost a separate little town, with marked characteristics, atmosphere, tastes and habits. How many, he wondered, behind those walls knew yearning, belief, imagination beyond the ruck and routine of familiar narrow thought? Rows upon rows, with their stunted, manufactured trees, hideous conservatories, bulging porches, ornamented windows—his wings beat against them all with the burning desire to set their inmates free. They caged themselves in deliberately. A few thousand years ago these people lived in mud huts, before that in caves, before that again in trees. Now they were "civilized." They dwelt in these cages. Oh, that he might tear away the thick dead bricks, and let in light and dew and stars, and the brave, free winds of heaven! Waken the deeper powers they carried unwittingly about with them through all their tedious sufferings! Teach them that they were greater than they knew!

The yearning was deep and true in him, as the houses followed and tried to bar his way. Many of the occupiers, he knew, would welcome help, would gaze with happy, astonished eyes at the wonder of their own greater selves set free. Not all, of course, were wingless. Yet the majority, he felt, were otherwise. They peered at him from behind thick curtains, hostile, sceptical, contented with their lot, averse to change. Mode, custom, habit chained them to the floor. He was aware of a collective obstinate grin of smug complacency, of dull resistance. Though a part of the community, of the race, of the world, of the universe itself, they denied their mighty brotherhood, and clung tenaciously to their idea of living apart, cut off and separate. They belonged to leagues, societies, clubs and circles, but the bigger oneness of the race they did not know. Of greater powers in themselves they had no faintest inkling. At the first sign of these, they would shuffle, sneer and turn away, grow frightened even.

The yearning to show them a bigger field of consciousness, to help them towards a realization of their buried powers, to let them out of their separate cages, beat through his being with a passionate sincerity. . . . In a hundred thousand years perhaps! Perhaps in a million! He knew the slow gait that Nature loved. The trend of an Age is not to be stemmed by one man, nor by twelve, who see over the horizon. The futility of trying pained him. Yet, if no one ever tried! Oh, for a few swift strokes of awful sacrifice—then freedom!

The words came back to him, and with them, from the same source, came others: "I sit and I weave. . . . I sit and I weave." . . . Whose, then, was this divine, eternal patience? . . .

There could be, it seemed, no hurried growth, no instant escape, no sudden leap to heaven. Slowly, slowly, the Ages turned the wheel. "Nor can other beings help," he remembered; "they can only tell what their own part is." . . . And as his clear mind saw the present Civilization like all its wonderful predecessors, tottering before his very eyes, threatening in its collapse, the extinction of knowledge so slowly, painfully, laboriously acquired, the deep heart in him rose as on wings of wind and fire, questing the stars above. There was this strange clash in him, as though two great divisions in his being struggled. A way of escape seemed just within his reach, only a little beyond the horizon of his actual knowledge. It fluttered marvellously; golden, alight, inviting. Its coming glory brushed his insight. It was simple, it was divine. There seemed a faint knocking against the doors of his mental and spiritual understanding. . . .

" 'N. H.'!" he cried, "Bright Messenger!"

He paused a moment and stood still. A new sound lay suddenly in the night. It came, apparently, from far away, almost from the air above him. He listened. No, after all it was only steps. They came nearer. A pedestrian, muffled to the ears, went past, and the steps died away on the resounding pavement round the corner. Yet the sound continued, and was not the echo of the steps just gone. It was, moreover, he now felt convinced, in the air above him. It was continuous. It reminded him of the musical droning hum that a big bell leaves behind it, while a suggestion of rhythm, almost of melody, ran faintly through it too.

Somebody's lines—was it Shelley's?—ran faintly in his mind, yet it was not his mind now that surged and rose to the new great rhythm:

> "'Tis the deep music of the rolling world
>   Kindling within the strings of the waved air
>   Æolian modulations. . . .
>   Clear, icy, keen awakening tones
>   That pierce the sense
>   And live within the soul. . . ."

He listened. It was a simple, natural, happy sound— simple as running water, natural as wind, happy as the song of birds. . . .

CHAPTER XX

H E became, again, vividly aware of the power and presence of "N. H."

He was not far from his house now on the shoulder of the hill. He turned his eyes upwards, where the three-quarter moon sailed above transparent cirrus clouds that scarcely dimmed her light. Like dappled sands of silver, they sifted her soft shining, moving slowly across the heavens before an upper wind. The sound continued.

For a moment or two, in the pale light of dawn, he watched and listened, then lowered his gaze, caught his breath sharply, and stood stock still. He stared in front of him. Next, turning slowly, he stared right and left. He stared behind as well.

Yes, it was true. The lines and rows of crowding houses trembled, disappeared. The heavy buildings dissolved before his very eyes. The solid walls and roofs were gone, the chimneys, railings, doors and porches vanished. There were no more conservatories. There were no lamp-posts. The streets themselves had melted. He gazed in amazement and delight. The entire hill lay bare and open to the sky.

Across the rising upland swept a keen fresh morning wind. Yet bare they were not, this rising upland and this hill. As far as he could see, the landscape flowed waist-deep in flowers, whose fragrance lay upon the air; dew trembled, shimmering on a million petals of blue and gold, of orange, purple, violet; the very atmosphere seemed painted. Flowering trees, both singly and in groves, waved in the breeze, birds sang in chorus, there was a murmur of streams and falling waters. Yet that other sound rose too, rose from the entire hill and all upon it, a continuous

gentle rhythm, as though, he felt, the actual scenery poured
forth its being in spontaneous, natural expression of sound
as well as of form and colour. It was the simplest, happiest
music he had ever heard.

Unable to deal with the rapture of delight that swept
upon him, he stood stock still among the blossoms to his
waist. Eyes, ears and nostrils were inadequate to report
a beauty which, simple though it was, overbore nerves and
senses accustomed to a lesser scale. Horizons indeed had
lifted, the joy and confidence of fuller life poured in. His
own being grew immense, stretched, widened, deepened, till
it seemed to include all space. He was everywhere, or
rather everything was happening somewhere in him all at
once. . . . In place of the heavy suburb lay this garden
of primal beauty, while yet, in a sense, the suburb itself
remained as well. Only—it had flowered . . . revealing the
subconscious soul the bricks and pavements hid. . . . Its
potential self had blossomed into loveliness and wonder.

The sound drew nearer. He was aware of movement.
Figures were approaching; they were coming in his direction, coming towards him over the crest of the hill, nearer
and nearer. Concealed by the forest of tall flowers, he
watched them come. Yet as Presences he perceived them,
rather than as figures, already borrowing power from them,
as sails borrow from a rising wind. His consciousness expanded marvellously to let them in.

Their stature was conveyed to him, chiefly, at first, by
the fact that these flowers, though rising to his own waist,
did not cover the feet of them, yet that the flowers in the
immediate line of their advance still swayed and nodded,
as though no weight had lain upon their brilliance. The
footsteps were of wind, the figures light as air; they shone;
their radiant presences lit the acres. Their own atmosphere,
too, came with them, as though the landscape moved and
travelled with and in their being, as though the flowers, the
natural beauty, emanated from them. The landscape *was*
their atmosphere. They created, brought it with them. It

seemed that they "expressed" the landscape and "were" the scenery, with all its multitudinous forms.

They approached with a great and easy speed that was not measurable. Over the crest of the living, sunlit hill they poured, with their bulk, their speed, their majesty, their sweet brimming joy. Fillery stood motionless watching them, his own joy touched with awed confusion, till wonder and worship mastered the final trace of fear.

Though he perceived these figures first as they topped the skyline, he was aware that great space also stretched behind them, and that this immense perspective was in some way appropriate to their appearance. Born of a greater space than his "mind" could understand, they flowed towards him across that windy crest and at the same time from infinitely far beyond it. Above the continuous humming sound, he heard their music too, faint but mighty, filling the air with deep vibrations that seemed the natural expression of their joyful beings. Each figure was a chord, yet all combining in a single harmony that had volume without loudness. It seemed to him that their sound and colour and movement wove a new pattern upon space, a new outline, form or growth, perhaps a flower, a tree, perhaps a planet. . . . They were creative. They expressed themselves naturally in a million forms.

He heard, he saw. He knew no other words to use. But the "hearing" was, rather, some kind of intimate possession so that his whole being filled and overbrimmed; and the "sight" was greater than the customary little irritation of the optic nerve—it involved another term of space. He could describe the sight more readily than the hearing. The apparent contradiction of distance and proximity, of vast size yet intimacy, made him tremble in his hiding-place.

His "sight," at any rate, perceived the approaching figures all round, all over, all at once, as they poured like a wave across the hill from far beyond its visible crest. For into this space below the horizon he saw as well, though, normally speaking, it was out of sight. Nor did he see one side only; he saw the backs of the towering forms as easily as the portion facing him; he saw behind them. It was not as with ordinary objects refracting light, the back and underneath and further edges invisible. All sides were visible at once. The space beyond, moreover, whence the mighty outlines issued, was of such immensity that he could think only of interstellar regions. Not to the little planet, then, did these magnificent shapes belong. They were of the Universe. The symbol of his valley, he knew suddenly, belonged here too.

Silent with wonder, motionless with worship, he watched the singing flood of what he felt to be immense, non-human nature-life pour past him. The procession lasted for hours, yet was over in a minute's flash. All categories his mind knew hitherto were useless. The faces, in their power, their majesty, the splendour even of their extent, were both appalling, yet infinitely tender. They were filled with stars, blue distance, flowers, spirals of fire, space and air, interwoven too, with shining geometrical designs whose intricate patterns merged in a central harmony. They brought their own winds with them.

Yet of features precisely, he was not aware. Each face was, rather, an immense expression, but an expression that was permanent and could not change. These were immutable, eternal faces. He borrowed from human terms the only words that offered, while aware that he falsely introduced the personal into that which was essentially impersonal.

There stole over him a strange certainty that what he worshipped was the grandeur of joyful service working through unalterable law—the great compassion of some untiring service that was deathless. . . . He stood *within* the Universe, face to face with its elemental builders, guardians, its constructive artizans, the impersonal angelic powers . . . the region, the state, he now felt convinced, to which "N. H." belonged, and whence, by some inexplicable chance, he had come to occupy a human body. . . . And the sounds

—the flash came to him with lightning conviction—were those essential rhythms which are the kernels of all visible, manifested forms. . . .

He was not aware that he was moving, that he had left the spot where he had stood—so long, yet for a single second only—and had now reached the corner of a street again. The flowers were gone, and the trees and groves gone with them; no waters rippled past; there was no shining hill. The moon, the stars, the breaking dawn remained, but he saw windows, walls and villas once again, while his feet echoed on dead stone pavements. . . .

Yet the figures had not wholly gone. Before a house, where he now paused a moment, the towering, flowing outlines were still faintly visible. Their singing still audible, their shapes still gently luminous, they stood grouped about an open window of the second story. In the front garden a big plane tree stirred its leafless branches; the tree and figures interpenetrated. Slowly then, the outlines grew dim and shadowy, indistinguishable almost from the objects in the twilight near them. Chimneys, walls and roofs stole in upon the great shapes with foreign, grosser details that obscured their harmony, confused their proportion, as with two sets of values. The eye refused to focus both at once. A roof, a chimney obtruded, while sight struggled, fluttered, then ended in confusion. The figures faded and melted out. They merged with the tree, the reddening sky, the murky air close to the house which a street lamp made visible. Suddenly they were lost—they were no longer there.

But the rhythmical sound, though fainter, still continued —and Fillery looked up.

It was a sound, he realized in a flash, evocative and summoning. Type called to type, brother to brother, across the universe. The house before him was his own, and the open window through which the music issued was the bedroom of "N. H."

He stood transfixed. Both sides of his complex nature operated simultaneously. His mind worked more clearly —the entire history of the "case" in that upstairs room passed through it: he was a doctor. But his speculative, emotional aspect, the dreamer in him, so greatly daring, all that poetic, transcendental, half-mystical part which classed him, he well knew, with the unstable; all this, long and dangerously repressed, worked with opposite, if equal pressure. From the subconscious rose violent hands as of wind and fire, lovely, fashioning, divine, tearing away the lid of the reasoning surface-consciousness that confined, confused them.

To disentangle, to define these separate functions, were a difficult problem even for the most competent psychiatrist. Creative imaginative powers, hitherto merely fumbling, half denied as well, now stretched their wings and soared. With them came a blinding clarity of sight that enabled him to focus a vast field of detail with extraordinary rapidity. Horizons had lifted, perspective deepened and lit up. In a few brief seconds, before his front door opened, a hundred details flashed towards a focus and shone concentrated:

The Vision, of course—the Figures had now melted into the night—had no objective reality. Suppressed passion had created them, forbidden yearnings had passed the Censor and dramatized a dream, set aside yet never explained, that heredity was responsible for. Both were born of his lost radiant valley. His Note Books held a thousand similar cases. . . .

But the speculative dreamer flashed coloured lights against this common white. The prism blazed. From the interstellar spaces came these radiant figures, from Sirius, immense and splendid sun, from Aldebaran among the happy Hyades, from awful Betelgeuse, whose volume fills a Martian orbit. Their dazzling, giant grandeur was of stellar origin. Yet, equally, they came from the dreadful back gardens of those sordid houses. Nature was Nature everywhere, in the nebulæ as in the stifled plane tree of a city court. That he saw them as "figures" was but his own private, personal interpretation of a prophecy the whole Universe announced. They were not figures necessarily; they were Powers. And "N. H." was of their kind.

He suddenly remembered the small, troubled earth whereon he lived—a neglected corner of the universe that was in distress and cried frantically for help. . . . Alcyone caught it in her golden arms perhaps; Sirius thundered against its little ears. . . .

He found his latchkey and fumblingly inserted it, but, even while he did so, the state of the planet at the moment poured into his mind with swift, concentrated detail; he remembered the wireless excitement of the instant—and smiled. Not that way would it come. The new order was of a spiritual kind. It would steal into men's hearts, not splutter along the waves of ether, as the "dead" are said to splutter to the "living." The great impulse, the mighty invitation Nature sent out to return to simple, natural life, would come, without "phenomena" from *within*. . . . He remembered Relativity—that space is local, space and time not separate entities. He understood. He had just experienced it. Another, a fourth dimension! Space as a whole was annihilated! He smiled.

His latchkey turned.

The transmutation of metals flashed past him—all substance one. His latchkey was upside down. He turned it round and reinserted it, and the results of advanced psychology rushed at him, as though the sun rushed over the horizon of some Eastern clime, covering all with the light of a new, fair dawn.

In a few seconds this accumulation of recent knowledge and discovery flooded his state of singular receptiveness—as thinker and as poet. The Age was crumbling, civilization passing like its predecessors. The little planet lay certainly in distress. No true help lay within it; its reservoirs were empty. No adequate constructive men or powers were anywhere in sight. It was exhausted, dying. Unless new help,

powers from a new, an inexhaustible source, came quickly
. . . a new vehicle for their expression. . . .

And wonder took him by the throat . . . as the key
turned in the lock with its familiar grating sound, and the
door, without actual pressure on his part, swung open.

Paul Devonham, a look of bright terror in his eyes, stood
on the threshold.

The expression, not only of the face but of the whole
person, he had seen once only in another human countenance
—a climber, who had slipped by his very side and dropped
backward into empty space. The look of helpless bewilderment as hands and feet lost final touch with solidity, the
air of terrible yet childlike amazement with which he began
his descent of a thousand feet through a gulf of air—the
shock marked the face in a single second with what he now
saw in his colleague's eyes. Only, with Devonham—Fillery
felt sure of his diagnosis—the lost hold was mental.

His outward control, however, was admirable. Devonham's voice, apart from a certain tenseness in it, was quiet
enough: "I've been telephoning everywhere. . . . There's
been a—a crisis——"

"Violence?"

But the other shook his head. "It's all beyond me quite,"
he said, with a wry smile. "The first outbreak was nothing
—nothing compared to this." The continuous sound of
humming which filled the hall, making the air vibrate oddly,
grew louder. Devonham seized his friend's arm.

"Listen!" he whispered. "You hear that?"

"I heard it outside in the street," Fillery said. "What
is it?"

Devonham glared at him. "God knows," he said, "I don't.
He's been doing it, on and off, for a couple of hours. It
began the moment you left, it seems. They're all about
him—these vibrations, I mean. He does it with his whole
body somehow. And"—he hesitated—"there's meaning in

it of some kind. Results, I mean," he jerked out with an effort.

"Visible?" came the gentle question.

Devonham started. "How did you know?" There was a thrust of intense curiosity in the eyes.

"I've had a similar experience myself, Paul. You opened the front door in the middle of it. The figures——"

"You saw figures?" Devonham looked thunderstruck. In his heart was obviously a touch of panic.

As the two men stood gazing into each other's eyes a moment silently, the sound about them increased again, rising and falling, its great separate rhythmical waves almost distinguishable. In Fillery's mind rose patterns, outlines, forms of flowers, spirals, circles. . . .

"He knows you're in the house," said Devonham in a curious voice, relieved apparently no answer came to his question. "Better come upstairs at once and see him." But he did not turn to lead the way. "That's not auditory hallucination, Edward, whatever else it is!" He was still clinging to the rock, but the rock was crumbling beneath his desperate touch. Space yawned below him.

"Visual," suggested Fillery, as though he held out a feeble hand to the man whose whole weight already hung unsupported before the plunge. His friend spoke no word; but his expression made words unnecessary: "We must face the facts," it said plainly, "wherever these may lead. No shirking, no prejudice of mine or yours must interfere. There must be no faltering now."

So plainly was this passion for truth and knowledge legible in the expression of the shocked but honest mind, that Fillery felt compassion overpower the first attitude of privacy he had meant to take. This time he must share. The honesty of the other won his confidence too fully for him to hold back anything. There was no doubt in his mind that he read his colleague's state aright.

"A moment, Paul," he said in a low voice, "before we go upstairs," and he put his hand out, oddly enough meeting

Devonham's hand already stretched to meet it. He drew him aside into a corner of the hall, while the waves of sound surged round and over them like a sea. "Let me first tell you," he went on, his voice trembling slightly, "my own experience." It seemed to him that any moment he must see the birth of a new form, an outline, a "body" dance across before his very eyes.

"Neither auditory nor visual," murmured Devonham, burning to hear what was coming, yet at the same time shrinking from it by the laws of his personality. "Hallucination of any kind, there is absolutely none. There's nothing transferred from your mind to his. This thing is real—original."

Fillery tightened his grip a second on the hand he held.

"Paul," he said gravely, yet unable to hide the joy of recent ecstasy in his eyes, "it is also—new!"

The low syllables seemed borne away and lifted beyond their reach by an immense vibration that swept softly past them. And so actual was this invisible wave that behind it lay the trough, the ebb, that awaits, as in the sea, the next advancing crest. Into this ebb, as it were, both men dropped simultaneously the same significant syllables: their lips uttered together:

"N. H." The wave of sound seemed to take their voices and increase them. It was the older man who added: "Coming into full possession."

The two stood waiting, listening, their heads turned sideways, their bodies motionless, while the soft rhythmical uproar rose and fell about them. No sign escaped them for some minutes; no words, it seemed, occurred to either of them.

Through the transom over the front door stole the grey light of the late autumn dawn; the hall furniture was visible, chairs, hat-rack, wooden chests that held the motor rugs. A china bowl filled with visiting cards gleamed white beside it. Soon the milkman, uttering his comic earthly cry, would clatter down the area staircase, and the servants would be up. As yet, however, but for the big soft sound, the house was perfectly still. This part of it, almost a separate wing, was completely cut off from the main building. No one had been disturbed.

Fillery moved his head and looked at his companion. The expression of both face and figure arrested him. He had taken off his dinner jacket, and the old loose golfing coat he wore hung askew; he had one hand in a pocket of it, the other thrust deep into his trousers. His glasses hung down across his crumpled shirt-front, his black tie made an untidy cross. He looked, thought Fillery, whose sense of the ludicrous became always specially alert in his gravest moments, like an unhappy curate who had presided over some strenuous and worrying social gathering in the local town hall. Only one detail denied this picture—the expression of something mysterious and awed in the sheet-white face. He was listening with sharp dislike yet eager interest. His repugnance betrayed itself in the tightened lips, the set of the angular shoulders; the panic was written in the glistening eyes. There were things in his face he could never, never tell. The struggle in him was natural to his type of mind: he had experienced something himself, and a personal experience opens new vistas in sympathy and understanding. But—the experience ran contrary to every tenet of theory and practice he had ever known. The moment of new birth was painful. This was his colleague's diagnosis.

Fillery then suddenly realized that the gulf between them was without a bridge. To tell his own experience became at once utterly impossible. He saw this clearly. He could not speak of it to his assistant. It was, after all, incommunicable. The bridge of terms, language, feeling, did not exist between them. And, again, up flashed for a second his sense of the comic, this time in an odd touch of memory —Povey's favourite sentence: "Never argue with the once-born!" Only to older souls was expression possible.

For the first time then his diagnosis wavered oddly. Why,

for instance, did Paul persist in that curious, watchful
stare . . . ?

Devonham, conscious of his chief's eyes and mind upon
him, looked up. Somewhere in his expression was a glare,
but nothing revealed his state of mind better than the fact
that he stupidly contradicted himself:

"You're putting all this into him, Edward," a touch
of anger, perhaps of fear, in the intense whispering voice.
"The hysteria of the studio upset him, of course. If you'd
left him alone, as you promised, he'd have always stayed
LeVallon. He'd be cured by now." Then, as Fillery made
no reply or comment, he added, but this time only the
anxiety of the doctor in his tone: "Hadn't you better go
up to him at once? He's your patient, not mine, remember!"

The other took his arm. "Not yet," he said quietly.
"He's best alone for the moment." He smiled, and it was
the smile that invariably won him the confidence of even
the most obstinate and difficult patient. He was completely
master of himself again. "Besides, Paul," he went on
gently. "I want to hear what you have to tell me. Some
of it—if not all. I want your Report. It is of value. I
must have that first, you know."

They sat on the bottom stair together, while Devonham
told briefly what had happened. He was glad to tell it,
too. It was a relief to become the mere accurate observer
again.

"I can summarize it for you in two words," he said:
"light and sound. The sound, at first, seemed wind—wind
rising, wind outside. With the light, was perceptible heat.
The two seemed correlated. When the sound increased, the
heat increased too. Then the sound became methodical,
rhythmical—it became almost musical. As it did so the
light became coloured. Both"—he looked across at the
ghostly hat-rack in the hall—"were produced—by him."

"Items, please, Paul. I want an itemized account."

Devonham fumbled in the big pockets of his coat and
eventually lit a cigarette, though he did not in the least

want to smoke. That watchful, penetrating stare persisted, none the less. Amid the anxiety were items of carelessness that almost seemed assumed.

"Mrs. Soames sent Nurse Robbins to fetch me," he resumed, his voice harshly, as it seemed, cutting across the waves of pleasant sound that poured down the empty stairs behind them and filled the hall with resonant vibrations. "I went in, turned them both out, and closed the door. The room was filled with a soft, white light, rather pale in tint, that seemed to emanate from nowhere. I could trace it to no source. It was equally diffused, I mean, yet a kind of wave-like vibration ran through it in faint curves and circles. There was a sound, a sound like wind. A wind was in the room, moaning and sighing inside the walls—a perfectly natural and ordinary sound, if it had been outside. The light moved and quivered. It lay in sheets. Its movement, I noticed, was in direct relation to the wind: the louder the volume of sound, the greater the movement of the air—the brighter became the light, and vice versa. I could not take notes at the actual moment, but my memory"—a slight grimace by way of a smile indicated that forgetting was impossible—"is accurate, as you know."

Fillery did not interrupt, either by word or gesture.

"The increase of light was accompanied by colour, and the increase of sound led into a measure—not actual bars, and never melody, but a distinct measure that involved rhythm. It was musical, as I said. The colour—I'm coming to that—then took on a very faint tinge of gold or orange, a little red in it sometimes, flame colour almost. The air was luminous—it was radiant. At one time I half expected to see fire. For there was heat as well. Not an unpleasant heat, but a comforting, stimulating, agreeable heat like—I was going to say, like the heat of a bright coal fire on a winter's day, but I think the better term is sunlight. I had an impression this heat must burst presently into actual flame. It never did so. The sheets of coloured light rose and fell with the volume of the sound. There were curves and waves and rising columns like spirals, but anything approaching a definite outline, form, or shape"—he broke off for a second—"figures," he announced abruptly, almost challengingly, staring at the white china bowl in front of him, "I could *not* swear to."

He turned suddenly and stared at his chief with an expression half of question, half of challenge; then seemed to change his mind, shrugging his shoulders a very little. But Fillery made no sign. He did not answer. He laid one hand, however, upon the banisters, as though preliminary to getting to his feet. The sound about them had been gradually growing less, the vibrations were smaller, its waves perceptibly decreasing.

Devonham finished his account in a lower voice, speaking rapidly, as though the words burnt his tongue:

"The sound, I had already discovered, issued from himself. He was lying on his back, the eyes wide open, the expression peaceful, even happy. The lips were closed. He was humming, continuously humming. Yet the sound came in some way I cannot describe, and could not examine or ascertain, from his whole body. I detected no vibration of the body. It lay half naked, only a corner of the sheet upon it. It lay quite still. The cause of the light and heat, the cause of the movement of air I have called wind— I could not ascertain. They came *through* him, as it were." A slight shiver ran across his body, noticed by his companion, but eliciting no comment from him. "I—I took his pulse," concluded Devonham, sinking his voice now to a whisper, though a very clear one; "it was very rapid and extraordinarily strong. He seemed entirely unconscious of my presence. I also"—again the faint shiver was perceptible —"felt his heart. It was—I have never felt such perfect action, such power—it was beating like an engine, like an engine. And the sense of vitality, of life in the room everywhere was—electrical. I could have sworn it was packed to the walls with—with others." Devonham never ceased to watch his companion keenly while he spoke.

Fillery then put his first question.

"And the effect upon yourself?" he asked quietly. "I

mean—any emotional disturbance? Anything, for instance, like what you *saw* in the Jura forests?" He did not look at his colleague; he stood up; the sound about them had now ceased almost entirely and only faint, dying fragments of it reached them. "Roughly speaking," he added, making a half movement to go upstairs. He understood the inner struggle going on; he wished to make it easy for him. For the complete account he did not press him.

Devonham rose too; he walked over to the china bowl, took up a card, read it and let it fall again. The sun was over the horizon now, and a pallid light showed objects clearly. It showed the whiteness of the thin, tired face. He turned and walked slowly back across the hall. The first cart went clattering noisily down the street. At the same moment a final sound from the room upstairs came floating down into the chill early air.

"My interest, of course," began Devonham, his hands in his pockets, his body rigid, as he looked up into his companion's eyes, "was very concentrated, my mind intensely active." He paused, then added cautiously: "I may confess, however—I must admit, that is, a certain increase of—of—well, a general sense of well-being, let me call it. The heat, you see. A feeling of peace, if you like it better—beyond the—fear," he blurted out finally, changing his hands from his coat to his trouser pockets, as though the new position protected him better from attack. "Also—I somehow expected—any moment—to see outlines, forms, something new!" He stared frankly into the eyes of the man who, from the step above him, returned his gaze with equal frankness. "And *you*—Edward?" he asked with great suddenness.

"Joy? Could you describe it as joy?" His companion ignored the reference to new forms. He also ignored the sudden question. "Any increase of——?"

"Vitality, you want to say. The word joy is meaningless, as you know."

"An intensification of consciousness in any way?"

But Devonham had reached his limit of possible confession. He did not reply for a moment. He took a step forward and stood beside Fillery on the stairs. His manner had abruptly changed. It was as though he had come to a conclusion suddenly. His reply, when it came, was no reply at all:

"Heat and light are favourable, of course, to life," he remarked. "You remember Joaquin Mueller: 'the optic nerve, under the action of light, acts as a stimulus to the organs of the imagination and fancy.'"

Fillery smiled as he took his arm and they went quietly upstairs together. The quoting was a sign of returning confidence. He said something to himself about the absence of light, but so low it was under his breath almost, and even if his companion heard it, he made no comment: "There was no moon at all to-night till well past three, and even then her light was of the faintest. . . ."

No sound was now audible. They entered a room that was filled with silence and with peace. A faint ray of morning sunlight showed the form of the patient sleeping calmly, the body entirely uncovered. There was an expression of quiet happiness upon the face whose perfect health suggested perhaps radiance. But there was a change as well, though indescribable—there was power. He did not stir as they approached the bed. The breathing was regular and very deep.

Standing beside him a moment, Fillery sniffed the air, then smiled. There was a perfume of wild flowers. There was, in spite of the cool morning air, a pleasant warmth.

"You notice—anything?" he whispered, turning to his colleague.

Devonham likewise sniffed the air. "The window's wide open," was the low rejoinder. "There are conservatories at the back of every house all down the row."

And they left the room on tiptoe, closing the door behind them very softly. Upon Devonham's face lay a curious expression, half anxiety, half pain.

CHAPTER XXI

D R. FILLERY, lying on a couch in his patient's bedroom, snatched some four to five hours' sleep, though,
if "snatched," it was certainly enjoyed—a deep, dream-
less, reposeful slumber. He woke, refreshed in mind and
body, and the first thing he saw, even before he had time
to stretch a limb or move his head, was two great blue eyes
gazing into his own across the room. They belonged, it
first struck him, to some strange being that had followed
him out of sleep—he had not yet recovered full consciousness and the effects of sleep still hovered; then an earlier
phrase recurred: to some divine great animal.

"N. H.," in his bed in the opposite corner, lay gazing
at him. He returned the gaze. Into the blue eyes came
at once a look of happy recognition, of contentment, almost
a smile. Then they closed again in sleep.

The room was full of morning sunshine. Fillery rose
quietly, and performed his toilet in his own quarters, but
on returning after a hurried breakfast, the patient still slept
soundly. He slept on for hours, he slept the morning
through; but for the obvious evidences of perfect normal
health, it might have been a state of coma. The body did
not even change its position once.

He left Devonham in charge, and was on his way to
visit some of the other cases, when Nurse Robbins stood
before him. Miss Khilkoff had "called to inquire after Mr.
LeVallon," and was waiting downstairs in case Dr. Fillery
could also see her.

He glanced at her pretty slim figure and delicate complexion, her hair, fine, plentiful and shiny, her dark eyes
with a twinkle in them. She was an attractive, intelligent,

experienced, young woman, tactful too, and of great use with extra sensitive patients. She was, of course, already hopelessly in love with her present "case." His "singing," so she called it to Mrs. Soames, had excited her "like a glass of wine—some music makes you feel like that—so that you could love everybody in the world." She already called him Master.

"Please say I will be down at once," said Dr. Fillery, watching her for the first time with interest as he remembered these details Paul had told him. The girl, it now struck him, was intensely alive. There was a gain, an increase, in her appearance somewhere. He recalled also the matron's remark—she was not usually loquacious with her nurses—that "he's no ordinary case, and I've seen a good few, haven't I? The way he understands animals and flowers alone proves that!"

Dr. Fillery went downstairs.

His first rapid survey of the girl, exhaustive for all its quickness—he knew her so well—showed him that no outward signs of excitement were visible. Calm, poised, gentle as ever, the same generous tenderness in the eyes, the same sweet firmness in the mouth, the familiar steadiness that was the result of an inner surety—all were there as though the wild scene of the night before had never been. Yet all those were heightened. Her beauty had curiously increased.

"Come into my study," he said, taking her hand and leading the way. "We shan't be disturbed there. Besides, it's ours, isn't it? We mustn't forget that you are a member of the Firm."

He was aware of her soft beauty invading, penetrating him, aware, too, somehow, that she was in her most impersonal mood. But for all that, her nature could not hide itself, nor could signs of a certain, subtle change she had undergone fail to obtrude themselves. In a single night, it seemed, she had blossomed into a wondrous ripe maturity; like some strange flower that opens to the darkness, the bud had burst suddenly into full, sweet bloom, whose coming only moon and stars had witnessed. There was moonlight now in her dark mysterious eyes as she glanced at him; there was the gold of stars in her tender, yet curious smile, as she answered in her low voice—"Of course, I always *was* a partner in the Firm"—there was the grace and rhythm of a wild flower swaying in the wind, as she passed before him into the quiet room and sank into his own swinging armchair at the desk. But there was something else as well.

A detail of his recent Vision slid past his inner sight again while he watched her. . . . "I thought—I felt sure —you would come," he said. He looked at her admiringly, but peace strong in his heart. "The ordeal," he went on in a curious voice, "would have been too much for most women, but you"—he smiled, and the sympathy in his voice increased—"you, I see, have only gained from it. You've mastered, conquered it. I wonder"—looking away from her almost as if speaking to himself—"have you wholly understood it?"

He realized vividly in that moment what she, as a young, unmarried girl, had suffered before the eyes of all those prying eyes and gossiping tongues. His admiration deepened.

She did not take up his words, however. "I've come to inquire," she said simply in an even voice, "for father and myself. He wanted to know if you got home all right, and how Julian LeVallon is." The tone, the heightened colour in the cheek, as she spoke the name no one had yet used, explained, partly at least, to the experienced man who listened, the secret of her sudden blossoming. Also she used her father, though unconsciously, perhaps. "He was afraid the electricity—the lightning even—had"—she hesitated, smiled a little, then added, as though she herself knew otherwise—"done something to him."

Fillery laughed with her then. "As it has done to you," he thought, but did not speak the words. The need of formula was past. He thanked her, adding that it was sweet yet right that she had come herself, instead of writing or telephoning. "And you may set your—your father's mind at rest, for all goes well. The electricity, of course," he added, on his own behalf as well as hers, "was—more than most of us could manage. Electricity explains everything except itself, doesn't it?"

He was inwardly examining her with an intense and accurate observation. She seemed the same, yet different. The sudden flowering into beauty was simply enough explained. It was another change he now became more and more aware of. In this way a ship, grown familiar during the long voyage, changes on coming into port. The decks and staircases look different when the vessel lies motionless at the dock. It becomes half recognizable, half strange. Gone is the old familiarity, gone also one's own former angle of vision. It is difficult to find one's way about her. Soon she will set sail again, but in another direction, and with new passengers using her decks, her corners, hatchways . . . telling their secrets of love and hate with that recklessness the open sea and sky make easy. . . . And now with the girl before him—he couldn't quite find his way about her as of old . . . it was the same familiar ship, yet it was otherwise, and he, a new passenger, acknowledged the freedom of sea and sky.

"And you—Iraida?" he asked. "It was brave of you to come."

She liked evidently the use of her real name, for she smiled, aware all the time of his intent observation, aware probably also of his hidden pain, yet no sign of awkwardness in her; to this man she could talk openly, or, on the contrary, conceal her thoughts, sure of his tact and judgment. He would never intrude unwisely.

"It was natural, Edward," she observed frankly in return.

"Yes, I suppose it was. Natural is exactly the right word. You have perhaps found yourself at last," and again he used her real name, "Iraida."

"It feels like that," she replied slowly. She paused. "I have found, at least, something definite that I have to do. I feel that I—must care for him." Her eyes, as she said it, were untroubled.

The well-known Nayan flashed back a moment in the words; he recognized—to use his simile—a familiar corner of the deck where he had sat and talked for hours beneath the quiet stars—to someone who understood, yet remained ever impersonal. And the person he talked with came over suddenly and stood beside him and took his hand between her own soft gloved ones:

"You told me, Edward, he would need a woman to help him. That's what you mean by 'natural'—isn't it? And I am she, perhaps."

"I think you are," came in a level tone.

"I know it," she said suddenly, both her eyes looking down upon his face. "Yes, I suppose I know it."

"Because *you*—need him," his voice, equally secure, made answer.

Still keeping his hand tight between her own, her dark eyes still searching his, she made no sign that his blunt statement was accepted, much less admitted. Instead she asked a question he was not prepared for: "You would like that, Edward? You wish it?"

She was so close against his chair that her fur-trimmed coat brushed his shoulder; yet, though with eyes and touch and physical presence she was so near, he felt that she herself had gone far, far away into some other place. He drew his hand free. "Iraida," he said quietly, "I wish the best—for him—and for you. And I believe this is the best —for him and you." He put his patient first. He was aware that the girl, for all her outer calmness, trembled.

"It is," she said, her voice as quiet as his own; and after a moment's hesitation, she went back to her seat again. "If you think I can be of use," she added. "I'm ready."

A little pause fell between them, during which Dr. Fillery

touched an electric bell beside his chair. Nurse Robbins appeared with what seemed miraculous swiftness. "Still sleeping quietly, sir, and pulse normal again," she replied in answer to a question, then vanished as suddenly as she had come. He looked into the girl's eyes across the room. "A competent, reliable nurse," he remarked, "and, as you saw, a pretty woman." He glanced out of the window. "She is unmarried." He mentioned it apparently to the sky.

The quick mind took in his meaning instantly. "All women will be drawn to him irresistibly, of course," she said. "But it is not *that*."

"No, no, of course it is not that," he agreed at once. "I should like you to see him, though not, however, just yet——" He went on after a moment's reflection, and speaking slowly: "I should like you to wait a little. It's best. There *has* been a—a certain disturbance in his being——"

"It's his first experience," she began, "of beauty——"

"Of beauty in women, yes," he finished for her. "It is. We must avoid anything in the nature of a violent shock——"

"He has asked for me?" she interrupted again, in her quiet way.

He shook his head. "And we cannot be sure that it was you—as *you*—he sought and is affected by. The call he hears is, perhaps, hardly the call that sounds in most men's ears, I mean."

The hint of warning guidance was audible in his voice, as well as visible in his eyes and manner. The laughter they both betrayed, a grave and curious laughter perhaps, was brief, yet enough to conceal stranger emotions that rose like dumb, gazing figures almost before their eyes. Yet if she knew inner turmoil, emotion of any troubling sort, she concealed it perfectly.

"I am glad," the girl said presently. "Oh, I am really

glad. I think I understand, Edward." And, even while
he sat silent for a bit, watching her with an ever-growing
admiration that at the same time marvelled, he saw the
wonder of great questions riding through her face. The
recollection of what she had suffered publicly in the Studio
a few hours before came into his mind again. In these
questions, perhaps, lay the only signs of the hidden storm
below the surface.

"Are there—are there such things as Nature-Beings,
Edward?" she asked abruptly. "We know this is his first
experience. Are there then——?" .

He was prepared a little for this kind of question by
her eyes. "We have no evidence, of course," he replied;
"not a scrap of evidence for anything of the sort. There
are people, however, so close to Nature, so intimate with
her, that we may say they are—strangely, inexplicably
akin."

"Has he a soul—a human soul like ours?" she asked
point blank.

"He is perhaps—not—quite—like us. That may be your
task, Iraida," he added enigmatically. He watched her
more closely than she knew.

She appeared to ponder his words for a few minutes;
then she asked abruptly: "And when do you think I ought
to come and see him? You will let me know?"

"I will let you know. A few days perhaps, perhaps a
week, perhaps longer. Some education, I think, is necessary first." He gazed at her thoughtfully, and she returned
his look, her dark eyes filled with the wonder that was
both of a child and of a woman, and yet with a security
of something that was of neither. "It will be a—a great
effort to you," he ventured with significant and sympathetic
understanding, "after—what happened. It is brave and
generous of you——" He broke off.

She nodded, but at once afterwards shook her head. She
rose then to go, but Dr. Fillery stopped her. He rose
too.

"Nayan, I now want *your* help," he said with more emotion than he had yet shown. "My responsibility, as you may guess, is not light—and——"

"And he is in your sole charge, you mean." She had willingly resumed her seat, and made herself comfortable with a cushion he arranged for her. He was aware chiefly of her eyes, for in them glowed light and fire he had never seen there before—but still in their depths.

"Well—yes, partly," he replied, lighting a cigarette, "though Paul is ready with help and sympathy whenever needed. But the charge, as you call it, is not mine alone: it is ours."

"Ours!" She started, though almost imperceptibly, as she repeated his word.

"Subconsciously," he said in a firm voice, "we three are similar. We are together. We obey half instinctively the unknown laws of"—he hesitated a moment—"of some unknown state of being." He added then a singular sentence, though so low it seemed almost to himself: "Had we been man and wife, Iraida, our child must have been —like him."

"Yes," she said, leaning forward a little in her chair, increased warmth, yet no blush, upon her skin. "Yes, Edward, we three are somehow together in this, aren't we? Oh, I feel it. It pours over me like a great wind, a wind with heat in it." Her hands clasped her knee, as they gazed at one another for a moment's silence. "I feel it," she repeated presently. "I'm sure of it, quite sure."

She stretched out a spirit hand, as it were, for an instant across the impersonal barrier between them, but he did not take it, pretending he did not see it.

"Ours, Nayan," he emphasized, again using the name that belonged to everyone. "Therefore, you see, I want you to tell me—if you will—what you felt, experienced, perceived—in the Studio last night." After watching her a little, he qualified: "Another day, if you would like to think it over. But some time, without fail. For my part,

I will confess—though I think you already know it—that
I brought him there on purpose——"

"To see my effect upon him, Edward."

"But in *his* interest, and in the interest of my possible
future treatment. His effect upon yourself was not my
motive. You believe that."

"I know, I know. And I will tell you gladly. Indeed,
I want to."

He was aware, as she said it, that it would be a satisfaction to her to talk; she would welcome the relief of
confession; she could speak to him as doctor now, as professional man, as healer, and this, too, without betraying
the impersonal attitude she evidently wore and had adopted
possibly—he wondered?—in self-protection. "Tell me
exactly what it is you would like to know, please, Edward,"
she added, and instinctively moved to the sofa, so that he
might occupy the professional swinging chair at the desk.

"What you saw, Nayan," he began, accepting the change
of position without comment, because he knew it helped
her. "What you saw is of value, I think, first."

He had all his usual self-control again, for he was now
on his throne, his seat of power; his inner attitude changed
subtly; he was examining two patients—the girl and himself. She sat before him demure, obedient, honest, very
sweet but very strong; if her perfume reached him he did
not notice it, the appeal of her loveliness went past him,
he did not see her eyes. He had a very comely and intelligent young woman facing him, and the glow, as it were,
of an intense inner activity, strongly suppressed, was the
chief quality in her that he noted. But his new attitude
made other things, too, stand out sharply: he realized there
was confusion in her own mind and heart. Her being was
not wholly at one with itself. This impersonal rôle meant
safety until she was sure of herself; and so far she had
been entirely and admirably non-committal. No girl, he
remembered, could look back upon what she had experienced

in the Studio, upon what she had herself said and done, before a crowd of onlookers too, without deep feelings of a mixed and even violent kind. That scene with a young man she had never seen before must bring painful memories; if it was love at first sight the memories must be more painful still. But was it a case of this sudden, rapturous love? What, indeed, were her feelings? What at any rate was her dominant feeling? She had felt his appeal beyond all question, but was it as Nayan or as Iraida that she felt it?

She was non-committal and impersonal, conscious that therein safety lay—until, having become one with herself, harmonious, she could feel absolutely sure. One hint only had she dropped—it was Nayan speaking—that her mothering, maternal instinct was needed and that she must obey its prompting. She must "care" for him. . . .

Dr. Fillery, meanwhile, though he might easily have probed and made discoveries without her knowing that he did so, was not the man to use his powers now. Unless she gave of her own free will, he would not ask. He would close eyes and ears even to any chance betrayal or unconscious revelation.

"When you first looked in, for instance? You had just come in from the street, I think. You opened the door on your way upstairs. Do you remember?"

She remembered perfectly. "I wanted to see who was there. You, I think, were chiefly in my thoughts—I was wondering if you had come." Her voice was even, her eyes quite steady; she chose her next words slowly: "I saw—to my intense surprise—a figure of light."

"Shining, you mean? A shining figure?"

She nodded her head, as one little hand put back a straying wisp of dark hair from her forehead. "A figure like flame," she agreed. "I saw it quite clearly. I saw everything else quite clearly too—the inner room, various people standing about, the piano, the thick smoke, everything as usual. I saw you. You were in the big outer room beyond, but your face was very distinct. You were staring—staring straight at me."

"True," put in Dr. Fillery; "I saw you in the doorway plainly."

"In the foreground, by itself apart somehow, though surrounded by people, was this shining, radiant outline. I thought it was a Vision—the first thing of that sort I had ever seen in my life."

"That was your very first impression—even before you had time to think?"

"Yes."

"It struck you as unusual?"

"I cannot say more than that. I knew by the light it was unusual. Then it moved—talking to Povey or Kempster or someone—and I realized in a flash who it was. I knew it must be your friend, the man you had promised to bring—Ju——"

"And then——?" he asked quickly, before she could pronounce the name.

"And then——"

She stopped, and her eyes looked away from him, not in the sense that they moved but that their focus changed as though she looked at something else, at something within herself, no longer, therefore, at the face in front of her. He waited; he understood that she was searching among deep, strange, seething memories; he let her search; and, watching closely, he presently saw the sight return into her eyes from its inward plunge.

"And when you knew who it was," he asked very quietly, "were you still surprised? Did he look as you expected him to look, for instance?"

"I had expected nothing, you see, Edward, because I had not been consciously thinking about his coming. No mental picture was present in me at all. But the moment I realized who it was, the light seemed to go—I just saw a young man standing there, with his head turned sideways to me. The light, I suppose, lasted for a second only—that first second. As to how he looked? Well, he looked, not only bigger—he *is* bigger than most men," she went on, "but he looked"—her voice hushed instinctively a little on the adjective—"different."

Her companion made a gesture of agreement, waiting in silence for what was to follow.

"He looked so extraordinary, so wonderful," she resumed, gazing steadily into his eyes, "that I—I can hardly put it into words, Edward, unless I use childish language." She broke off and sighed, and something, he fancied, in her wavered for a second, though it was certainly neither the voice nor the eyes. A faint trembling again perhaps ran through her body. Her account was so deliberately truthful that it impressed him more than he quite understood. He was aware of pathos in her, of some vague trouble very poignant yet inexplicable. A breath of awe, it seemed, entered the room and moved between them.

"The childish words are probably the best, the right ones," he told her gently.

"An angel," she said instantly in a hushed tone, "I thought of an angel. There is no other word I can find. But somehow a helpless one. An angel—out of place."

He looked hard at her, his manner encouraging though grave; he said no word; he did not smile.

"Someone not of this earth quite," she added. "Not a man, at any rate."

Still more gently, he then asked her what she felt.

"At first I couldn't move," she went on, her voice normal again. "I must have stood there ten minutes fully, perhaps longer"—her listener did not correct the statement—"when I suddenly recovered and looked about for you, Edward, but could not see you. I needed you, but could not find you. I remember feeling somehow that I had lost you. I tried to call for you—in my heart. There was no answer. . . . Then—then I closed the door quietly and went upstairs to change from my street clothes."

She paused and passed a hand slowly across her forehead. Dr. Fillery asked casually a curious question:

"Do you remember *how* you got upstairs, Nayan?"

Her hand dropped instantly; she started. "It's very odd you should ask me that, Edward," she said, gazing at him with a slightly rising colour in her face, an increase of fire glowing in her eyes; "very odd indeed. I was just trying to think how I could describe it to you. No. Actually I do not remember how I got upstairs. All I know is—I was suddenly in my room." A new intensity appeared in voice and manner. "It seemed to me I flew—or that—something—carried me."

"Yes, Nayan, yes. It's quite natural you should have felt like that."

"Is it? I remember so little of what I actually felt. I wonder—I wonder," she went on softly, with an air almost of talking to herself, "if it will ever come back again—what I felt then——"

"Such moments of subliminal excitement," Dr. Fillery reminded her gently, "have the effect of obliterating memory sometimes——"

"Excitement," she caught him up. "Yes, I suppose it was excitement. But it was more, much more, than that. Stimulated—I think that's the word really. I felt caught away somewhere, caught away, caught up—as if into the rest of myself—into the whole of myself. I became vast"—she smiled curiously—"if you know what I mean—in several places at once, perhaps, is better. It was an immense feeling—no, I mean a feeling of immensity——"

"Happy?" His voice was low.

Her eyes answered even before her words, as the memory came back a little in response to his cautious suggestion.

"A new feeling altogether," she replied, returning his clear gaze with her frank, innocent eyes that had grown still more brilliant. "A feeling I have never known before." She talked more rapidly now, leaning forward a little in her chair. "I felt in the open air somehow, with

flowers, trees, hot burning sunshine and sweet winds rushing to and fro. It was something bigger than happiness
—a sort of intoxicating joy, I think. It was liberty, but
of an enormous spiritual kind. I wanted to dance—I believe I did dance—yes, I'm sure I did, and with hardly
anything on my body. I wanted to sing—I sang downstairs, of course——"

"I heard," he put in briefly. He did not add that she
had never sung like that before.

"The moment I came into the room, yes, I remember
I went straight to the piano without a word to anyone."
She reflected a moment. "I suppose I had to. There was
something new in me I could only express by music—
rhythm, that is, not language."

"It was natural," Dr. Fillery said again. "Quite natural,
I think."

"Yes, Edward, I suppose it was," she answered, then sank
back in her chair, as though she had told him all there was
to tell.

Dr. Fillery smoked in silence for a few minutes, then
rose and touched the bell as before, and, as before, Nurse
Robbins appeared with the same miraculous speed. There
was a brief colloquy at the door; the woman was gone
again, and the doctor turned back into the room with a
look of satisfaction on his face. All, apparently, was going
well upstairs. He did not sit down, however; he stood
looking out of the window at the drab wintry sky of motionless clouds, his back to his companion. It was midday, but
the light, while making all things visible, was not light;
there was no shine, no touch of radiance, no hint of sparkle
beneath the canopy of sullen cloud. The English winter's
day was visible, no more than that. Yet it was not the
English day, nor the clouds, nor the bleak dead atmosphere
he looked at. In a single second his sight travelled far,
far away, covering an enormous interval in space and time,
in condition too. He saw a radiant world of sun-drenched
flowers "tossing with random airs of an unearthly wind";

he saw a foam of forest leaves shaking and dancing against a deep blue sky; he say a valley whose streams and emerald turf knew not the touch of human feet. . . . The familiar symbols he saw, but inflamed with new meaning.

"Thank you, Edward, thank you"—she was just behind him, her hands upon his shoulders. "You understand everything in the world!" she added, "and out of it," but too low for him to hear.

He came back with an effort, turning towards her. They were standing level now and very close, eyes looking into eyes. He felt her breath upon his face, her perfume rose about him, her lips were moving just in front of him— yet, for a second, he did not know who she was. It was as though *she* had not come with him out of that valley, not come back with him. . . . An insatiable longing seized him—to return and find her, stay with her. The ache of an intolerable yearning was in his heart, yet a sudden flash of understanding that brought a bigger, almost an unearthly joy in its train. At the call of some service, some duty, some help to be rendered to humanity, the three of them together—he, "N. H.," the girl—were in temporary exile from their rightful home. The scent of wild flowers rose about him. He suddenly remembered, recognized, and gave a little start. He had left her behind in the valley—Iraida; it was Nayan who now stood before him.

He uttered a dry little laugh. "You startled me, Nayan. I was thinking. I didn't hear you." She had just thanked him for something—oh, yes—because he had left her alone for a moment, giving her time to collect herself after the long cross-examination.

He took both her hands in his.

"*Our* patient then—isn't it?" he asked in a firm voice, looking deep into her luminous eyes. He saw no fire in them now.

"I'll do all I can, Edward."

She returned the pressure of his hands. His keen insight, operating in spite of himself, had read her clearly.

It was mother, child and woman he had always known.
The three, however, were already in process of disentangle-
ment. For the first time during their long acquaintance,
what now stood so close before him was—the woman. Yet
behind the woman like an enveloping shadow stood the
mother too. And behind both, again, stood another wild,
gigantic, lovely possibility. Was it, then, the child that he
had left playing in the radiant valley? . . . The child, he
knew, was his always, always, even if the woman was another's. . . . He laughed softly. These, after all, were but
transitory states in human, earthly evolution, concerned with
play, with a production of bodies and so forth. . . .

He had lost himself in her deep eyes. Her gaze lay
all over him, over his entire being, like a warm soft covering that blessed and healed. She was so close that it seemed
he drew her breath in with his own. She made a movement
then, a tiny gesture. He let go the hands his own had held
so long. He turned from the window and from her. He
was trembling.

"What came later," he resumed in his calm, almost in
his professional voice, "you probably do not remember?"
He went towards his desk. "We need not talk about that.
No doubt, in your mind, it all remains a blurred impression——"

She interrupted, following him across the room. "What
happened, Edward," she said very quietly in her lowest
tone, "*I know*. It was all told to me. But my memory,
as you say, is so faint as to be worthless really. What I
do remember is this"—she tapped her open palm with two
fingers slowly, as she spoke the words—"light, heat, a smell
of flowers and a rushing wind that lifted me into some
kind of exhilarating liberty where I felt—the intense joy
of knowing myself somehow free—and greater, oh, far
greater—than I am—now." Then she suddenly whispered
again too low for him to catch—"angelic." A smile, as of
glory, rippled across her face.

His voice, coming quickly, was cool, its tone measured:

"And you will come to see him the moment I let you know," he interrupted abruptly. "It may be a few days, it may be a week. The instant it seems wise——" He was entirely practical again.

She went to the door with him. "I'll come, of course," she answered, as he opened the door.

"I'll let myself out, Edward—please. I know the way. There's no good being a partner if one doesn't know the way out——" She laughed.

"And in, remember!" he called down the little passage after her, as, with a smile and a wave of the hand, she was gone.

He went back to his desk, drew a piece of paper towards him, and jotted a few notes down in briefest fashion. The expression on his rugged face was enigmatical perhaps, but the sternness at least was clear to read, and it was this, combining with an extraordinary tenderness, that drew out its nobility:

"Intensification of consciousness, involving increased activity of every centre; hearing, sight, touch and smell, all affected. Slight exteriorization of consciousness also took place. No signs of split or divided personality, but an increase of coherence rather. The central self active —aware of greater powers in time and space, hence sense of joy, heat, light, sound, motion. Distinct subliminal up-rush, followed by customary loss of memory later. Her *whole* being, together with neglected tracts as yet untouched by experience—her *entire* being—reached simultaneously. Knew herself for the first time a woman—but something more as well. Unearthly complex, visible.

"Appeal made direct to subconscious self. Unfavourable reactions—none. Favourable reactions—increased physical and mental strength. . . ."

He laid down his pencil as with a gesture of impatience at its uselessness, and sat back in the chair, thinking.

The effect "N. H." had upon other people was here again confirmed. That, at least, seemed reasonably clear.

Vitality was increased; heart and mind caught up an extra gear; thought leaped, if extravagantly, towards speculation; emotion deepened, if ecstatically, towards belief. All the normal reactions of the system were speeded up and strengthened. Consciousness was intensified.

More than this—with some it was extended, and subliminal powers were set free. In his own experience this had been the case; the sight, hearing, even a mild degree of divination, had opened in his being. It had, similarly, taken place with Devonham, an unlikely subject, who fought against acknowledging it. Father Collins, too, he suspected —he recalled his behaviour and strange language—had known also a temporary extension of faculty outside the normal field. He remembered, again, the Customs official, Charing Cross Station, and a dozen other minor instances. . . . Indications as yet were slight, he realized, but they were valuable.

Such abnormal experiences, moreover, each one interpreted, respectively, in the terms of his own individual being, of his own temperament, his own personal shibboleths. The law governing unusual experience operated invariably.

Was not his own particular "vision" easily explained? It might indeed, had it happened earlier, have found a place in his own book of Advanced Psychology. He reflected rapidly: He believed the industrial system lay at the root of Civilization's crumbling, and that man must return to Nature—therefore his yearnings dramatized themselves in personified representations of the beauty of Nature.

He could trace every detail of his Vision to some intense but unrealized yearning, to some deep hope, desire, dream, as yet unfulfilled. Always these yearnings and wishes unfulfilled!

Colour, form and sound again—he used them one and all in his treatment of special cases, and felt hurt by the ignorant scoffing and denial of his brother doctors. Hence their present dramatization.

His immense belief, again, in the results upon the Race when once the subliminal powers should have reached the stage where they could be used at will for practical purposes—this, in its turn, led him to hope, perhaps to believe, that this strange "Case" might prove to be some fabulous bright messenger who brought glad tidings. . . . All, all was explicable enough!

A smile stole over his face; he began to laugh quietly to himself. . . .

Yes, he could explain all, trace all to something or other in his being, yet—he knew that the real explanation . . . well—his cleverest intellectual explanation and analysis were worthless after all. For here lay something utterly beyond his knowledge and experience. . . .

The note of another searcher recurred to him.

"Each human being has within himself that restless creative phantasy which is ever engaged in assuaging the harshness of reality. . . . Whoever gives himself unsparingly and carefully to self-observation will realize that there dwells within him something which would gladly hide up and cover all that is difficult and questionable in life, and thus procure an easy and free path. Insanity grants the upper hand to this something. When once it is uppermost, reality is more or less quickly driven out."

But he knew quite well that although he belonged to what he called the "Unstable," the "something" which Jung referred to had by no means obtained "the upper hand." The vista opening to his inner sight led towards a new reality. . . . Ah! If he could only persuade Paul Devonham to see what *he* saw . . . !

CHAPTER XXII

LADY GLEESON had heard from a Promethean what had transpired in the studio after she had left, and her interest was immensely stimulated. These details she had not known when she had driven her hero home, and had felt so strangely drawn to him that she had kissed him in front of Dr. Fillery as though she caressed a prisoner under the eyes of the warder.

She made her little plans accordingly. It was some days, however, before they bore fruit. The telephone at last rang. It was Dr. Fillery. The nerves in her quivered with anticipation.

Devonham, it appeared, had been away, and her "kind letters and presents," he regretted to find, had remained unanswered and unacknowledged. Mr. LeVallon had been in the country, too, with his colleague, and letters had not been forwarded. Oh, it would "do him good to see people." It would be delightful if she could spare a moment to look in. Perhaps for a cup of tea to-morrow? No, to-morrow she was engaged. The next day then. The next day it was. In the morning arrived a brief letter from Mr. Le-Vallon himself: "You will come to tea to-morrow. I thank you.—JULIAN LeVALLON."

Yet there was something both in Dr. Fillery's voice, as in this enigmatic letter, that she did not like. She felt puzzled somewhere. The excitement of a novel intrigue with this unusual youth, none the less, was stimulating. She decided to go to tea. She put off a couple of engagements in order to be free.

A servant let her in. She went upstairs. There was

no sign of Dr. Fillery nor, thank heaven, of Devonham either. Tea, she saw, was laid for two in the private sitting-room. LeVallon, seated in an arm-chair by the open window, looked "magnificent and overpowering," as she called it. He rose at once to greet her. "Thank you," he said in his great voice. "I am glad to see you." He said it perfectly, as though it had been taught him. He took her hand. Her ravishing smile, perhaps, he did not notice. His face, at any rate, was grave.

His height, his broad shoulders, his inexperienced eyes and manner again delighted Lady Gleeson.

The effect upon her receptive temperament, at any rate, was instantaneous. That he showed no cordiality, did not smile, and that his manner was constrained, meant nothing to her—or meant what she wished it to mean. He was somewhat overcome, of course, she reflected, that she was here at all. She began at once. Sitting composedly on the edge of the table, so that her pretty silk stockings were visible to the extent she thought just right, she dangled her slim legs and looked him straight in the eyes. She was full of confidence. Her attitude said plainly: "I'm taking a lot of trouble, but you're worth it."

"Mr. LeVallon," she purred in a teasing yet determined voice, "why do you ignore me?" There was an air of finality about the words. She meant to know.

LeVallon met her eyes with a look of puzzled surprise, but did not answer. He stood in front of her. He looked really magnificent, a perfect study of the athlete in repose. He might have been a fine Greek statue.

"Why," she repeated, her lip quivering slightly, "do you ignore me? I want the truth," she added. She was delighted to see how taken aback he was. "You don't dislike me." It was not a question.

Into his eyes stole an expression she could not exactly fathom. She judged, however, that he felt awkward, foolish. Her interest doubtless robbed him of any *savoir faire* he might possess. This talk face to face was a little

too much for any young man, but for a simple country
youth it was, of course, more than disconcerting.

"I'm Lady Gleeson," she informed him, smiling precisely
in the way she knew had troubled so many other men.
"Angela," she added softly. "You've had my books and
flowers and letters. Yet you continue to ignore me. Why,
please?" With a different smile and a pathetic, childish,
voice: "Have I offended you somehow? Do I displease
you?"

LeVallon stared at her as though he was not quite certain
who she actually was, yet as though he ought to know,
and that her words now reminded him. He stared at her
with what she called his "awkward and confused" expression, but which Fillery, had he been present, would have
recognized as due to his desire to help a pitiful and hungry
creature—that, in a word, his instinct for service had been
a little stirred.

The scene was certainly curious and unusual.

LeVallon, with his great strength and dignity, yet something tender, pathetic in his bearing, stood staring
at her. Lady Gleeson, brimming with a sense of easy
victory, sat on the table-edge, her pretty legs well forward,
knowing herself divinely gowned. She had her victim,
surely, at a disadvantage. She felt at the same time a faint
uneasiness she could not understand. She concealed it,
however.

"I suffer here," he said suddenly in a quiet tone.

She gave a start. It was the phrase he had used before.
She thrilled. She hitched her skirt a fraction higher.

"Julian, poor boy," she said—then stared at him. "How
innocent you are!" She said it with apparent impulse,
though her little frenzied mind was busy calculating. There
came a pause. He said nothing. He was, apparently, quite
innocent, extraordinarily, exasperatingly innocent.

In a low voice, smiling shyly, she added—as though it
cost her a great effort:

"You do not recognize what is yours."

"You are sacred!" he replied with startling directness, as though he suddenly understood, yet was stupidly perplexed. "You already have your man."

Lady Gleeson gulped down a spasm of laughter. How slow these countrymen could be! Yet she must not shock him. He was suffering, besides. This yokel from the woods and mountains needed a little coaxing. It was natural enough. She must explain and teach, it seemed. Well —he was worth the trouble. His beauty was mastering her already. She loved, in particular, his innocence, his shyness, his obvious respect. She almost felt herself a magnanimous woman.

"My man!" she mentioned. "Oh, he's finished with me long ago. He's bored. He has gone elsewhere. I am alone"—she added with an impromptu inspiration—"and free to choose."

"It must be pain and loneliness to you."

LeVallon looked, she thought, embarrassed. He was struggling with himself, of course. She left the table and came up close to him. She stood on tiptoe, so that her breath might touch his face. Her eyes shone with fire. Her voice trembled a little. It was very low.

"I choose—*you*," she whispered. She cast down her shining eyes. Her lips took on a prim, inviting turn. She knew she was irresistible like that. She stood back a step, as if expecting some tumultuous onslaught. She waited.

But the onslaught did not come. LeVallon, towering above her, merely stared. His arms hung motionless. There was, indeed, expression in his face, but it was not the expression that she expected, longed for, deemed her due. It puzzled her, as something entirely new.

"Me!" he repeated, in an even tone. He gazed at her in a peculiar way. Was it appraisement? Was it halting wonder at his marvellous good fortune? Was it that he hesitated, judging her? He seemed, she thought once for an instant, curiously indifferent. Something in his voice startled her.

The moment's pause, at any rate, was afflicting. Her spirit burned within her. Only her supreme belief in herself prevented a premature explosion. Yet something troubled her as well. A tremor ran through her. LeVallon, she remembered, was—LeVallon.

His own thought and feeling lay hidden from her blunt perception since she read no signs unless they were painfully obvious. But in his mind—in his feeling, rather, since he did not think—ran evidently the sudden knowledge of what her meaning was. He understood. But also, perhaps he remembered what Fillery had told him.

For a long time he kept silent, the emotions in him apparently at grips. Was he suddenly going to carry her away as he had done to that "little Russian poseuse"? She watched him. He was intensely busy with what occupied his mind, for though he did not speak, his lips were moving. She watched him, impatience and wonder in her, impatience at his slowness, wonder as to what he would do and say when at last his simple mind had decided. And again the odd touch of fear stole over her. Something warned her. This young man thrilled her, but he certainly was strange. This was, indeed, a new experience. Whatever was he thinking about? What in the world was he going to say? His lips were still moving. There was a light in his face. She imagined the very words, could almost read them, hear them. There! Then she heard them, heard some at any rate distinctly: "You are an animal. Yet you walk upright. . . ."

The scene that followed went like lightning.

Before Lady Gleeson could move or speak, however, he also said another thing that for one pulsing second, and for the first time in her life, made her own utter worthlessness become appallingly clear to her. It explained the touch of fear. Even her one true thing, her animal passion, was a trumpery affair:

"There is nothing in you I can work with," he said with gentle, pitying sympathy. "Nothing I can use."

Then Lady Gleeson blazed. Vanity instantly restored self-confidence. It seemed impossible to believe her ears.

What had he done? What had he said that caused the explosion? He watched her abrupt, spasmodic movements with amazemnt. They were so ugly, so unrhythmical. Their violence was so wasteful.

"You insult me!" she cried, making these violent movements of her whole body that, to him, were unintelligible. "How dare you? You——" The breath choked her.

"Cad," he helped her, so suddenly that another mind not far away might almost have dropped the word purposely into his own. "I am so pained," he added, "so pained." He gazed at her as though he longed to help. "For you, I know, are valuable to him who holds you sacred—to—your husband."

Lady Gleeson simply could not credit her ears. This neat, though unintentional, way of transferring the epithet to her who deserved it, left her speechless. Her fury increased with her inability to express it. She could have struck him, killed him on the spot. Her face changed from white to crimson like some toy with a trick of light inside it. She seemed to emit sparks. She was transfixed. And the shiver that ran through her was, perhaps, for once, both sexual and spiritual at once.

"You insult me," she cried again helplessly. "You insult me!"

"If there was something in you I could work with— help——" he began, his face showing a tender sympathy that enraged her even more. He started suddenly, looking closer into her blazing eyes. "Ah," he said quickly below his breath, "the fire—the little fire!" His expression altered. But Lady Gleeson, full of her grievance, did not catch the words, it seemed.

"—In my tenderest, my most womanly feelings," she choked on, yet noticing the altered expression on his face. "How *dare* you?" Her voice became shrill and staccato. Then suddenly—mistaking the look in his eyes for shame—

she added: "You shall apologize. You shall apologize at once!" She screamed the words. They were the only ones that her outraged feelings found.

"You show yourself, my fire," he was saying softly in his deep resonant voice. "Oh, I see and worship now; I understand a little."

His look astonished her even in the middle of her anger —the pity, kindness, gentleness in it. The bewilderment she did not notice. It was the evident desire to be of service to her, to help and comfort, that infuriated her. The superiority was more than she could stand.

"And on your knees," she yelped; "on your knees, too!"

Drawing herself up, she pointed to the carpet with an air of some tragedy queen to whom a lost self-respect came slowly back. "Down there!" she added, as the gleaming buckle on her shoe indicated the spot. She did not forget to show her pretty stockings as well.

The picture was comic in the extreme, yet with a pathetic twist about it that, had she possessed a single grain of humour, must have made her feel foolish and shamed until she died, for his kneeling position rendered her insignificance so obvious it was painful in the extreme. LeVallon clasped his hands; his face, wearing a dignity and tenderness that emphasized its singular innocence and beauty, gazed up into her trivial prettiness, as she sat on the edge of the table behind her, glaring down at him with angry but still hungry eyes.

"I should have helped and worshipped," his deep voice thrilled. "I am ashamed. Always—you are sacred, wonderful. I did not recognize your presence calling me. I did not hear nor understand. I am ashamed."

The strange words she did not comprehend, even if she heard them properly. For one moment she knew a dreadful feeling that they were not addressed to her at all, but the sense of returning triumph, the burning desire to extract from him the last ounce of humiliation, to make him suffer as much as in her power lay, these emotions deadened any perceptions of a subtler kind. He was kneeling at her feet, stammering his abject apology, and the sight was wine and food to her. Though she could have crushed him with her foot, she could equally have flung herself in utter abandonment before his glorious crouching strength. She adored the scene. He looked magnificent on his knees. He was. She believed she, too, looked magnificent.

"You apologize to me," she said in a trembling voice, tense with mingled passions.

"Oh, with what sadness for my mistake you cannot know," was his strange reply. His voice rang with sincerity, his eyes held a yearning that almost lent him radiance. Yet it was the sense of power he gave that thrilled Lady Gleeson most. For she could not understand it. Again a passing hint of something remote, incalculable, touched her sense of awe. She shivered slightly. LeVallon did not move.

Appeased, yet puzzled, she lowered her face, now pale and intense with eagerness, towards his own, hardly conscious that she did so, while the faint idea again went past her that he addressed his astonishing words elsewhere. Blind vanity at once dismissed the notion, though the shock of its brief disthroning had been painful. She found satisfaction for her wounded soul. A man who had scorned her, now squirmed before her beauty on his knees, desiring her—but too late.

"You have *some* manhood, after all!" she exclaimed, still fierce, the upper lip just revealing the shining little teeth. Her power at last had touched him. He suffered. And she was glad.

"I worship," he repeated, looking through her this time, if not actually past her. "You are sacred, the source of all my life and power." His pain, his worship, the aching passion in him made her forget the insult. Upon that face upturned so close to hers, she now breathed softly.

"I'll try," she said more calmly. "I'll try and forgive you—just this once." The suffering in his eyes, so close against her own, dawned more and more on her. "There, now," she added impulsively, "perhaps I will forgive you—altogether !"

It was a moment of immense and queenly generosity. She felt sublime.

LeVallon, however, made no rejoinder; one might have thought he had not heard; only his head sank lower a little before her.

She had him at her mercy now; the rapt and wonderful expression in his eyes delighted her. She bent slightly nearer and made as though to kiss him, when a new idea flashed suddenly through her mind. This forgiveness was a shade too quick, too easy. Oh, she knew men. She was not without experience.

She acted with instant decision upon her new idea, as though delay might tempt her to yield too soon. She straightened up with a sudden jerk, touched his cheek with her hand, then, with a swinging swish of her skirts, but without a single further word, she swept across the room. She went out, throwing him a last glance just before she closed the door. At his kneeling figure and upturned face she flung this last glance of murderous fascination.

But LeVallon did not move or turn his head; he made no sign; his attitude remained precisely as before, face upturned, hands clasped, his expression rapt and grave as ever. His voice continued:

"I worship you for ever. I did not know you in that little shape. O wondrous central fire, teach me to be aware of you with awe, with joy, with love, even in the smallest things. O perfect flame behind all form. . . ."

For a long time his deep tones poured their resonant vibration through the room. There came an answering music, low, faint, continuous, a long, deep rhythm running in it. There was a scent of flowers, of open space, a fragrance of a mountain top. The sounds, the perfume, the touch of cool refreshing wind rose round him, increasing with every minute, till it seemed as though some energy informed them. At the centre he knelt steadily, light glowing faintly in his face and on his skin. A vortex of energy swept round him. He drew upon it. His own energy was increased and multiplied. He seemed to grow more radiant. . . .

A few minutes later the door opened softly and Dr. Fillery looked in, hesitated for a second, then advanced into the room. He paused before the kneeling figure. It was noticeable that he was not startled and that his face wore no expression of surprise. A smile indeed lay on his lips. He noticed the scent of flowers, a sweetness in the air as after rain; he felt the immense vitality, the exhilaration, the peace and power too. He had made no sound, but the other, aware of his presence, rose to his feet.

"I disturbed you," said Fillery. "I'm sorry. Shall I go?"

"I was worshipping," replied "N. H." "No, do not go. There was a little flash"—he looked about him for an instant as if slightly bewildered—"a little sign—something I might have helped—but it has gone again. Then I worshipped, asking for more power. *You* notice it?" he asked, with a radiant smile.

"I notice it," said Fillery, smiling back. He paused a moment. His eye took in the tea-things and saw they were untouched; he felt the tea-pot. It was still warm. "Come," he said happily; "we'll have some tea together. I'll send for a fresh brew." He rang the bell, then arranged the chairs a little differently. "Your visitor?" he asked. "You are expecting someone?"

"N. H." looked round him suddenly. "Oh!" he exclaimed, "but—she has gone!"

His surprise was comical, but the expression on the face changed in his rapid way at once. "I remember now. Your Lady Gleeson came," he added, a touch of gentle sadness in his voice, "I gave her pain. You had told me. I forgot——"

"You did well," Fillery commented with smiling approval as though the entire scene was known to him, "you did very

well. It is a pity, only, that she left too soon. If she had
stayed for your worship—your wind and fire might have
helped——"

"N. H." shook his head. "There is nothing I can work
with," he replied. "She is empty. She destroys only.
Why," he added, "does she walk upright?"

But Lady Gleeson held very different views upon the
recent scene. This magnificent young male she had put in
his place, but she had not finished with him. No such being
had entered her life before. She was woman enough to see
he was unusual. But he was magnificent as well, and,
secretly, she loved his grand indifference.

She left the house, however, with but an uncertain feeling that the honours were with her. Two days without a
word, a sign, from her would bring him begging to her
little feet.

But the "begging" did not come. The bell was silent, the
post brought no humble, passionate, abandoned letter. She
fumed. She waited. Her husband, recently returned to
London and immensely preoccupied with his concessions,
her maid too, were aware that Lady Gleeson was impatient.
The third, the fourth day came, but still no letter.

Whereupon it occurred to her that she had possibly gone
too far. Having left him on his knees, he was, perhaps,
still kneeling in his heart, even prostrate with shame and
disappointment. Afraid to write, afraid to call, he knew
not what to do. She had evidently administered too severe
a lesson. Her callers, meanwhile, convinced her that she
was irresistible. There was no woman like her in the
world. She had, of course, been too harsh and cruel with
this magnificent and innocent youth from the woods and
mountains. . . .

Thus it was that, on the fourth day, feeling magnanimous
and generous, big-hearted too, she wrote to him. It would
be foolish, in any case, to lose him altogether merely for a
moment's pride:

"DEAR MR. LEVALLON,—I feel I must send you a tiny word to let you know that I really have forgiven you. You behaved, you know, in a way that no man of my acquaintance has ever done before. But I feel sure now you did not really mean it. Your forest and mountain gods have not taught you to understand civilized women. So—I forgive.

"Please forget it all, as I have forgotten it.—Yours,

"ANGELA GLEESON.

"P. S.—And you may come and see me soon."

To which, two days later, came the reply:

"DEAR LADY GLEESON,—I thank you.

JULIAN LEVALLON."

Within an hour of its receipt, she wrote:

"DEAR JULIAN,—I am so glad you understand. I knew you would. You may come and see me. I will prove to you that you are really forgiven. There is no need to feel embarrassed. I am interested in you and can help you. Believe me, you need a woman's guidance. All—*all* I have, is yours.

"I shall be at home this afternoon—alone—from 4 to 7 o'clock. I shall expect you. My love to you and your grand wild gods!—Yours,   "ANGELA.

"P. S.—I want you to tell me more about your gods. Will you?"

She sent it by special messenger, "Reply" underlined on the envelope. He did not appear at the appointed hour, but the next morning she received his letter. It came by ordinary post. The writing on the envelope was not his. Either Devonham or Fillery had addressed it. And a twinge of unaccustomed emotion troubled her. Intuition, it seems, survives even in the coarsest, most degraded feminine nature, ruins of some divine prerogative perhaps. Lady Gleeson, at any rate, flinched uneasily before she opened the long expected missive:

"DEAR LADY GLEESON,—Be sure that you are always under the protection of the gods even if you do not know them. They are impersonal. They come to you through passion but not through that love of the naked body which is lust. I can work with passion because it is creative, but not with lust, for it is destructive only. Your suffering is the youth and ignorance of the young uncreative animal. I can strive with young animals and can help them. But I cannot work with them. I beg you, listen. I love in you the fire, though it is faint and piti-ful.   "JULIAN."

Lady Gleeson read this letter in front of the looking-glass, then stared at her reflection in the mirror.

She was dazed. But in spite of the language she thought "silly," she caught the blunt refusal of her generous offer. She understood. Yet, unable to believe it, she looked at her reflection again—then, impulsively, went downstairs to see her husband.

It really was more than she could bear. The man was mad, but that did not excuse him.

"He is a beast," she informed her husband, tearing up the letter angrily before his eyes in the library, while he watched her with a slavish admiration that increased her fury. "He is nothing but an animal," she added. "He's a—a——"

"Who?" came the question, as though it had been asked before. For Sir George wore a stolid and a patient expression on his kindly face.

"That man LeVallon," she told him. "One of Dr. Fillery's cases I tried to—to help. Now he's written to me——"

George looked up with infinite patience and desire in his kindly gaze.

"Cut him out," he said dryly, as though he was accustomed to such scenes. "Let him rip. Why bother, anyway, with 'patients'?"

And he crossed the room to comfort her, knowing that presently the reaction must make him seem more desirable than he really was. . . .

"Never in my house again," she sighed, as he approached her lovingly, his fingers in his close brown beard. "He is simply a beast—an animal!"

CHAPTER XXIII

IT was, perhaps, some cosmic humour in the silent, beautiful stars which planned that Nayan's visit should follow upon the very heels of Lady Gleeson's call. Those vast Intelligences who note the fall of even a feather, watching and guarding the Race so closely that they may be said in human terms to love it, arranged the details possibly, enjoying the result with their careless, sunny laughter. At any rate, Dr. Fillery quickly sent her word, and she came. To lust "N. H." had not reacted. How would it be with love?

The beautiful girl entered the room slowly, shyly, as though, certain of herself, she was not quite certain what she was about to meet. Fillery had told her she could help, that she was needed; therefore she came. There was no thought of self in her. Her first visit to Julian LeVallon after his behaviour in the Studio had no selfish motive in it. Her self-confidence, however, went only to a certain point; in the interview with Fillery she had easily controlled herself; she was not so sure that her self-control would be adequate now. Though calm outwardly, an inexpressible turmoil surged within.

She remembered his strength, virility and admiration—as a woman; his ingenuous, childlike innocence, an odd appealing helplessness in it somewhere, touched the mother in her. That she divined this latter was, perhaps, the secret of her power over men. Independent of all they had to offer, she touched the highest in them by making them feel they had need of the highest in herself. She obtained thus, without desiring it, the influence that Lady Gleeson, her antithesis, lacked. They called her Nayan the Impersonal.

The impersonal in her, nevertheless, that which had withstood the cunning onslaught of every type of male successfully, had received a fundamental shock. Both her modesty and dignity had been assailed, and in public. Others, women among them, had witnessed her apparent yielding to LeVallon's violence and seen her carried in his arms; they had noted her obvious willingness, had heard her sympathetic cry. She knew quite well what the women thought —Lady Gleeson had written a little note of sympathy—the men as well, and yet she came at Fillery's call to visit, perhaps to help, the offender who had caused it all.

As she opened the door every nerve she possessed was tingling. The mother in her yearned, but the woman in her sent the blood rushing from her heart in pride, in resentment, in something of anger as well. How had he dared to seize her in that awful way? The outrage and the love both tore at her. Yet Nayan was not the kind to shirk self-revelation when it came. She brought some hidden secret with her, although as yet herself uncertain what that secret was.

Fillery met her on the threshold with his sweet tact and sympathy as usual. He had an authoritative and paternal air that helped and comforted her, and, as she took his hand at once, the look she gave him was more kind and tender than she knew. The last trace of self, at any rate, went out of her as she felt his touch.

"Here I am," she said; "you sent for me. I promised you."

He replied in a low tone: "There's no need to refer to anything, of course. Assume—I suggest—that he has forgotten all that happened, and you—have forgotten too."

He was aware of nothing but her eyes. The softness, the delicate perfume, the perfect voice, even the fur and flowers—all were summed up in her eyes alone. In those eyes he could have lost himself perhaps for ever.

He led her into the room, a certain abruptness in his manner.

"I shall leave you alone," he whispered, using his professional voice. "It is best that he should see you quite alone. I shall not be far away, but you will find him perfectly quiet. He understands that you are"—his tone changed upon the adjective—"sacred."

"Sacred," she murmured to herself, repeating the word, "sacred."

They smiled. And the door closed behind her. Across the room rose the tall figure of the man she had come to see, dressed in dark blue, a low white shirt open at the neck, a blue tie that matched the strong, clear eyes, the wondrous hair crowning the whole like a flame. The slant of wintry sunlight by chance just caught the great figure as it rose, lightly, easily, as though it floated up out of the floor before her.

And, as by magic, the last uncertainty in her disappeared; she knew herself akin to this radiant shape of blue and gold; knew also—mysteriously—in a way entirely beyond her to explain—knew why Edward Fillery was dear to her. Was it that something in the three of them pertained to a common origin? The conviction, half thought, half feeling, rose in her as she looked into the blue eyes facing her and took the outstretched hand.

"You strange lost being! No one will understand you— here. . . ."

The words flashed through her mind of their own accord, instantly, spontaneously, yet were almost forgotten the same second in the surge of more commonplace feeling that rose after. Only the "here" proved their origin not entirely forgotten. It was the selfless, mothering instinct that now dominated, but the division in her being had, none the less, been indicated as by a white piercing light that searched her inmost nature. That added "here" laid bare, she felt, some part of her which, with all other men, was clothed and covered away.

Realized though dimly, this troubled her clear mind, as she took the chair he offered, the conviction that she must

tend and care for, even love this strange youth, as though
he were in exile and none but herself could understand him.
She heard the deep resonant voice in the air in front of her:

"I am not lost now," he said, with his radiant smile, and
as if he perceived her thought from the expression in her
face. "I wished to take you away—to take you back. I
wish it still."

He stood gazing down at her. The deep tones, the shining eyes, the towering stature with its quiet strength—these,
added to the directness of the language, confused her for
a moment. The words were so entirely unexpected. Fillery
had led her to suppose otherwise. Yet before the blazing
innocence in his face and manner, her composure at once
returned. She found no words at first. She smiled up into
his eyes, then pointed to a chair. Seated he would be more
manageable, she felt. His upright stature was so overpowering.

"You had forgotten——" he went on, obeying her wish
and sitting down, "but I could not know that you had forgotten. I apologize"—the word sounded oddly on his lips,
as though learned recently—"for making you suffer."

"Forgotten!"

A swift intuition, due to some as yet undecipherable kinship, told her that the word bore no reference to the Studio
scene. Some larger meaning, scaled to an immenser map,
came with it. An unrealized emotion stirred faintly in her
as she heard. Her first sight of him as a figure of light
returned.

"But that is all forgiven now," she replied calmly in her
firm, gentle voice. "We need not speak of it. You understand now" — she ended lamely — "that it is not possible——"

He listened intently, gravely, as though with a certain
effort, his head bent forward to catch every syllable. And
as he bent, peering, listening, he might have been some
other-worldly being staring down through a window in the
sky into the small confusions of earth's affairs.

"Yes," he said, the moment she stopped speaking, "I understand now. I shall never make you suffer again. Only—I could not know that you had forgotten—so completely."

"Forgotten?" she again repeated in spite of herself, for the way he uttered the word again stirred that nameless, deep emotion in her. Their attitudes respectively were changing. She no longer felt that she could "mother" this great figure before her.

"Where we belong," he answered in his great quiet voice. *"There,"* he added, in a way that made it the counterpart of her own spontaneous and intuitive "here." "It is so easy. I had forgotten too. But Fillery, dear Fillery, helps me to remember, and the stars and flowers and wind, these help me too. And then you—when I saw *you* I suddenly remembered more. I was so happy. I remembered what I had left to come among men and women. I knew that Fillery and you belonged 'there' with me. You, both, had come down for a little time, come down 'here,' but had remained too long. You had become almost as men and women are. I remembered everything when I saw your eyes. I was so happy in a moment, as I looked at you, that I felt I must go back, go home. The central fire called me, called us all three. I wanted to escape and take you with me. I knew by your eyes that you were ready. You called to Fillery. We were off."

He paused a moment, while she listened in breathless silence.

"Then, suddenly, you refused. You resisted. Something prevented. The Messengers were there when suddenly"— an expression of yearning pain clouded his great eyes a moment—"you forgot again. I forgot too, forgot everything. The darkness came. It was cold. My enemy, the water, caught me."

He stopped, and passed his hands across his forehead, sighing, his eyes fixed upon vacancy as with an intense effort to recover something. "And I still forget," he went on, the yearning now transferred from the eyes to the lowered voice. "I can remember nothing again. All, all is gone from me." The light in his face actually grew dimmer as he slowly uttered the words. He leaned back in his big arm-chair. Again, it occurred to her, it was as if he drew back from that window in the sky.

A curious hollow, empty of life, seemed to drop into the room between them as his voice ceased.

While he had been speaking, the girl watched and listened with intense interest and curiosity. She remembered he was a "patient," yet no touch of uneasiness or nervousness was in her. His strange words, meaningless as they might seem, woke deep echoes of some dim buried recognition in her. It amazed and troubled her. This young man, this sinner against the conventions whom she had come to comfort and forgive, held the reins already. What had happened, what was happening, and how did he contrive it? She was aware of a clear, divining knowledge in him, a power, a directness she could not fathom. He seemed to read her inside out. It was more than uncanny; it was spiritual. It mastered her.

During his speech he remained very still, without gesture, without change of expression in his face; he made no movement; only his voice deepened and grew rhythmical. And a power emanated from him she hardly dared resist, much less deny. His voice, his words, reached depths in her she scarcely knew herself. He was so strong, so humble, so simple, yet so strangely peaceful. And—suddenly she realized it—so far beyond her, yet akin. She became aware that the figure seated in the chair, watching her, talking, was but a fraction of his whole self. He was—the word occurred to her—immense. Was she, too, immense?

More than troubled, she was profoundly stimulated. The mothering instinct in her for the first time seemed to fail a little. The woman in her trembled, not quite sure of itself. But, besides these two, there was another part of her that listened and felt joy—a white, radiant joy which, if she allowed, must become ecstasy. Whence came this hint of unearthly rapture? Again there rose before her the two significant words: "There" and "Here."

"I do not quite understand," she replied, after a moment's pause, looking into his eyes steadily, her voice firm, her young face very sweet; "I do not fully understand, perhaps. But I sympathize." Then she added suddenly, with a little smile: "But, at any rate, I did not come to make you apologize—Julian. Please be sure of that. I came to see if I might be of any use—if there was anything I might do to make——"

His quick interruption transfixed her.

"You came," he said in a distinct, low tone, "because you love me and wish me to love you. But we do love already, you, dear Fillery, and I—only our love is in that great Service where we all three belong. It is not of this—it is not *here*——" making an impatient gesture with his hand to indicate his general surroundings.

He broke off instantly, noticing the expression in her face.

She had realized suddenly, as he spoke, the blind fury of reproduction that sweeps helpless men and women everywhere into union, then flings them aside exhausted, useless, its purpose accomplished. Though herself never yet caught by it, the vivid realization made her turn from life with pity and revulsion. Yet—were these thoughts her own? Whence did they come, if not? And what was this new blind thing straining in her mind for utterance, bursting upwards like a flame, threatening to split it asunder even in its efforts to escape? "What are these words we use?" darted across her. "What do they mean? What is it we're talking about *really?* I don't know quite. Yet it's real, yes, real and true. Only it's beyond our words. It's something I know, but have forgotten. . . ." That was *his* word again: "Forgotten"! While they used words together, something in her went stumbling, groping, thrusting towards a great shining revelation for which no words existed. And a strange, deep anguish seized her suddenly.

"Oh!" he cried, "I make you suffer again. The fire leaves you. You are white. I—I will apologize"—he slipped on to his knees before her—"but you do not understand. It was not your sacredness I spoke of." Already on his knees before her, but level with her face owing to his great stature, gazing into her eyes with an expression of deep tenderness, humility, almost suffering, he added: "It was our other love, I meant, our great happy service, the thing we have forgotten. You came, I thought, to help me to remember *that*. The way home—I saw you knew." The light streamed back into his face and eyes.

The tumult and confusion in the girl were natural enough. Her resourcefulness, however, did not fail her at this curious and awkward moment. His words, his conduct were more than she could fathom, yet behind both she divined a source of remote inspiration she had never known before in any "man." The beauty and innocence on the face arrested her faculties for a second. That nameless emotion stirred again. A glimmer of some faint, distant light, whose origin she could not guess, passed flickering across her inner tumult. Some faculty she could not name, at any rate, blew suddenly to white heat in her. This youth on his knees before her had spoken truth. Without knowing it even herself, she had given him her love, a virgin love, a woman's love hitherto unawakened in her by any other man, but a love not of this earth quite—because of him who summoned it into sudden flower.

Yet at the same time he denied the need of it! He spoke of some marvellous great shining Service that was different from the love of man and woman.

This too, as some forgotten, lost ideal, she knew was also true.

Her mind, her heart, her experience, her deepest womanly nature, these, she realized in a glowing instant of extraordinary divination, were at variance in her. She trembled; she knew not what to do or say or think. And again, it came to her, that the visible shape before her was but the insignificant fraction of a being whose true life spread actively and unconfined through infinite space.

She then did something that was prompted, though she did not know it thus, by her singleness of heart, her purity of soul and body, her unique and natural instinct to be of use, of service, to others—the accumulated practice and effort of her entire life provided the action along a natural line of least resistance: she bent down and put her arm and hand round his great shoulder. She lowered her face. She kissed him most tenderly, with a mother's love, a woman's secret passion perhaps, but yet with something else as well she could not name—an unearthly yearning for a greater Ideal than anything she had yet known on earth among humanity. . . . It was the invisible she kissed.

And LeVallon, she realized with immense relief, justified her action, for he did not return the kiss. At the same time she had known quite well it would be thus. That kiss trembled, echoed, in her own greater unrealized self as well.

"What is it," she whispered, a mysterious passion surging up in her as she raised him to his feet, "that you remember and wish to recover—for us all? Can you tell me? What is this great, happy, deathless service that we have forgotten?" Her voice trembled a little. An immense sense of joy, of liberty, shook out its sunlit wings.

His expression, as he rose, was something between that of a child and a faithful yearning animal, but of a "divine animal," though she did not know the phrase. Its purity, its sweetness, its power—it was the power she noticed chiefly—were superb.

"I cannot tell, I cannot remember," his voice said softly, for all its resonant, virile depth. "It is some state we all have come from—into this. We are strangers here. This brain and intellect, this coarse, thick feeling, this selfishness, this want of harmony and working together—all this is new and strange to us. It is of blind and clumsy children. This love of one single person for one other single person—it is so pitiful. We three have come into this for a time, a little time. It is pain and misery. It is prison. Each one works only for himself. There is no joy. They know nothing of our great Service. We cannot show them. Let us go back——"

Another pause fell between them, another of those singular hollows she had felt before. But this time the hollow was not empty. It was brimmed with surging life. The gulf between her earthly state and another that was nameless, a gulf usually unbridgeable, the fixed gulf, as an old book has it, which may not be crossed without danger to the Race, for whose protection it exists—this childhood simile occurred to her. And a sense of awe stirred in her being. It was the realization that this gulf or hollow now brimmed with life, that it could be crossed, that she might step over into another place—the sense of awe rose thence, yet came certainly neither from the woman nor the mother in her.

"I am of another place," Le Vallon went on, plucking the thought naked from her inmost being. "For I am come here recently, and the purpose of my coming is hidden from me, and memory is dark. But it is not entirely dark. Sometimes I half remember. Stars, flowers, fire, wind, women —here and there—bring light into the darkness. Oh," he cried suddenly, "how wonderful they are—how wonderful you are—on that account to me!"

The voice held a strange, evoking power perhaps. A thousand yearnings she had all her life suppressed (because they interfered with her duty—as she conceived it—here and now, fluttered like rising flames within her as she listened. His voice now increased in volume and rhythm, though still quiet and low-pitched; it was as if a great wind poured behind it with tremendous vibrations, through it, lifting her out of a limited, cramped, everyday self. A delicious warmth of happy comfort, of acceptance, of enthusiasm glowed in her. And LeVallon's face, she saw, had become radiant, almost as though it emanated light. This light entered her being and brought joy again.

"Joy!" he said, reading her thought and feeling. "Joy!"

"Joy! Another place!" she heard herself repeating, her eyes now fixed upon his own.

She felt lighter, caught up and away a little, lifted above the solid earth; as if it was heat that lightened, and wind that bore her upwards. Everything in her became intensified.

"Another state, another place"—her voice seemed to borrow something of the rhythm in his own, though she did not notice it—"but not away from earth, this beautiful earth?" With a happy smile she added, "I love the dear kind earth, I love it."

The light on his face increased:

"The earth we love and serve," he said, "is beautiful, but here"—he looked about him round the room, at the trees waving through the window, at the misty sky above draping the pale light of the sun—"here I am on the surface only. There is confusion and struggle. Everything quarrels against everything else. It is discord and disorder. There is no harmony. Here, on the surface, everything is separate. There is no working together. It is all pain, each little part fighting for itself. Here—I am outside—there is no joy."

It was the phrase "I am outside" that flashed something more of his meaning into her. His full meaning lay beyond actual words perhaps; but this phrase fell like a shock into that inmost self which she had deliberately put away.

"*You are from inside,* yes," she exclaimed, marvelling afterwards that she had said it; "within—nearer to the centre——!"

And he took the abrupt interruption as though they both understood and spoke of the same one thing together, having found a language born of similar great yearnings and of forgotten knowledge, times, states, conditions, places.

"I come," he said, his voice, his bright smile alive with the pressure of untold desire, "from another place that is— yes—inside, nearer to the centre. I have forgotten almost everything. I remember only that there was harmony, love, work and happiness all combined in the perfect liberty of our great service. We served the earth. We helped the life upon it. There was no end, no broken fragments, no failure." The voice touched chanting. "There was no death."

He rose suddenly and came over to her side, and instinctively the girl stood up. What she felt and thought as she heard the strange language he used, she hardly knew herself. She only knew in that moment an immense desire to help her kind, an intensification of that great ideal of impersonal service which had always been the keynote of her life. This became vividly stimulated in her. It rose like a dominating, overmastering passion. The sense of ineffectual impotence, of inability to accomplish anything of value against the stolid odds life set against her, the uselessness of her efforts with the majority, in a word, seemed brushed away, as though greater powers of limitless extent were now at last within her reach. This blazed in her like fire. It shone in her big dark eyes that looked straight into his as they stood facing one another.

"And that service," he went on in his deep vibrating, half-singing tone, "I see in dear Fillery and in you. I know my own kind. We three, at least, belong. I know my own." The voice seemed to shake her like a wind.

At the last two words her soul leaped within her. It seemed quite natural that his great arm should take her breast and shoulder and that his lips should touch her cheek and hair. For there was worship in both gestures.

"Our greater service," she whispered, trembling, "tell me of that. What is it?" His touch against her was like the breath of fire.

Her womanly instincts, so-called, her maternal love, her feminine impulses deserted her. She was aware solely at that moment of the proximity of a being who called her to a higher, to, at any rate, a different state, to something beyond the impoverished conditions of humanity as she had hitherto experienced it, to something she had ever yearned and longed for without knowing what it was. An extraordinary sense of enormous liberty swept over her again.

His voice broke and the rhythm failed.

"I cannot tell you," he replied mournfully, the light fading a little from his eyes and face. "I have forgotten. That other place is hidden from me. I am in exile," he added slowly, "but with you and—Fillery." His blue eyes filled with moisture; the expression of troubled loneliness was one she had never seen before on any human face. "I suffer," he added gently. "We all suffer."

And, at the sight of it, the yearning to help, to comfort, to fulfil her rôle as mother, returned confusingly, and rose in her like a tide. He was so big and strong and splendid. He was so helpless. It was, perhaps, the innocence in the great blue eyes that conquered her—for the first time in her life.

But behind, beside the mother in her, stirred also the natural woman. And beyond this again, rose the accumulated power of the entire Race. The instinct of all the women of the planet since the world began drove at her. Not easily may an individual escape the deep slavery of the herd.

The young girl wavered and hestitated. Caught by so many emotions that whirled her as in a vortex, the direction of the resultant impetus hung doubtful for some time. During the half hour's talk, she had entered deeper water than she had ever dared or known before. Life hitherto, so far as men were concerned, had been a simple and an easy thing that she had mastered without difficulty. Her real self lay still unscarred within her. Freely she had given the mothering care and sympathy that were so strong in her, the more freely because the men who asked of her were children, one and all, children who needed her, but from whom she asked nothing in return. If they fell in love, as they usually did, she knew exactly how to lift their emotion in a way that saved them pain while it left herself untouched. None reached her real being, which thus remained unscathed, for none offered the lifting glory that she craved.

Here, for the first time facing her, stood a being of another type; and that unscathed self in her went trembling at the knowledge. Here was a power she could not play with, could not dominate, but a power that could play with her as easily as the hurricane with the flying leaf. It was not his words, his strange beauty, his great strength that mastered her, though these brought their contribution doubtless. The power she felt emanated unconsciously from him, and was used unconsciously. It was all about him. She realized herself a child before him, and this realization sweetened, though it confused her being. He so easily touched depths in her she had hardly recognized herself. He could so easily lift her to terrific heights. . . . Various sides of her became dominant in turn. . . .

The inmost tumult of a good woman's heart is not given to men to read, perhaps, but the final impetus resulting from the whirlpool tossed her at length in a very definite direction. She found her feet again. The determining factor that decided the issue of the struggle was a small and very human one. He appealed to the woman in her, yet what stirred the woman was the vital and afflicting factor that—he did not need her.

He wished to help, to lift her towards some impersonal ideal that remained his secret. He wished to *give*—he could give—while she, for her part, had nothing that he needed. Indeed, he asked for nothing. He was as independent of her as she was independent of these other men.

And the woman, now faced for the first time with this entirely new situation, decided automatically—that he should learn to need her. He must. Though she had nothing that he wanted from her, she must on that very account give all. The sacrifice which stands ready for the fire in every true feminine heart was lighted there and then. She had found her master and her god. Half measures were not possible to her. She stood naked at the altar. But in her sacrifice he, too, the priest, the deity, the master, he also should find love.

Such is the woman's power, however, to conceal from herself the truth, that she did not recognize at first what this decision was. She disguised it from her own heart, yet quite honestly. She loved him and gave him all she had to give for ever and ever: even though he did not ask nor need her love. This she grasped. Her rôle must be one of selfless sacrifice. But the deliberate purpose behind her real decision she disguised from herself with complete success. It lay there none the less, strong, vital, very simple. She would teach him love.

Alone of all men, Edward Fillery could have drawn up this motive from its inmost hiding place in her deep subconscious being, and have made it clear to her. Dr. Fillery, had he been present, would have discerned it in her, as, indeed, he did discern it later. He had, for that matter, already felt its prophecy with a sinking heart when he planned bringing them together: Iraida might suffer at LeVallon's hands.

But Fillery, apparently, was not present, and Nayan Khilkoff remained unaware of self-deception. LeVallon "needs your care and sympathy; you can help him," she remembered. This she believed, and Love did the rest.

So intricate, so complex were the emotions in her that she realized one thing only—she must give all without thought of self. "When half gods go the gods arrive" sang in her heart. She was a woman, one of a mighty and innumerable multitude, and collective instinct urged her irresistibly. But it hid at the same time with lovely care the imperishable desire and intention that the arriving god should—*must*—love her in return.

The youth stood facing her while this tumult surged within her heart and mind. Outwardly calm, she still gazed into the clear blue eyes that shone with moisture as he repeated, half to himself and half to her:

"We are in exile here; we suffer. We have forgotten."

His hands were stretched towards her, and she took them in her own and held them a moment.

"But you and I," he went on, "you and I and Fillery—shall remember again—soon. We shall know why we are here. We shall do our happy work together here. We shall then return—escape."

His deep tones filled the air. At the sound of the other name a breath of sadness, of disappointment, touched her coldly. The familiar name had faded. It was, as always, dear. But its potency had dimmed. . . .

The sun was down and a soft dusk covered all. A faint wind rustled in the garden trees through the open window.

"Fillery," she murmured, "Edward Fillery!—— He loved me. He has loved me always."

The little words—they sounded little for the first time— she uttered almost in a whisper that went lost against the figure of LeVallon towering above her through the twilight.

"We are together," his great voice caught her whisper in the immense vibration, drowning it. "The love of our happy impersonal service brings us all together. We have forgotten, but we shall remember soon."

It seemed to her that he shone now in the dusky air. Light came about his face and shoulders. An immense vitality poured into her through his hands. The sense of strange kinship was overpowering. She felt, though not in terms of size or physical strength, a pigmy before him, while yet another thing rose in gigantic and limitless glory as from some inner heart he quickened in her. This sense of exaltation, of delirious joy that tempted sweetly, came upon her. He *must* love her, need her in the end. . . .

"Julian," she murmured softly, drawn irresistibly closer. "The gods have brought you to me." Her feet went nearer of their own accord, but there was no movement, no answering pressure, in the hands she held. "You shall never know loneliness again, never while I am here. The gods—your gods—have brought us together."

"*Our* gods," she heard his answer, "are the same." The words trembled against her actual breast, so close she was now leaning against him. "Even if lost, it is they who sent us here. I know their messengers——"

He broke off, standing back from her, dropping her hands, or, rather, drawing his own away.

"Hark!" he cried. The voice deep and full, yet without loudness, thrilled her. She watched him with terror and amazement, as he turned to the open window, throwing his arms out suddenly to the darkening sky against which the trees loomed still and shapeless. His figure was wrapped in a faint radiance as of silvery moonlight. She was aware of heat about her, a comforting, inspiring warmth that pervaded her whole being, as from within. The same moment the bulk of the big tree shook and trembled, and a steady wind came pouring into the room. It seemed to her the wind, the heat, poured through that tree.

And the inner heart in her grew clear an instant. This wind, this heat, increased her being marvellously. The exaltation in her swept out and free. She saw him, dropped from alien skies upon the little teeming earth. The sense of his remoteness from the life about them, of her own remoteness too, flashed over her like wind and fire. An immense ideal blazed, then vanished. It flamed beyond her grasp. It beckoned with imperishable loveliness, then faded instantly. Wind caught it up once more. With the fire an overpowering joy rose in her.

"Julian!" she cried aloud. "Son of Wind and Fire!"

At the words, which had come to her instinctively, he turned with a sudden gesture she could not quite interpret, while there broke upon his face a smile, strange and lovely, that caught up the effect of light about him and seemed to focus in his brilliant eyes. His happiness was beyond all question, his admiration, wonder too; yet the quality she chiefly looked and expected—was *not* there.

She chilled. The joy, she was acutely conscious, was not a personal joy.

"You," he said gently, happily, emphasizing the word, "you are not pitiful," and the rustle of the shaking trees outside the window merged their voice in his and carried it outward into space. It was as if the wind itself had spoken. Across the garden dusk there shot a sudden effect of light, as though a flame had flickered somewhere in the sky, then passed back into the growing night. There was a scent of flowers in the air. "You," he cried, with an exultation that carried her again beyond herself. "You are not pitiful."

"Julian——!" she stammered, longing for his arms. She half drew away. The blood flowed down and back in her. "Not pitiful!" she repeated faintly.

For it was to her suddenly as if that sighing wind that entered the room from the outer sky had borne him away from her. That wind was a messenger. It came from that distant state, that other region where he belonged, a state, a region compared to which the beings of earth were trumpery and tinsel-dressed. It came to remind him of his home and origin. The little earth, the myriad confused figures struggling together on its surface, he saw as "pitiful." From that window in the sky whence he looked down he watched them. . . .!

She knew the feeling in him, knew it, because some part of her, though faint and deeply hidden, was akin. Yet she was not wholly "pitiful." He had discerned in her this faint, hidden strain of vaster life, had stirred and strengthened it by his words, his presence. Yet it was not vital enough in her to stand alone. When wind and fire, his elements, breathed forth from it, she was afraid.

"You are not pitiful," he had said, yet pitiful, for all that, she knew herself to be. On that breath of sighing wind he swept away from her, far, far away where, as yet, she could not follow. And her dream of personal love swept with it. Some ineffable hint of a divine, impersonal glory she had known went with him from her heart. The personal was too strong in her. It was human love she desired both to give and ask.

Unspoken words flared through her heart and being: "Julian, you have no soul, no human soul. But I will give you one, for I will teach you love——"

He turned upon her like a hurricane of windy fire.

"Soul!" he cried, catching the word out of her naked heart. "Oh, be not caught with that pitiful delusion. It is this idea of soul that binds you hopelessly to selfish ends and broken purposes. This thing you call soul is but the dream of human vanity and egoism. It is worse than love. Both bind you endlessly to limited desires and blind ambitions. They are of children."

He rose, like some pillar of whirling flame and wind, beside her.

"Come out with me," he cried, "come back! You teach me to remember! Our elemental home calls sweetly to us, our elemental service waits. We belong to those vast Powers. They are eternal. They know no binding and they have no death. Their only law is service, that mighty service which builds up the universe. The stars are with us, the nebulæ and the central fires are their throne and altar. The soul you dream of in your little circle is but an idle dream of the Race that ties your feet lest you should fly and soar. The personal has bandaged all your eyes. Nayan, come back with me. You once worked with me there—you, I and Fillery together."

His voice, though low, had that which was terrific in it. The volume of its sound appalled her. Its low vibrations shook her heart.

"Soul," she said very softly, courage sure in her, but tears close in her burning eyes, "is my only hope. I live for it. I am ready to die for it. It is my life!"

He gazed at her a moment with a tenderness and sympathy she hardly understood, for their origin lay hidden beyond her comprehension. She knew one thing only—that he looked adorable and glorious, a being brought by the wise powers of life, whatever these might be, into the keeping of her love and care. The mother and the woman merged in her. His redemption lay within her gentle hands, if it lay at the same time upon an altar that was her awful sacrifice.

"Son of wind and fire!" she cried, though emotion made her voice dwindle to a breathless whisper. "You called to my love, yet my love is personal. I have nothing else to give you. Julian, come back! O stay with me. Your wind and fire frighten, for they take you away. Service I know, but your service—O what is it? For it leaves the bed, the hearthstone cold——"

She stopped abruptly, wondering suddenly at her own words. What was this rhythm that had caught her mind and heart into an unknown, a daring form of speech?

But the wind ran again through the open window fluttering the curtains and the skirts about her feet. It sighed and whispered. It was no earthly wind. She saw him once again go from her on its quiet wings. He left her side, he left her heart. And an icy realization of *his* loneliness, his exile, stirred in her. . . . For a moment, as she looked up into his shining face silhouetted in the dusk against the window, there rose tumultuously in her that maternal feeling which had held all men safely at a distance hitherto. Like a wave, it mastered her. She longed to take him in her arms, to shield him from a world that was not his, to bless and comfort him with all she had to give, to have the right to brush that wondrous hair, to open those lids at dawn and close them with a kiss at night. This ancient passion rose in her, bringing, though she did not recognize it, the great woman in its train. She walked up to him with both hands outstretched:

"All my nights," she said, with no reddening of the cheek, "are as our wedding night!"

He heard, he saw, but the words held no meaning for him.

"Julian! Stay with me—stay here!" She put her arms about him.

"And forget——!" he cried, an inexpressible longing in his voice. He bent, none the less, beneath the pressure of her clinging arms; he lowered his face to hers.

"I will teach you love," she murmured, her cheek against

his own. "You do not know how sweet, how wonderful it is. All your strange wisdom you shall show me, and I will learn willingly, if only I may teach you—love."

"You would teach me to forget," he said in a voice of curious pain, "just as you—are forgetting now."

He gently unclasped her hands from about his neck, and went over to the open window, while she sank into a chair, watching him. She again heard the wind, but again no common, earthly wind, go singing past the walls.

"But *I* will teach you to remember," he said, his great figure half turning towards her again, his voice sounding as though it were in that sighing breath of wind that passed and died away into the silence of the sky.

The strange difficulty, the immensity, of her self-appointed task, grew suddenly crystal clear in her mind. Amid the whirling, aching pain and yearning that she felt it stood forth sharp and definite. It was imperious. She loved, and she must teach *him* love. This was the one thing needful in his case. Her own deep, selfless heart would guide her.

There was pain in her, but there was no fear. Above the conventions she felt herself, naked and unashamed. The sense of a new immense liberty he had brought lifted her into a region where she could be natural without offence. He had flung wide the gates of life, setting free those strange, ultimate powers which had lain hidden and unrealized hitherto, and with them was quickened, too, that mysterious and awful hint which, beckoning ever towards some vaster life, had made the world as she found it unsatisfactory, pale, of meagre value.

As the strange drift of wind passed off into the sky, she moved across the room and stood beside him, its dying chant still humming in her ears. That song of the wind, she understood, was symbolic of what she had to fight, for his being, though linked to a divine service she could not understand, lay in Nature and apart from human things:

"Think, Julian," she murmured, her face against his

shoulder so that the sweet perfume as of flowers he exhaled came over her intoxicatingly, "think what we could do together for the world—for all these little striving ignorant troubled people in it—for everybody! You and I together working, helping, lifting them all up——!"

He made no movement, and she took his great arm and drew it round her neck, placing the hand against her cheek. He looked down at her then, his eyes peering into her face.

"That," he said in a deep, gentle voice that vibrated through her whole body, "yes, that we will do. It is the service—the service of our gods. It is why I called you. From the first I saw it in you, and in——"

Before he could speak the name she kissed his lips, pulling his head lower in order to reach them: "Think, Julian," she whispered, his eyes so close to hers that they seemed to burn them, "think what our child might be!"

The wind came back across the tossing trees with a rush of singing. Her hair fluttered across their two faces, as it entered the room, drove round the inner walls, then, with a cry, flew out again into the empty sky. She felt as if the wind had answered her, for other answer there came none. Far away in the spaces of that darkening sky the wind rushed sailing, sailing with its impersonal song of power and of triumph. . . . She did not remember any further spoken words. She remembered only, as she went homewards down the street, that Julian had opened the door upon some unspoken understanding that she had lost him because she dared not follow recklessly where he led, and that the steady draught, it seemed, had driven forcibly behind her—as though the wind had blown her out.

It was only much later she realized that the figure who had then overtaken her, supported, comforted with kind ordinary words she hardly understood at the moment and yet vaguely welcomed, finally leaving her at the door of her father's house in Chelsea, was the figure of Edward Fillery.

CHAPTER XXIV

A S upon a former occasion some twenty-four hours before, "N. H." seemed hardly aware that his visitor
had left, though this time there was the vital difference—
that what was of value had not gone at all. The essence
of the girl, it seemed, was still with him. It remained. The
physical presence was to him apparently the least of all.

He returned to his place at the open window of the
darkening room, while night, with her cooler airs, passed
over the world on tiptoe. He drew deep breaths, opened
his arms, and seemed to shake himself, as though glad to
be free of recent little awkward and unnatural gestures that
had irked him. There was happiness in his face. "She
is a builder, though she has forgotten," ran his thought with
pleasure, "and I can work with her. Like Fillery, she
builds up, constructs; we are all three in the same service,
and the gods are glad. I love her . . . yes . . . but she"—
his thoughts grew troubled and confused—"she speaks of
another love that is a tight and binding little thing . . . that
catches and confines. It is for one person only . . . one
person for one other. . . . For two . . . only for two persons! . . . What is its meaning then?"

Of her words and acts he had understood evidently a
small part only; much that she had said and done he had
not comprehended, although in it somewhere there had certainly lain a sweet, faint, troubling pleasure that was new
to him.

His thought wavered, flickered out and vanished. For
a long time he leaned against the window with his images,
thinking with his heart, for when alone and not stirred by

the thinking of others close to him, he became of a curious childlike innocence, knowing nothing. His "thinking" with others present seemed but a reflection of *their* thinking. The way he caught up the racial thinking, appearing swiftly intelligent at the time (as with Fillery's mind), passed the instant he was alone. He became open, then, to bigger rhythms that the little busy thinkers checked and interrupted. But this greater flow of images, of rhythms, this thinking with the heart—what was it, and with what things did it deal? He did not know. He had forgotten. To his present brain it was alien. He grasped only that it was concerned with the rhythms of fire and wind apparently, though hardly, perhaps, of that crude form in which men know them, but of an inner, subtler, more vital heat and air which lie in and behind all forms and help to shape them—and of Intelligences which use these as their vehicles, their instruments, their bodies.

In his "images" he was aware of these Intelligences, perceived them with his entire being, shared their activities and nature: behind all so-called forms and shapes, whether of people, flowers, minerals, of insects or of stars, of a bird, a butterfly or a nebula, but also of those *mental* shapes which are born of thought and mood and heart—this host of Intelligences, great and small, all delving together, building, constructing, involved in a vast impersonal service which was deathless. This seemed the mighty call that thundered through him, fire and wind merely the agencies with which he, in particular, knew instinctively his duties lay.

For his work, these images taught him, was to increase life by making the "body" it used as perfect as he could. The more perfect the form, the instrument, the greater the power manifesting through it. A poor, imperfect form stopped the flow of this manifesting life, as though a current were held up and delayed. For instance, his own form, his present body, now irked, delayed and hampered him, although he knew not how or why or whence he had come to be using it at this moment on the earth. The instinctive desire to escape from it lay in him, and also the instinctive recognition that two others, similarly caught and imprisoned, must escape with him. . . .

The images, the rhythms, poured through him in a mighty flood, as he leaned by the open window, his great figure, his whole nature too, merging in the space, the wind, the darkness of the soft-moving night beyond. . . . Yet darkness troubled him too; it always seemed unfamiliar, new, something he had never been accustomed to. In darkness he became quiet, very gentle, feeling his way, as it were, uneasily.

He was aware, however, that Fillery was near, though not, perhaps, that he was actually in the room, seated somewhere among the shadows, watching him. He felt him close in the same way he felt the girl still close, whether distance between them in space was actually great or small. The essential in all three was similar, their yearnings, hopes, intentions, purposes were akin; their longing for some service, immense, satisfying, it seemed, connected them. The voice, however, did not startle when it sounded behind him from an apparently empty room:

"The love she spoke of you do not understand, of course. Perhaps you do not need it. . . ."

The voice, as well as the feeling that lay behind, hardly disturbed the images and rhythms in their wondrous flow. Rather, they seemed a part of them. "N. H." turned. He saw Dr. Fillery distinctly, sitting motionless among the shadows by the wall.

"It is, for you, a new relationship, and seems small, cramping and unnecessary——"

"What is it?" "N. H." asked. "What is this love she seeks to hold me with, saying that I need it? Dear Fillery," he added, moving nearer, "will you tell me what it is? I found it sweet and pleasant, yet I fear it."

"It is," was the reply, "in its best form, the highest quality *we* know——"

"Ah! I felt the fire in it," interrupted "N. H." smiling.

"I smelt the flowers." His smile seemed faintly luminous across the gloom.

"Because it was the best," replied the other gently. "In its best form it means, sometimes, the complete sacrifice of one being for the welfare of another. There is no self in it at all." He felt the eyes of his companion fixed upon him in the darkness of the quiet room; he felt likewise that he was bewildered and perplexed. "As, for instance, the mother for her child," he went on. "That is the purest form of it we know."

"One being feels it for *one* other only," "N. H." repeated apparently ignoring the reference to maternal love. "Each wants the other for himself *alone!* Each lives for the other only, the rest excluded! It is always two and two. Is that what she means?"

"She would not like it if you had the same feeling for another—woman," Fillery explained. "She would feel jealousy—which means she would grudge sharing you with another. She would resent it, afraid of losing you."

"Two and two, and two and two," the words floated through the shadows. The ideal seemed to shock and hurt him; he could not understand it. "She asks for the whole of me—all to herself. It is lower than insects, flowers even. It is against Nature. So small, so separate——"

"But Nature," interrupted Dr. Fillery, after an interval of silence between them, "is not concerned with what we call love. She is indifferent to it. Her purpose is merely the continuance of the Race, and she accomplishes this by making men and women attractive to one another. This, too," he explained, "we call love, though it is love in its weakest, least enduring form."

"That," replied "N. H.," "I know and understand. She builds the best form she can."

"And once the form is built," agreed the other, "and Nature's aim fulfilled, this kind of love usually fades out and dies. It is a physical thing entirely, like the two atoms we read about together a few days ago which rush together automatically to produce a third thing." He lowered his voice suddenly. "There was a great teacher once," he went on, "who told us that we should love everybody, everybody, and that in the real life there was no marriage, as we call it, nor giving in marriage."

It seemed that, as he said the words, the darkness lifted, and a faint perfume of flowers floated through the air.

"N. H." made no comment or reply. He sat still, listening.

"I love her," he whispered suddenly. "I love her in *that* way—because I want everybody else to love her too—as I do, and as you do. But I do not want her for myself alone. Do you? You do not, of course. I feel you are as I am. You are happy that I love her."

"There is morality," said Fillery presently in a low voice, glad at that moment of the darkness. "There is what we call morality."

"Tell me, dear Fillery, what that is. Is it bigger than your 'love'?"

Dr. Fillery explained briefly, while his companion listened intently, making no comment. It was evidently as strange and new to him as human love. "We have invented it," he added at the end, "to protect ourselves, our mothers, our families, our children. It is, you see, a set of rules devised for the welfare of the Race. For though a few among us do not need such rules, the majority do. It is, in a word, the acknowledgment of the rights of others."

"It had to be invented!" exclaimed "N. H.," with a sigh that seemed to trouble the darkness as with the sadness of something he could scarcely believe. "And these rules are needed still! Is the Race at that stage only? It does not move, then?"

Into the atmosphere, as the low-spoken words were audible, stole again that mysterious sense of the insignificance of earth and all its manifold activities, human and otherwise, and with it, too, a remarkable breath of some larger reality, starry-bright, that lay shining just beyond all known horizons. Fillery shivered in spite of himself. It seemed to him for an instant that the great figure looming opposite through the darkness extended, spread, gathering into its increased proportions the sky, the trees, the darkened space outside; that it no longer sat there quite alone. He recalled his colleague's startling admission—the touch of panic terror.

"Slowly, if at all," he said louder, though wondering why he raised his voice. "Yet there is *some* progress."

He had the feeling it would be better to turn on the light, as though this conversation and the strange sensations it produced in him would be impossible in a full blaze. He made a movement, indeed, to find the switch. It was the sound of his companion's voice that made him pause, for the words came at him as though a wave of heat moved through the air. He knew intuitively that the other's intense inner activity had increased. He let his hand drop. He listened. Their thoughts, he was convinced, had mingled and been mutually shared again. There was a faint sound like music behind it.

"We have worked such a little time as yet," fell the words into the silence. "If only—oh! if only I could remember more!"

"A little time!" thought Fillery to himself, knowing that the other meant the millions of years Nature had used to evoke her myriad forms. "Try to remember," he added in a whisper.

"What I do remember, I cannot even tell," was the reply, the voice strangely deepening. "No words come to me." He paused a moment, then went on: "I am of the first, the oldest. I know that. The earth was hot and burning—burning, burning still. It was soft with heat when I was summoned from—from other work just completed. With a vast host I came. Our Service summoned us. We began at the beginning. I am of the oldest. The earth was still hot—burning, burning——"

The voice failed suddenly.

"I cannot remember. Dear Fillery, I cannot remember.

It hurts me. My head pains. Our work—our service—yes, there *is* progress. The ages, as you call them—but it is such a little time as yet——" The voice trailed off, the figure lost its suggestion of sudden vastness, the darkness emptied. "I am of the oldest—*that* I remember only. . . ." It ceased as though it drifted out upon the passing wind outside.

"Then you have been working," said Fillery, his voice still almost a whisper, "you and your great host, for thousands of years—in the service of this planet——" He broke off, unable to find his words, it seemed.

"Since the beginning," came the steady answer. "Years I do not know. Since the beginning. Yet we have only just begun—oh!" he cried, "I cannot remember! It is impossible! It all goes lost among my words, and in this darkness I am confused and entangled with your own little thinking. I suffer with it." Then suddenly: "My eyes are hot and wet, dear Fillery. What happens to them?" He stood up, putting both hands to his face. Fillery stood up too. He trembled.

"Don't try," he said soothingly; "do not try to remember any more. It will come back to you soon, but it won't come back by any deliberate effort."

He comforted him as best he could, realizing that the curious dialogue had lasted long enough. But he did not produce a disconcerting blaze by turning the light on suddenly; he led his companion gently to the door, so that the darkness might pass more gradually. The lights in the corridor were shaded and inoffensive. It was only in the bedroom that he noticed the bright tears, as "N. H.," examining them with curious interest in the mirror, exclaimed more to himself than to Fillery: "She had them too. I saw them in her eyes when she spoke to me of love, the love she will teach me because she said I needed it."

"Tears," said Fillery, his voice shaking. "They come from feeling pain."

"It is a little thing," returned "N. H.," smiling at himself, then turning to his friend, his great blue eyes shining wonderfully through their moisture. "Then she felt what I felt—we felt together. When she comes to-morrow I will show her these tears and she will be glad I love. And she will bring tears of her own, and you will have some too, and we shall all love together. It is not difficult, is it?"

"Not very," agreed Fillery, smiling in his turn; "it is not very difficult." He was again trembling.

"She will be happy that we all love."

"I—hope so."

It was curious how easily tears came to the eyes of this strange being, and for causes so different that they were not easy to explain. He did not cry; it was merely that the hot tears welled up.

Even with Devonham once it happened too. The lesson in natural history was over. Devonham had just sketched the outline of the various kingdoms, with the animal kingdom and man's position in it, according to present evolutionary knowledge, and had then said something about the earth's place in the solar system, and the probable relation of this system to the universe at large—an admirable bird's-eye view, as it were, without a hint of speculative imagination in it anywhere—when "N. H.," after intent listening in irresponsive silence, asked abruptly:

"What does it believe?" Then, as Devonham stared at him, a little puzzled at first, he repeated: "That is what the Race *knows*. But what does it *believe?*"

"Believe," said Devonham, "believe. Ah! you mean what is its religion, its faith, its speculations!"—and proceeded to give the briefest possible answer he felt consistent with his duty. The less his pupil's mind was troubled with such matters, the better, in his opinion.

"And their God?" the young man inquired abruptly, as soon as the recital was over. He had listened closely, as he always did, but without a sign of interest, merely waiting for the end, much as a child who is bored by a poor fairy tale, yet wishes to know exactly how it is all going to finish. "They *know* Him?" He leaned forward.

Devonham, not quite liking the form of the question, nor the more eager manner accompanying it, hesitated a moment, thinking perhaps what he ought to say. He did not want this mind, now opening, to be filled with ideas that could be of no use to it, nor help in its formation; least of all did he desire it to be choked and troubled with the dead theology of man-made notions concerning a tumbling personal Deity. Creeds, moreover, were a matter of faith, of auto-suggestion as he called it, being obviously divorced from any process of reason. He had, nevertheless, a question to answer and a duty to perform. His hesitation passed in compromise. He was, as has been seen, too sincere, too honest, to possess much sense of humour.

"The Race," he said, "or rather that portion of it into which you have been born, believes—on paper"—he emphasized the qualification—"in a paternal god; but its real god, the god it worships, is Knowledge. Not a Knowledge that exists for its own sake," he went on blandly, "but that brings possessions, power, comfort and a million needless accessories into life. That god it worships, as you see, with energy and zeal. Knowledge and work that shall result in acquisition, in pleasure, that is the god of the Race on this side of the planet where you find yourself."

"And the God on paper?" asked "N. H.," making no comment, though he had listened attentively and had understood. "The God that is written about on paper, and believed in on paper?"

"The printed account of this god," replied Devonham, "describes an omnipotent and perfect Being who has existed always. He created the planet and everything upon it, but created it so imperfectly that he had to send later a smaller god to show how much better he *might* have created us. In doing this, he offered us an extremely difficult and laborious method of improvement, a method of escaping from his own mistake, but a method so painful and unrealizable that it is contrary to our very natures—as he made them first." He almost smacked his lips as he said it.

"The big God, the first one," asked "N. H." at once. "Have they seen and known Him? Have they complained?"

"No," said Devonham, "they have not. Those who believe in him accept things as he made them."

"And the smaller lesser God—how did He arrive?" came the odd question.

"He was born like you and me, but without a father. No male had his mother ever known."

"He was recognized as a god?" The pupil showed interest, but no emotion, much less excitement.

"By a few. The rest, afraid because he told them their possessions were worthless, killed him quickly."

"And the few?"

"They obeyed his teaching, or tried to, and believed that they would live afterwards for ever and ever in happiness——"

"And the others? The many?"

"The others, according to the few, would live afterwards for ever and ever—in pain."

"It is a demon story," said "N. H.," smiling.

"It is printed, believed, taught," replied Devonham, "by an immense organization to millions of people——"

"Free?" inquired his pupil.

"The teachers are paid, but very little——"

"The teachers believe it, though?"

"Y-yes—at least some of them—probably," replied Devonham, after brief consideration.

"And the millions—do they worship this God?"

"They do, on paper, yes. They worship the first big God. They go once or twice a week into special buildings, dressed in their best clothes as for a party, and pray and sing and tell him he is wonderful and they themselves are miserable and worthless, and then ask him in abject humility for all sorts of things they want."

"Do they get them?"

"They ask for different things, you see. One wants fine weather for his holidays, another wants rain for his crops. The prayers in which they ask are printed by the Government."

"They ask for this planet only?"

"This planet conceives itself alone inhabited. There are no other living beings anywhere. The Earth is the centre of the universe, the only globe worth consideration."

Although "N. H." asked these quick questions, his interest was obviously not much engaged, the first sharp attention having passed. Then he looked fixedly at Devonham and said, with a sudden curious smile: "What you say is always dead. I understand the sounds you use, but the meaning cannot get into me—inside, I mean. But I thank you for the sound."

There was a moment's pause, during which Devonham, accustomed to strange remarks and comments from his pupil, betrayed no sign of annoyance or displeasure. He waited to see if any further questions would be forthcoming. He was observing a phenomenon; his attitude was scientific.

"But, in sending this lesser God," resumed "N. H." presently, "how did the big One excuse himself?"

"He didn't. He told the Race it was so worthless that nothing else could save it. He looked on while the lesser God was killed. He is very proud about it, and claims the thanks and worship of the Race because of it."

"The lesser God—poor lesser God!" observed "N. H."

"He was bigger than the other." He thought a moment. "How pitiful," he added.

"Much bigger," agreed Devonham, pleased with his pupil's acumen, his voice, even his manner, changing a little as he continued. "For then came the wonder of it all. The lesser God's teachings were so new and beautiful that the position of the other became untenable. The Race disowned him. It worshipped the lesser one in his place."

"Tell me, tell me, please," said "N. H.," as though he

noticed and understood the change of tone at once. "I listen.
The dear Fillery spoke to me of a great Teacher. I feel
a kind, deep joy move in me. Tell me, please."

Again Devonham hesitated a moment, for he recognized
signs that made him ill at ease a little, because he did not
understand them. Following a scientifi& textbook with his
pupil was well and good, but he had no desire to trespass
on what he considered as Fillery's territory. "N. H." was
his pupil, not his patient. He had already gone too far, he
realized. After a moment's reflection, however, he decided
it was wiser to let the talk run out its natural course, instead
of ending it abruptly. He was as thorough as he was sincere, and whatever his own theories and prejudices might
be in this particular case, he would not shirk an issue, nor
treat it with the smallest dishonesty. He put the glasses
straight on his big nose.

"The new teachings," he said, "were so beautiful that,
if faithfully practised by everybody, the world would soon
become a very different place to what it is."

"Did the Race practise them?" came the question in a
voice that held a note of softness, almost of wonder.

"No."

"Why not?"

"They were too difficult and painful and uncomfortable.
The new God, moreover, only came here 2,000 years ago,
whereas men have existed on earth for at least 400,000."

"N. H." asked abruptly what the teachings were, and
Devonham, growing more and more uneasy as he noted
the signs of increasing intensity and disturbance in his
pupil, recited, if somewhat imperfectly, the main points of
the Sermon on the Mount. As he did so "N. H." began
to murmur quietly to himself, his eyes grew large and
bright, his face lit up, his whole body trembled. He began
that deep, rhythmical breathing which seemed to affect the
atmosphere about him so that his physical appearance increased and spread. The skin took on something of radi-

ance, as though an intense inner happiness shone through it. Then, suddenly, to Devonham's horror, he began to hum.

Though a normal, ordinary sound enough, it reminded him of that other sound he had once shared with Fillery, when he sat on the stairs, staring at a china bowl filled with visiting cards, while the dawn broke after a night of exhaustion and bewilderment. That sound, of course, he had long since explained and argued away—it was an auditory hallucination conveyed to his mind by LeVallon, who originated it. Interesting and curious, it was far from inexplicable. It was disquieting, however, for it touched in him a vague sense of alarm, as though it paved the way for that odd panic terror he had been amazed to discover hidden away deeply in some unrealized corner of his being.

This humming he now listened to, though normal and ordinary enough—there were no big vibrations with it, for one thing—was too suggestive of that other sound for him to approve of it. His mind rapidly sought some way of stopping it. A command, above all an impatient, harsh command, was out of the question, yet a request seemed equally not the right way. He fumbled in his mind to find the wise, proper words. He stretched his hand out, as though to lay it quietly upon his companion's shoulder— but realized suddenly he could not—almost he dared not— touch him.

The same instant "N. H." rose. He pushed his chair back and stood up.

Devonham, justly proud of his equable temperament and steady nerves, admits that only a great effort of self-control enabled him to sit quietly and listen. He listened, watched, and made mental notes to the best of his ability, but he was frightened a little. The outburst was so sudden. He is not sure that his report of what he heard, made later to Fillery, was a verbatim, accurate one:

"Justice we know," cried "N. H." in his half-chanting voice that seemed to boom with resonance, "but this—this

mercy, gentle kindness, beauty—this unknown loveliness—
we did not know it!" He went to the open window, and
threw his arms wide, as though he invoked the sun. "Dimly
we heard of it. We strive, we strive, we weave and build
and fashion while the whirl of centuries flies on. This
lesser God—he came among us, too, making our service
sweeter, though we did not understand. Our work grew
wiser and more careful, we built lovelier forms, and knew
not why we did so. His mighty rhythms touched us with
their power and happy light. Oh, my great messengers of
wind and fire, bring me the memory I have lost! Oh, where,
where——?"

He shook himself, as though his clothes, perhaps his body
even, irked him. It was a curious coincidence, thought
Devonham, as he watched and listened, too surprised and
puzzled to interfere either by word or act, that a cloud, at
that very moment, passed from the face of the sun, and
a gust of wind shook all the branches of the lime trees
in the garden. "N. H." stood drenched in the white clear
sunshine. His flaming hair was lifted by the wind.

"Behind, beyond the Suns He dwells and burns for ever.
Oh, the mercy, kindness, the strange beauty of this personal
love—what is it? These have been promised to *us* too——!"

He broke off abruptly, bowed his great head and shoulders,
and sank upon his knees in an attitude of worship. Then,
stretching his arms out to the sky, the face raised into the
flood of sunlight, while his voice became lower, softer, almost hushed, he spoke again:

"Our faithful service, while the circles swallow the suns,
shall lift us too! You, who sent me here to help this little,
dying Race, oh, help me to remember——!"

His passion was a moving sight; the words, broken
through with fragments of his chanting, singing, had the
blood of some infinite, intolerable yearning in them.

Devonham, meanwhile, having heard outbursts of this
strange kind before with others, had recovered something
of his equanimity. He felt more sure of himself again.

The touch of fear had left him. He went over to the window. The attack, as he deemed it, was passing. A thick cloud hid the sun again. "There, there," he said soothingly, laying both hands upon the other's shoulders, then taking the arms to help him rise. "I told you His teachings were very beautiful—that the world would become a kind of heaven if people lived them." His voice seemed not his own; beside the volume and music of the other's it had a thin, rasping, ugly sound.

"N. H." was on his feet, gazing down into his face; to Devonham's amazement there were tears in the eyes that met his own.

"And many people *do* live them—try to, rather," he added gently. "There are thousands who really worship this lesser God to-day. You can't go far wrong yourself if you take Him as your model an——"

"How He must have suffered!" came the astonishing interruption, the voice quiet and more natural again. "There was no way of telling what he knew. He had no words, of course. You are all so difficult, so caged, so—dead!"

Devonham smiled. "He used parables." He paused a moment, then went on "Men have existed on the planet, science tells us, for at least 400,000 years, whereas *He* came here only 2,000 years ago——"

"Came *here*," interrupted the pupil, as though the earth were but one of a thousand places visited, a hint of contempt and pity somewhere in his tone and gesture. "We made His way ready then! We prepared, we built! It was for that our work went on and on so faithfully."

He broke off. . . .

Devonham experienced a curious sensation as he heard. In that instant it seemed to him that he was conscious of the movement of the earth through space. He was aware that the planet on which he stood was rushing forward at eighteen miles a second through the sky. He felt himself carried forward with it.

"What was His name?" he heard "N. H." asking. It

was as though he was aware of the enormous interval in space traversed by the rolling earth between the first and last words of the sudden question. It trailed through an immense distance towards him, after him, yet at the same time ever with him.

"His name—oh—Jesus Christ, we call him," wondering at the same moment why he used the pronoun "we."

"Jesus—Christ !"

"N. H." repeated the name with such intensity and power that the sound, borne by deep vibrations, seemed to surge and circle forth into space while the earth rushed irresistibly onwards. A faintly imaginative idea occurred to Devonham for the first time in his life—it was as though the earth herself had opened her green lips and uttered the great name. With this came also the amazing and disconcerting conviction that Nature and humans were expressions of one and the same big simple energy, and that while their forms, their bodies, differed, the life manifesting through them was identical, though its degree might vary. For an instant this was of such overpowering conviction as to be merely obvious.

It passed as quickly as it came, though he still was dimly conscious that he had travelled with the earth through another huge stretch of space. Then this sense of movement also passed. He looked up. "N. H." was in his chair again at the table, reading quietly his book on natural history. But in his eyes the moisture of tears was still visible.

Devonham adjusted his glasses, blew his nose, went quickly to another room to jot down his notes of the talk, the reactions, the general description, and in doing so dismissed from his mind the slight uneasy effects of what had been a "curious hallucination," caused evidently by an "unexplained stimulation" of the motor centres in the brain.

CHAPTER XXV

THE full account of "N. H.," with all he said and did, his effect upon others, his general activities in a word, it is impossible to compress intelligibly into the compass of these notes. A complete report Edward Fillery indeed accumulated, but its publication, he realized, must await that leisure for which his busy life provided little opportunity. His eyes, mental and physical, were never off his "patient," and "N. H.," aware of it, leaped out to meet the observant sympathy, giving all he could, concealing nothing, yet debarred, it seemed, by the rigid limitations of his own mental and physical machinery, as similarly by that of his hearers, from contributing more than suggestive and tantalizing hints. Of the use of parable he, obviously, had no knowledge.

His relations with others, perhaps, offered the most significant comments on his personality. Fillery was at some pains to collect these. The reactions were various, yet one and all showed this in common, a curious .verdict but unanimous : that his effect, namely, was greatest when he was not there. Not in his actual presence, which promised rather than fulfilled, was his power so dominating upon mind and imagination as after the door was closed and he was gone. The withdrawal of his physical self, its absence—as Fillery had himself experienced one night on Hampstead Heath as well as on other occasions—brought his real presence closer.

It was Nayan who first drew attention to this remarkable characteristic. She spoke about him often now with Dr. Fillery, for as the weeks passed and she realized the uselessness, the impossibility, of the plan she had proposed to herself, she found relief in talking frankly about him to her older friend.

"Always, always after I leave him," she confessed, "a profound and searching melancholy gets hold of me, poignant as death, yet an extraordinary unrealized beauty behind it somewhere. It steals into my very blood and bones. I feel an intense dissatisfaction with the world, with people as they are, and a burning scorn for all that is small, unworthy, petty, mean—and yet a hopelessness of ever attaining to that something which *he* knows and lives so easily." She sighed, gazing into his eyes a moment. "Or of ever making others see it," she added.

"And that 'something,'" he asked, "can you define it?"

She shook her head. "It's in me, within reach even, but —the word he used is the only one—forgotten."

"Perhaps—has it ever occurred to you?—that he simply cannot describe it. There are no words, no means at his disposal—no human terms?"

"Perhaps," she murmured.

"Desirable, though?" he urged her gently.

She clasped her hands, smiling. "Heavenly," she murmured, closing her eyes a moment as though to try and recall it. "Yet when I'm with him," she went on, "he never *quite* realizes for me the state of wonder and delight his presence promises. His personality suggests rather than fulfils." She paused, a wistful, pained expression in her dark eyes. "The failure," she added quickly, lest she seem to belittle him of whom she spoke, "of course lies in myself. I refuse, you see—I can't say why, though I feel it's wise— to let myself be dominated by that strange, lost part of me he stimulates."

"True," interposed Dr. Fillery. "I understand. Yet to have felt this even is a sign——"

"That he stirs the deepest, highest in me? This hint of divine beauty in the unrealized under-self?"

He nodded. There was an odd touch of sadness in their talk. "I've watched him with many types of people," he went on thoughtfully, almost as though thinking aloud in his rapid way, "I've talked with him on many subjects. The meanness, jealousy, insignificance of the Race shocks and amazes him. He cannot understand it. He asked me once 'But is no one *born* noble? To be splendid is such an effort with them!' Splendour of conduct, he noticed, is a calculated, rarely a spontaneous splendour. The general resistance to new ideas also puzzles him. 'They fear a rhythm they have never felt before,' as he put it. 'To adopt a new rhythm, they think, must somehow injure them.' That the Race respects a man because he possesses much equally bewilders him. 'No one serves willingly or naturally,' he observed, 'or unless someone else receives money for drawing attention loudly to it.' Any notion of reward, of advertisement, in its widest meaning, is foreign to his nature."

He broke off. Another pause fell between them, the girl the first to break it:

"He suffers," she said in a low voice. "Here—he suffers," and her face yearned with the love and help she longed to pour out beyond all thought of self or compensation, and at the same time with the pain of its inevitable frustration; and, watching her, Dr. Fillery understood that this very yearning was another proof of the curious impetus, the intensification of being, that "N. H." caused in everyone. Yet he winced, as though anticipating the question she at once then put to him:

"You are afraid for him, Edward?" her eyes calmly, searchingly on his. "His future troubles you?"

He turned to her with abrupt intensity. "If *you*, Iraida, could not enchain him——" He broke off. He shrugged his shoulders.

"I have no power," she confessed. "An insatiable longing burns like a fire in him. Nothing he finds here on earth, among men and women, can satisfy it." A faint blush stole up her neck and touched her cheeks. "He is different. *I* have no power to keep him here." Her voice sank suddenly to a whisper, as though a breath of awe passed into her.

"He is here now at this very moment, I believe. He is with us as we talk together. I feel him." Almost a visible thrill passed through her. "And close, so very close—to *you.*"

Dr. Fillery made no sign by word or gesture, but something in his very silence gave assent.

"And not alone," she added, still under her breath. It seemed she looked about her, though she did not actually move or turn her head. "Others—of his kind, Edward—come with him. They are always with him—I think sometimes." Her whisper was fainter still.

"You feel that too!" He said it abruptly, his voice louder and almost challenging. Then he added incongruously, as though saying it to himself this time, "That's what I mean. I've known it for a long time——"

He looked at the girl sharply with unconcealed admiration. "It does not frighten you?" he asked, and in reply she said the very thing he felt sure she would say, hoping for it even while he shrank:

"Escape," he heard in a low, clear voice, half a question, half an exclamation, and saw the blood leave her face.

The instinctive "Hush!" that rose to his lips he did not utter. The sense of loss, of searching pain, the word implied he did not show. Instead, he spoke in his natural, everyday tone again:

"The body irks him, of course, and he may try to rid himself of it. Its limitations to him are a prison, for his true consciousness he finds outside it. The explanation," he added to himself, "of many a case of suicidal mania probably. I've often wondered——"

He took her hand, aware by the pallor of her face what her feelings were. "Death, you see, Nayan, has no meaning for him, as it has for us who think consciousness out of the body impossible, and he is puzzled by our dread of it. 'We,' he said once, 'have nothing that decays. We may be stationary, or advance, or retreat, but we can never end.' He derives—oh, I'm convinced of it—from another order.

Here—amongst us—he is inarticulate, unable to express himself, hopeless, helpless, in prison. Oh, if only——"

"He loves *you*," she said quickly, releasing her hand. "I suppose he realizes the eternal part of you and identifies himself with that. In you, Edward, lies something very close to what he is, akin—he needs it terribly, just as you——" She became confused.

"Love, as we understand it," he interrupted, his voice shaking a little, "he does not, cannot know, for he serves another law, another order of being."

"That's how I feel it too."

She shivered slightly, but she did not turn away, and her eyes kept all their frankness.

"Our humanity," she murmured, "writes upon his heart in ink that quickly fades——"

"And leaves no trace," he caught her up hurriedly. "His one idea is to help, to render service. It is as natural to him as for water to run down hill. He seeks instinctively to become one with the person he seeks to aid. As with us an embrace is an attempt at union, so he seeks, by some law of his own being, to become identified with those whom he would help. And he helps by intensifying their consciousness—somewhat as heat and air increase ordinary physical vitality. Only, first there must be something for him to work on. Energy, even bad, vicious, wrongly used, he can work on. Mere emptiness prevents him. You remember Lady Gleeson——"

"We—most of us—are too empty," she put in with quiet resignation. "Our sense of that divine beauty is too faint——"

"Rather," came the quick correction, "he stands too close to us. His effect is too concentrated. The power at such close quarters disturbs and overbalances."

"That's why, then, I always feel it strongest when he's left."

He glanced at her keenly.

"In his presence," she explained, "it's always as though

I saw only a part of him, even of his physical appearance, out of the corner of my eye, as it were, and sometimes——" She hesitated. He did not help her this time. "As if those others, many others, similar to himself, but invisible, crowding space about us, were intensely active." Her voice hushed again. "He brings them with him—as now. I feel it, Edward, now. I feel them close." She looked round the empty room, peering through the window into the quiet evening sky. Dr. Fillery also turned away. He sighed again. "Have you noticed, too," he went on presently, yet half as if following his own thoughts, and a trifle incongruously, "the speed and lightness his very movements convey, and how he goes down the street with that curious air of drawing things after him, along with him, as trains and motors draw the loose leaves and dust——"

"Whirling," her quick whisper startled him a little, as she turned abruptly from the window and gazed straight at him. He smiled, instantly recovering himself. "A good word, yes—whirling—but in the plural. As though there were vortices about him."

It was her turn to smile. "That might one day carry him away," she exclaimed. They smiled together then, they even laughed, but somewhere in their laughter, like the lengthening shadows of the spring day outside, lay an incommunicable sadness neither of them could wholly understand.

"Yet the craving for beauty," she said suddenly, "that he leaves behind in me"—her voice wavered—"an intolerable yearning that nothing can satisfy—nothing—here. An infinite desire, it seems, for—for——"

Dr. Fillery took her hand again gently, looking down steadily into the clear eyes that sought his own, and the light glistening in their moisture was similar, he fancied for a moment, to the fire in another pair of shining eyes that never failed to stir the unearthly dreams in him.

"It lies beyond any words of ours," he said softly. "Don't struggle to express it, Iraida. To the flower, the star, we are wise to leave their own expression in their own particular field, for we cannot better it."

A sound of rising wind, distant yet ominous, went past the window, as for a moment then the girl came closer till she was almost in his arms, and though he did not accept her, equally he did not shrink from the idea of acceptance—for the first time since they had known one another. There was a smell of flowers; almost in that wailing wind he was aware of music.

"Together," he heard her whisper, while a faint shiver —was it of joy or terror?—ran through her nerves. "All of us—when the time comes—together." She made an abrupt movement. "Just as we are together now! Listen!" she exclaimed.

"We call it wind," she whispered. "But of course—really—it's behind—beyond—inside—isn't it?"

Dr. Fillery, holding her closely, made no answer. Then he laughed, let go her hands, and said in his natural tone again, breaking an undesirable spell intentionally, though with a strong effort: "We are in space and time, remember. Iraida. Let us obey them happily until another certain and practical thing is shown us."

The faint sound that had been rising about them in the air died down again.

They looked into each other's eyes, then drew apart, though with a movement so slight it was scarcely perceptible. It was Nayan and Dr. Fillery once more, but not before the former had apparently picked out the very thought that had lain, though unexpressed, in the latter's deepest mind— its sudden rising the cause of his deliberate change of attitude. For she had phrased it, given expression to it, though from an angle very different to his own. And her own word, "escape," used earlier in the conversation, had deliberately linked on with it, as of intentional purpose.

"He must go back. The time is coming when he must go back. We are not ready for him here—not yet."

Somewhat in this fashion, though without any actual

words, had the idea appeared in letters of fire that leaped
and flickered through a mist of anguish, of loss, of loneliness, rising out of the depths within him. He knew whence
they came, he divined their origin at once, and the sound,
though faint and distant at first, confirmed him. Swiftly
behind them, moreover, born of no discoverable antecedents,
it seemed, rose simultaneously the phrase that Father Collins
loved: "A Being in his own place is the ruler of his fate."
Father Collins, for all his faults and strangeness, was a
personality, a consciousness, that might prove of value. His
extraordinarily swift receptiveness, his undoubted telepathic
powers, his fluid, sensitive, protean comprehension of possibilities outside the human walls, above the earthly ceiling,
so to speak. . . . Value suddenly attached itself to Father
Collins, as though the name had been dropped purposely
into his mind by someone. He was surprised to find this
thought in him. It was not for the first time, however, Dr.
Fillery remembered.

In Nayan's father, again, an artist, though not a particularly subtle one perhaps, lay a deep admiration, almost
a love, he could not explain. "There's something about
him in a sense immeasurable, something not only untamed
but untamable," he phrased it. "His gentleness conceals
it as a summer's day conceals a thunderstorm. To me it's
almost like an incarnation of the primal forces at work in
the hearts of my own people"—he grew sad—"and as
dangerous probably." He was speaking to his daughter,
who repeated the words later to Dr. Fillery. The study of
Fire in the elemental group had failed. "He's too big, too
vast, too formless, to get into any shape or outline *my* tools
can manage, even by suggestion. He dominates the others
—Earth, Air, Water—and dwarfs them."
"But fire ought to," she put in. "It's the most powerful
and splendid, the most terrific of them all. Isn't it? It
regenerates. It purifies. I love fire——"
Her father smiled in his beard, noticing the softness in

her manner, rather than in her voice. The awakening in
her he had long since understood sympathetically, if more
profoundly than she knew, and welcomed.

"He won't hurt you, child. He won't harm Nayushka
any more than a summer's day can hurt her. I see him
thus sometimes," he mumbled on half to himself, though
she heard and stored the words in her memory; "as an
entire day, a landscape even, I often see him. A stretch
of being rather than a point; a rushing stream rather than
a single isolated wave harnessed and confined in definite
form—as *we* understand being here," he added curiously.
"No, he'll neither harm nor help you," he went on; "nor
any of us for that matter. A dozen nations, a planet, a
star he might help or harm"—he laughed aloud suddenly
in a startled way at his own language—"but an individual
never!" And he abruptly took her in his arms and kissed
her, drying her tears with his own rough handkerchief.
"Not even a fire-worshipper," he added with gruff tenderness, "like you!"

"There's more of divinity in fire than in any other earthly
thing we know," she replied as he held her, "for it takes
into itself the sweetest essence of all it touches." She looked
up at him with a smile. "That's why you can't get it into
your marble perhaps." To which her father made the significant rejoinder: "And because none of us has the least
conception what 'divine' and 'divinity' really mean, though
we're always using the words! It's odd, anyhow," he
finished reflectively, "that I can model the fellow better from
memory than when he's standing there before my eyes.
At close quarters he confuses me with too many terrific
unanswerable questions."

To multiply the verdicts and impressions Fillery jotted
down is unnecessary. In his own way he collected; in his
own way he wrote them down. About "N. H.," all agreed
in their various ways of expressing it, was that vital suggestion of agelessness, of deathlessness, of what men call
eternal youth: the vigorous grace of limbs and movements,

the deep simple joy of confidence and power. None could picture him tired, or even wearing out, yet ever with a faint hint of painful conflict due to immense potentialities—"a day compressed into a single minute," as Khilkoff phrased it—straining, but vainly, to express themselves through a limited form that was inadequate to their use. A storm of passionate hope and wonder seemed ever ready to tear forth from behind the calm of the great quiet eyes, those green-blue changing eyes, which none could imagine light-less or unlamping; and about his whole presentment a surplus of easy, overflowing energy from an inexhaustible source pressing its gifts down into him spontaneously, fire and wind its messengers; yet that the human machinery using these—mind, body, nerves—was ill adapted to their full expression. To every individual having to do with him was given a push, a drive, an impetus that stimulated that individual's chief characteristic, intensifying it.

This to imaginative and discerning sight. But even upon ordinary folk, aware only of the surface things that de-liberately hit them, was left a startling impression as of someone waving a strange, unaccustomed banner that made them halt and stare before passing on—uncomfortably. He had that nameless quality, apart from looks or voice or manner, which arrested attention and drew the eyes of the soul, wonderingly, perhaps uneasily, upon itself. He left a mark. Something defined him from all others, leaving him silhouetted in the mind, and those who had looked into his eyes could not forget that they had done so. Up rose at once the great unanswerable questions that, lying ever at the back of daily life, the majority find it most comfortable to leave undisturbed—but rose in red ink or italics. He started into an awareness of greater life. And the effect remained, was greatest even, after he had passed on.

It was, of course, Father Collins, a frequent caller now at the Home, betraying his vehement interest in long talks with Dr. Fillery and in what interviews with "N. H." the latter permitted him—it was this protean being whose mind, amid wildest speculations, formed the most positive conclusions. The Prometheans, he believed, were not far wrong in their instinctive collective judgment. "N. H." was not a human being; the occupant of that magnificent body was not a human spirit like the rest of us.

"Nor is he the only one walking the streets to-day," he affirmed mysteriously. "In shops and theatres, trains and buses, tucked in among the best families," he laughed, although in earnest, "and even in suburbia I have come across other human bodies similarly inhabited. What they are and where they come from exactly, we cannot know, but their presence among us is indubitable."

"You mean you recognize them?" inquired Dr. Fillery calmly.

"One unmistakable sign they possess in common—they are invariably inarticulate, helpless, lost. The brain, the five senses, the human organs—all they have to work through—are useless to express the knowledge and powers natural to them. Electricity might as well try to manifest itself through a gas-pipe, or music through a stone. One and all, too, possess strange glimmerings of another state where they are happy and at home, something of the glory à la Wordsworth, a Golden Age idea almost, a state compared to which humanity seems a tin-pot business, yet a state of which no single descriptive terms occur to them."

"Of which, however, they can tell us nothing?"

"Memory, of course, is lost. Their present brain can have no records, can it? Only those of us who have perhaps at some time, in some earlier existence possibly, shared such a state can have any idea of what they're driving at."

He glanced at Fillery with a significant raising of his bushy eyebrows.

"There have been no phenomena, I'm glad to say," put in the doctor, aware some comment was due from him, "no physical phenomena, I mean."

"Nor could there be," pursued the other, delighted. "He has not got the apparatus. With all such beings, their power, rather than perceived, is *felt*. Sex, as with us, they also cannot know, for they are neither male nor female." He paused, as the other did not help him. "Enigmas they must always be to us. We may borrow from the East and call them *devas,* or class them among nature spirits of legend and the rest, but we can, at any rate, welcome them, and perhaps even learn from them."

"Learn from them?" echoed Fillery sharply.

"They are essentially *natural,* you see, whereas we are artificial, and becoming more so with every century, though we call it civilization. If we lived closer to nature we might get better results, I mean. Primitive man, I'm convinced, did get certain results, but he was a poor instrument. Modern man, in some ways, is a better, finer instrument to work through, only he is blind to the existence of any beings but himself. A bridge, however, might be built, I feel. 'N. H.' seems to me in close touch with these curious beings, if"—he lowered his voice—"he is not actually one of them. The wind and fire he talks about are, of course, not what *we* mean. It is heat and rhythm, in some more essential form, he refers to. If 'N. H.' is some sort of nature spirit, or nature-being, he is of a humble type, concerned with humble duties in the universe——"

"There are, you think, then, higher, bigger kinds?" inquired the listener, his face and manner showing neither approval nor disapproval.

Father Collins raised his hands and face and shoulders, even his eyebrows. His spirits rose as well.

"If they exist at all—and the assumption explains plausibly the amazing intelligence behind all natural phenomena—they include every grade, of course, from the insignificant fairies, so called, builders of simple forms, to the immense planetary spirits and vast Intelligenes who guide and guard the welfare of the greater happenings." His eyes shone, his tone matched in enthusiasm his gestures.

"A stupendous and magnificent hierarchy," he cried, "but all, all under God, of course, who maketh his angels spirits and his ministers a flaming fire. Ah, think of it," he went on, becoming lyrical almost as wonder fired him, "think of it now especially in the spring! The vast abundance and insurgence of life pouring up on all sides into forms and bodies, and all led, directed, fashioned by this host of invisible, yet not unknowable, Intelligences! Think of the prolific architecture, the delicacy, the grandeur, the inspiring beauty that are involved. . . .!"

"You said just now a bridge might be built," Dr. Fillery interrupted, while the other paused a second for breath.

Father Collins, nailed down to a positive statement, hesitated and looked about him. But the hesitation passed at once.

"It is the question merely," he went on more composedly, "of providing the apparatus, the means of manifestation, the instrument, the—body. Isn't it? Our evolution and theirs are two separate—different things."

"I suppose so. No force can express itself without a proper apparatus."

"Certain of these Intelligences are so immense that only a series of events, long centuries, a period of history, as we call it, can provide the means, the body indeed, through which they can express themselves. An entire civilization may be the 'body' used by an archetypal power. Others, again—like 'N. H.' probably—since I notice that it is usually the artist, the artistic temperament *he* affects most—require beauty for their expression—beauty of form and outline, of sound, of colour."

He paused for effect, but no comment came.

"Our response to beauty, our thrill, our lift of delight and wonder before any manifestation of beauty—these are due only to our perception, though usually unrecognized except by artists, of the particular Intelligence thus trying to express itself——"

Dr. Fillery suddenly leaned forward, listening with a

new expression on his face. He betrayed, however, no sign of what he thought of his voluble visitor. An idea, none the less, had struck him like a flash between the eyes of the mind.

"You mean," he interposed patiently, "that just as your fairies use form and colour to express themselves in nature, we might use beauty of a mental order to—to——"

"To build a body of expression, yes, an instrument in a collective sense, through which 'N. H.' might express whatever of knowledge, wisdom and power he has——"

"Will you explain yourself a little more definitely?"

Father Collins beamed. He continued with an air of intense conviction:

"The Artist is ever an instrument merely, and for the most part an unconscious one; only the greatest artist is a conscious instrument. No man is an artist at all until he transcends both nature and himself; that is, until he interprets both nature and himself in the unknown terms of that greater Power whence himself and nature emanate. He is aware of the majestic source, aware that the universe, in bulk and in detail, is an expression of it, itself a limited instrument; but aware, further—and here he proves himself great artist—of the stupendous, lovely, central Power whose message stammers, broken and partial, through the inadequate instruments of ephemeral appearances.

"He creates, using beauty in form, sound, colour, a better and more perfect instrument, provides this central Power with a means of fuller expression.

"The message no longer stammers, halts, suggests; it flows, it pours, it sings. He has fashioned a vehicle for its passage. His art has created a body it can use. He has transcended both nature and himself. The picture, poem, harmony that has become the body for this revelation is alone great art."

"Exactly," came the patient comment that was asked for.

"One thing is certain: only human knowledge, expressed

in human terms, can come through a human brain. No mind, no intellect, can convey a message that transcends human experience and reason. Art, however, can. It can supply the vehicle, the body. But, even here, the great artist cannot communicate the secret of his Vision; he cannot talk about it, tell it to others. He can only *show* the result."

"Results," interrupted Dr. Fillery in a curious tone; "what results, exactly, would you look for?" There was a burning in his eyes. His skin was tingling.

"What else but a widening, deepening, heightening of our present consciousness," came the instant reply. "An extension of faculty, of course, making entirely new knowledge available. A group of great artists, each contributing his special vision, respectively, of form, colour, words, proportion, could together create a 'body' to express a Power transcending the accumulated wisdom of the world. The race could be uplifted, taught, redeemed."

"You have already given some attention to this strange idea?" suggested his listener, watching closely the working of the other's face. "You have perhaps even experimented—— A ceremonial of some sort, you mean? A performance, a ritual—or what?"

Father Collins lowered his voice, becoming more earnest, more impressive:

"Beauty, the arts," he whispered, "can alone provide a vehicle for the expression of those Intelligences which are the cosmic powers. A performance of some sort—possibly —since there must be sound and movement. A bridge between us, between our evolution and their own, might, I believe, be thus constructed. Art is only great when it provides a true form for the expression of an eternal cosmic power. By combining—we might provide a means for their manifestation——"

"A body of thought, as it were, through which our 'N. H.' might become articulate? Is that your idea?"

Behind the question lay something new, it seemed, as

though, while listening to the exposition of an odd mystical
conception, his mind had been busy with a preoccupation,
privately but simultaneously, of his own. "In what way
precisely do you suggest the arts might combine to provide
this 'body'?" he asked, a faint tremor noticeable in the
lowered voice.

"That," replied Father Collins promptly, never at a loss,
"we should have to think about. Inspiration will come to
us—probably through *him*. Ceremonial, of course, has
always been an attempt in this direction, only it has left
the world so long that people no longer know how to construct a real one. The ceremonials of to-day are ugly,
vulgar, false. The words, music, colour, gestures—everything must combine in perfect harmony and proportion
to be efficacious. It is a forgotten method."

"And results—how would they come?"

"The new wisdom and knowledge that result are suddenly there *in* the members of the group. The Power has
expressed itself. Not through the brain, of course, but,
rather, that the new ideas, having been *acted* out, are suddenly there. There has been an extension of consciousness.
A group consciousness has been formed, and——"

"And there you are!" Dr. Fillery, moving his foot
unperceived, had touched a bell beneath the table. The
foot, however, groped and fumbled, as though unsure of
itself.

"You learn to swim—by swimming, not by talking about
it." Father Collins was prepared to talk on for another
hour. "If we can devise the means—and I feel sure we
can—we shall have formed a bridge between the two
evolutions——"

Nurse Robbins entered with apologies. A case upstairs
demanded the doctor's instant attendance. Dr. Devonham
was engaged.

"One thing," insisted Father Collins, as they shook hands
and he got up to go, "one thing only you would have to
fear." He was very earnest. Evidently the signs of

struggle, of fierce conflict in the other's face he did not notice.

"And that is?" A hand was on the door.

"If successful—if we provide this means of expression for him—we provide also the means of losing him."

"Death?" He opened the door with rough, unnecessary violence.

"Escape. He would no longer need the body he now uses. He would *remember*—and be gone. In his place you would have—LeVallon again only. I'm afraid," he added, "that he already *is* remembering——!"

His final words, as Nurse Robbins deftly hastened his departure in the hall, were a promise to communicate the results of his further reflections, and a suggestion that his cottage by the river would be a quiet spot in which to talk the matter over again.

But Dr. Fillery, having thanked Nurse Robbins for her prompt attendance to his bell, returned to the room and sat for some time in a strange confusion of anxious thoughts. A singular idea took shape in him—that Father Collins had again robbed his mind of its unspoken content. That sensitive receptive nature had first perceived, then given form to the vague, incoherent dreams that lurked in the innermost recesses of his hidden self.

Yet, if that were so—— and if "N. H." already was "remembering"——!

A wave of shadow crept upon him, darkening his hope, his enthusiasm, his very life. For another part of him knew quite well the value to be attributed to what Father Collins had said.

Instinctively his mind sought for Devonham. But it did not occur to him at the moment to wonder why this was so.

CHAPTER XXVI

SPRING had come with her sweet torment of delight, her promises, her passion, and London lay washed and perfumed beneath April's eager sun. An immense, persuasive glamour was in the sky. The whole earth caught up a swifter gear, as the magic of rich creative life poured out of "dead" soil into flower, insect, bird and animal. The prodigious stream omitted no single form; every "body" pulsed and blossomed at full strength. The hidden powers in each seed emerged. And it was from the inanimate body of the earth this flood of increased vitality rose.

Into Edward Fillery, strolling before breakfast over the wet lawn of the enclosed garden, the tide of new life rose likewise. It was very early, the flush of dawn still near enough for the freshness of the new day to be everywhere. The greater part of the huge city was asleep. He was alone with the first birds, the dew, the pearl and gold of the sun's slanting rays. He saw the slates and chimneys glisten. Spring, like a visible presence, was passing across the town, bringing the amazing message that all obey yet no man understands.

> "This is its touch upon the blossomed rose,
>   The fashion of its hand shaped lotus-leaves;
> In dark soil and the silence of the seeds
>   The robe of spring it weaves.
>
> "It maketh and unmaketh, mending all;
>   What it hath wrought is better than had been;
> Slow grows the splendid pattern that it plans,
>   Its wistful hands between."

The lines came to his memory, while upon his mind fell lovely and wonderful impressions. It was as though the subconsciousness of the earth herself emerged with the spring, producing new life, new splendour everywhere. Out of a single patch of soil the various roots drew material they then fashioned into such different and complicated outlines as daisy, lily, rose, and a hundred types of tree. From the same bit of soil emerged these intricate patterns and designs, these different forms. At this very moment, while his feet left dark tracks across the silvery lawn, the process was going steadily forward all over England. Beneath those very feet up rushed the power into all conceivable bodies. Colour, music, form, marvellously organized, making no mistakes, were turning the world into a vast, delicious garden.

Form, colour, sound! From his own hidden region rose again the flaming hope and prophecy. He stooped and picked a daisy, examining with rapt attention its perfect little body. Who, what made this astonishing thing, that was yet among the humbler forms? What intelligence devised its elaborate outline, guarded, cared for, tended it, ensured its growth and welfare? He gazed at its white rays tipped with crimson, its several hundred florets, its composite design. The spring life had been pouring through it until he picked it. Through the huge mass of earth's body its tiny roots had drawn the life it needed. This power was now cut off. It would die. The process, as with everything else, was "automatic and unintelligent!" It seemed an incredible explanation. The old familiar question troubled him, but he saw it abruptly now from a new angle.

"We built it," came a voice so close that it seemed behind him, for when at first he turned, startled, and yet not startled, he saw no figure standing; "we who work in darkness, yet who never die, the Hidden Ones who build and weave inside and out of sight. You have destroyed our work of ages. . . ."

A pang of sudden regret and anguish seized him. He stood still and stared in the direction whence he thought the voice had come, but no form, no outline, no body that could have produced a sound, a voice, was visible. A blackbird flew with its shrill whistle over the enclosing wall, and the gardener, up unusually early, was now moving slowly past the elms at the far end, some two hundred yards away. The old man, he remembered, had been telling him only the day before that the life in his plants this year had been prodigious and successful beyond his whole experience. It puzzled him. Something of reverence, of superstition almost, had lain in the man's voice and eyes.

"Who are you?" whispered Fillery, still holding the "dead" broken flower in his hand and staring about him. He was aware that the sound from which the voice had come, detaching itself, as it were, into articulate syllables out of a general continuous volume, had not ceased. It was all about him, softly murmuring. Was it in himself perhaps? An intense inner activity, like the pressure of an enveloping tide, that was also in space, in the soil, the body of the planet, rose in him too. And it seemed to him that his mind was suddenly in process of being shaped and fashioned into a new "body of understanding"; a new instrument of understanding.

> " This is its work upon the things ye see:
>   The unseen things are more; men's hearts and minds,
>   The thoughts of peoples and their ways and wills,
>   These, too, the great Law binds."

"I know," he exclaimed, this time with acceptance that omitted the doubt he had first felt. "I know who you are" . . . and even as he said the words, there dropped into him, it seemed, some knowledge, some hint, some wonder that lay, he well knew, outside all human experience. It was as though some cosmic power brushed gently against and through his being, but a power so alien to known human categories that to attempt its expression in human terms—language, reason, imagination even—were to mutilate it. Yet, even for its partial, broken manifestation, human terms were alone available, since without these it must remain unperceived, he himself unaware of its existence.

He *was*, however, aware of its presence, its existence. All that was left to him therefore was his own personal interpretation. Herein, evidently, lay the truth for him; this was the meaning of his "acceptance." It was, in some way, a renewal of that other vision he called the Flower Hill and Flower Music experience.

"I know you," he repeated, his voice merging curiously in the general underlying murmur of the morning. "You belong to the bodiless, the deathless ones who work and build and weave eternally. Form, sound, colour are your instruments, the elements your tools. You wove this flower," he fingered the dying daisy, "as you also shaped this body"—he tapped his breast—"and—you built as well this mind——"

He stopped dead. Two things arrested him: the feeling that the ideas were not primarily his own, but derived from a source outside himself; and a sudden intensification of the flaming hope and prophecy that burst up as with new meaning into the words "mind" and "body."

The broken body of the flower slipped from his fingers and fell upon the body of the earth. He looked down at its now empty form through which no life flowed, and his eye passed then to his own body beating with intense activity, and thence to the bodies of the trees, the darting birds, the gigantic sun now peering magnificently along the heavens. Body! A body was a form through which life expressed itself, a vehicle of expression by means of which life manifested, an instrument it used. But a body of thought was a true phrase too. And with the words, shaped automatically in his brain, a new light flashed and flooded him with its waves.

"A body of thought, a mental body"—the phrase went

humming and flowing strangely through him. A body of thought! Father Collins, he remembered, had used some such wild language, only it had seemed empty words without intelligible meaning. Whence came the intense new meaning that so suddenly attached itself to the familiar phrase? Whence came the thrilling deep conviction that new, greater knowledge was hovering near, and that for its expression a new body must be devised? And what was this new knowledge, this new power? Whence came the amazing certainty in him that a new way was being shown to him, a means of progress for humanity that must otherwise flounder always to its average level of growth, development, then invariably collapse again?

"We built it," ran past him through the air again, or rose perhaps from the stirred depths of his own subconscious being, or again, dropped from a hidden rushing star. "The more perfect and adequate the form, the greater the flow of life, of knowledge, of power it can express. No mind, no intellect, can convey a message that transcends human experience. Yet there is a way."

The new knowledge was there, if only the new vehicle suited to its expression could be devised. . . .

The stream of life pouring through him became more and more intense; some power of perception seemed growing into white heat within him; transcending the limited senses; becoming incandescent. This tide of sound, inaudible to ordinary ears, was the music which is inseparable from the rhythm that underlies all forms, the music of the earth's manifold activities now pouring in vibrations huge and tiny all round and through him. He turned instinctively.

"You . . . !" exclaimed the doctor in him, as though rebuke, reproval stirred. "You here . . . !"

It seemed to him that the figure of "N. H.," embodying as it were a ray of sunlight, stood beside him.

"We," came the answer, with a smile that took the sparkling sunlight through the very face. "We are all about you," added the voice with a rhythm that swamped all denial, all objection, bringing an exultant exhilaration in their place. "We come from what always seems to you a Valley of sun and flowers, where we work and play behind the appearances you call the world."

"The world," repeated Fillery. "The universe as well."

The voice, the illusion of actual words, both died away, merging in some perplexing fashion into another appearance, perhaps equally an illusion so far as the senses were concerned—the phenomenon men call sight. Instead of hearing, that is, he now suddenly saw. Something in the arrangement of light caught his attention, holding it. The deep, central self in him, that which interprets and de-codes the reports the senses bring, employed another mode.

The figure of "N. H." still was definite enough in form indeed, yet at the same time taking the rays into itself as though it were a body of light. There was no transparency, of course, nor was this clear radiance seen by Fillery for the first time, but rather that his natural shining was caught up and intensified by the morning sunshine. A body of light, none the less, seemed a true description of what Fillery now saw. This sunshine filled the air, the space all round him, the entire lawn and garden shone in a sparkling flood of dancing brilliance. It blazed. The figure of "N. H." was merely a portion of this blazing. As a focus, but one of many, he now thought of it. And about each focus was the toss and fling of lovely, ever-rising spirals.

Across the main stream came then another pulsing movement, hardly discernible at first, and similar to an underswell that moves the sea against the wave—so that the eye perceives it only when not looking for it. This contrary motion, it soon became apparent, went in numerous, almost countless directions, so that, within and below its complicated wave-tracery, he was aware of yet other motions, crossing and interlacing at various speeds, until the space about him seemed to whirl with myriad rhythms, yet without the least confusion. These rhythms were of a hundred different magnitudes, from the very tiny to the gigantic, and while the smallest were of a radiant brilliance that made the sunshine pale, the larger ones seemed distant, their light of an intenser quality, though of a quality he had never seen before. These were strangely diffused, these bigger ones—"distant" was the word that occurred to him, although that inner brilliance which occurs in dreams, in imaginative moments, the nameless glow that colours mental vision, described them better. Moreover they wore colours the human eye had never seen, while the smallest rhythms were lit with the familiar colours of the prism.

He stood absorbed, fascinated, drinking in the amazing spectacle, as though the glowing spirals of fire communicated to his inmost being a heat and glory of creative power. He was aware of the creative stream of spring in his own heart, pouring from the body of the earth on which he stood, drenching mind, nerves and even muscles with concentrated life. His subconscious being rose and stretched its wings. All, all was possible. A sensation of divine deathlessness possessed him. The limitations of his ordinary human faculties and powers were overborne, so that he felt he could never again face the mournful prison that caged him in. The meaning of escape became plain to him.

He saw the invisible building Intelligences at work.

He was aware then suddenly of purpose, of intention. The seeming welter of the waves of coloured light, of the immense and tiny rhythms, the intricate streams of vibrating, pulsing, throbbing movements were, he now perceived, marvellously co-ordinated. There was a focus, a vortex, towards which all rushed with a power so prodigious that a sense of terror touched him. He suddenly became conscious of a pattern forming before his eyes, hanging in empty space, shining, soft with light and beauty. It became, he saw, a geometric design. An idea of crystals, frost-forms, a spider's web hung with glistening dewdrops shot across his memory. The spirals whirled and sang about it.

This outline, he next perceived, was the focus to which the light, heat, colour all contributed their particular touch and quality. It glowed now in the centre of the vortex. So overwhelming, however, was the sense of the stupendous power involved that, as he phrased it afterwards, it seemed he watched the formation of some mighty sun. It was the whirling of those billion-miled sheets of incandescent fires that attend the birth of a nebula he watched. The power, at any rate, was gigantic.

He stood trembling before a revelation that left him lost, shelterless, bereft of any help that his little self might summon—when, suddenly, with an emotion of strange tenderness, he saw the great rhythms become completely dominated by the very smallest of all. The same instant the pattern grew sharply outlined, perfect in every detail, as though the focus of powerful glasses cleared—and the pattern hung a moment exquisitely fashioned in space beneath his eyes before it sank slowly to the ground. It remained in an upright position on the grass at his feet—a daisy, growing in the earth, alive, its tiny delicate face taking the sunlight and the morning wind.

With a shock he then realized another thing: it was the very daisy he had broken, uprooted, killed a few minutes before.

He stooped, one hand outstretched as though to finger its wee white petals, but found instead that he was listening—listening to a sweet faint music that rose from the surface of the lawn, from grass and flowers, running in waves and circles, like the vibrations of gentle wind across a thousand strings. It was similar, though less in volume, to the sound he had heard in the presence of "N. H." He rose slowly to an upright position, dazed, bewildered, yet rapt with the wonder of the whole experience.

"N. H. !" he heard his voice exclaim, its sound merging

in the growing volume of music all about him. "N. H. !"
he cried again. "This is your work, your service . . . !"

But he could not see him; his figure was no longer
differentiated from the ever-moving sea of light that filled
space wherever he looked. The same play of brilliance
shone and glistened everywhere, whirling, ever shifting as
in vortices of intricate geometrical designs, dancing, inter-
penetrating, and with a magnificence of colour that caught
his breath away. There were remarkable flashings, and
two of these flashings blazed suddenly together, forming an
immense physiognomy, an expression, rather, as of a
mighty face. The same instant there were a hundred of
these mighty brilliant visages that pierced through the sea
of whirling colour and gazed upon him, close, terrific, with
a power and beauty that left thought without even a ghost
of language to describe them. Their glory lay beyond all
earthly terms. He recognized them. These mighty outlines
he had seen before.

His mind then made an effort; he tried to think; memory
and reason strove with emotion and sensation. The forms,
the faces, the powers at once grew fainter. They faded
slowly. The whirling vortices withdrew in some extraordinary way, the colour paled, the sound grew thinner,
ever more distant, the great weaving designs dissolved. The
lovely spirals all were gone. He saw the garden trees again,
the flower beds. Space emptied, showing the morning sunshine on roofs and chimney-pots.

"We have rebuilt, remade it," he heard faintly, but he
heard also the roar and boom of the gigantic rhythms as
they withdrew, not spatially, so much as from his consciousness that was now contracting once more, till only
the fainter sounds of the smaller singing patterns, the
Flower Music as he had come to call it, reached his ears.
Words and music, like voices known in dreams, seemed
interwoven. He remembered the huge faces, with their
bright confidence and glory, rising through the sunlight,
peering as through a mirror at him, radiant and of imperish-

able beauty. The words, perhaps, he attached himself, his own interpretations of their ringing motions.

The sounds died away. He reeled. The expansion and subsequent contraction of consciousness had been too rapid, the whole experience too intense. He swayed, unsure of his own identity. He remembered vaguely that tears filled his eyes and rolled down his cheeks, that the destruction of a lovely form had caused him a peculiar anguish, and that its recreation produced an intolerable joy, bringing tears of happiness. An arm caught him as he swayed. The accents of a voice he knew were audible close beside him. But at first he did not understand the words, feeling only a dull pain they caused.

"Their imperishable beauty! Their divine loveliness!" he stammered, recognizing the face and voice. He flung his arms wide, gazing into the now empty air above the London garden. "The great service they eternally fulfil —oh, that we all might——" He made a gesture towards the other houses with their sightless, shuttered windows.

"I know, I know," came in the familiar tones. "But come in now, come in, Edward, with me. I beg you— before it is too late." Paul Devonham's voice shook so that it was hardly recognizable. The skin of his face was white. He wore a haggard look.

"Too late!" repeated the other; "it is always too late. The world will never see. Their eyes are blinded." An intolerable emotion swept him. He stared suddenly at his colleague, an immense surprise in him. "But you, Paul!" he exclaimed. "You understand! Even you——!"

Devonham led him slowly into the house. There was protection in his manner, in voice and gesture there was deep affection, respect as well, but behind and through these flickered the signs of another unmistakable emotion that Fillery at first could hardly credit—of pity, was it? Of something at any rate he dared not contemplate.

"Even I," came in quick, low tones, "even I, Edward, understand. You forget. I was once alone with him"—

the voice sank to a rapid whisper—"in the mountain valley."
Devonham's expression was curious. He raised his tone
again. "But—not now, not now, I beg of you. Not yet,
at any rate. You will be cast out, judged insane, your work
destroyed, your career ruined, your reputation——" His
excitement betrayed itself in his bright eyes and unusual
gestures. He was shaken to the core. Fillery turned upon
him. They were in the corridor now. He flung his arm
free of the restraining hand.

"You know!" he cried, "yet would keep silent!" His
voice choked. "You saw what I saw: new sources open,
the offer made, the channels accessible at our very door,
yet you would refuse——"

"Not one in ten million," came the hard rejoinder,
"would believe." The voice trembled. "We have no proof.
Their laws of manifestation are unknown to us, and such
glimpses are but glimpses—useless and dangerous." He
whispered suddenly: "Besides—what are they? What,
after all, are we dealing with?

"We can experiment," interrupted his companion
quickly.

"How? Of what possible value?"

"You felt what I felt? In your own being you experienced the revelation too, and yet you use such words!
New forces, new faculties, Beings from another order of
incalculable powers to ennoble, to bless, to inspire! The
creation of higher forms through which new, greater life
and knowledge, shall manifest!"

He could hardly find the words he sought, so bright was
the hope and wonder in his heart still. "Think—at a
time like this—what humanity might gain. *Creative* powers,
Paul, creative! Acting directly on the subconscious selves
of everybody, intensifying every individual, whether he
understands and believes or not! The gods, Paul—and
nothing less—— You saw the daisy——"

Devonham seized both of his companion's hands, as he
heard the torrent of wild, incoherent words: "You'll have

the entire world against you," he interrupted. "Why seek
crucifixion for a dream?" Then, as his hands were again
flung off, he turned, a finger suddenly on his lips. "Hush,
hush, Edward!" he whispered. "The house is sleeping still.
You'll wake them all."

There was a new, strange authority about him. Dr.
Fillery controlled himself. They went upstairs on tiptoe.

"Listen!" murmured Devonham, as they reached the first-
floor landing. "That's what woke me first and led me
to his room, but only to find it empty. He was already
gone. I saw him join you on the lawn. I watched from
the open window. Then—I lost him. . . . Listen!" He
was trembling like a child.

The sound still echoed faintly, distant, rising and falling,
sweet and very lovely, and hardly to be distinguished from
the musical hum of wind that sighs and whispers across
the strings of an æolian harp. To one man came incredible
sensations as they paused a moment. Dim though the landing was, there still seemed a tender luminous glow pervad-
ing it.

"They're everywhere," murmured Fillery, "everywhere
and always about us, though in different space. Through
and behind and inside everything that happens, helping,
building, constructing ceaselessly. Oh, Paul, how can you
doubt and question value? Behind every single form and
body, physical or mental, they operate divinely——"

"Mental! Edward, for God's sake——"

Devonham stepped nearer to him with such abruptness
that his companion stopped. The pallor of the assistant's
face so close arrested his words a moment. They held
their breath, listening together side by side. The sounds
grew fainter, died away in the stillness of the early morning, then ceased altogether. It was not the first time they
had listened thus to the strange music, nor was it the first
time that Fillery entered the room alone. As once before,
his colleague remained outside, watching, waiting, half
seduced, it seemed, yet vehemently against a sympathetic

attitude. He watched his chief go in, he saw the expression on his face. Upon his own, behind a mild expectancy, lay a look of pain.

"Empty!" He heard the startled exclamation.

And instantly Devonham was at his side, a firm hand upon his arm, his eyes taking in an unused bed, a window opened wide, a glow of light and heat the early sunshine could not possibly explain. The perfume, as of flowers in the air, he noted too, and a sense of lightness, freshness, sweetness about the atmosphere that produced happiness, exhilaration. The room throbbed, as it were, with invisible waves of some communicable power even he could not deny. But of "N. H.," the recent occupant, there was no sign.

"In the garden still. I lost sight of him somehow. I told you."

Fillery crossed quickly to the window, his colleague with him, looking out upon a lawn and paths that held no figure anywhere. The gardener was not in sight. Only the birds were visible among the daisies. The quiet sunlight lay as usual upon leaves and flowers waving in the breeze. "He came in," Fillery went on rapidly under his breath. "He must have slipped back when——"

The sound of steps and voices behind them in the corridor brought both men round with a quick movement, as Nurse Robbins, her arm linked in that of "N. H.," stood in the open doorway. Her face was radiant, her eyes alight, her breath came unevenly, and one might have thought her caught midway in some ecstatic dance that still left its joy and bliss stamped on her pretty face. Only she looked more than pretty; there was beauty, a fairy loveliness about her that betrayed an intense experience of some inner kind.

At the sight of the two doctors she rapidly composed herself, leading her companion quietly into the room. "He was upstairs, sir," she said respectfully but breathlessly somewhat, and addressing herself, Fillery noticed, to Devonham and not to himself. "He was going from room to room, talking to the patients—er—singing to them. It was the singing woke me——"

"Upstairs!" exclaimed Devonham. "He has been up there!"

She broke off as Fillery came forward and took "N. H." by the hands, dismissing her with a gesture she was quick to understand. Devonham went with her hurriedly, intent upon a personal inspection at once.

"Your service called you," said Fillery quietly, the moment they were alone. "I understand!" Through the contact of the hands waves of power entered him, it seemed. About the face was light, as though fire glowed behind the very skin and eyes, producing the effect almost of a halo.

"They came for me, and I must go." The voice was deep and wonderful, with prolonged vibrations. "I have found my own. I must return where my service needs me, for here I can do so little."

"To your own place where you are ruler of your fate," the other said slowly. "Here you——"

"Here," came the quick interruption, while the voice lost its resonance, fading as it were in sadness, "here I—die." Even the radiance of his face, although he smiled, dimmed a little on that final word. "I can help where I belong— not here." The light returned, the music came back into the amazing voice.

"The daisy," whispered Fillery, joy rising in him strangely.

"Nature," floated through the air like music, "is my place. With human beings I cannot work. It is too much, and I only should destroy. They are not ready yet, for our great rhythms injure them, and they cannot understand."

Trembling with emotions he could neither define nor control, Fillery led him to the window.

"Even in this little back-garden of a London house," he murmured, "among, so to speak, the humble buttercups and daisies of our life! The creative Intelligences at work, building, ever building the best forms they can. You re-make a broken daisy"—his voice rose, as the great shining face so close lit with its flaming smile—"you re-make as well our broken minds. In the subconscious hides our creative power that you stimulate. It is with that and that alone you work. It hides in all of us, though the artist alone perceives or can use it. It is with that you work——"

"With you, dear Fillery, I can work, for you help me to remember. You feel the big rhythms that we bring."

Dr. Fillery started, peered about him, listened hard. Was it the trees, shaking in the morning wind, that rustled? Was it a voice? The dancing leaves reflected the sunshine from a thousand facets. The sound accompanied, rather than interrupted, his own speech. He turned back to "N. H." with passionate enthusiasm.

"Using beauty—the artists—the creative powers of the Race," he went on, "we shall create together a new body, a new vehicle, through which your powers can express themselves. The intellect cannot serve you . . . it is the creative imagination of those who know beauty that you seek. You are inarticulate in this wretched body. We shall make a new one——"

"They have come for me and I must go——"

"We will work together. Oh, stay—stay with me——!"

"I have found the way. I have remembered. I must go back——"

The wind died down, the leaves stopped rustling, the sunshine seemed to pale as though a cloud passed over the sky. The words he had heard resolved themselves into the morning sounds, the singing of the birds. Had they been words at all? Bewilderment, like a pain, rushed over him. He knew himself suddenly imprisoned, caught.

"I have remembered," he heard in quiet tones, but the voice dead, no resonance, no music in it. And across the room he saw suddenly Paul Devonham just inside the door, returned from his inspection. Beside him stood—LeVallon.

An extraordinary reaction instantly took place in him.

A lid was raised, a shutter lifted, a wall fell flat. He hardly knew how to describe it. Was it due to the look of anxiety, of tenderness, of affectionate, of protective care he saw plainly upon his colleague's face? He could not say. He only knew for certain in that instant that Paul Devonham's main preoccupation was with—himself; that the latter regarded him exactly as he regarded any other —yes, that was the only word—any other patient; that he looked after him, tended, guarded, cared for him—and that this watchful, experienced observation had been going on now for a long, long time.

The authority in his manner became abruptly clear as day. Devonham watched over him; also he watched him. For days, for weeks, this had been his attitude. For the first time, in this instant, as he saw him lead away LeVallon into his own room and close the door, Fillery now perceived this. He experienced a violent revulsion of mind. In a flash a hundred details of the recent past occurred to him, chief among them the fact that, more and more, the control of the Home and its occupants had been taken over, Fillery himself only too willing, by his assistant. A moment of appalling doubt rose like a black cloud. . . .

He heard Paul telling LeVallon to begin his breakfast, just as the door closed, and he noted the authoritative tone of voice. The next minute he and his colleague were alone together.

"Paul," said the chief quickly, but with a calm assurance that anticipated a favourable answer, "*they,* at any rate, are all right?"

Devonham nodded his head. "No harm done," he replied briefly. "In fact, as you know, he rather stimulates them than otherwise."

"I know."

He felt, for the first time in their years of close relationship, a breath of suspicion enter him. There was a look upon his colleague's face he could not quite define. It baffled him.

"Of course, I know——"

He stopped, for the undecipherable look had strengthened suddenly. He thought of a gaoler.

"Paul," he said quickly, "what's the matter? What's wrong with you?"

He drew back a pace or two and watched him.

"With me—nothing, Edward. Nothing at all." The tone was grave with anxiety, yet had this new authority in it.

A feeling of intolerable insecurity came upon him, a sensation as though he balanced on air, yet its cause, its origin, easily explained: the support of his colleague's mind was taken from him. Paul's attitude was clear as day to him. He *was* a gaoler. . . . He recalled again the recent detail, brightly significant—that Nurse Robbins had turned to Paul, rather than to himself.

"With—*me*, then—you think?" His voice hardly sounded like his own. He looked about him for support, found an arm-chair, sat down in it. "You're strange, Paul, very strange," he whispered. "What do you mean by 'there's something wrong with *me'?*"

Devonham's expression cleared slightly and a kindly, sympathetic smile appeared, then vanished. The grave look that Fillery disliked reappeared.

"What d'you mean, Paul Devonham?" came the repetition, in a louder, more challenging voice. "You're watching me—as though I were"—he laughed without a trace of mirth—"a patient." He leaned forward. "Paul, you've been watching me for a long time. Out with it, now. What is it?"

Devonham, who had kept silent, drew some papers from his pocket, a bundle of rolled sheets.

"Of course," he said gently, "I always watch you. For that's how I learn. I learn from you, Edward, more than from anybody I know."

But Dr. Fillery, his eyes fixed upon the sheaf of papers, had recognized them. His own writing was visible along the uneven edges. They were the description he had set

down of his adventure on Flower Hill, of the scenes between "N. H." and Lady Gleeson, between "N. H." and
Nayan, the autobiographical description with "N. H." and
Nurse Robbins soon after his arrival, when Fillery had so
amazingly found his own mind—as he believed—identified
with his patient's.

Devonham snapped off the elastic band that held the
sheaf together. "Edward, I've read them. We have no
secrets, of course. I've read them carefully. Every word—
my dear fellow."

"Yes, yes," replied the other, while something in him
wavered horribly. "I'm glad. They were meant for you to
read, for of course we have no secrets. I—I do not expect
you to agree. We have never quite seen eye to eye—have
we?" His voice shook. "You terrible iconoclast," he
added, betraying thus the nature of the fear that changed
his voice, then recognizing with vexation that he had done
so. "You believe nothing. You never will believe anything.
You cannot understand. With joy you would destroy what
I and others believe—wouldn't you, Paul——?"

The deep sadness, the gravity on the face in front of him
stopped the tirade.

"I would save you, Edward," came the earnest, gentle
words, "from yourself. The powers of auto-suggestion, as
we know in our practice—don't we?—are limitless. If you
call that destroying——"

From the adjoining room the clatter of knives and forks
was audible. Dr. Fillery listened a moment with a smile.

"Paul," he asked, his voice firm and sure again, "is your
chief patient in that room," indicating the door with his
head, "or—in this?"

"In this," was the reply. "A wise man is always his own
patient and 'Physician, heal thyself' his motto." He sat
down beside his chief. His manner changed; there was
affection, deep solicitude, something of passionate entreaty
even in voice and eyes and gestures. "There are features
here," he said in lowered tones, "Edward, we have not

understood, perhaps even we can never understand; but we have not, I think, sufficiently guarded against one thing—auto-suggestion. The rôle it plays in life is immense, incalculable; it is in everything we do and think, above all in everything we believe. It is peculiarly powerful and active in—er—unusual things——"

"The sound—the sounds—you've heard them yourself," broke in his companion.

Devonham shrugged his thin shoulders. "He sings—in a peculiar way." As an aside, he said it, returning to his main sermon instantly. "Let us leave details out," he cried; "it is the principle that concerns us. Edward, your complex against humanity lies hard and rigid in you still. It has never found that full recognition by yourself which can resolve it. Your work, your noble work, is but a partial expression. The kernel of this old complex in you remains unrelieved, undischarged—because still unrecognized. And, further, you are continually adding to the repression which"—even Devonham paused a second before using such a word to such a man—"is poisoning you, Edward, poisoning you, I repeat."

"You saw—you saw the rebuilding of—the daisy"—an odd whisper of insecurity ran through the quiet words, a statement rather than a question—"you realize, at any rate, that chance has brought us into contact with Powers, creative Powers, of a new order——"

"Let us omit all details just now," interrupted the other, a troubled, indecipherable look on his face. "The undoubted telepathy between your mind and mine nullifies any such——"

"——powers of which we all have some faint counterpart, at any rate, in our subliminal selves." Fillery had not heard the interruption. "Powers by means of which we may build for the Race new forms, new mental bodies, new vehicles for life, for God, to manifest through—more perfect, more receptive——"

Devonham had suddenly seized both his hands and was

leaning closer to him. Something compelling, authoritative, peculiarly convincing for a moment had its undeniable effect, again stopping the flow of hurried, passionate, eager words.

"There is one new form, new body," and the intensity in voice and eyes drove the meaning deep, deep into his listener's mind and heart. "I wish to see you build. One, and one only—physical, mental, spiritual. But you cannot build it, Edward—alone!"

"Paul!" The other held up a warning hand; the expression in his eyes was warning too. Their effect upon Devonham, however, was nil. He was talking with a purpose nothing could alter.

"She is still waiting for you," he went on with determination, "and already you have kept her waiting—overlong." In the tone, in the hard clear eyes as well, lay a suggestion almost of tears.

He opened the door into the breakfast-room, but Fillery caught his arm and stopped him. They could hear Nurse Robbins speaking, as she attended as usual to her patient's wants. Coffee was being poured out. There was a sound of knives and plates and cups.

"One minute, Paul, one minute before we go in." He drew him aside. "And what, *Doctor* Devonham, may I ask, would you prescribe?" There was a curious mixture of gentle sarcasm, of pity, of patient tolerance, yet at the same time of sincere, even anxious, interest in the question. The face and manner betrayed that he waited for the answer with something more than curiosity.

There was no hesitancy in Devonham. He judged the moment ripe, perhaps; he was aware that his words would be listened to, appreciated, understood certainly, and possibly, obeyed.

"Expression," he said convincingly, but in a lowered voice. "The fullest expression, everywhere and always. Let it all come. Accept the lot, believe the lot, welcome the lot, and thus"—he could not conceal the note of passionate entreaty, of deep affection—"avoid every atom of *repression*. In the end—in the long run—your own best judgment *must* prevail."

They smiled into each other's eyes for a moment in silence, while, instinctively and automatically, their hands joined in a steady clasp.

"Bless you, old fellow," murmured the chief. "As if I didn't know! It's the treatment you've been trying on me for weeks and months. As if I hadn't noticed!"

As they entered the breakfast-room, Nurse Robbins, with flushed face and sparkling eyes, was pouring out the coffee, leaning close over her patient's shoulder as she did so. Fresh roses were in her cheeks as well as on the table.

"This is its touch upon the blossomed maid," whispered Fillery, with the quick hint of humour that belongs only to the sane. At the same time the light remark was produced, he well knew, by a part of himself that sought to remain veiled from recognition. Any other triviality would have done as well to cloak the sharp pain that swept him, and to lead his listener astray. For in that instant, as they entered, he saw at the table not "N. H.," but LeVallon—the backward, ignorant, commonplace LeVallon, an empty, untaught personality, yet so receptive that anything—*anything*—could be transferred to him by a strong, vivid mind, a mind, for instance, like his own. . . .

The sight, for a swift instant, was intolerable and devastating. He balanced again on air that gave him no support. He wavered, almost swayed. "N. H.," in that horrible and painful second, did not exist, and never had existed. The unstable mind, he comforted himself, experiences dislocating extremes of attitude . . . for, at the same time as he saw himself shaking and wavering without solid support, he saw the figure of Paul Devonham, big, important, authoritative, dominating the uncertainties of life with calm, steady power.

In a fraction of a second all this came and went. He sat down beside LeVallon, his eyes still twinkling with his trivial little joke.

" 'N. H.,' " he whispered to Devonham quickly, "has— escaped at last."

"LeVallon," came the whispered reply as quickly, "is cured at last." And, to conceal an intolerable rush of pain, of loss, of loneliness that threatened tears, he pointed to the dropped eyes and blushing cheeks of the pretty nurse across the table.

CHAPTER XXVII

TO Edward Fillery, the deep pain of frustration baffling all his mental processes, the end had come with a strange, bewildering swiftness. He knew there had been a prolonged dislocation of his being, possibly, even a partial loss of memory with regard to much that went on about him, but he could not, did not, admit that no value or reality had attached to his experiences. The central self in him had projected a limb, an arm, that, feeling its way across the confining wall of the prison house, groping towards an unbelievably wonderful revelation of new possibilities, had abruptly now withdrawn again. The dissociation in his personality was over. He was, in other words, no longer aware of "N. H." Like Devonham, he now did not "perceive" "N. H.," but only LeVallon. But, unlike Devonham, he *had* perceived him. . . .

He had met half-way a mighty and magnificent Vision. Its truth and beauty remained for him enduring. The revelation had come and gone. That its close was sudden, simple, undramatic, above all untheatrical, satisfied him. "N. H." had "escaped," leaving the commonplace LeVallon. in his place. But, at least, he had known "N. H."

His whole being, an odd, sweet, happy pain in him, yearned ever to the glorious memory of it all. The melancholy, the peculiar shyness he felt, were not without an indefinite pleasure. His nature still vibrated to those haunting and inspiring rhythms, but his normal, earthly faculties, he flattered himself, were in no sense permanently disorganized. Professionally, he still cared for LeVallon, disenchanted dust though he might be, compared to "N. H." . . . He approved of Devonham's proposal to take him

367

for a few days to the sea. He also approved of Paul's
advice that he should accept Father Collins' invitation to
spend a day or two at his country cottage. The Khilkoffs
would be there, father and daughter. The Home, in charge
of an assistant, could be reached in a few hours in case of
need. The magic of Devonham's wise, controlling touch
lay in every detail, it seemed. . . .

He saw the trio—for Nurse Robbins was of the party—
off to Seaford. "The final touches to his cure," Paul mentioned slyly, with a smile, as the guard whistled. But of
whose cure he did not explain. "He'll bathe in the sea," he
added, the reference obvious this time. "And—when we
return—I shall be best man. I've already promised!" There
was a triumph of skilled wisdom in both sentences.

"The time isn't ripe yet, Edward, for too magnificent
ideas. And your ideas have been a shade too magnificent,
perhaps." He talked on lightly, even carelessly. And, as
usual, there was purpose, meaning, "treatment"—his friend
easily discerned it now—in every detail of his attitude.

Fillery laughed. Through his mind ran Povey's sentence,
"Never argue with the once-born!" but aloud he said, "At
any rate, I've no idea that I'm Emperor of Japan or—or
the Archangel Gabriel!" And the other, pleased and satisfied that a touch of humour showed itself, shook hands
firmly, affectionately, through the window as the train
moved off. LeVallon raised his hat to his chief and smiled
—an ordinary smile. . . .

With the speed and incongruity of a dream these few
days slipped by, their happenings vivid enough, yet all set
to a curiously small scale, a cramped perspective, blurred a
little as by a fading light. Only one thing retained its brilliance, its intense reality, its place in the bigger scale, its
vast perspective remaining unchanged. The same immense
sweet rhythm swept Iraida and himself inevitably together.
Some deep obsession that hitherto prevented had been withdrawn.

She had called that very morning—Paul's touch visible here again, he believed, though he had not asked. He looked on and smiled. After the ordeal of breakfast with Devonham and LeVallon her visit was announced. It was Paul, after a little talk downstairs, who showed her in. With the radiance of a spring wild-flower opening to the early sunshine, her unexpected visit to his study seemed clothed. Unexpected, yes, but surely inevitable as well. With the sweet morning wind through the open window, it seemed, she came to him, the letter of invitation from Father Collins in her hand. His own lay among his correspondence, still untouched. Her perfume rose about him as she explained something he hardly heard or followed.

"You'll come, Edward, won't you? You'll come too."

"Of course," he answered. But it was a song he heard, and no dull spoken words. She ran dancing towards him through a million flowers; her hair flew loose along the scented winds; her white limbs glowed with fire. He danced to meet her. It was in the Valley that he caught her hands and met her eyes. "It's happened," he heard himself saying. "It's happened at last—just as you said it must. *Escape!* He has escaped!"

"But we shall follow after—when the time comes, Edward."

"Where the wild bee never flew!" . . .

"When the time comes," she repeated.

Her voice, her smile, her eyes brought him back sharply into the little room. The furniture showed up again. The Valley faded. He noticed suddenly that for the first time she wore no flowers in her dress as usual.

"Iraida!" he exclaimed. "Then—you knew!"

She bent her head, smiling divinely. She took both his hands in hers. At her touch every obstacle between them melted. His own private, personal inhibition he saw as the trivial barriers a little child might raise. His complex against humanity, as Paul called it, had disappeared. Their minds, their beings, their natures became most strangely one, he felt, and yet quite naturally. There was nothing they did not share.

"With the first dawn," he heard her say in a low voice. "Never—never again," he seemed to hear, "shall we destroy his—their—work of ages."

"A flower," he whispered, "has no need to wear a flower!"

He was convinced that she too had shared an experience similar to his own, perhaps had even seen the bright, marvellous Deva faces peering, shining. . . . He did not ask. She said no more. Life flowed between them in an untroubled stream. . . .

Like the flow of a stream, indeed, things went past him, yet with incidents and bits of conversation thus picked out with vivid sharpness. The dissociation of his being was still noticeable here and there, he supposed. The swell after the storm took time to settle down. Slowly, however, the waves that had been projected, leaping to heaven, returned to the safe, quiet dead level of the normal calm. . . . The depths lay still once more. And his melancholy passed a little, lifted. He knew, at any rate, those depths were now accessible.

"I've seen over the wall a moment," he said to himself. "Paul is both right and wrong. What I've seen lies too far ahead of the Race to be intelligible or of use. I should be cast out, crucified, my other, simpler work destroyed. To control rhythms so powerful, so different to anything we now know, is not yet possible. They would shatter, rather than construct." He smiled sadly, yet with resignation. There was pain and humour in his eyes. "I should be regarded as a Promethean merely, an extremist Promethean, and probably be locked up for contravening some County Council bye-law or offending Church and State. That's where he, perhaps, is right—Paul!" He thought of him with affection and pity, with understanding love. "How wise and faithful, how patient and how skilled—within his limits. The stable are the useful; the stable are the leaders;

the stable rule the world. People with steady if unvisioned eyes like Paul, with money like Lady Gleeson. . . . But, oh!"—he sighed—"how slow, ye gods! how slow!" . . .

The visit was a strange one. Nayan sat between him and her father in the motor. It was not far from London, the ancient little house among the trees where Father Collins secreted himself from time to time upon occasional "retreats."

Within the grounds it might have been the centre of the New Forest, but for the sound of tramcar bells that sometimes came jangling faintly through the thick screen of leaves. There were old-world paved courtyards with sweet playing fountains, miniature lawns, tangles of flowers, small sunken gardens with birds of cut box and yew, stone nymphs, and a shaggy, moss-grown Pan, whose hand that once held the pipes had broken off. Suburbia lay outside, yet, by walking wisely, it was possible to move among these delights for half an hour, great trees ever rustling overhead, and a clear small stream winding peacefully in and out with gentle lapping murmurs. Nature here lay undisturbed as it had lain for centuries.

The little ancient house, moreover, seemed to have grown up with the green things out of the soil, so naturally, it all belonged together. The garden ran indoors, it seemed, through open doors and windows. Butterflies floated from courtyard into drawing-room and out again, leaves blew through dining-room windows, scurrying to another little bit of lawn; the sun and wind, even the fountains' spray, found the walls no obstacle as though unaware of them. Bees murmured, swallows hung below the eaves. It was, indeed, a healing spot, a natural retreat. . . .

"I really believe the river rises in your library," exclaimed Fillery, after a tour of inspection with his host, "and my bedroom is in the heart of that big chestnut across the lawn. Do my feet touch carpet, grass, or bark when I get out of bed in the morning?"

"I've learnt more here," began Father Collins, "than at all the conferences and learned meetings I ever attended. . . ."

The group of four stood in the twilight by the playing fountain where the dignified stone Pan watched the paved little court, listening to the splash of the water and the wind droning among the leaves. The lap of the winding stream came faintly to them. The stillness cast a spell about them, dropping a screen against the outer world.

"Hark!" said Father Collins, holding a curved hand to his ear. "You hear the music . . .?"

> " 'Why, in the leafy greenwood lone
> Sit you, rustic Pan, and drone
> On a dulcet resonant reed?' "

He paused, peering across to the stone figure as for an answer. All stood listening, waiting, only wind and water breaking the silence. The bats were now flitting; overhead hung the saffron arch of fading sunset. In a deep ringing voice, very gruff and very low, Father Collins gave the answer:

> " 'So that yonder cows may feed
> Up the dewy mountain passes,
> Gathering the feathered grasses.'

"That's Pan's work," he said, laughing pleasantly, "Pan and all his splendid hierarchy. Always at work, though invisibly, with music, colour, beauty! . . ."

It was scraps like this that stood out in Fillery's memory, adding to his conviction that Paul had enlisted even this strange priest in his deep-laid plan. . . .

"Each man is saturated with certain ideas, thoughts, phrases in a line of his own. These constitute his groove. To go outside it makes him feel homeless and uncomfortable. Accustomed to its measurements and safe within them, he interprets all he hears, reads, observes, according to his particular familiar shibboleths, to which, as to a standard of infallible criticism, he brings slavishly all that is offered for the consideration of his judgment. A new Idea stands little chance of being comprehended, much less adopted. Tell him new things about the stars, the Stock Exchange, the Stigmata—up crops his Standard of approval or disapproval. He cannot help himself. His judgment, based upon the limited content of his groove, operates automatically. He condemns. An entirely new idea is barely glanced at before it is rejected for the rubbish heap. How, then, can progress come swiftly to a Race composed of such individuals? Mass-judgment, herd-opinion governs everything. He who has original ideas is outcast, and dwells lonely as the moon. How slow, ye Gods! How slow!" . . .

Only Fillery could not remember, could not be certain, whether it was his host or himself that used the words. Father Collins, as usual, was saying "all sorts of things," but addressed himself surely, to old Khilkoff most of the time, the Russian, half angry, half amused, growling out his comments and replies as he sat smoking heavily and enjoying the peaceful night scene in his own fashion. . . .

It was odd, none the less, how much that the wild priest gabbled coincided with his own, with Fillery's, thoughts at the moment. A peculiar melancholy, a mood of shyness never known before, lay still upon him. The beauty of the silent girl beside him overpowered him a little; too wonderful to hold, to own, she seemed. Yet they were deliciously, uncannily akin. All his former self-created denials and suppressions, hesitations and refusals had vanished. "N. H."—He wondered?—had provided him with the fullest expression he had ever known. A boundless relief poured over him. He was aware of wholesome desire rising behind his old high admiration and respect. . . .

He watched her once standing close to Pan's broken outline among the shadows, touching the mossy arm with white fingers, and he imagined for an instant that she held the vanished pipes.

"After an experience with Other Beings," Father Collins's endless drone floated to him, "shyness, they say, is felt. Silence descends upon the whole nature" . . . to which, a little later, came the growling comment with its foreign accent: "Talk may be pleasurable—sometimes—but it is profitable rarely. . . ."

The talk flowed past and over him, occasional phrases, like islands rising out of a stream, inviting his attention momentarily to land and listen. . . . The girl, he now saw, no longer stood beside the broken stone figure. She was wandering idly towards the farther garden and the trees.

He burned to rise and go to her, but something held him. What was it? What could it be? Some strange hard little obstacle prevented. Then, suddenly, he knew what it was that stopped him: he was waiting for that familiar pet sentence. Once he heard that, the impetus to move, the power to overcome his strange shyness, the certainty that his whole being was at last one with itself again, would come to him. It made him laugh inwardly while he recognized the validity of the detail—final symptoms of the obstructing inhibitions, of the obstinate original complex.

The outline of the girl was lost now, merged in the shadows beyond. He stirred, but could not get up to go. A fury of impatience burned in him. Father Collins, he felt, dawdled outrageously. He was talking—jawing, Fillery called it—about extraordinary experiences. "Gradually, as consciousness more and more often extends, the organs to record such extensions will be formed, you see. . . . If our inventive faculties were turned inwards, instead of outwards for gain and comfort as they now are, we might know the gods. . . ."

The sculptor's growl, though the words were this time inaudible, had a bite in them. The other voice poured on like thick, slow oil:

"What, anyhow, is it, then, that urges us on in spite of all obstacles, denials, failures . . . ?"

Then came something that seemed leading up to the pet

sentence that was the signal he waited for—nearer to it, at
any rate:

". . . It's childish, surely, to go on merely seeking more
of what we have already. We should seek something
new. . . ."

A call, it seemed, came to him on the wind from the dark
trees. But still he could not move.

But, at last, out of a prolonged jumble of the two voices,
one growling, the other high pitched, came the signal he
somehow waited for. Even now, however, the speaker
delayed it as long as possible. He was doing it, of course,
on purpose. This was intentional, obviously.

". . . Yes, but a thing out of its right place is without
power, life, means of expression—robbed of its context
which alone gives it meaning—robbed, so to speak, of its
arms and legs—*without a body*. . . ."

There, at least, was the definite proof that Father Collins
was doing this of deliberate, set purpose!

"Go on! Yes, but, for God's sake, say it! I want to be
off!" Fillery believed he shrieked the words, but apparently
they were inaudible. They remained unnoticed, at any rate.

". . . Hence the value of order, tidiness, you see. Often
a misplaced thing is invisible until replaced where it belongs. It is, as we say, lost. No movement is meaningless,
no walk without purpose. All your movements tend towards
your proper place. . . ."

A breeze blew the fountain spray aside so that its splashing ceased for a brief second. From the rustling leaves
beyond came a faint murmur as of distant piping. But—
into the second's pause had leaped the pet sentence:

"Only a being in his *own* place is the ruler of his fate."

The signal! He was aware that the Russian cleared his
throat and spat unmusically, aware also that Father Collins,
a queer smile just discernible on his face in the gloom,
turned his head with a gesture that might well have been
an understanding nod. Both sound and gesture, however,
were already behind him. He was released. He was across

the paved courtyard, past the fountain, past the stone figure of the silent old rough god—and off!

And as he went, finding his way instinctively among the dark trees, that pet sentence went with him like a clarion call, as though sweet piping music played it everywhere about him. A thousand memories shut down with a final snap. In the stage of his mind came a black-out upon a host of inhibitions. There was an immense and glorious sense of relief as though bitter knots were suddenly disentangled, and some iron kernel of resistance that had weighted him for years flowed freely at last in a stream of happy molten gold. . . .

He found her easily. Where the trees thinned at the farther edge he saw her figure, long before he came up with her, outlined against the fading saffron. He saw her turn. He saw her arms outstretched. He came up with her the same minute, and they stood in silence for a long time, watching the darkness bend and sink upon the landscape.

For, here, at this one edge of the tiny estate, the real open country showed. Beyond them, in the twilight, lay the silent fields like a gigantic brown and yellow carpet whose shaken folds still seemed to tremble and run on beneath the growing moon. Along a farther ridge the trees and hedges passed in a ragged procession of strange figures, defined sharply against the sky—witches, queens and goblins on the prowl, the ancient fairyland of the English countryside.

They still stood silent, side by side, touching almost, their heat and perfume and atmosphere intermingling, looking out across the quiet scene. He was aware that her mind stole into his most sweetly, and that without knowing it his hand had found her own, and that, presently, she leaned a little against him. Their eyes, their mental sight as well, saw the same things, he knew. The first stars peeped out, and they looked up at them as one being looks, together.

"The wonder that you saw—in him," he heard himself saying. It was a statement, not a question.

"Was yourself, of course," her voice, like his own, in the rustle of the leaves, came softly. It continued his own thought rather than replied to it. "The part you've held down and hidden away all these years."

Her divination came to him with staggering effect. "You always knew then?"

"Always. The first day we met you took me into the firm."

He was aware that everything about him pulsed and throbbed with life, intelligence in every stick and stone. Angelic beings marched on their wondrous business through the sky. A mighty host pursued their endless service with a network of huge and tiny rhythms. The spirals of creative fire soared and danced. . . .

The moon emerged, sailing, sailing, as though no wind could stop her lovely flight. She fled the stars themselves. The clouds turned round to look at her, as, clearing their hair, she passed onwards with her radiant smile. Heading into the bare bosom of the sky, she blazed in her triumph of loneliness, her icy prow set towards some far, unknown, unearthly goal, which is the reason why men love her so.

"And my theories—our theories?" he murmured into the ear against his lips. "The way that has been shown to us?"

Both arms were now about her, and he held her so close that her words were but a warm perfumed breath to cover his face as her hair was covering his eyes.

"We shall follow it together . . . dear."

It was as if some angel, stepping down the sky, came near enough to fold them in a great rhythm of fire and wind. Bright, mighty faces in a crowd rose round them, and, through her hair, he saw familiar visible outlines of all the common things melt out, showing for one gorgeous instant the flashings and whirlings that was the workshop of Their deathless service.

"Look! Look!" he whispered, pointing from the darkening earth to the stars and sailing moon above. "They're everywhere! You can see them too? The bright messengers?"

For answer, she came yet closer against his side, holding him more tightly to her, lifting her lips to his, so that in her very eyes he saw the marvellous fire shine and flash. "We shall build together, you and I," she whispered very softly, "and with Their help, the sweetest and most perfect body ever known. . . ."

But behind the magic of her words and voice, behind their meaning and the steadying, understanding sympathy he easily divined, he heard another sound, familiar as a dream, yet fraught with some haunting significance he already was forgetting—almost *had* entirely forgotten. From the centre of the earth it seemed to rise, a magnificent, deep, stupendous rhythm that created, at least, the impression of a voice:

"I weave and I weave . . . !" rolled forth, as though the planet uttered. He stood waiting, transfixed, listening intently.

"You heard?" he whispered.

"Everything," she said, tight in his arms at once again, her lips on his. "The very beating of your heart—your inmost thoughts as well."

THE END

www.ingramcontent.com/pod-product-compliance
Lightning Source LLC
Chambersburg PA
CBHW032142010726
47494CB00002B/321